I0618461

Dar Tania II: Set's Dream

Look for these other great titles!

Dar Tania – October 2016, "a 100 page story", 105 pages
Malcor's Story – November 2016, 400+ pages
Bomoki's Gate – April 2017, 550+ pages
Dar Tania II: Set's Dream – August 2017, 250+ pages
Other Forsaken Isles "100 Page Stories" – November 2017 on
Merakoran Agenda - 2018

For more information about the stories set in the Forsaken Isles, its characters, author, or whatever else inspires you to contact Dar Malcor:

darmalcor.weebly.com

Send an email and join my email list as well at darmalcor.weebly.com
If you enjoy the story, please leave a review on Amazon and Good Reads; thank you!

Edited by Tony Reynolds and Ben Duffy

Table of Contents

Morbatten during the Reign of Dar Tania

Author's Preface

You'll enjoy this book more if you've read Dar Tania. If you have not, that book tells the story of Dar Tania, a 19-year-old girl who becomes the first high priestess of the Goddess Tiamat. She begins assembling the barbarian tribes into an empire under god emperor Alerius. Alerius is the fire dragon patriarch who serves Tiamat as an avatar in the world. In that story, Dar begins to learn what it means to be a cleric and, with the help of a paladin named Sean, they begin identifying and training paladins. In that story, Syliri the medusa was introduced as a friend and aid to Alerius.

Syliri is an eldar medusa. Alerius saved her from the madness of "Set's Dream." Trapped in abyssal sleep, Set dreams and his nightmares spawn the monsters that fill the worlds of the Forsaken Isles. Eldar creatures, like Syliri and the dragons, did not fall into Set's Dream and become mortal. By not falling, they were able to retain their immortal will-based powers, though there are various twists to how their Eldar powers manifest. Readers of Malcor's Story will remember the Khasran Lich and how powerful he was. Part of the lich's power, different from Syliri's, is that the lich was using magic mastered before Time. By the same token, the Tanian dragons, especially the Eldar Court of Patriarchs, function as unascended gods. Syliri never learned magic. When all other medusae fell, Alerius saved Syliri from falling. Also, Syliri had the maedar to contend with.

Before Time, the medusae were enslaved to their male counterparts, called the *maedar*. The maedar fully embraced Set's worship. They hunted down and captured the medusae, and bred them in harems for armies. They were experimented on, tortured, bred, and made to fight against each other for the maedars' enjoyment. Syliri led a rebellion that destroyed all maedar before Time moved. Bull gorgons, cockatrices, and other petrifying creatures (also stunning or paralyzing) were just normal creatures to the maedar, the way cows and chickens are normal to us. They were livestock and raised as food. Syliri's rebellion and overthrow caught Alerius' attention and was the reason he saved her.

So, how does Set's Dream work and why does it matter? Though explained in other books, consider the somewhat random and brutal nature of monsters, even wild animals like a grizzly bear. They are this way because they do not experience the same world we do. The terror we feel when confronted with a wild animal is the remnant of Set's Dream in our primordial makeup. It triggers adrenalin and fear. Our pulse races and sounds amplify. If we fight, shock and other primed senses allow us to continue with only a vague awareness of pain. If we survive, the pain comes later. That moment of fear is what creatures in Set's Dream experience their entire lives. The grizzly bear does not see us as a non-threat. It sees us as the most threatening thing ever. By the same token, Syliri's sisters who fell see humans as maedar. That humans run in terror from them, or attack them with weapons, makes it worse by reinforcing the wrong belief that humans are actual maedar. Fallen medusae never have a chance to have a positive encounter and, the next time, the terror of Set's Dream is magnified by the real memory of what happened last time.

It's not all bad though. Certain magics, like *charm* or *summoning* spells, allow the creatures to see the caster as they are. Freed of Set's Dream for a while, the caster appears non-terrible and safe. Even in the dream, positive interactions, like giving food and water to a wounded wolf, can become reinforced enough that the animal eventually relaxes. They still view the caretaker as a threat but the small non-traumatized parts of their brain recognize the pattern of "this particular horrible monster brings me good things." Only the caretaking of a god can allow true sentience and moral agency to exist for those trapped in Set's Dream. Alerius and Syliri both hope that Syliri will become the goddess of the fallen medusae someday.

Syliri has an extra-cautionary side to Set's Dream. Some of the creatures, and eldar too, caught in Set's Dream before Time became powerful in it. Like the maedar, the medusae thrived in their use of the dream to augment their petrification ability, strength, speed, regeneration, and other powers. Where the maedar learned how to manipulate it to enslave others, the medusae were enslaved by it, and they loved its ability to capture their prey in stone. When Syliri finally broke free and led her sisters in rebellion, she did so by embracing Set's Dream at a level – and understanding of the consequences – no other medusa had before. It's as addicting to her as the most addictive drug imaginable. Alerius saved her from falling, but he also saved her from becoming just as bad as the maedar were. Hating the maedar, Syliri has no desire to be like them but the power is beyond tempting to her. Thanks to Alerius, she has learned some control.

In Morbatten, Syliri keeps a "garden" of petrified monsters and strange beasts that make up the world. This allows Dar Tania and her fighters to get up close and study these creatures as statues. Since Dar Tania elevated the barbarian tribes to a new nation just five years ago, Syliri and the Taysoran ranger, Bruce, have fallen in love. Together, they go out and explore the lands Alerius considers part of Morbatten. Hunting for anything that could hurt the tribespeople, and also on the lookout for new additions to the zoo, they encounter a slaad.

There are not many, if any, books written about the Slaadi. If you do an internet search on them, you'll find pictures of fanged and clawed frogs. That's not really what they are. They're the ultimate worshipper of Set.

Leave it to an abyssal god to take a simple Pha Rannic creation, like amphibians, and twist it into travesty of slaads.

The more powerful the slaad creating a transformant, and the more powerful the infected host, the more powerful the slaad that comes from this. A slaad's own progression is limited only by their rate of consumption of intelligence. Because the fastest way to do this is to strengthen a chosen host, infect it, and then consume it directly, you have to imagine the Slaadi are a vast multi-level marketing scheme... of self-consumption. The safest advancement for any slaad is to grow a stable of lower level Slaadi and then consume them. When enough intelligence is consumed, an Azuros can rise to an Embros/red, which can rise to an Anthracos/gray, which can rise to an Atramenti/midnight.

At Azuros, the slaad acquires the knowledge and memories of those consumed. Driven by this trinity of "please Master," "eat knowledge," and "get gold," the Azuros becomes aware of this self-consumptive chain and grow increasingly paranoid about preserving their own lives and identity. Enchantments in gold retain their properties across all realms. After all, a slaad, even the Fecundus, can alter its appearance. They're the ultimate manipulators, as are any who serve Set.

For those familiar with Greek mythology, or contemporary fantasy writings, my portrayal of Syliri may be confusing. She is not a monster, because Alerius has freed her from Set's Dream. She can shapeshift, though not very well. She has a humanoid form that she prefers when interacting with the people of Morbatten. She can also turn into a giant half-snake and half-humanoid. Her upper half remains humanoid. A few of her hair snakes are sentient, like the one Bruce names "Kelly." When Syliri petrifies, she is using Set's Dream, and hates it – and herself – for loving the power it brings her. Unlike other eldar in my writings up to this point, Syliri cannot use magic. Eldar magic is an expression of the eldar's immortal will, which for Syliri is petrification through Set's Dream.

Special thanks to Athena for gracing our mythologies with such a capricious story as Medusa. I'd also like to thank my illustrator Darko, my editors Tony and Ben, and those who have fired my imagination throughout my youth.

Chapter 1 – Syliri and Bruce on Patrol

"I can see this entire area dotted with farms and homesteads," Bruce said to Syliri. Lying on the ground, the two looked over the ravine edge. It commanded a scenic valley view crisscrossed by a river. The valley followed the Cordabad South River but here, it had widened enough that the mountains rising up the eastern side created a natural backdrop and breathtaking view. Autumn leaves crunched under them as the ranger shifted to get a better view. "The dragon didn't lie. This area is four regions: valley, river, mountains, and hot springs. Quattrain; at least the name makes sense."

Syliri found it strange that Bruce, the Ranger, hated cities, even other people. "For someone who hates civilization, your imagination seems fixated on it." Syliri mimicked him, "Oh look, Syliri. This would be a great site for a stronghold! Look over there! I can see cattle grazing!" She elbowed him playfully. "I look and see hiding places for giants to ambush us. I see a river through a valley on a beautiful fall day. I see mountains. That's all I see out here for five years now."

Bruce rolled to face her. The faint green cast of her skin and the occasional serpentine scale along her bare arms up to her face made her look exotic and otherworldly in the bright daylight. Syliri wore a forest green head scarf that bound and quieted the snakes writhing about where human hair normally fell. The loose fabric blew in the wind. "I see the woman I love." He stated it factually, without pause. "Since that first day."

She smirked and caught his eye. "Giants," she said. "Lots of giants. Only giants." As a human, Bruce's energy always made her smile. Listening to him say what he could someday see in the valley, she could also see farm fields, even smell the mill at work grinding seeds into flour.

He scanned the valley more carefully. "I count eight giants. They seem well-organized. So far, no sign of anything larger than hill giants. That's good. I hate stone giants." He pulled himself forward into a crouch and reached back for her hand. It still struck her how this human ranger seemed so completely unaffected by her monstrous nature. Even after five years of being together on missions just like this one, Bruce's unconscious treatment of her like a lover left her feeling awestruck, and – when honest with herself - confused.

Far too many humans, just like Bruce, had taken sword and shield to destroy her and her sisters. Until Bruce, she could not even imagine holding hands with a human. If not for Alerius' fascination with them, her bitterness would long ago have turned to hate. As a medusa, her hate would fill the world with statues of fighters and those sent to slay her. She shook the thoughts from her head. *I'm not that type of gorgona. I'm here, with Bruce. He's holding my hand. It's sweet.* Still, she had to force images of him turning against her from her mind. Set's Dream worked that way. Always there, it poisoned good moments. Any crack in her thinking and the Dream would pull her back into that terrible world.

Time quieted and she unwillingly fixated on her green-tinted scales against his tan skin. The scaled ridges along her fingers entwined in his calloused ones made her question, yet again, the reality of this. *What if Set has finally found a more insidious way to infiltrate nightmares into my waking moments?* Her stomach clenched. She loved being with Bruce, but the constant onslaught of thoughts like this, coupled to her instinctive urge to protect herself by petrifying him, made it mentally exhausting. The gold ring Alerius gifted her before her first date with Bruce twinkled on her hand. The golden ring crossed her three middle fingers, each adorned with a polished emerald. She recalled Alerius' words to her five years ago when he gave her the emerald ring. "This will fortify your self-control. Bruce is remarkable. I hope he knows how special you are." Remembering Alerius' words helped chase some of her dark thinking away.

Syliri wished to freeze this good moment forever, but quickly pushed it away from her thoughts. *That's how it begins. This is how it always begins and then, suddenly, I am standing surrounded by stone.* "You don't see," she squeezed his hand as he pulled her up, "any other monsters? Perhaps something so terrible and horrible you need to kill it?" When teasing him this way, she always felt a giddy rush of dread that he might say the wrong thing. *I'm testing him, yet again. It's not fair to him,* she thought. *He deserves someone who isn't always actively thinking, "I must not petrify him."*

He ignored her test. "I'm not sure the giants deserve to die," he said rubbing his beard. "They are a threat though, should they realize how close they are to Dar Tania and the others. Still," he kissed her hand before letting go. "We could always just note them on the map. I'm sure Dar would love to come down with a force of new paladins against hill giants. Of course, that's the same as my killing them though, right? So today, do I chose to kill them now with you, or later with an army of Dar's paladins?"

Bruce pulled his sword out about halfway and noted the blue runes gleaming all along its edge. "My sword wants to kill them." He replaced it in the scabbard. "I wonder when I'll be done killing innocent creatures. You?"

Syliri crouched next to him and put her head on his shoulder. She whispered, "Would it surprise you if I told you that I've never killed anything?"

"Come on, it's time to head down. They're rotating their shift positions," Bruce said. "And, yes. It would surprise me. How is petrifying a creature different than killing them?"

The leaves made loud crunching sounds under their feet. Syliri tried to walk quietly, wondering for the hundredth time how Bruce, in all his armor, made less noise than she did. "I'm not wearing armor. Explain to me again how you're so quiet?"

"I'm not quiet," he replied. "The key is that I'm more quiet than you; we are more quiet than the giants are. We're essentially inaudible to them. Stupid beasts." He paused and pulled her close for a kiss.

They made their way down the steep edge until they slid to the bottom in a spray of leaves. Somehow, Bruce found footholds and grabbed onto tree roots to slow down. He always caught her too, always just before she slipped and needed his help. They moved forward until Bruce stopped and pointed to a nearly invisible line through the undergrowth drowning under the falling leaves. "A giant came through right here," he said. "Or, some other very large creature."

They followed the line and Syliri tried to mimic Bruce's stepping pattern. "So," she said slip-pressing her foot into the ground sideways rather than stepping straight down, "you use each step to push the leaves aside. This creates a cleared area before you step down into that area?"

Bruce nodded. "If you want to be extra ranger-like you can vary your gait and go side to side a bit. In fall, that makes your trail impossible to follow. It also creates random noise that more naturally blends into nature." He caressed one of the more curious and aggressive snakes in her hair. He called that one "Kelly the Cobra." The snake loved his touch as much as she did. "Think about your snakes, they hiss randomly. It makes it easy to pretend they aren't even there. I don't even notice them anymore. You want your own noise to be like that. If all the snakes hissed at the same time, or in a pattern, you'd definitely notice that."

Suddenly, Bruce raised his hand in a fist. He stopped and slowly moved them both behind a clump of bushes. He pointed to a grouping of trees. Though not tall, the trees stood the height of three men. At first, Syliri could not see anything worth all the fuss, but then a movement caught her eye.

A giant hand scratched under a belt of putrid animal pelts tied together around the hill giant's waist like a belt. She realized the trees were actually a single tree, more correctly a giant. If they wind blew their way, Syliri knew she would smell the monster. The barely cleaned pelts dribbled pus and worms as the giant scratched. It had so many leafy branches shoved into its armor and rotting clothes that she had confused it for a small stand of trees. The giant picked its nose and then snorted before spitting.

Bruce mouthed the word, "Guard." His facial expression told her that, later, she would listen to him complain – again – about the need for silent hand communication. Bruce had strong feelings about it. Their experiments with it had so far had failed for anything beyond basic information like "Stop," "5 enemies over there," or "Take cover." He wanted to be able to communicate entire sentences, the "poetry of combat" he called it, in sign language.

Bruce checked his sword and looked relieved it was not glowing red. That meant the giants in this area remained unaware of them. His Merakoran blade glowed blue in the presence of giants. When any giant had active evil or hostile intent towards Bruce, the runes changed to red. He completely withdrew his blade and signaled they would attack from opposite sides. She nodded as he quieted the runes so they would stop shining.

Syliri crept up on the giant's left side. She got as close as she could before she just stood up and walked forward, pretending her gown had entangled along a spiky bush. The giant froze and slowly reached for his club. *They really are stupid*, Syliri thought. The almost sheer white fabric of her dress tore on the plants. *I'm glad I listened to Dar and wore linen wraps under my clothing like she does.* Dar had wanted her to wear armor but, being a medusa, Syliri never felt the need.

"Stupid thorns," she muttered loud enough for the giant to hear. She twisted to and fro trying to untangle the pretend thorns. Her white linen wraps snagged on enough sticks to make it at least believable.

The giant stepped forward, trying to be quiet, and raised its club. It gave Syliri a great view of Bruce as he sprinted full charge at the giant's back. Only when it was too late did the giant notice the attacking ranger. The sword ignited in a red halo and then it was over. Bruce stabbed perfectly into the monster's lower spine. Instantly paralyzed from the waist down, the giant fell over sideways trying to swing its club at Bruce.

Bruce rolled and dodged to the side. Unbalanced and not yet aware of its paralysis, the giant floundered about trying to smash Bruce. A slashing cut above the giant's wrist removed the club. When a fist smashed at him, Bruce stabbed his sword through the wrist into the ground and said in their guttural, grunting language, "I can do this all day. Live, or die?" He dodged back as the red runes on his sword began to fade to blue.

The giant calmed, only now noticing it could not move its legs. It sniffed and then tears began to rain down its face. "Why kill?" it said sniffling. The tears left clean streaks down its face. "Want to live!" He fumbled at its waist pocket. "Give shiny rocks to live," he whimpered.

"You speak our language, good. You have a leader?" Bruce asked.

Syliri walked up. They had never had a giant talk to them before. Seeing her, the giant licked its lips hungrily before remembering its sorry plight. "Here," he said to her. The grunting and snorting around the giant's speech made it hard to understand. It dumped a sack of gold ore onto the dirt and leaves. "Shiny rocks."

"Focus," Bruce said. "Do you have a leader?"

The giant's eyes darted back and forth between Syliri and Bruce's blood-streaked sword. The sword went completely blue as the giant lost its desire to fight. The beast shook its head. "Yes, leader. Bull Stomper. He give you more shiny rocks."

"Is Bull Stomper like you, a hill giant?" Bruce struggled to pronounce the word they had for themselves. Its closest meaning in Taysoran Common would be "lord of mountains." Taysoran Common changed this to "big stinky enemies."

The giant kept losing its focus whenever it looked at Syliri. "She pretty," he said at last. "Tasty too, I bet. Hungry."

"No food here. Is Bull Stomper a lord of mountains?" he asked again. This time he flicked his sword in front of the giant's eyes.

With some pain but no fear, the giant said, "Yes. No, I mean no. Not us. Bull Stomper have no hair, no furs. Has horns." The giant wiggled his fingers, "Makes magic. My toes don't wiggle," the giant said forlornly.

Syliri saw Bruce getting ready to strike. The giant sensed it too. In the tension of the moment, Syliri heard a whimper of agony and imagined Bruce's body broken as the giant bit his head off. Her eyes tensed at the giant and her snakes reared up. Inside, she screamed, *No! Not now, not this way! Bruce is a giant-slayer. Don't do this.* The ecstasy of the dream rose up and colored her world yellow. Bruce's sword moved slowly through the molasses-colored world of Set's Dream...then changed as the giant's position reversed with Bruce's. Syliri tried to close her eyes, but could not. The horror of Bruce's death, even as her logical mind rejected it, made it so she could not look away.

A loud thud sounded and Syliri felt something pressed over her eyes. It was the cobra snake, held by Bruce's hand to cover her eyes. "It's dead, Syl. I killed it. You don't need to do this. Let it go."

Trembling, Syliri grasped at the emerald ring and felt reality assert itself. The yellow and brown tint to the world faded slowly and the cobra covered her eyes. Bruce patted Kelly covering her face. "Syl, I can handle a hill giant. Are you okay?"

Syliri dropped to her knees and held her hands to her face. She could not petrify herself. The snake helped, but she knew where she was. The power of her memory told her where Bruce stood, which leaves had become stone, the giant's corpse, she could see them all and the power within her attempted to lash out at everything around. Bruce stepped back a bit as the leaves under and around her crinkled and turned to gray stone. "Syl, it's okay. How can I help?"

Whenever Syliri used her gaze attack, her teeth elongated to fangs and her other senses amplified. She could sense Bruce's body heat next to the fading energy mass of the hill giant. She could smell his fright. *No, he's not scared. Have faith in him*, her mind shouted. Syliri beat her hands against her eyes, drawing an angry hiss from the cobra. She sensed again and found only concern. His heart, loud and constant to her ears, beat rhythmically. The hill giant battle affected him no more than a walk through the woods.

Bruce saw her incline her head towards the giant. "He was getting ready to try something. I had to end him. You almost beat me to the punch. Like the others, his face is looking right at you. By the way, if you ever do that to me, I'm going to smile at the last instant, just to mix it up. It's not fair that you only get to see these horrible 'no, don't petrify me' reactions all the time."

Syliri's voice, twisted and rasping, said, "Killing the giant, am I going to have to listen to you complain about morality all night?"

Bruce began wiping his sword on the giant's pelts, and then changed his mind as stone took hold everywhere, even the decapitated head. He said, "Well, that's our first giant in Quattrain that won't ever trouble the innocents of Morbatten. You know, it's not normal that the dragon calls them that - *innocents*," Bruce said, referring to how the red dragon Alerius referred to the normal people of Morbatten. "I'm hoping I can distract you and help you focus on something else." The radius of petrification stopped. "Well done. That's much better than the vampire coven."

Syliri tried to laugh even though she did not feel like it. She wanted to seem more human for him. "Well, it was your crappy idea to allow ourselves to be captured. When they realized what I was, when they dared me saying my power would not work on them, I had a moral obligation to end them."

"Yes, and the fact you also petrified the fire from their torches, and the metal chains binding us, and a vampire in gas form watching… you know, it's too bad none of them survived. How will the vampire world know to leave you alone? I assume the dragons know you're more powerful than the medusae sung about by bards."

Syliri watched him clean his sword through her other senses. Its blade still glowed blue. "It's not normal you refuse to call him anything other than 'dragon.' He's like a big brother to me. The GOD EMPEROR," she stressed his correct title, "has always looked at the world that way – there are those like us who can advance a god's purpose, and then those that can only participate passively. I suppose there's another class: enemies." She picked up one of the chunks of gold ore. "This is quality gold," she noted.

Bruce sat down and looked intently at the hill giant's face. "I hope I did the right thing. This one seemed harmless enough." Bruce measured the distance between the giant's eyes with his hands. "A large one too. One of the biggest I've ever seen up close. He's been eating well. You know what else is odd? Alerius refers to you as 'my precious Syliri.' In Taysor, those are words a lover might use, but when Alerius says it, all I can think of is a dragon sitting on a pile of gold."

"You did the right thing," she said. "The giant would not have hesitated to capture me, do unspeakable things to me, and when I could offer no more sport, they'd eat me. The eating isn't evil. The torture leading up to it is. If you spared this one and it took an innocent, Alerius would kill you. He might even eat you. He eats humans, you know. Especially Taysoran rangers that let his people die. So, consider this act pure and pre-emptive self-defense. And, he is a dragon. And he talks about all his treasures like that. I rather consider it a compliment." She made a face at the ranger. "You're upset Alerius doesn't consider you treasure." She laughed softly. She moved up to him and caressed the stubble on his face. "I treasure you. Sadly, you're kind of dirty. You need a bath."

He nodded. "Okay, I can justify this taken life." He jumped to his feet. "And there are more. If we take this Bull Stomper of theirs, the hill giants will probably flee this area. Devil? Demon? What's your guess?"

Syliri placed the large gold nugget into her backpack. "Devil. A demon would never let them live. A devil though. A devil could organize them, get them mining. I'm going with devil. Or something like a devil. Of course, it's hard to imagine a devil being content with hill giants and some gold when a dragon-ruled empire of humans is just up north."

Bruce pointed east. "The giants come from the mountains over there. You can see where the giants crossed the river. The dragon notated possible giants on his map there."

Syliri squinted but did not see anything other than rolling valley floor and a shining river. Seven other giants no doubt would die before they reached the river. Bruce never left his back unprotected in the wild.

* * *

Shak D'Rath, the first paladin of Tiamat, yelled out for divine healing. Dar Tania's blessing burst forth in his heart, energizing his limbs, and giving him a second wind. In front of him, five just barely initiated paladins raised shields and readied blunted spears. Their simulated combat with wooden and blunted weapons resulted in broken bones, lacerations, and lots of bloodshed. When it ended, Shak and a sole survivor squared off. Otor and Wess, two paladins from the second class, stood ready to jump in and have a go at Shak. With the high priestess watching, they wanted to impress.

When the last novice fell, Otor charged forward and caught Shak's blow on his gauntlet. It saved the novice from a broken nose, maybe a concussion. "If I had been old enough and therefore faster, I'd be in your class," Otor grunted at Shak.

"Not true, you passed all the tests, Otor, but failed to do so with faith. I was in your assessment." Shak spun and kicked at Otor. His metal boot connected with Otor's arm block. It sent Shak stumbling forward and Otor backpedaled to keep his balance in the heavy plate armor. "Join us, Wess."

Wess and Otor now circled Shak from opposite sides looking for an opening. Slowly, the tempo of their attacks and feints increased until the two landed a few blows on Shak. Shak grinned through bloodied lips at them. "Well done, now try to keep up." Shak blinked and suddenly was not there anymore. Before Otor could call out a warning to Wess, who had not seen this style of combat, Shak body-slammed Otor face first into the grass. Wess charged forward but Shak was already gone. The next attack and then all the attacks blurred together as Shak stepped in and out of Time's flow to strike at them.

The two paladins went back to back, a strong defensive posture. Though Wess seemed confused by what was happening, Otor managed a few blocks. A crack of bone and screams of agony interrupted Dar's quiet explanation of the technique to the five paladins watching with her. Annoyance crossed her face but before she could halt the fight, another bone crack resounded.

Dar pulled her hair back into a knot. "Shak, stop breaking bones! I cannot heal these until they're set correctly." She signaled for one of her priestesses to go and get the bone setter. "It's too much." The bone setter should have been with them from the beginning. Shak's impatience meant they had started without the old lady from the Dire Wolf tribe.

Ignoring her, Shak called out for divine fire. "That's it," Dar swore. She stepped out of the River's flow, enjoying how the torrent of energy caressed her skin. It reminded her of a river flowing with energy instead of water; gods accessed the world in this in-between-the-moment place. She reappeared between the three paladins and caught Shak's wooden sword, pushing it aside before it connected with Otor's head.

Shak's momentum in the attack carried him forward into Dar. Though he spun sideways from Dar's throw, he still smashed into her. Silvery light flickered around Dar where Shak's armor pressed into her and it then threw both Shak and the other paladin away from her. Though only briefly visible, Dar's goddess armor glimmered for a moment and then went invisible again. The paladins pointed and whispered excitedly. They had heard the priestesses acquired this invisible faith-based armor at some point, but had never seen it.

The divine armor only became apparent when Dar stopped wearing armor after a year of training with the paladins. During a combat drill three years ago, Sean's attack had broken the hardened leather shoulder pauldrons Dar wore back then. His next attack would have hit the exposed shoulder. Instead, a flash of light and repulsion threw Sean's wooden training sword out of his hand. In the moment, the flash of light took the shape of a dragon tail smashing his sword back and away. Emboldened but not understanding what just happened either, Dar's counterattack pressed Sean until he summoned his holy avenger. Subsequent attacks were mostly deflected but after one made it through the strange armor and almost killed Dar, they stopped. Dar had knelt and ordered them to continue attacking her. Sean refused to attack her again, but Shak and the others had gone at it. Not a single wooden training sword broke through, unless Dar allowed it. Metal blades yielded the same outcome.

Shak recovered his footing mid-air and almost drove forward again after landing. Against the racing of his heart and the fatigue of his battle training, he took a deep breath – just like Captain Sean had shown them – and prayed in his heart and mind. He felt the Queen's adoration but also the ever-present wish that he submit to the high priestess. He noticed the burn char of Dar's hand on his practice sword. "You must be angry," he said pointing to the black handprint.

Dar did look angry. Her fiery hair and red lips seemed dim compared to the burning in her eyes. "You need to learn control! This is training, not combat."

Dar's hand ignited with fire and Shak became aware that she moved in Time around him. His paladin resistance to magic vanished. Shak felt its loss and knew he could try to step out of the river and confront Dar, but would fail. He knew Dar's anger from other training and combat situations, but it had never been directed at him like this. Shak dropped to his knees and held his hands out to either side. "You and Sean pressed me until I nearly broke. Why would the new knights have anything less?"

His tone and words were totally respectful. Dar sensed no intent to mock or challenge her though she remembered how he ignored her command and express instructions to not train this way unless a bone setter were present. She pointed to the unconscious, broken, and battered initiates. "If you don't see the difference, maybe Sean overestimated your judgement. A paladin, and I'm going to quote your commander here, 'must fight for a cause.' Is the cause of this battle to test them to death?" Before Shak could answer, she snapped at him. "No! It's to gain experience with basic combat skills and see how they respond in combat to divine healing. There is a time and place for them to be tested like you were. That time and place is not every drill, every day, every time." She ran her hands through her hair and let the autumn wind blow along her neck. Like Shak, she took a deep breath. "Is that what you want – to see them all tested to death?" she asked quietly.

Shak blinked and then dropped to the ground, pressing his face to the dirt. The Tanian formal bow showed total submission. "Only on your command, Priestess!"

"How many times did you die?" Dar asked. "Eight?" Dar sneered the word knowing Shak knew she knew how many times. She had restored him twelve times. The trial had nearly exhausted her. Even now, she wondered if Shak's trial had stopped because of his reaching his maximum for healing, or her reaching her maximum for healing. Tiamat whispered that the answer was a limitation with Shak, not her.

"No, Priestess! I died twelve times!"

Behind Dar, the initiates whispered and she detected a faint tone of anxiety. Dar whirled to face them. "As you learn and grow in Tiamat's grace, you will be able to die more and more. We cannot measure a wound, but death is absolute. To the faithful, death is an inconvenience. I need my paladins unafraid of death and totally trusting that their goddess will restore them to continue fighting. So, we test you. You will be tested until you are dead. This combat drill with Shak and Commander Sean – this is to strengthen you. You're not paladins yet. Why?" She prayed for them all, except Otor and Wess with their broken bones, and healed them all. They moved into line alongside Shak.

Dar pointed to Shak and then the others. "When the bone setter gets here, you will watch and you will help. I need my paladins to be able to set their own bones. Unafraid of death and unconcerned with pain, your body is your Temple of War." She brushed dirt and blood from Shak's face. He had been sorely wounded too. "I ask of you each these questions. You do not know your limits. If you don't know your limits, how can I or your commanders trust you in war? The god emperor did not set this nation in motion for you to run off and die permanently in your first real fight. So, you will train and then we will test you to learn – how much pain, how much death can your faith endure? Shak, tell them about your first death."

Shak said loudly, "My first test – I died almost immediately. After being restored just two more times, I fell unconscious. My second test, I lasted twelve times!"

"And across an entire day and night of continuous fighting against Commander Sean, Bruce, and Dread Lord Ynt'taris. Second, not knowing your limits and not trusting each other to stretch those limits, you cannot endure the dragons. When we have trust, when you can endure the dragons and their terrible presence, then you will be my paladins. This also tests my priestesses: how much healing can they provide to you, my dearest knights?"

The bone setter arrived and Dar said, "I'll see you all at the Temple site tomorrow, at sunrise."

Behind her departure, the bone setter started her terrible work. Dar walked for many long minutes accompanied by the sounds of leaves crunching under foot and the screams of the five paladins-to-be until she could no longer hear them. Though her words felt right, something in her mind bothered her. She considered it and an hour later realized the truth: Shak had improved massively between his first and second rites. All of the paladins did. But, their progress ceased after that initial burst.

Speaking to herself, she said, "If I kill Shak twelve times now, he will still fall the twelfth time." Workers alongside the walkway to the grand staircase eyed her, wondering whom she spoke with. And all of the paladins seemed locked in their current development, not just Shak. Though they improved in other areas, such as memorizing scripture and how to tend wounds, their combat prowess – which should be growing daily towards the divine – remained where it was after a short burst of improvement.

With only her own progress to measure it against, Dar realized that her priestesses had a similar problem. They grew in their powers and faith quickly, then stagnated. Dar alone remained the only one capable of calling a divine flamestrike. Even the god emperor had deigned to not speak to the others, considering them not yet ready for a more personal relationship. She could not figure it out and Tiamat offered her no answers. She found herself envying Sean's Pragmatist Order, with their scriptures and commentaries going back into the early stages of Merakor. *No doubt,* she thought, *they would just pop open some ancient book and it would all be spelled out in plain language.* She knew it bothered Sean too, who took it as a personal insult that his students' progress stalled.

It can't be permanent. Could it? After Shak's first improvement, Dar required all new paladins to go through similar testing. Of a hundred tested, only a few failed to be revived after the first time. The others all endured between two and ten resurrections. Dar remembered Sean watching it all years ago during Shak's trial, his face impassive and hard to read. It was a year after they rescued the Halflings and they had just routed a coven of vampires from the edges of the southern swamp they named "Quat." Dar remembered how she trembled while reaching out to the Goddess yet again to call Shak back to life. When the young paladin drew his first breath, Dar had looked up at the Commander. "How many times can you be healed?" she asked of Sean.

"I don't know my maximum. Pha Rann does not have this obsession over testing limits the way you seem to, Dar. On a quest, I once fell four times. Then we defeated our enemy. Only a crazy person would push death's boundary. At some point, you're either torturing the paladins or recruiting priestesses with a penchant for enjoying the knights' pain. You don't want sadists for clerics. Trust me, it's a bad mix. Taysor does not do this. I find it... nauseating. I wish you would stop. You're going to break their morale."

The chastisement under his words had stung her. "I thought we were doing the right thing," she said. "The Queen approves."

Sean turned his back to her. "Your Queen approves their advancement by this brutal method? All my time here and I've questioned, a few times, the designation of your Queen as evil. Watching this though reassures me. What good god would use pain to drive improvement?"

Dar walked away and spat over her shoulder, "If you don't like it, help us find a better way."

Later that night, she found Sean and apologized to him. And, it became another unspoken topic in their relationship. Over the years, she knew Sean had a list of forbidden topics with her too. She mentally went through them: resurrection as a training tool, necromantic reversals of healing, the nature of Tiamat and Bahamut's relationship, love, Sean's vows of chastity, the difference in their auras when they stepped out of the River's flow… and it went on and on. Dar found herself getting depressed. "I've only known him five years and this list is already getting hard to remember. In five more years, we'll have so many things we don't talk about, we'll actually need Bruce's hand language to communicate."

* * *

The goblins feared Bull Stomper. At the end of the tall but narrow tunnel, a goblin screamed. Set against the shrill cry of pain, a deep rumble sounded, "Work faster. No lazy ones get food. Lazy ones *are* food." Wet rending and then slurping sounds quieted not just the unlucky meal but the hundreds of miners working the narrow shaft. Bull Stomper growled out, "I'm still hungry and hear no mining." All the goblins hastily resumed work, scratching at the crumbly white rock around the harder white stones flecked with gold. Iron digging spikes and chisels rested on the ground as part of each miner's toolset. As Bull Stomper drew near, many of the goblins grabbed these iron spikes and began cracking rocks apart. It made them look busy and productive. It also gave them a small measure of defense and comfort.

Bull Stomper kicked the goblins while walking down the line to the end of the tunnel. At the end, Bull Stomper slammed his fist into the stone face there and said, "This needs to be three paces farther along by tomorrow or I'll feed you to the other miners," he growled. The goblins there chipped away at the end section trying to extend it. A larger goblin, one called a hobgoblin, stood guard over them with a crossbow loaded and ready to fire.

The hobgoblin nodded to Bull Stomper and then hit one of the workers in the head with the butt of his crossbow. "We're making good time, Bull Stomper. Good time," he said. "Could always use more of these squibs though." To the hobgoblin, Bull Stomper looked like a twisted human with oily black skin and devil-like horns growing along his arms. Lacking a nose, Stomper's head framed a circular fanged mouth below overly-large eyes, like a frog's. Two lines of small horns grew back from his eyes to end just at a bony ridge that continued down his spine. Golden bracers embedded with gems slipped along veiny forearms marked by circular scars. A hobgoblin skull, polished, hung on Stomper's belt. It was the last overseer, who had not worked fast enough.

Bull Stomper placed his ear against the stone and growled. "We need another thirty paces. At least." He snapped at the hobgoblin, "How many today?"

"Four, Bull Stomper. With the additional three they just promised, that'll be seven paces today." It hurt the overseer to think in numbers. The overseer rubbed his neck and gulped. "Give me more squibs, or drugs. Food helps. I'm working them near to death as it is. We'll get thirty paces in ten days." The hobgoblin grunted, "No, numbers. Days. Bull Stomper, I can get them to work faster if I can have more of the drug."

Bull Stomper watched their progress for a few moments before he unlatched the skull at his belt. With his other hand, he drew his black claw across his arm and let blood run into the skull. "Drugs," Stomper laughed. "Here you go. Let me know when you break through."

The overseer watched Stomper leave, glad to be left in charge. Things had gotten much worse since Stomper arrived. "I miss the wars," he harrumphed. "Here, drink this." He shoved the blood-filled skull towards the tunnel diggers.

None of them wanted to drink it, but after a few threats and a beating, one finally did. The blood's effect hit immediately. The goblin's emaciated body went rigid. Next, sweating – lots of sweating, and trembling throughout its body hit in waves. The overseer gave him back his digging tools and pointed at the wall. "Kill the wall," he whispered to the goblin.

With a frenzy of bloodlust and rage, the goblin attacked the wall as if his life depended on it. After maybe ten minutes, the goblin dropped the tools and began clawing at the wall, biting at the stone. In moments, only bloody pulp and gore showed where the digger had been. Still, the short burst of activity created a hole half an arm deep. Widening it would be easy. The overseer smiled. "So predictable. You!" The next goblin had to be forced to drink, and to the same effect. Some lasted minutes, others lasted longer. They each attacked the wall until they died or fell unconscious.

Days passed and by the time they breached the section, all goblins the overseer could catch and force to drink lay in a wet heap of corpses before the wall. An iron spike at last stabbed through and fresh cave air blew back into the mining tunnel. Seeing he had murdered the wall at last, the digger quickly widened the hole by biting at the edges and tried to burrow through.

The hobgoblin almost shot him the butt, but then took an iron spike and stabbed it into the hapless creature's lower back. Using the spike to pull the goblin back, the overseer yelled, "No one enters. Get Stomper."

Bull Stomper arrived quickly. "You've done well, overseer. I'm pleased you did not enter this place." Stomper gave the hobgoblin a key and smiled. "Take your pick." The key would open a cell full of females and food.

The overseer happily accepted. A key meant wealth and power in the clans beyond even their chieftain. "How else may I serve you, Stomper?"

"Nothing. Go. Enjoy," Stomper said. Turning his gaze down the tunnel, Bull Stomper snarled, "No one enters, unless you're sick of living." He paused for a moment and enchanted with his hands over the heap of dead goblins. One by one, arms and legs twitched back to life and began shoving to clear a way out. Sick green light filled their eyes and the reanimated dead clawed their way free of the pile. Stomper pointed to the tools and said, "Get back to work mining gold." The expressionless tone of his voice gave the surviving goblins chills. When their zombie brethren stumbled back to mechanically chip away at the rock, the hunger emanating from their dead eyes was too much. One and then another tried to run away. Stomper smiled and let the zombies feast on those fleeing. "All of you, work!"

Stomper entered the new cavern. It was very large but threaded by large columns that made it seem tight, like a forest. Pools of cold water rippled and splashed as he walked through it. Not needing light to see, he looked around and walked around stalagmites to a large central pool. This one sat still and calm. A faint radiance shimmered from its deep center. "Just like the master said," Stomper said, squatting down. He touched the liquid. Nothing happened and he laughed. A leather pouch from his belt melted away when he dipped it in the pool. "Acid." He placed one of the gold rocks into the pool and watched as the stone crumbled away leaving only gold in his hand. He laughed again. His master Ylgolth had said, *When you find the cave of acid lights, you will drink deeply and bathe. That will mark your ascension to Azuros.*

Stomper dove in head first. His scant clothing, he felt it all disintegrate and melt away from him. When he reemerged, he willed there to be light and laughed at how easy it was. His will sent small globes of red light dancing throughout the cavern. He laughed again. Before, he would have had to cast a spell and make hand gestures. Except for his gold jewelry and the gold in his hands, everything had dissolved, even the goblins' bones. He squeezed the gold into a tiny ball and chuckled again. Things were going well. He cupped the acid in his hands, took a deep breath, and then drank.

He felt nothing at first, but a warm feeling followed by pain in his bowels made him choke. He tried to avoid screaming, but when the acid ate through his stomach, he could not stand it anymore. His melting stomach gave way to other organs until he could see inside his bowels. Stomper tried to cradle himself in pain but then he could not breathe as his throat melted away. He screamed in terrible rasping agony and then threw himself into the pool, drinking. Ylgolth said this would hurt and that he must drink. How did he say it? *Your body's pain is a sacrifice to your new form. The more pain, the stronger your Azuros form will be.* Stomper clawed and raked at his body to increase his pain.

Outside, the goblin miners shuddered. Stomper never screamed, never showed pain. The loud splashing noise and ending of the scream - had he died? One held an iron spike and gibbered to the others, "Kill Stomper?" The others shrank back. A few began chipping away at the gold ore. No one wanted to challenge Bull Stomper. Their last champion, a large goblin they called "Bull," Stomper had killed by, well, stomping him to death.

From the pool, shadows rose up touching the walls in the ill-lit tunnel. It looked like Stomper but larger. Their hearts fell. It was Stomper, alive. Large wings burst from his back. The faint radiance of the pool illuminated winged Stomper for the goblins to see. Always fearsome, Bull Stomper projected a new sensation now – cold and numbing hunger.

"I did it!" Stomper shrieked. "Now, for my next metamorphosis - *Embros.*" As he walked back to the tunnel, the wings folded and draped over his body. The numerous spines and horns of his *Fecundus* form, melted back into perfect grey skin. Even the horn ridges on his head, so prominent before, folded back. "Pure and perfect, I am reborn." Stomper pointed to a goblin and demanded, "Before, did I look green, well – green like your kind?" A long bony tail twisted out from the base of Stomper's spine. Sharp bone ridges gleamed as the appendage moved on its own.

The goblin, terrified of becoming another meal, shook its head and said, "N, no-o. Not green. You look blue, like sky now."

This pleased Bull Stomper. "I wish to see my reflection, but never mind. You are the new overseer." Stomper put his hand on the goblin's torso. His spiny fingers curled nearly all the way around. Webbing there reminded the goblin of a frog. When Stomper removed his hand, he pointed to the spiral of cauterized cuts and said, "I have marked you for power and glory. Serve me and you will become more powerful than your mightiest chieftain. Now, get these miners back to mining and remember – no one enters the cavern!"

Bull Stomper blew out of the mine. His new form, with longer legs and arms, allowed him to walk at his old running speed. To the hapless miners, only droplets of acid and pain suggested he had even been there at all. The other goblins groveled before their new overseer, hissing in pain where acid dripped onto them. "Mine the gold faster!" their new overseer screamed. "I am merciful! You all dig gold, and I give you food and females!"

Deep in the mining complex, Stomper found the hobgoblin stuffing food into his mouth. The hunger besetting Stomper since his transformation made his stomach growl. The overseer flinched at the sound and turned just in time to see a large claw reaching for his face. The unfamiliar creature looked like a frog-touched demon and the hobgoblin screamed even as a thumb talon speared his throat into his brain. At first bite, Stomper congratulated himself. "Feeding them well does make them taste better." He reached for one of the goblin slaves ferrying food and other rewards to the hobgoblin. "But, I'm still hungry."

* * *

Bruce and Syliri leaned back against a fallen tree. A small fire crackled softly in front of them. She shuddered when Bruce ran his fingers through the snakes that should have been human hair. The snakes pushed against his hand, enjoying the feeling. "All these years and no one has ever played with your hair? There's always some kid somewhere playing with snakes. I can't believe never." They talked about their earliest memories. Mostly Bruce did as Syliri only had first memories. The eldar did not have births or young phases; they just happened.

"Hair?" she laughed. "No, how could they? Alerius tried many times to introduce me to members of the tribes. It never went well. Eventually, he apologized and told me to come and go as I wanted. It was easier to stay in the mountain, on the outside looking in. Being alone isn't a bad thing," She kissed his hand and leaned into him. Several of her more independent serpents curled up around Bruce's head wanting more attention.

"If more humans spent more time alone, we'd no doubt be a better race." Bruce kissed her forehead but had to kiss Kelly before the cobra would move to the side and let him. "I think your snakes are jealous. You know that that was a cobra, right?"

She did not. "I have twenty-nine snakes along my head. I've never thought of them as anything different than me. Do you name your fingers?" She touched his ring finger. "Is this your cobra?"

He laughed softly. "The things you say would get you in trouble in Taysor. So, Alerius. And a medusa. How did that happen? You told me you'd explain it on this mission. My head is already full of maedera and medusae and gorgons. But the dragon thing? I just don't get it yet." They had this conversation nearly every mission.

Syliri pinched his ring finger. It looked so perfectly human. Her own fingers looked scaled and ugly, too long, too skinny. She sighed, "Maybe someday I'll figure out this shapeshifting thing and give you a proper form to love."

"Don't do that," Bruce reassured her. "You get like this and shut down. Please don't. It's not about the form. We live in a world of magic. Anyone with magic can be any form. It's not the form I love."

When he spoke like this, it made her want to freeze the moment forever. She suppressed the urge to petrify him. He felt it, her self-control and kissed her forehead again. "You'll grow tired of this at some point," she cajoled him. "I bet there aren't many couples in Taysor where the woman has to actively resist turning her love to stone in any moment of emotion."

Bruce shrugged. "Humans have their issues too. I'm the last one to tell you if petrification is even worse than how some humans treat one another. All I know is that I have wandered this world and know I will never find someone like you. I see what you're doing, by the way. It won't work. I still want to know about Alerius."

She punched his leg. "Okay, I used to be a dragon, I think. That surprises you? Most eldar were dragons at one point or another you know. I followed Alerius always. I cannot remember a moment before Time when I was not near Alerius. His fire and heat, they made it easier for me to move, to be me. At some point, I became fascinated with stone. Turning things to stone, turning them back, turning them into different things."

She fell quiet for a while, lost in the crackling flames past her hand holding Bruce's. "When Time flowed," she shrugged. "I had left my dragon form for this one. I must have encountered snakes or been trying to make snakes – smaller dragons – when Time moved. It trapped me like this. I nearly went mad. I kept trying to return to my dragon form and could not. Then, the maedar came. Alerius saved me from ending myself." While talking, she picked up a stone and it morphed from dragon to medusa to snake to stone in her hand. As she did so, her mood darkened and she shuddered. "I hate doing that but it felt appropriate to show you this again. It helps me remember that I control, am not controlled by what the maedar forced my sisters and I to be. You cannot imagine the horror of those misogynists."

"I should thank the dragon then," Bruce said smugly. "Never thought a colored dragon would do something I appreciated."

"Shhh," Syliri said. "Alerius has been like a big brother to me. He's not just a dragon. If you keep trying to see him that way, either he'll get angry with you or you'll fail to understand the most important thing about him, about me, about the eldar."

"I hate it when you make these distinctions. Yes, I'm not like you. But, then no one has ever been quite like us. So, what am I missing this time?"

"Time, it came at us like a murderer. If someone attacked you, wouldn't you fight back?" He agreed. "And if you killed the murderer, would you be evil?"

"No, of course not," Bruce said. "But you're making an argument that, while it may have been true in the Dragon Wars, is not true in this world today, where Time flows. You can't kill Time."

"Oh Bruce, the grandest of all lies is that Time is natural. Of course, you can kill it; sure, not everyone. But, for you – you could. If I transition to the ethereal, I'll see you dying. And, you'll see me being killed too - too slowly to matter. I'll live forever cursed, watching those I love be slain by this natural thing you call 'aging.' It's a curse, Bruce. That's how I see it, how Alerius sees it. When we get back, I'm going to ask Dar or Sean to help you see this. I've never been able to 'access the River' as Alerius, and now Dar too, calls it."

Bruce laughed. "Maybe. Okay, maybe. But, what if you're wrong? What if the red dragon only sees opportunity? After all, if you were being chased by a murderer you could not beat and someone powerful like Alerius shows up and says, 'Hey, I can save you!' Not only would you accept his help, but you'd be grateful. Dare I say, Alerius would seem," and he pointed up to the sky, "heavenly. But, he's not heavenly. He's a fire-breathing red dragon that wants to hand this world over to a hell lord. And, for all his help, you're still here even if you're dying slowly. You can call Time a murderer, but for the rest of us mortals, we call it living. The time we have isn't murder; it's a gift. You matter to me. Our handful of time, it's everything to me."

Syliri sighed. "You don't understand. You should talk to Alerius about the archmage Veltrestan."

"Why? Who's Veltrestan?"

"He was the Merakoran mage credited with creating the magic that detects the inherent good or evil nature of someone or something. Bruce, I saw it myself. It's not like we were all sitting in dark caves during Merakor's rise and fall, watching the barbarians learn how to swim. That entire place, Merakor was – joyous. Like nothing I could imagine and have yet to encounter again. In that state, to devise a spell to detect good or evil – as if mortal motivations were so well-packaged – is an incorrect philosophy. After all, if you cast that stupid spell on me, I come across as evil. Why? What have I done to you, to the Taysorans, to anyone that would make me identify as evil?"

Bruce started to answer, but Syliri threw him down by the fire and straddled him. The snakes shot forward stopping just shy of biting Bruce's face. A few rested their fangs on his skin. "I am not evil, though I can understand why humans like Veltrestan might identify my fallen sisters as such. I come across as Evil because I lingered too close to the nexal gate of Warp when Time flowed. It was an accident. I could have been by Creation; then I'd come across in that stupid spell as good. Is the world really so black and white for you? One eldar is here – Good. Another is over there – oops, sorry: Evil. It seems kind of arbitrary from our perspective. Then, you toss Tiamat into it. She defeated a hell lord and carved an entire dominion out of Hell. If one of the arrogant Cuthberic knights did this, they'd be lauded as heroes! You'd have paraded commemorating them. Don't deny it!"

He sat up to encircle her waist with his arms. "Good, evil. It only matters to me that I behave righteously, in my own way and make the world a better place around me. I can't speak to grand conflict, hell lords, and demons. It's all beyond me, but yes, in Taysor, the Cuthberics would lord it over everyone. In our time together, I haven't seen you do evil and that's enough for me, even if your overall life is evil and you're doomed to hell." He winked at her. "Right now though, I feel like misbehaving. Misbehavior is my inherent nature. Syl, you are absolutely on my scales of misbehaving tonight."

Syliri laughed and let him roll her to the side.

Chapter 2 – Hrax Terrej

"It's exhausting, isn't it?" Shak commented to Otor and Wess. Just days after their fight, the healing, and Dar's chastisement, the three paladins found themselves with Bomoki on the south and eastern edge of Home. A series of small creeks and rivers created a bog against the eastern mountains that eventually dropped to the Sea of Ymac farther out. Because the Halflings never came here, but had plans to look into rare mushrooms that might grow someday in a place like this, the Morbattanian patrols came out to look for signs of encroachment by possible threats. "I wonder if all Halflings are scared of trolls?" Shak mused.

Bomoki leaned back against a tree and picked his nails. "You all look like death just barely recovered. Too much healing, I take it?" When no one answered, Bomoki spat on the ground. "Your god emperor would not approve of this distance you keep from me. Magic is very much a part of his plans for you."

Otor and Wess carefully studied a map to find their bearings, even though Bomoki had brought them to a well-known landmark established by Sean and Gerin several years back. Shak undid a clasp on his breastplate and carefully removed it. "Let's remove our armor for a bit. We're not effective like this," Shak said. "Bomoki, it all takes some getting used to. Remember, we grew up with legends and tales of magic, but they all came from the god emperor and the Court of Patriarchs. We considered it miracles and blessings. It's a bit jarring to suddenly have a normal person doing things we worshipped as divine just a handful of years ago."

"Hardly normal," Bomoki said. He walked over to Shak and helped him remove his back plates. "Even though your people seem created for Tiamat, you have yet to find a single Tanian able to use magic."

"Thank you," Shak said as he caught a handle and helped Bomoki lower the heavy steel. "With the Goddess, maybe we don't need magic though it sure is handy to," Shak wiggled his fingers to mimic Bomoki casting a spell, "woosh, and we're a two week horse ride away from where we were. I don't suppose you were given orders to retrieve us after we complete this atonement."

This time smirking, Bomoki said, "I was not. It's stupid you needed to atone at all. You're fighters. So what if a few bones get broken? My guess is that they've already decided how long you'll be out here and I'll be sent to retrieve you at that time. So, that being said, enjoy yourselves." Bomoki mimicked Shak's finger wiggling, then vanished.

"What exactly are we supposed to do out here?" Wess asked. "I never heard of atonement until suddenly the high priestess is lecturing us."

Shak dropped his shoulder armor, the heavy pauldrons clanking as they rested atop his breastplate. The other two had similarly begun removing the heavy plate mail. Shak said, "It's a paladin thing. The Commander once told us a story of a Pha Rannic paladin who broke a vow. His atonement was an extreme version of that vow, to be obeyed absolutely while on a quest. After the quest, his paladin powers returned to him. From that and other stories, I get the sense that Sean's religion uses atonement for bigger, grander things than our getting a bit carried away."

Wess and Otor laughed. They had been training together long enough that, Wess in particular, they enjoyed the moments when training became actual fighting. In the tribes, they grew up this way. The entire culture struggled to embrace sparring as a valid form of training. Wess said, "When the bone setter adjusted my arm and wrist, one of Dar Tania's acolytes lectured me about becoming addicted to pain and the relief of healing. Whatever that means."

Shak nodded. "I was lectured by Dar and the Commander on this several times. You do actually need to be careful of that. Just like we can only be revived so many times, the priestesses can only heal us so many times. If we needlessly suffer wounds, we make them needlessly expend faith, not for the Goddess' glory, but because we were reckless."

Otor sat down on a fallen tree and began unbuckling the steel greaves wrapping about his lower legs. "I always feel like I'm walking on air after I drop this stuff. You know, reckless for us isn't really reckless for you anymore, Shak. In our last fight, I saw my old friend from the tribes but there was definitely something else. Things that I could have blocked or dodged before, they just worked out for you, or at least, against me."

"How do you guys handle it all?" Wess asked. "It's not a lack of faith for me. I mean, the dragons, the high priestess, they're all right there. What is there to believe in? The first time I was nearly killed in training, I remember praying for healing, and it just happened. I barely think about it anymore."

Shak patted the younger knight on the shoulder and helped him remove the last bit of his armor. "Remember, you were chosen from all the fighters because of faith. Even if you take it for granted, you have to hold it foremost in your heart and mind. Everything we do is for Tiamat."

Wess shrugged his plate off and asked, "And for Tiamat, what are we doing here again?"

Shak began to laugh and after a moment tried to say, "Appeasing the high priestess." But, Otor joined in and it became contagious for Wess. After a recovering a bit, Shak finally said, "Appeasing the high priestess because she hates it when we break bones. She's probably watching us now and deciding how many more days we'll be stuck out here."

As if prophetic, a flock of birds flew over them and scat from one landed on Shak's head. He burst into laughter again.

Three days passed with the trio hauling their plate armor south along the bog. The bog and pools of water dropped southwards and eventually drained into the ground. Riding, many days further south it reappeared as part of the Rain River. A smell lingered in the bog and, though they did not notice it anymore, it masked other smells. At night, they whispered because of a keen sense of watching eyes. Otor said that third night, "I did a patrol with Gerin here in the spring. It's so noisy you can barely hear someone talking next to you. I wonder if we'll run into one of Gerin's patrols."

Wess asked, "Gerin was in your class, right Shak?"

"He was. He killed almost as many of the thieves and ogres as I did back when we found Summer's people. He's a good man, a good friend, and strong knight."

Wess marveled, "He gave up being a chieftain to become a knight?"

Shak nodded. "Like I said, he's a good man. He was the only one from the chieftains who made it through the tests. For a time, I actually thought he might beat me when we did that race up the mountain."

"I heard Gerin was being pushed as a husband for Dar Tania a while ago," Otor commented. "What's going to happen with that whole situation? Whenever I return home, my own tribe seems tense about it."

Shak poked at the fire. "I don't know what happens. My tribe is also on edge. Except for the god emperor, there's never been a single person in charge of the tribes. That so many foreigners keep coming in has Wolf on alert. Bomoki, and those like him, they make it worse. I trust Dar knows what she is doing though. I'd be lying if I said I didn't want some kind of a confrontation to happen. Dar, by herself, would rip the chieftains to pieces. They know this. Even if they somehow won, there is no way the dragons would stand by and let it happen."

They began to speculate about what would happen in such a challenge. During a heated discussion about which side the Commander would take, they heard a loud cracking sound to their east. Moments later, the pool of water some twenty paces in that direction made a washing noise as water lapped up on the edge of the bog. With no wind, Shak pointed to their swords and armor and they carefully pulled it back from the fire behind trees they had prepared as places of safe retreat if attacked from the bog. Shak and Otor quickly donned their armor with a minimum of noise and then helped Wess. With his upper armor still not completed, they heard another loud cracking sound and then a wet thud that trembled the ground. All went quiet until a giant log came flying out of the darkness to smash through their camp. A shower of sparks from the fire shot into the sky.

Shak signaled for quiet and they all drew their swords. The thrown log still had roots attached at the base and was almost as wide around as Shak's torso. Shak mouthed the word "giant" but Otor did not understand. A moment later, there was another thud and another uprooted tree smashed through their clearing. This one slammed into the trees the three paladins had moved behind. Everything went still and then goat-sized rocks began raining down into their clearing. Watching in the dim light of their ruined fire, Shak could see the general area they came from. Their attacker must be standing in the bog. A cluster of rocks on the far side of the pool matched the general size of these rocks. Tree branches and debris rained down around them as rock after rock smashed around them.

Shak pointed to the bog and then himself. He made a curving gesture with his hand to the left towards the bog. He pointed to Otor and Wess and made a similar gesture. He hoped they understood that he wanted to flank their assailant.

Shak prayed to Takhissis and then ran. He hoped Otor would understand what to do. Reaching cover behind another tree and still seeing rocks smashing towards their fire, Shak grew bolder and ran to the thinner trees and scraggly bushes along the bog's edge. With a clear moonlit night, Shak quickly spotted a pale-skinned giant ripping stones from the far edge of the bog and throwing them. Grateful they had surveyed the bog enough to know how large the wet area was, Shak ran to the giant's left to a narrow bridge of firmer land that divided the bog in half.

"Attack!" Shak screamed, hoping Otor and Wess were likewise moving to the giant's right. The initial thud and wet sound was the giant slipping into the bog. It looked stuck, or at least sitting. The next rock barely missed Shak, who had to dodge low.

Shak reached the same side as the giant and noted strange spiral scars on the creatures left side shoulder and chest. He also saw Otor leading the charge at the giant's other side. Focused on Shak, the giant seemed oblivious to the other two. Shak prayed and his sword ignited in Tiamat's flames. The spiral markings on the giant came alive with reflected light from the avenging sword blade. Shak wondered what they meant.

The giant lifted a large boulder from the ground and at the last minute decided to use it as a bludgeon to smash Shak. A feint to the side and a lucky slip on the wet ground allowed Shak to dodge and cut up at the giant's fingers. The sword dug a trench along the outer two fingers and then the smell of blood reached Shak's nostrils. He realized that the blood smelled rotten.

Grunting, the giant slid the rock against Shak. The might behind that simple gesture slammed Shak into the air. Tumbling and twisting, Shak prayed to Tiamat and though he landed in the muck, the ground felt firm beneath his feet. He wiped rotting leaves from his eyes and saw Otor slice into and up the lower hip of the giant. Wess also attacked, but missed as he tried to dodge the giant sweeping his other hand at them.

The giant really is giant, Shak thought, marveling at its size. Used to the dragons and the garden creatures, seeing one actually trying to kill them gave him a new appreciation for Syliri's lectures about the giants. The markings and strange skin color threw him but Shak felt sure this must be a hill or stone giant, the smallest of giantkind.

"Let's all attack at the same time! I'll distract it and try to keep its attention on me. Remember, we can scratch at it with our swords all day, but we need to cut its throat or some other weak point to defeat it." Shak charged.

The giant completely ignored Shak and rolled over to remove his foot from the bog. The other foot kicked out and though it missed, it sent a tidal splash of mud at Shak. Shak realized he could try to dodge it, but instead, he prayed to Tiamat and stepped out of the moment. Rising up from the River, Shak noted the giant's aura seemed dark green and sick. He easily moved away from the splash, and re-entered the River to jump atop the giant's back leg. Maggot-infested pelts draping the giant's groin gave him enough leverage to vault onto the giant's back.

Otor and Wess pressed their own attacks when the giant braced himself to kick at Shak. Wess made two slicing cuts at the giant's wrist and shouted in triumph as blood sprayed forth. Otor charged the giant's center with his sword over his head and drew a deep and bloody gash from the giant's exposed rib cage down to the opposite hip. The giant now screamed in pain and sought to crush Otor by dropping flat.

Wess cried out, "Otor, look out!"

Otor dropped to his knees, sliding on the wet ground, and braced his sword over his head. The giant grunted and then Shak drove his burning sword into the base of the giant's neck.

"Ouch," the giant grumbled. It twisted his body, shaking it like a wet dog drying. The force of it threw Shak to the side who left his sword buried to the hilt in the giant's back of the giant's neck. The flames went out the moment Shak's hand left it.

Wess felt his body tremble. It had surprised him that he passed the tests. While it brought great honor to his family, he had never considered himself anything other than a fisherman. Sparring, training, none of it prepared him for this. The Fish Tribe moved a lot between the Cordabad and the coast. In his tribe the warriors, not the fishermen, fought monsters. With fingers trembling so badly Wess could hardly hold his sword, he saw the giant tilt its head and focus on him. Though wounded terribly, and in pain, the giant looked terrible beyond any nightmare Wess could remember.

Wess prayed to Tiamat. The simple song of faith, one of Dar's hymns based on an ancient folk song, filled his mind and then, the name Takhissis came to his lips. "Takhissis, grant me power!" Wess screamed. Fire and light exploded in his heart and limbs. Wess, the fisherman who worshipped Tiamat, became Wess, a paladin of Takhissis in that moment. His vision narrowed to just the giant's eye. His charge seemed to slow everything else. He noticed his own reflection growing in the giant's lens. *I look really good*, Wess thought. Not knowing why or how he knew, Wess saw himself leap sword first into the giant's eye. Somehow, he cleared the ground in his heavy plate armor and speared the exact center of his own reflection in that dark pool.

The giant screamed in agony this time and reared up, trying to regain his footing and stand. Blood and gel ooze seeped from the blinded orb and the many wounds it had already suffered were too much. The monster could not see Wess, nor Otor somewhere below where the pain skewered his gut. Shak though, Shak it could see.

Shak prayed gratitude to the Goddess for the gift of another paladin. Shak found a branch buried in muck and tried to remember Sean's many teachings on this topic. "Feel the sword, Shak," he said to himself. "See the fire." Though nothing happened, Shak attacked the giant with the muddy and fragile stick. "Takhissis, aid me!" Shak prayed as he charged. Just as he cut at the giant's knee tendons, the branch flickered and then burst into fire. "For Your glory!" Shak screamed as he cut and slashed into the giant's bent knee.

Feeling a new burning pain in his knee amid the agony elsewhere in its body, the giant tried to roll to the side and crush Shak with it. Sensing the giant's hulk moving towards him, Shak scrabbled through the bloody mud and barely avoided being crushed. He saw Wess come falling out of the giant's eye even as the giant swatted at the knight. The sick crunch of broken bones resounded where Wess landed askew on his legs. The giant's hand, attempting to swat at Wess, turned into a fist to pummel the ground. Otor was nowhere to be seen still and Shak prayed for his friend. Though a camaraderie had quickly developed in the first class, Otor was the first fellow knight Shak had really connected with. Injuries aside, Otor was the first to not pull punches and Shak respected the bulldog attitude he brought to everything.

Though exhausted from using the River, Shak whispered a prayer at Dar's wisdom for testing him so many times and ways that Shak knew he could do it again. In the moment of the giant's fist arcing down to kill Wess, Shak caught and pulled Wess free.

Blinded by blood and liquid from the eye, Wess did not see Shak save him, but felt a sudden jarring as he slid across the ground and then a trembling as the giant's knuckles buried deep into the mud and rocks. Finally, Wess' eyes cleared and he saw Shak looking back at the giant. He held a small and molded branch in his hand.

The giant turned to face them so that it could see with its other eye. "What is that?" Wess called out pointing. In the center of the spiral markings, a snake-like creature had begun to crawl out. In the darkness and sporadic light from Shak's firesword, it would have been easy to miss.

"Get it," Shak ordered. The branch ignited in Shak's hand and Shak charged. With exhaustion and fatigue weighing on him now, Shak focused all of his will into hearing Tiamat's guidance. Though no answer came, he told himself that She guided his footsteps. She set the stage of this battle. She would decide who won, and who died.

Shak slid past the giant's hand and thrust it along the back. Leaving the firesword embedded there, and lacking even a stick now, another firesword appeared in both of his hands. Shak rose up to cross-cut the giant's throat. An unlucky slip made him miss.

And then, the giant brought both its hands together to smash Shak. The jarring force and rupturing of Shak's eardrums tested his faith, but he told himself, *Dar can heal my hearing. I am Takhissis' sword against this giant.*

The giant picked him up in both hands and began squeezing while shaking the paladin. Shak ignored it and concentrated on his body as a sword. *If I can wield a stick as a firesword, why not my body?*

Wess eyed the tiny snake as it wriggled free and dropped to the ground. Against the giant's stumbling combat and the crushing strike against Shak, Wess crawled forward to grab the snake, his broken leg trailing behind. This pain, the broken bone pain, he knew that though it hurt, it would be mended. He remembered Dar telling him that poison would not affect him anymore. *It'll still hurt to get bitten*, he thought. The snake felt rigid and oily. It made his skin crawl to hold it, even through his gauntlets.

A bright fire erupted behind him and then heat washed over the bog. The giant screeched and dropped Shak, whose entire body glowed with fire, just like Dar's hair and eyes. Two fireswords extended from Shak's arms and the knight leapt at the giant. This time, one of the swords sliced open the giant's throat, eliciting a rasping gurgle. The giant's attempt to hold the wound shut allowed Shak and Wess to finish it off.

When it at last fell backwards into the bog, they found Otor kneeling in prayer. The knight still held his sword over his head. Coated from head to toe in blood and abdominal organs, Otor's face had turned purple while holding his breath. At Shak's touch, Otor heaved, gulping in air. Exhausted, he fell over. Both his legs below the knees had been pressed into the ground and shattered by the giant's weight.

Otor dry heaved trying to breathe. At last, he asked, "We won?" and yelled it again when Shak indicated he could not hear.

Wess shouted back to them, "Shak's deaf. But, yes, we won. My legs are broken too."

Otor began to laugh. After a moment, Shak and Wess joined in. The camaraderie they shared after brutal training returned to them so easily, even with a dead giant bleeding out near them. Only after the nature of their wounds, and their general dire situation, began to pull at them did Shak signal they needed to move. A fight like this would no doubt draw attention from all over the bog. Shak stood and tried to help Otor, but the knight's legs would not bear any weight. Shak pointed to the blood spilling out from the greaves and indicated to Wess they needed to remove Otor's armor. They found multiple fractures and realized that, while they might splint a broken leg, Otor's situation would require actual bone setting.

Wess was not in much better shape though only one leg had actually broken. The shock and pain in the other stemmed from severe bending. Shak pointed to it and noted that it would be all right. He worked quickly to splint Wess' broken leg and then the sprained one. By the time he finished, Otor had fallen asleep, with fitful breathing. The improvised tourniquets had slipped and Otor's pulse fluttered to Shak's touch. Shak shook his head and silently prayed to Tiamat. Commander Sean could heal even dire wounds by prayer and touch. *Maybe Tiamat will allow...?* Shak felt nothing and realized that until the atonement completed, he had to put less faith in himself and more in the Queen. The irony struck him while he removed his hands from Otor. Faith could heal, but the atonement required penance. In this case, his faith would go unanswered. He sighed loudly.

Igniting his firesword, Shak cauterized the bleeding portions of Otor's wounds and then redid the tourniquets. He signaled to Wess to pray and to move out of the bog. Stripping their heavy armor off, Shak heaved Otor onto his shoulders and carried them out of the bog. Wess struggled in the slippery mud. When Shak went back, he found Wess fallen to the side. Thinking he might have passed out from pain or blood loss, Shak ran over to him. The absence of hearing bothered him. The bog should be very loud. Silence always meant something bad was about to happen.

He found Wess locked in a silent fight for his life. The tadpole snake had broken out of the leather sack at Wess' belt. Its tail wrapped around the knight's throat, Wess looked purple and about to pass out. The head of the snake showed a circular mouth of fangs and strained to bite into Wess. Multiple bites dribbled blood and a faint green ichor along Wess' arms, forehead, and throat. Shak reached down and grabbed the snake from Wess. Dismayed the snake retained its chokehold, Shak jerked back as the snake suddenly stopped attacking Wess and instead bit at Shak's hands. The teeth latched onto his forearm and began digging in.

Instantly, Shak felt ill. It began in his stomach. He almost vomited. Next, a feeling of dizziness struck him and he saw a vast world of beige sand dunes blowing glass marbles against an alien sky. A voice tolled in his mind and then Shak ignited the snake as if an avenging firesword. It shrieked and the mental connection ended when the creature burned to ash in Shak's hand. Shak dropped to the ground near Wess, pleased to see Wess still lived though yellow blisters from the fire circled his neck. Shak helped Wess stand and then, like Otor, heaved Wess onto his shoulders and carried him to Otor.

Shak dug through his gear and found a small metal flask. The precious healing potion, a new thing in Morbatten since Dar Tania, strengthened Otor enough that Shak felt the knight might live if Dar came soon. Otor smiled weakly at Shak and said, "You should take some for yourself." Shak pointed to his ears and shook his head.

Like Commander Sean had many times, Shak put his hand on Otor's head and prayed. Nothing happened except a sense of chastisement. Shak said, "I'm sorry. My faith is not enough to heal like the Commander. If this were a mission, we've failed."

Wess touched Shak's shoulder and said, "I know you can't hear me, but we're alive. That's a victory." Wess embraced Shak and Otor.

"Any ideas on that snake?" Shak asked. "I don't remember that from the statues." When the other two knights shook their heads, Shak noted, "We'll describe it to Dar Tania and the Commander. It's a new thing. We didn't beat the giant until that fell free. We were just annoying it."

The three knights remained huddled together until Otor and Wess at last fell asleep. Bereft of their armor and with night's chill coming on, Shak ignited two fireswords and stood above the two. The swords' light might draw or ward off another attack. *I must trust in Tiamat. I must not let my friends die.* He prayed and corrected himself, *I must not let Tiamat's paladins die. I am but a tool in for you, my Queen. I send my gratitude for the fireswords' warmth. Please let them live, or take my life instead.*

The next morning, Bomoki teleported Dar Tania and Veroi, chief priestess after Dar, into the clearing. Shak dropped to his knees but kept the fireswords burning. The two priestesses checked on Otor and Wess and asked a few questions before they noted the dried blood around Shak's ears. Seeing Shak's mess of bruises, Dar pulled Shak to his feet and embraced him. Only when he embraced her back did Tiamat's healing warmth ignite his soul.

Shak felt the healing energy, but this time the healing power felt different. He realized it had been years since he viewed it as the miraculous event it was. When the divine surge of health reached the snake bite in his forearm, Shak felt it halt. Dar must have felt it too because she had to pray again, several times more, before the bite healed. Shak felt a malicious presence leave his body and realized his entire arm felt cold, like ice water. When his hearing at last returned, he heard Dar say, "I should not be surprised that Bone Breaker Shak, in atonement for breaking bones, would return so many more broken bones."

An acerbic reply rose up in Shak's throat, but he held his silence and dropped to his knees before Dar. "We were attacked by a hill giant bearing a strange parasite. We barely won. I am pleased to report that Wess, at long last, communed with the Queen and fought as a paladin."

Dar looked at Veroi. "Not your usual response, Shak D'Rath. Thank you for tending to Otor and Wess. You have done well." She kissed the top of his forehead. "You have fulfilled your atonement, all of you."

During their ministrations to Otor and Wess, Bomoki retrieved the hill giant corpse, using many small blue disks of energy to lift and bring the corpse to them. He began poking at it. "When you're done with the knights, there's something you need to see here," Bomoki called out.

Like Shak, Dar struggled to heal Wess. The young paladin had suffered many more attacks by the snake. Overcoming that fell power exhausted Veroi and nearly drained Dar. "Otor, I had thought to save myself for you, but we cannot heal you without tending to your bones. As such, I'm going to pray to Tiamat and we will put you to sleep." Otor tried to say thank you, but instantly fell asleep.

Shak supported Wess on his broken leg and watched. "Dar," Shak said. "I felt that resistance in my arm, where the snake attacked me. It felt like no venom…"

"It wasn't venom. It was a spiritual attack against your soul." She pointed to Shak's arm. "If you imagine your body – not this one but the ideal one you'd have if you were an Eldar – your arm became infected and was dying. Untended for much longer, you spirit arm would have actually died. Same with you Wess."

Veroi moved to Wess' other side to help him hobble over to the giant. "The mage looks impatient, Dar."

"Let's go see. Wess, congratulations on your first combat kill," Dar said over her shoulder.

They found Bomoki with his arm deep in the center of the spiral cuts. He seemed to be reaching for something but when he pulled his hand out, it was empty. "This hill giant, compared to the several statues in the garden, is the size of a stone giant. It should not be this big. Also, there's a cavity in the center of his armpit, like what I'd expect for a heart. But," Bomoki pointed to the giant's other side. "That's where the giant's heart is. Did you see anything in the battle?"

"Tell them, Wess," Shak said.

Wess described how the snake had struggled to escape from the center of the spiral scars. "Shak said it to me, but I did not register it in combat. The giant really only lost to us when that snake, or worm or whatever, left the giant."

Bomoki pointed to Wess' face and arms. "Maybe it wanted a better host?"

Dar said, "We can ask the giant. I have some strength left. If the Queen wills it, I should be able to ask the giant's spirit a few questions." She bowed her head and began to hum. When draconian words entered her humming, they sounded unlike any draconian words the knights had ever heard or studied. When Dar stopped, nothing happened and she grew frustrated. "We should be able to see a mist around the giant, maybe even a ghost. There's nothing." Dar smashed her fist on the giant's leg. "Veroi, combine with me. Let's bring it back as an undead."

That more complicated and longer prayer to reanimate the giant also failed. Veroi swooned at the prayer's ending and Bomoki caught her. Blue disks of energy swarmed around Wess to steady the knight from falling on top of Veroi. Seeing the disks shooting at them, Shak tensed for combat and the disks popped out of existence as their magic dispelled so close to a paladin. Bomoki swore. "Stupid paladin. I'm trying to help." Dar caught Wess though. "Idiots. One day, if you believe this vision, you'll all need to come to terms with magic. The god emperor," Bomoki jabbed his finger at Dar, "even she sees it. A spear forged in magic, wielding magic and faith." Bomoki leaned Veroi down to the ground beside the giant. When she thanked him, he stormed off. "I'm going to prepare another *teleport* spell. I'm not the god emperor, not yet. We'll need to be in a clear area and I'll need to be able to hold Otor's hand. Ten minutes."

"It's been a long night, mage," Shak answered. He bristled at the tone Bomoki used to address Dar Tania, but she did not seem to notice.

Dar snapped her fingers. "I'll have to confirm this with the god emperor, but the only way these prayers would fail is if there were no soul left. This snake, whatever it was, it destroyed the giant's soul."

Wess' eyes went wide. "And if you hadn't come, even destroying the snake, I'd have died?"

Dar nodded. "The nature of the wounds to your soul were severe. You would have died or become like this giant within a few days. Maybe three days, I'd guess."

Shak found Dar and quietly said, "My Dar, high priestess, I will never again engage in reckless training. I'm sorry. This long night, I have seen parts of myself that require more tempering."

Dar wiped mud from his face. "I know. That's the nature of atonement, paladin. Tiamat does this to us all, even to me. Even to the god emperor."

Shak bowed his head as he considered his ordeal at the level of the god emperor.

* * *

Two hill giants herded twenty goblins ahead of them. The narrow ravine trail snaked east into the increasingly jagged mountains. Steep hillsides gave way to mountain rock and forced them to jump and scrabble along fields of boulders. Far down below, jagged trees and still raging rivers waited for any careless missteps. It required careful stepping by the giants though the puny goblins moved along it easily enough. At the head of the column, Bull Stomper walked lost in thought, occasionally twitching his new wings wrapped like a cloak along his back. A goblin tripped and almost died when the giant's foot slammed down near his body. The goblin rolled aside and then the giant picked him up by the head and threw him back into the group with a curse.

Though Stomper walked at a leisurely stride, the rest ran to keep up. They had done this often enough that no one wanted to fall behind. Their leader had killed and eaten enough stragglers over the years that all ran to keep pace. The trail began to wind upwards and they stopped for a pause in a large clearing at its high point. "We'll stop here and rest," Stomper said.

The clearing in the mountain pass had grown over the years as Stomper's crew cut trees for fire. Down below and still eastwards, a steaming lake ringed by yellow, orange, and red stone waited for them. The water there boiled hot and blasted columns of steam high into the air. Sometimes, the steam blasts would pierce the perpetual haze of that area. No food existed by the boiling lake, and so they always stopped here to rest and eat. The welcome smell of brimstone lingered just enough to tell them how close they were. The goblins called it the *melting place*. It's where they found Stomper one day. The goblin chief named Bull had tried to capture Stomper thinking him a lost elf with green-cast skin and a horn mutation. The goblins were familiar with chaos marks. Stomper had proven anything but and within days ruled the goblin tribes.

This night, they feasted, even the goblins ate well, on fresh meat. Disbelieving it at first, when Stomper summoned woodland creatures for their feast and offered meat to them, they fell into the meal with gusto. Normally, they ate maggot-infested meat sticking to bone. All too often, they recognized the meat as their fellow miners or others who ran afoul of Stomper and his giants. The succulent smell of roasted game filled their camp and they dug in knowing Stomper might change his mind at any moment.

A giant trudged over to Stomper who looked back across the river and valley westwards. "What you see?" the giant asked. "Need us to check?"

Stomper shook his head and said, "No, it's a small campfire, too small to worry about. I'm trying to remember when we sent out parlays to the other tribes, if any were over there. It's not giant. It's not goblin. I wonder," Stomper said squinting.

"I run. Send word, on your command," the giant said.

"It's fine," Stomper said as he turned back to their bonfire and tore a leg off the elk spitted over the fire. "Too far to worry about. The witch, Bet Mirgul, she will deal with them." Stomper rubbed his hands together and wondered if Bet had not already set her sights on whoever had made that fire. The witch possessed an uncanny ability to make things happen. *I need to ask my Master who, what Bet is. Maybe she's a spy watching me?* Uncertain anxiety, a new feeling for Stomper, filled his gut. He rubbed his stomach and took a deep breath, surprised at how this new feeling made it hard to breathe. After all, he had seen Bet's original form. At that thought, something kindled in his mind and he knew: *I too can change my shape.* For now, he decided to keep this knowledge to himself.

The hill giant smacked his lips. "Witch lady, she make tasty food." The giant pointed to the circular scars along Stomper's left side. They made spiral patters from the lower part of his face onto his shoulder and torso. "She make marks like that on chief, and young fighter. What mean?"

Stomper clapped the giant on his shoulder. "Power. The marks mean power. For them and for me. It's a perfect alliance."

"I get marks?" the giant asked hopefully.

For a moment, Stomper matched the giant's eyes. When their gazes met, the giant felt the ground go soft and quake softly. The giant fell over backwards trying to keep his balance but failed. Stomper turned his gaze away and said, "No. You're too clumsy." The giant jumped up ready to argue. However, the vertigo lingered and the giant remembered the last one to challenge Stomper's leadership. The chieftain's brother, one of their clan's strongest, had died in a challenge just like this. Stomper had pointed and, boom!, a loud crack and searing flash of light. Charred flesh, jerking and twitching in arcs of lightning, showed clearly that any other challenges would fail. The thought of not challenging Stomper, it seemed like a good idea. The giant nodded and walked back to the bonfire to eat, just like he had feasted that evening on the challenger's flesh.

The next day, they arrived in the area of boiling pools and colored stones. Geothermal springs fed the lower part of the valley filling it with the stench of brimstone to the point their eyes watered. Stomper picked his way through the water carelessly, unworried by the temperature or acidity. The others carefully followed as best they could. At several places, the giants jumped and then tossed the goblins over large sections of scalding acid. When a goblin eventually tripped and fell face first into a pool, the group stopped and then began laughing. The giants joked about 'accidentally dropping' more of the goblins, but Stomper cut their play short. When the death throes faded, a giant picked the corpse up by its leg. Boiling water warped and blistered the skin, but the face and arm that landed in the water showed clean white bone. Brains slowly dribbled out of the eye sockets. "Hey Stomper! Snack?" Receiving no reply, the giant discarded the carcass into the pool. "No more tripping!"

The group hiked like this for hours before scrambling up an escarpment of smooth stone. On the other side, they found Stomper crouched by the largest pool of boiling acid. He stirred it with his finger. In the smoky haze of daylight streaming through the mist all around, Stomper looked demonic and even more terrifying. Even the giants had not grown accustomed to his new winged appearance. The overly-wide fanged smile did not help. "Gather around," he waved them towards the edge with his webbed fingers. "Don't worry, I just want to show you something."

Nervously, the goblins moved forward with the giants pushing those in back. When Stomper lifted his fist from the water, they saw a gleaming twisted ball of gold there. He removed more gold ore, taken from the mine, that lay in a leather sack nearby. He repeated the process. "This pool connects to the one in the caves," he said. "Look. The acid leaves only gold behind." Seeing the rock dissolve leaving gold behind, the goblins got more excited and moved forward. "Now, boys."

The giants and Stomper hurled the goblins into the acid pool. Their howls of pain and shock quickly went silent as gagging death pulled the goblins under the acid. Many goblins died this way over the many trips. The giants pointed and made bets about which might last longest. The acid ran red as skin melted and then currents in the pool quickly cleared it. Stomper sat down along the edge in an attitude of meditation. "Giants, step back and do not watch what happens next. See nothing, hear nothing, say nothing." Twenty goblins was his largest offering yet. Ylgolth would come.

They nodded and stomped away behind the melted rocks and far off from their leader. Watching them to ensure he was alone, Stomper then waded into the acid and swam to a small cluster of rocks just barely breaking the acid lake. Too small to be an island, the rocks barely allowed Stomper to stand on them. He began moving the rocks around to make a circular platform just barely above the acid's surface. Once clear, Stomper sat down in the center and closed his eyes.

"Great teacher, Ylgolth. Hear me. I have fed your waters and await further instruction." Stomper continued to repeat this, focusing on the name. "Ylgolth," he whispered over and over. Gradually, the acid around him stopped boiling. By the time the sun fell into the western skies behind, a wavering image took shape before Stomper on the mirror-like surface. Still Stomper continued. By midnight, the form became discrete. When a pale grey hand, bearing a large blinking eye on its back, broke the surface of the pool's mirror-like reflection, Stomper caught the hand and helped pull Master Ylgolth through into the world of Tehra.

Like Stomper, Ylgolth had grey, almost black skin and wings. The similarity ended there as Ylgolth had needle-like spikes, as if fur, covering its entire body. Giant horns rose up in sweeping curves around his head. Where Stomper carried almost nothing, Ylgolth sat draped in gold and glittering gems across from him, levitating just over the acid lake. A squat frog-like head with eyes side apart blinked, and then another set of eyes opened just above the nose bridge. The eyes within eyes made it hard to focus on Ylgolth's face. Clawed hands, webbed like a frog's, reached out and Stomper saw them open with suckers along the inside of the palm.

Ylgolth smiled. "Do you still go by that ridiculous name they call you?" Nearly twice as large as Stomper, Ylgolth wore dread like a cloak and power emanated as a pulsing rhythm in the air all around. "Hrax Terrej. That was the name I gave you when you chewed free of your mother's belly."

Stomper mouthed the words, reverently. "Hrax Terrej. I am – Hrax Terrej! Thank you, great lord." Hrax bowed his head low. The sound of his real name spoken by one of his own made his skin shiver and he trembled with the pleasure of it.

Ylgolth looked around at the molten rocks, the high mountains, and the blue sky. "Our realms are not like this. I find it uncomfortable. As you grow, you too will begin to find this world weighing on you. That will be when you know it is time to come home to your family, Azuros. Tell me of the gold."

Hrax held out the small crushed balls of gold. "I am following a great tunnel of gold. With the acid pool acquired, we can refine it much faster."

"How much gold and time?"

Hrax looked at the sky and thought for a moment, "In the reckoning of this world, at least a month to extract and purify all we have mined so far." Hrax gestured and an illusion of stacked gold bars appeared. It stacked four paces square on its sides and three paces high. "This is how much I estimate we have mined so far. The tunnel continues along the vein for some extra distance. I have no idea how far or how much gold there could be."

Ylgolth nodded. "It is time to focus on what we have," Ylgolth said pointing to the illusionary pile. "It would please me if you were to go faster. The gold must then be transported into the cavern pool where I can retrieve it during visits like this. What must you have to go faster?"

The intensity of the question and the offer surprised Hrax. "I need more goblins. I've tried other workers, but goblins are small and fast. I need more."

"No, you need something else. The goblins, the giants, they all taste wrong in the *acid reginus*." Ylgolth cupped his hands and lifted the clear acid from the pool. Letting it wash down Hrax's head, he continued, "The gold is more than precious. It is absent in our world and yet it retains form, shape, and magic in all worlds. You were the first of our children to find it. I desire you to work faster and then find another location. I want it all."

Hrax cupped his hands and brought up acid. The sky and Ylgolth reflected in the small mirror of liquid in his hands. "A world of acid but gold endures in all planes. Master Ylgolth, I will find a way to go faster."

"Your words and desire please me. I'm sure there are other creatures who can do what the goblins do but will nourish you as well. I had hoped my transformant worm in your mother would have resulted in your current Azuros form. Still, at least you weren't a worthless Fecundus for very long. Find and take something stronger than the goblins. Make them work. Mark the smartest. Remember, our kind feeds on intelligence, not strength. As an Azuros, you may spawn with lesser beasts if needed. Raise up a horde and claim for me this world's treasure." Ylgolth pointed to the facial and shoulder scars marking Hrax since birth and stayed with him through his Azuros transformation. They made a spiral from a center position just inside his shoulder. "Mark the smartest. Impregnate the smartest females. My consort, Bet Mirgul, is too careful. Maybe the goblins will give you Fecundi. I think not. From the goblins, you will get transformants and slaves. The giants though – they should provide you Fecundi. How is Bet Mirgul?"

"She serves, as you ordered. There are two in the tribe she deems good enough." Hrax realized he grew hungry talking this way. "You forbade impregnation before."

"You are Azuros now. The time of my teaching you ends soon. I have a thousand-thousand like you, but only you found gold. I shall come and ensure you gain all you need to secure the gold. Then, you are on your own… until you defeat other Azuros and begin learning what is required to ascend to Embros; it is our way. It is my way to empower your rebellion against me. I pray that day is far off. I do not wish to eat you, Hrax."

Hrax bowed low again, "I do not wish to be eaten. It shall be as you command, great Ylgolth."

Ylgolgth's giant form slipped under the night sky's reflection glimmering atop the acid's surface. The bright stars hurt Hrax's eyes. He called out, "Giants! What are those tiny giants to the north called?"

Careful to stay unseen, one called back, "Humans. Tasty. You want?"

"Yes, bring me as many as the clan can get. Hurry. We will replace the goblins with 'humans.' Human," he said again. "They do sound tasty. Find me a variety to eat. I hunger."

* * *

Bruce and Syliri noted the cavern's entrance on the map, which Bruce continued to sketch and add detail to as they worked their way east towards the river. "If my memory of Alerius' map is right, the mountains here wend their way to the ocean amidst a series of hot springs." Bruce scratched at his beard. "You're sure you don't want me to shave this?" he asked Syliri.

"I like the beard. I can feel it on my face. Let it grow," she encouraged him. "Hot springs. Alerius thought it suitable for black dragons and wyverns."

"Yes, hot springs occur near volcanoes and other areas where there used to be volcanos. Sometimes you can't even see the volcano because it's buried so far underground. It seems like a great place for black dragons to be." He looked at her, "I don't suppose Alerius has any black dragon friends down here?"

"You say 'black dragon' like it's a bad thing, Bruce. And it should not surprise you that, yes, Alerius has black dragon friends. In the Dragon Wars, all of the patriarchs made sacrifices and not just colored dragons. Alerius is quite friendly with two of the black dragon patriarchs. The one here that watches over the dwarves goes by the human nickname, Screem." Syliri watched Bruce carefully and said, "Screem watches over the dwarves of Stone the same way Alerius watches over Dar Tania's people."

Bruce tried to mask his reaction to learning of a black dragon patriarch. "Does Stone know? They must."

When Syliri shook her head, Bruce chuckled at his own and their ignorance. "I feel like, whenever we get into topics like this, you tell me things that directly contradict everything I learned as a boy growing up in the faith of Pha Rann. So, a black dragon...clearly Screem does not rule them? Though, I guess I'd have stayed if it made sense to me. Krentismar matches my own view of things so much more naturally."

"Screem watches and guards. If the dwarves knew of him, then yes, I suppose that Screem might insist on ruling. Though, even Mallaforax does not rule the elves. I don't want to fight with you," Syliri said. "Not this way about religion and philosophy. But, you have to admit that it's different living in the world than how your Taysoran scriptures and clerics talk about the world."

Syliri spread her arms wide and spun in a circle. "While I have no doubt we spin," she said spinning still so that her gown flared around her hips, "according to Pha Rann's creation, I doubt the clerics really know for sure anymore. I've heard them preach. They talk like there are these things about the world that are accepted facts of the world. Yet, we spin. Your Literalist Order denies we spin. Your Pragmatist Order says it's a mystery whether we spin by Pha Rann's will or by the laws of nature created by Pha Rann. Yet, we spin. While I cannot doubt their faith, belief and facts are two very different things. Did you know – Alerius and all other colored dragons existed in bound pairs, for example? In the Dragon Wars, those surviving pairs either gave up the female to Tiamat or went into hiding. It's why Tiamat only represents five colored types when there are many more than five colored dragon types. So, tell me, Ranger of Krentismar. Does the world spin? What does Pha Rann and the doctrine of Heaven say about the metallics – did they exist in pairs?"

Bruce eyed the relatively flat stretch of land ahead of them. Autumn had killed back undergrowth and made it easy to see quite far under the trees' barren branches. "All of the metallics united under Bahamut and Pha Rann. Everyone knows that. Though, you'll tell me otherwise."

"Yes, otherwise. Not all metallics wanted to. They became coloreds. That's why gold and red dragons have the same breath weapon."

Bruce sighed and with a resigned look said, "And the metallics went to Heaven. But, Bahamut realized he could not let Tehra be solely populated by the offspring of Tiamat so he sent a few back. Also, otherwise?"

Syliri laughed. "Not all dragons could ascend to Heaven. Bahamut took those strong enough to leave Tehra. The rest, he abandoned here. Later, the other gods named them 'caretakers.' Alerius considers them orphans. The truth, unsaid in your doctrine, is that the metallics left behind were left here because they were too weak to go to Heaven. So tell me, do all the 'good gods' abandon the weak? Is strength and might the key to gaining Heaven's sweet embrace?"

"Your Alerius' view no doubt," Bruce said. "Tiamat did not abandon any?"

"Tiamat did not abandon any of the dragons, actually, unless you consider all of them as being abandoned. She left the patriarchs, the strongest of the strong, behind to watch over and guide them. Alerius and the patriarchs chose to stay behind and protect them. The only ones who went with Tiamat were the bound-pair females of the chosen patriarchs."

Bruce raised his eye brow on one side and looked at her skeptically. "Alerius does not protect other dragons."

"Why do you think he's building a Temple? Is there a temple of metallics?" Syliri pressed back at him. "The temples will provide a consecration of all dragons to Tiamat. It's spiritual, not physical protection. Morbatten, an entire empire dedicated to the dragons, becomes protection for all dragons."

Bruce kissed her. "Enough religion, Syl. Enough. It all sounds very wonderful – for Tiamat. You have one more thing to say? Okay, let me have it."

"Why are there no clerics of Bahamut?"

"Bahamut is part of Pha Rann's pantheon of Good, that's why. In Heaven, it's all shared. Cleric of Pha Rann, cleric of Bahamut, who cares?"

Syliri poked him, "Then, tell me, why are you a ranger of Krentismar and not of Pha Rann?"

They walked forward carefully as they talked. "Because Krentismar does not care if I fall in love with a medusa, and Pha Rann probably does, at least some of the Orders and Sects do." They continued like this for what felt like miles until at last Bruce slowed. He drew and nocked an arrow in his long bow. The bow and arrow both bore runes similar to the ones on Bruce's sword. In the wind, a distant echo of voices came. So softly at first that Syliri barely noticed it, even concentrating, Bruce confirmed it. "Hill giants, up ahead. An encampment maybe."

Bruce continued forward, moving them through trees. At first, Syliri did not know why, but then she saw a ring of giants leaning against the trees, resting their arms along upper branches as they slouched their body weight against the main trunk. Bruce pointed and numbered the five that he could see. About fifty paces ahead of them, two guards stood close enough that they could not pass. The ground dipped here and showed the well-marked use of frequent travel by the giants. Bruce pulled them back into a clump of piney bushes. He touched the arrow and whispered a magical word. The arrow pulsed softly at the sound of its activation word.

Bruce shot it at the ground, but instead of sticking in the earth, the arrow reappeared in his hand. It continued to throb with energy, as if still in flight. "Wait here," Bruce said.

The woodsman moved stealthily into a line with one of the giants and aimed the arrow at one. Bracing the arrow so that it rested atop two branches, Bruce returned. Together, Syliri and Bruce crept towards the sentinel line. Only when they had gotten as close as they could did Bruce speak the arrow's magical word again.

The giant across from them grunted. An arrow stuck into its lower hip pelts. Grunting, the giant pulled it out. The other, the one closest to Bruce and Syliri, walked over to see. Together they began eyeing the forest, trying to see who had shot at them. Ripping the arrow free, the wounded giant pointed and the two charged the direction of the arrow's flight. They did not notice the ranger, or his friend, slip past them.

Safely inside the guard perimeter, and after a few minutes, Bruce whispered, "Retrieve." The arrow reappeared in his hand. It stank like giant. "Nasty," Bruce said. He pointed to Syliri. "Tell me, Syl, if you were a giant, you wouldn't be this gross, right?"

Syliri laughed softly, "You're a giant-slayer. If I were a giant, I'd be pure and dreadful. Your stony slayer heart would melt and you'd love me forever. Though, I'm sure you'd still find me filthy and disgusting. They really aren't so bad. You're going to have to come to terms with the kerchki, you know."

"Yeah right. Like that'll ever happen. Fire giants. Leave it to Sean to bring us to a land full of fire giants I can't kill. Politics! At least the kerchki are a worthy enemy." Though speaking, Bruce continued to eye the land around them. So far as he could tell, the hill giants had not placed any more guards. The din of hill giant activity and bluster grew louder as they carefully picked their way forward.

Syliri learned, long ago, that humans possess far greater reserves of patience than she had ever given them credit for. Bruce worked his way forward, barely making noise, leaving no trace. Somehow, he also led her in the same quiet and trackless way. She marveled at his meticulous forest craft. As a medusa, her role in Morbatten had always been simple: collect and catalog. It struck her as odd that Bruce took such care to not be noticed when she could easily petrify the entire hill giant tribe. Bruce would certainly not hesitate to kill his way through the bunch if needed. As a giant slayer, he probably wanted to kill them. *Well*, she conceded. *He'd be conflicted about it. Probably talk to Sean.* She could hear Sean telling him that all hill giants are evil and to put it out of his mind already.

The flat road ended at a cluster of large boulders. Cresting the sharp edge of a large boulder at the top of the pile, Syliri looked down into a large clearing devoid of trees. A raging bonfire in the center held a giant metal pot into which the hill giants threw living cattle, goblins, fish, even plants. The novel sight of giants cooking forced her to stifle a laugh. An older looking giant lay, disemboweled by the fire, with its fellows cutting and tearing it apart. Chunk by chunk, they tossed the body into the metal cauldron. Amidst laughing, bellowing roars, and occasionally head butts, they somehow filled the pot. "I count seventy-two," she said to Bruce. "I can take them all right now if you want me to." Her snakes hissed menacingly. The cobra even snapped at Bruce.

He shook his head. "We need to know why they're here. Alerius' map did not note this many. A dragon would have noticed this type of gathering. Where's Bull Stomper?" Next to her, Bruce scanned the group. "Besides the giants, the witch one and that young one over there," he pointed. "He has those weird marks. None of the others do. Oh wait, that must be the chieftain there. He has them too. Do you know what they mean?"

"The markings look familiar but I'm not placing them with hill giants. Maybe it's a tribal tattoo? I've seen spiral marks on the left side like this before though. I'm sure of it. Sorry, Bruce. It's not coming to me now."

A crude chair of flat rocks lay stacked up and draped with ratty animal pelts. Antlers and skulls shoved into the chair denoted it clearly as the leader's seat. Bruce said, "I'm sure you'll remember, Syl. We'll wait here. The question with hill giants, besides why so many, is what brought them together. They aren't exactly social creatures. They'd normally stay here so long only if they could fill their bellies. You can see how they've deforested this entire section around their camp. I wonder how they're getting food. This area will become a desert if they stay too long."

"Are you still thinking Bull Stomper is a devil?" Syliri asked. "I'm not getting a sense of devils. They leave marks. The giants, for example, look off but not tortured. A devil's cruelty would have wounded all of them by now. A demon could not hold them together this long."

"I hope it's that easy," Bruce muttered. "Here, let's settle in. So long as they don't spot us, we'll stay and observe until we learn what Bull Stomper is. I want to see him." Time passed in silence before Bruce nudged Syl. "Hey, look at the witch."

A malnourished female giant, bent and gnarled, hobbled forward on a shaved tree she used as a staff. She dragged a bear in her other hand. It roared and bellowed. "Its back is broken," Bruce whispered. He raised his bow but Syliri prevented him from firing. Unlike the other female giants, the hag's complexion looked ill and grey. Black bruises all over her exposed body suggested infection. Wrinkles in the skin created flaps with parts of her forearm nearly dragging on the ground. The other giants quieted, some licking their lips. The bonfire calmed at her approach though the bear's roaring became a pitiful mew of fear.

The witch pulled the bear towards her. They could not hear her, but saw her lips moving. The bear's broken back healed and then it began to enlarge. When it reached almost double, the witch speared her walking log through its heart and levered it into the cauldron. The giants erupted in applause and catcalls, pelting the bear with rocks and muck. The witch pointed at it and laughed. Enlarged, the bear struggled to escape the boiling stew in spite of its wound. The hot metal pot burned its paws and after several escape attempts where the giants threw rocks that smashed it back in, it drowned in the stew and stopped moving.

"This is how they're staying here so long. The witch is magically prolonging their food. No bear would linger anywhere near such a group. I bet she uses her magic to lure them in as well. Curse her! You could tell the bear was terrified. That wasn't hunting or a clean kill. She twisted the summoning spell; she murdered it."

This side of Bruce fascinated Syliri. The barbarians cared about nature and the natural world too. But, they did not feel it the way Bruce did. Bruce took it personally. Every part of him hurt for the bear's violation and death. She took his hand and said, "Unless you want me to petrify them, there are too many."

For the rest of the day, they watched, took notes, and when night fell they realized that, as bad as it was watching the hill giants prepare a meal, watching them actually eat was worse.

Chapter 3 – Evil Answers

Ynt'taris spun around, looking at himself in the mirror. His preferred human form, that of a small girl barely eleven years old, danced there. He looked back at Alaura with a question in his eyes. Alaura said, "Your hair is still too dark. Taysorans do not really have black hair like Morbattanians. Lighten it to be more brown, like a chestnut."

Ynt'taris' hair color shifted towards red and then a mix of brown and red. "Will this work? I can see your meaning when you say 'chestnut' but I haven't exactly studied to know the color."

Alaura smiled and pulled a strand of hair out to the side, looking at it in the sunlight through a nearby window. "That works well." She had laid out some clothes on the desk in her stone house. Dresses, frocks, and other clothes knit and embroidered with symbols of the sun and decorative designs contrasted starkly from the woodsman attire Ynt'taris usually wore. Most Morbattanians dressed in wrapped leathers tied in bands. Even women did this. Anything that hindered movement or could become entangled did not make sense at a cultural level. For a moment, Alaura pondered something she had read in the older writings of Alerius. "It's funny how a dragon could affect fashion by immediately catching anyone wearing clothing he felt was impractical. Over centuries and generations of this, your people here, they're baffled at Taysoran clothing. Yet, not a single one of them would relate it to the Coming of Age rituals against the god emperor."

Ynt'taris picked up a cream dress bearing bright yellow and beaming sun patterns embroidered along its hem. Alaura laughed, trying to avoid the line where the ice patriarch might think she mocked him. It was a very fine line. She pointed to the dress and said, "I'm not saying it's wrong, dread lord, but I can hardly imagine the white dragon patriarch skipping about Taysor in a sun dress." She stifled a laugh and failed. She laughed even harder.

Ynt'taris glared at her and then slowly, he laughed too. "Maybe if I put my hair up in twin pony tails, like this?" Alaura loved this awkward side of Ynt'taris; his rare attempts at humor made them special.

Alaura triggered her sketching spell and behind her, a quill drew Ynt'taris onto a blank piece of parchment. "No one will recognize you, Master Ynt'taris. The little girl that humbled Roland's house versus this? You're safe. I'm surprised you have not wandered Taysor before now. Oh, of course, your eyes."

Ynt'taris' shoulders slumped. So many attempts and he could not yet present eyes even slightly human. In the small girl's form, it looked unnerving. Ynt'taris answered her question. "The gold dragon that watches Taysor, Oranstakar, did not want us to. But, with trade open now, the gold dragon can hardly track all our movements. I'm going to wander Taysor's streets and see for myself if this sun religion has resulted in a kinder, better society. I judge societies by how they treat their children. I expect Taysor will disgust me. What if I keep my eyes closed? I can navigate by scent and sound. They'll think I'm a blind girl."

Alaura's paladin guard knocked on the door to let her know a visitor had arrived. The two knocks meant a Taysoran guest. She opened the door and admitted a cleric of Pha Rann. The cleric bowed to Alaura, "My Queen." He saw the little girl too and ignored her. Alaura's attendant, Lilli, and the paladin guard elbowed the cleric and his eyes went wide. "Apologies. You must be the dread lord Ynt'taris?" He dropped to his best Morbattanian pose used by Dar Tania's people.

"By how they treat their children," Ynt'taris said to Alaura. "This is what I'm expecting to find: a society that wishes its children were invisible and without regard." The little girl jumped out the window with an over-the-shoulder wave at Alaura. A blast of wind blew back through the window with the sound of mighty dragon wings.

"I did not realize," the cleric said walking over and looking out the window. A titanic white dragon climbed into the sky towards the north. "Of course, they told me about you and your, ummm, teacher?" He turned back to Alaura and bowed, presenting a rolled parchment with the King's Seal. "My name is Warner van Struzer. My friends call me Van. My Queen, I come to join your retinue and assist however I may."

Alaura took in his charismatic good looks and easygoing words. He looked well-educated, attractive, and bore insignia of a cleric of Pha Rann. She noted the order's symbol. "I see you're a Pragmatist, like Commander Sean? Look," she said sitting down behind her desk. She pulled out a sketch book. Opening it, she pointed to a drawing on the first page. "This is…"

Van smiled, "Edward of Farholm, yes. I know him."

She flipped to the next page and, without waiting for a reaction, Alaura said, "LeRoy ker Dann, nephew of the King."

They did this one more time with another sketch before Alaura asked, "Did the king send you with the mission of marrying me?"

Van grinned and let his smile say everything. "Queen Alaura, it's hardly a mission to visit and serve you. Truthfully, I came here expecting to study, assist, and learn from this new dragon empire. King Nathaniel told me you were becoming a sage, are in fact already a sage. I share an interest along the same lines though my lore interest is theological, especially Merakor's theology. If it just so happens that we can serve our King this other way - because it's what our King wants, I'd deem that a worthy side adventure. Besides, Edward is a friend. He told me what you did to him. Nathaniel asked me to tell you that after me, there will not be anyone else sent. So, pardon my bluntness and lack of etiquette, but either this works out or you're on your own."

Van sat down opposite her and opened his backpack. He moved slowly, clearly wanting Alaura to understand what he said. If she refused the king, as a Queen in line to the Taysoran throne, the king could disavow her. It amounted to exile. She would lose her position. The Winter War would become actual war. From his bag, Van withdrew a small book wrapped many times in protective cloth. Though small, the book's skin glittered darkly. It showed a mix of ancient age and magic preservation. He smiled seeing her interest. "Unlike Edward and LeRoy though, I brought you a proper gift, though I can only loan it to you." He held it out and then pulled it back. "After all the stories I've heard about you and Ynt'taris, I kind of hope you tell Nathaniel 'no' and keep me on as a fellow sage. You see, I have a bit of an ultimatum from my family as well. I guess having two kingdoms without wedded leadership is making the King and his Council antsy."

"What is it?" Alaura asked reaching out her hand to the book.

Van pointed to the ancient runes engraved on the front cover, touching them tenderly. "Merakoran. It tells the tale of the blind dragon. Careful, it has a trick to open it."

Her interest piqued, Alaura took the book reverently. Books this old rarely appeared outside of mage laboratories and royal vaults. The clasp unlocked a second after Alaura took it. She looked up at Van with a smirk to see him looking genuinely impressed. "This is wonderful. Thank you." She waved Lilli off with instructions to return with paper. "I need a blank book at least two hundred pages." The attendant raced off to get the requested materials.

Van pointed to the open clasp. "Impressive. I am, frankly, stunned. One of the reasons I came to see you was to ask aid of the Morbatten dragons to open this. I thought they would be interested in this story, whatever it is." Van leaned forward, "How did you open it? Can you read it?"

Alaura pointed to a place in the spine and the clasp. Both contained a tiny dragon claw. "I pressed these at the same time. As to reading it, not really. I don't want to try with magic in case it damages the book. Once we have a few copies made, we'll request aid. I've found the god emperor enjoys being involved in the revelation, less so in the problems working towards it." Alaura paged through it and then stopped towards the middle. It did not match the other page's material type. "It's a loose page," Alaura said. "And blank. I don't recognize this material. Do you? I think the rest of this book is pressed plant leaves, like papyrus, or an exotic vellum, but unique to Merakor. Ynt'taris would know. Van," she said turning to face him with the page in her hand. "Like Edward and LeRoy, I will always choose Ynt'taris over you. Do not upset him or embarrass me again. You see, Alerius wants what Taysor has. Spark does not care. But, Ynt'taris, you see Ynt'taris hates Taysor. He sees you all as Prince Rolands. You must find a way for him to see you the way he sees Commander Sean. That is to say, not hated, but not loved either."

"I understand, Queen Alaura." She passed the loose page to Van who held it up to light and then sniffed it. "It smells new, and like freshly tanned leather." He held it up against the light by the window. "It reminds me of albino skin. I once saw one in an autopsy during my healer studies. It was like looking at wounds and bruises through a window of skin. And look, the crease from its fold is gone. There's magic at work here."

Alaura continued to page through the Merakoran book while Van looked at the loose page from various directions. He tried folding it again. While it folded just fine, once flattened, the crease vanished within seconds. "May I borrow a pen?"

Alaura pushed a writing tablet and quill towards him. "I think this book is an interview with the blind dragon. It has to be fictional. But, we can test it and compare to what Ynt'taris and the god emperor know."

No sooner did Van's ink touch the page than all of the ink in the quill vanished. It surprised him to the point he fumbled the tablet on his lap and spilled ink all over his white vestments. Van grumbled and fussed until his finger sliced open on the edge of the crisp sheet. He drew in a sharp breath and sucked his finger. It would hurt when writing. He sighed as a thin red line appeared. "I keep asking if the Temple can adopt darker colors. Since they won't and I'm here in Morbatten, I think today is my last day wearing white." His white tassets ran with black ink. On a whim, he touched the strange paper to his stained clothes and laughed triumphantly when the page sucked it out of his white clothes. It left them gleaming.

The page remained clear and clean until a single drop of Van's blood touched it. Van gasped and jerked his hand back from the page as, from that single cut, a line of blood shot out to drench its surface. He shrieked in pain. "It feels like my finger is being cut off!" He dropped the paper to the desk and squeezed his small cut to stop the bleeding.

"You look pale, Van," Alaura commented coming around to check him. "Maybe it's cursed. What else and to what purpose would a single page be enchanted to feed on so much blood?"

Van leaned forward to pick up the paper but got dizzy. "I feel like I've been drained of blood. There is some kind of curse or warding magic active for sure."

Alaura cast a simple spell to detect cursed magic. The page did not glow. "We know it's magic so I won't bother with detecting that." As she said this, a rune unlike anything they had ever seen before, cast in Van's blood, appeared on the page's center. After a moment, it resolved into their own language. It read:

For what, would you know?

* * *

Sean surveyed the carnage since his visit last year. Giant rocks, inconvenient trees, and an unruly river were gone, removed from the wild plateau two days' fast ride south of the Temple site. Summer, the Halflings' leader rescued by Dar Tania five years' prior, smiled and cheered. Mothers brought their children forward, asking him, "Please Commander Sean, would you bless our children in Pha Rann's name? We don't get many of Pha Rann's clerics through here." As each asked, Sean reached down to pull them up onto his horse and blessed them. It made them happy. It was Sean's favorite part about visiting Home.

The large oxen, dragging the last annoying boulder to the side, snorted when Sean reached the hill's summit. In all directions, the plateau stood cleared and ready. "Captain," Summer said, reaching out with his good hand. The blind Halfling had not recovered his eyesight and had refused Dar's offer to heal his amputated hand. Grasping tightly to Sean, Summer waved his arm stump around them. "I can see a glorious concourse of rolling meadows, orchards, and farms here."

Behind them, a mage cleared his throat. "As soon as you give the command, Sean, I am ready to have the earth elementals complete this project." Under his breath, he muttered, "…and I can get back to my studies."

Sean took Summer's arms and oriented him to Bomoki's voice. Summer said, "Bomoki, we're almost ready for that. This late in the year, we can't really plant anything and we need to understand how water will flow with the trees and rocks removed. I think we'll be there after the next rain storm."

Sean looked up at the clear sky. It did not usually rain in Morbatten in autumn. Blue skies and puffy white clouds created a perfect day, but not one with rain. Sean saw Bomoki frown, and begin flipping through his spell book. He thought he heard Bomoki mutter that if the Halflings interjected even a single new request, he was quitting and going back to Taysor. The Halflings' reluctance to use magic to clear Home for agriculture had been a surprise, even to Alerius.

Sean wondered what Bomoki was looking for but addressed the Halfling leader. "Summer, this would be so much easier if we could settle your people. It has to be terrible living in rough huts and tents when we could provide stone houses magically overnight. With this done, and after a rain, will we be able to permanently settle you?"

Summer chuckled and replied, "Not even then. We will not live centrally in a city like you humans. Once we know the lay lines and how water flows through the soil, we'll let nature tell us where and what type of plant will thrive. Around those, we'll settle into the rolling land and build our homes. I'm sure to you, it's a weird way of approaching farming, but you'll see. It's the Halfling way and it produces better crop yields than you can imagine. Plus, and I have explained this to the mage many times, we derive our strength from the land's happiness and health. Maybe if humans followed our example, you'd live longer."

Sean was about to ask more when Bomoki's voice rang out in draconian. With his fingers spread out to the sky, Bomoki pointed at a cloud on the eastern horizon. The mage began shouting at the cloud in draconian. Sean barely understood draconian, not having any desire to learn it. But, even he could tell Bomoki had begun a spell to make it rain. "Come, Summer. The impatient mage is calling you your rainstorm." Sean ordered the Morbattanian paladins with him to wrap things up and seek shelter with the Halflings. He added that they should take extra precautions. Bomoki's magic had a reputation for overkill.

By the time they reached their tents, the first drop of rain fell and still Bomoki screamed at the sky. Summer sat down in the tent and said, "Captain Sean, even by human standards, that mage is reckless. I'm not sure this rainstorm will bring us what we need. Magic like this, because it's not natural, may not work. But, we'll see."

The torrential downpour lasted for three hours. When it ended, it collapsed as a furious stormwind that sent tents flying. Then, the sun reappeared and the clouds fell back to how it had been before the storm. Within minutes, except for the wet ground, the sky returned to how it was before the spell. Everywhere, Halflings poked their heads outside and then walked the length of the fields. The only druid in their group to survive the dark journey to Morbatten, named Brook Summerstone, climbed up the hill. She looked intently all around until Bomoki demanded to know what she was doing.

When the ground dried at last, hours later, she called out, "We are good, Summer. The magic rain worked. Our crop plans were correct. There might be some mistakes on the lay lines since the magic rain won't trigger those, but we can compensate for it. The roads though," she stopped abruptly because Summer had started yelling.

"Captain, tell your mage -"

But, it was too late. Bomoki heard Brook. The plan for roads had been decided in anticipation of this. Sean ran for the mage, who had retrieved a tall staff. "No, wait!" Sean called out. Bomoki looked straight at him and struck the staff on the ground with a defiant smirk.

The god emperor named it, the *Elemental Staff of Earth*. Hitting the ground, helical tendrils of mud swirled up the staff and withdrew a cluster of diamonds along its shaft. "You were told to wait for Brook and Summer's approval, Bomoki!" Sean shouted to the mage.

"The god emperor said 'with all due haste.' And that was four years ago. The plan is correct. The druid said so. I'm doing this now."

The diamonds gone, the ground beneath them trembled gently. From the staff's bottom the mud reformed into flat rock. It grew out around Bomoki in a circle almost a hundred paces in diameter. For Sean and the others, the transformation from wet grass to flat stone made them lose balance. As the circle reached the hill top's perimeter, roads shot out towards the north, south, east and west. Those roadways raced away from Bomoki and the staff, occasionally making ninety degree turns.

Brook joined them. "Square turns are not a very Halfling design," she said to Bomoki. "Nature abhors it. Our plans had the roads making gentle turns, not sharp square turns."

Concentrating on the magic, Bomoki muttered, "You should have said this when we mapped it all out two years ago." He groaned. "The eastern edge is reached." A while later, he whispered, "Home is now connected to the Southern Highway. As ordered, there is a rough bridge over the Cordabad

River." About an hour later, Bomoki began to tremble and shake so badly Sean thought he might collapse. At last, the mage whispered, "It is done. All roads are completed."

Bomoki fumbled for a water skin slung over his shoulder. After a long drink, Bomoki bowed to Summer. "Summer, Home has its roads, its farmlands. It's been a pleasure doing this for the god emperor. Good-bye." His voice hoarse from spellcasting, Bomoki whispered a last spell and vanished.

Sean frowned. Maybe sensing it, Summer said, "You've got some trouble with that one."

"At least we never described where we'd live," Brook added. "I'm sure if we had, we'd have stone houses everywhere. Ugly stone houses built by a mage in haste. We'd be lucky to have windows or doors. Not that I'm opposed to stone, but we aren't human or dwarf." She bowed low to Captain Sean. "Thank you. Thank you so much for watching over us through this. I know it's been a long five years for you, but it really has meant everything to us." She turned and pointed to the Morbattanian paladins. "Really, we direct our thanks to you all. I know our lives must seem very boring, but I hope the monsters you fought to keep us safe helped pass the time. We, I, cannot express our appreciation enough. Just know that parts of Home will be named after you and this team of heroes."

"Your expression of thanks is enough for me, and for my team," Sean said bowing back to her. "So long as you remember the Battle of Umber Hill and how our patrol leader, Gerin, defeated an umber hulk, we are happy." Gerin and his team grinned and punched each other's shoulders. The moment caught at Sean. *They're so young.* He focused back on Summer and Brook, "The two-year patrol rotation worked perfectly for the knights. I will be returning to Morbatten tomorrow and expect to see you all again in a month's time." Sean squeezed Summer's hand and bowed respectfully to Brook. "It's a shame you lost your priest to the ogres. Brook, you'd be and are most welcome to come study at the Temple of the Sun should you wish to become a cleric, or put forth Halflings who could be."

During their talk and the elemental conversion of the land to their designs, all three hundred and fifty of the Halflings joined them on the hill top. Summer said, "We'll be filing a report of grievances for the god emperor regarding Bomoki during this project."

"Please do," Sean answered. "Wisdom is found with biting teeth," he added, referring to a common adage shared between the Taysoran people and those, like the Halflings, coming from Merakor.

The Halflings waved good bye to Captain Sean.

Syliri and Bruce watched for two days as the giants gorged themselves on anything they could eat. Even leaves and moss found their way into the large pot. Syliri grimaced, and to distract herself, started a grim but humorous commentary on the giants' food choices. When they tossed a few live goblins into the cauldron, she fell silent. Growing bored and running low on food themselves, Bruce suggested they follow the southwestern path of the giants coming and going. They also noticed the occasional yellow glint of gold.

"I wonder where they're getting gold from. Let's find out," he suggested. The group of goblins, seeing their brothers picked up and thrown into the soup, tried to escape. Their mangled screams as the giants grabbed and crunched them dead was too much for either to watch. The witch giant enacted a spell and one of the dead goblins jerked back to life. Mindlessly, it began to shove its fellows towards the fire. While this amused the giants, it disgusted Bruce. When the hag picked up the zombie goblin and began to eat it, and the zombie quietly helped her, Bruce shuddered. "Yes, it's time for us to leave this unclean place. Stomper would have come by now if he were coming. We should have heard something if they were expecting him soon."

Avoiding the giants proved easy. None of the beasts suspected intruders so close to their camp. The farther out they got, the more likely they would run into a giant actually paying attention. The giants had so trampled the ground towards the mountains across the river that Bruce and Syliri were able to traverse it quickly. Bruce's stomach growled and Syliri laughed at him. That night, as they settled down, Bruce set a series of snares. "Tomorrow, at the river, maybe we can get some fish. The giants have eaten everything." He looked back at Syliri. She walked easily through the forest with a faint smile on her face. "That's why hill giants and stone giants hate each other. The hill giants consume everything until they reach the mountains. The stone giants stop them there. As the hill giants multiply, they destroy their own food base. The stone giants then eat the hill giants."

"Are there any stone giants here?" Syliri asked.

"Not that the dragons marked. We'll see. They tend to draw each other together."

The next morning, Bruce's snares had caught a variety of small game too wily and small for the giants to go after. Bruce prepared them quickly and set them to cook in a small metal skillet. A draconian rune in the pan gave off magical heat. They walked as their food cooked. "I do love how the dragons figured out to apply magic to common things like this," Bruce said, biting into a small rabbit. "Perfectly cooked, all the time. No fire, no smoke. Why has this not been done in Taysor?"

Syliri could not help herself. With a voice dripping in sarcasm she answered, "Because for as much as you talk about your pantheon in Heaven sharing power, the actual people worshipping those gods do not. Share power, that is. It takes a dragon to create correct behavior. Someone has to be bad, for the greater good." Bruce snorted and cracked a joke about wolves understanding correct sheep behavior. "Just remember, it's your own scriptures that teach you to be a sheep. Baaaaa," she imitated a lamb. After that, Bruce walked in quiet.

They crossed the river easily enough. The giants used large boulders to make an impromptu crossing. Leaping along these, they reached the other side without issue. On the far side, Bruce scanned the ground and pointed to some mud prints. "Different than giants. This pair of footprints is with the giants, but look. They're smaller, well, look." He pointed to sharp end points in the mud at the heel and toes. "Either this one, probably Bull Stomper, is wearing hob-nailed boots or else had talons, almost bird-like, for feet."

"Alerius would occasionally have one of the tribes come down and explore as a test. The giants and goblins always made it hard for them to make much progress. I'm surprised though. The last report I remember, they noted lots of different goblinoids." Syliri asked, "Did the giants eat them all? We're only seeing goblins and hill giants."

Bruce nodded, "Part of what makes goblinoids what they are is a hunger for meat – any meat. They really don't care. Well, they care when there is plenty of other food like fish or monsters. This group has been active and held here long enough that they probably ate the kobolds. I'm surprised we haven't seen hobgoblins or orcs though. Even ogres."

Several times, they moved off the path to take cover as a hill giant ran in either direction. The path generally worked its way into a box canyon about a thousand feet up the side of the first mountain. They could see a small plume of dust there. From further back, Bruce thought he could see a trail going deeper into the mountain range. Up ahead, a third giant could be seen racing towards them. "Let's ask this one a few questions, Syl."

Fetching a coil of magical rope out of his bag, he tied one end to a large tree and then they crossed the road ready to pull it taught about their shoulder height. "I could just take him directly," Syliri said.

"Where's the fun in that?" Bruce retorted. "Besides, I'm the giant slayer."

"I think you just don't like seeing me in my other form. Scared?" Syliri referred to her eldar form where her lower body transformed into a titanic serpent.

"Frankly, yes. I'm just a human after all. Your nature changes when you do that. It's not just your form that shifts, you know."

The first time Syliri had shown him her eldar form, Bruce's sword had activated. It gave Bruce nightmares. It was weeks before he had been able to be near Syliri. At first, she had thought his repulsion exaggerated. Alerius had intervened at last saying, "Rangers, I wish Morbatten had more of them. These humans develop a keen sense for the natural world. Remember – for them, they don't see this world poisoned by Time. Bruce does not understand the Eldar. His heart loves you, but it will take some time before he can accept that you are also a timeless eldar. Let this be, Syliri. Until he can stand with you freed of the poison, he will not understand that he too has the potential to be timeless, formless, and infinite."

Bruce gave the signal and they both pulled the rope taut. The giant's foot caught the rope perfectly. Though it pulled hard enough to break their arms and they let go, the giant stumbled and then rolled in the gravel and mud. An arrow thunked into the ground by its face. Bruce growled in their guttural language. "Don't move or you'll be riddled by a hundred of these."

The giant carefully moved his head to see his attackers, but Syliri and Bruce remained masked in the forest. Another arrow shot out, this one glancing off the giant's forehead between its eyes. "The next arrow goes into your eye," Bruce said mimicking a different dialect and voice, from a different location. "We have a few questions. Answer them and you'll be on your way unharmed."

The beast sat up on its knees and nodded.

Bruce asked, "Where can we find Bull Stomper?"

In his own language, the giant answered. "He's up in the mountains, the hot melted stones. He'll be coming back to the gold mine any time now. You smell delicious," the beast said, giving up on sighting them. His fingers dug into the ground slowly looking for a rock.

Bruce shot three arrows. One struck the webbing between its fingers and the other two just barely blocked its grab for a boulder. Already Bruce moved to a different location and in another voice said, "One more attempt like that and we'll kill you. Is Bull Stomper a hill giant?"

The giant laughed. "He was at first. Now, he's higher, a devil beast. Let me go."

"Leave, now. When you get to the feasting place, tell them all – the rangers are here to kill them. If they leave this place and head south or west, we'll let you live. There's no food here anyway."

This time, Syliri called out in Elvish and fired an arrow at the giant. The missile landed right in front of the giant in the mud. Bruce translated, "The elves in our group want to kill you now. I suggest you leave, quickly!"

The giant fled towards the enclave where the group feasted. Stepping out of the forest to gather their arrows, Bruce winked at her. "You can tell that even the giants want to leave. If this Bull Stomper is a devil, this trip just became more interesting. I bet the dragons would love to add a devil statue to their collection."

"Depends on the type of devil. We already have most types. I'll recognize it when we finally see this Stomper devil. There are other monsters than devils though. The ability to gather hill giants hardly seems interesting. Threatening to Morbatten, maybe. From what we've seen so far, our novice fighters could take this group."

They continued debating what type of devil would gather hill giants and goblins together until they could see the mine tunnel. Sunset behind them provided a clear view of a large and crudely supported mine. Debris piles around both sides showed it actively being worked. Quartz crystals and rough stone had been dumped in equal measure along the ravine edge. While they watched, a goblin came out with a basket on its shoulder and dumped it to the ravine side pile. A few stones fell down and the goblin kicked at the pile.

"Will your ranger code allow you to kill goblins?" Syliri asked.

"I was just thinking about that. They appear to be enslaved to the giants, who are being forced to do un-hill-giant like things by Bull Stomper. The greatest threat here to us all is Stomper. If we remove that threat, the giants and goblins will no doubt leave this area by themselves. They're not a threat to us, certainly not to Morbatten."

"The god emperor will want the gold mine," Syliri said. "Sean would kill the goblins."

"He might, I'm not sure he would in this case. The devil – most certainly, yes." Five more goblins came out to dump their baskets.

"I could petrify them all. We take out Stomper, I could release them and we'll see what they do. Seems like a waste to me though. Of all the eldar, only Grimsh ever cared about the goblins even then, and except for creating them, he lost interest. If their own god doesn't care, why should we?"

"I like to think we have a higher moral code than Grimsh," Bruce said, kissing her shoulder. "Let's follow this group into the mine. They look tired and hungry. I bet they won't even notice us."

They pulled their cloaks over their heads and quickly fell in behind the goblins. Too weary and hungry to care, the goblins walked mechanically until they began sitting down to continue working. Bruce pointed out a zombie, recently dead and reanimated, digging too. "Devil," he mouthed.

The rough mine proved crude beyond belief. Tree trunks and large sticks had been wedged against the ceiling and walls in places that, if bumped at all, rained down enough material to be alarming. Faint yellow gold streaks glimmered here and there, though obvious gold had already been taken. Smoky lamps burning fat filled the tunnel with the stench of flesh and grease. While the goblins seemed resigned to how awful the mine's condition was, both Bruce and Syliri had to breathe shallowly to avoid gagging and coughing. Their eyes watered.

Still, they passed by many goblins working away at the tunnel edges as if in a charmed state. None noticed the two strangers. Ahead, a cool breeze became noticeable and soon, they stepped into a crystal cavern full of soft silver luminescence. To their right, a better-fed and stronger goblin said, "Stomper, I," and then stabbed at them with a spear.

The hissing of snakes and Syliri's quick reflexes caught the spear tip an inch away from Bruce's chest. He jumped back in surprise. The familiar sight of a creature, beyond terrified, met his gaze as Syliri's eyes and the snakes around her head gazed intently at the guard. "No, Bruce!" she called out in warning. Her hand covered Bruce's eyes a second after the cobra blocked him from meeting Syliri's petrification gaze. Unable to breathe through stone lungs, the goblin gurgled and then completely petrified. The yellow light in Syliri's and her snakes' eyes faded. She caught the statue before it tumbled over off balance, and laid it gently to the side. "I bet the goblins won't even notice," she whispered. Some of the snakes in her hair hissed at the statue, and under the dim orange light, Syliri's hands molded the stone back into a semblance of guard-on-duty. The instinctive use of her power for defense came with less price that when Set's Dream seduced her into it.

Bruce swept her up in a hug, careful not to look in her eyes. "I'm sorry you had to do that," he whispered. "I know how much you hate that part of your nightmare."

Syliri tried to say something, anything, but the tears had started. She buried her face in his arms while the snakes hissed at him. Kelly latched onto his hand, but did not bite through his skin. Turning a creature to stone immersed Syliri in Set's Dream.

Bruce nodded, admiring her handiwork. "All the stories I've heard about medusae, not a single story mentioned that you could reshape and change them. In Merakor, there was a story about a medusa who had set up an art studio of perfect sculptures. It's told as a horror story, about how great Merakor was to find and end her tyrannical murder of innocents. Fallen, right?"

Syliri nodded into his shoulder. Her whisper was soft but sad. "All of my sisters fell when Time flowed. They went mad, like that artist. She was my friend, my sister. I knew her name. Now, she's just the 'Medusa of Merakor.' Before Time, petrification created a permanency of form that endured beyond fleeting moments of will. Other eldar could not undo it. It's why I'm so grateful to Alerius. You have no idea how frightening and rage-inducing it is to see all you love and cherish begin dying all at once. Knowing that you cannot undo it, where just moments before you could make them beautiful. My sisters and I, we dreamed of a beautiful world. Since, when this happens, I barely control it and I see the world that drove them insane. It's all they see. I hate it! I hate Set. I hate being what he made me into. You have no idea how regal, glorious, beautiful I was. Before... my sisters... before all of this."

"You still are beautiful, Syl." Bruce held her until she pushed back from him, still not meeting his gaze. It would be hours before she would trust herself to look at him, at anything. They placed the guard back by the entrance and Bruce hollered back into the tunnel, "No more interruptions!" His mimicry of the goblin guard and its language would work given the near catatonic state of the miners.

The large crystal cavern held a central pool, which spilled light and shadows into the entire cave. They moved towards the pool but stopped when they saw a goblin body by the edge. It looked to have crawled forward to drink. The dead body rested perfectly against the still liquid. They could see it had dissolved perfectly through its hands and the lower part of its head. "It's been dead long enough that there's no more blood," Bruce noted. "Potent acid."

Taking a crystal, he splashed some of the water onto the goblin and noted that the hair and skin immediately began to melt away. "Deadly, to me at least. It's too bad we don't have a gnome here. They would be able to tell us what kind of acid this is and how deadly."

Small piles of gold, perfectly culled from stone, lay around the edge of the pool. The miners had figured out how to use the flat sections of crystals to dip ore into the acid. Bruce pointed at it. "They're refining the ore. This must be aqua regia. Well, something like it, obviously different. I've never seen it occur naturally, yet I feel nothing off about this place. The world is truly full of mystery."

Syliri put her hand into the acid. "No!" Bruce called but she smiled at him and told him to be quiet.

"I'm immune to acid." She picked up some of the unrefined ore and submerged it. Within seconds, only pure gold remained in her hand. "Let me check something else. Help me?" Careful to not touch Bruce with her acid wet hand, she began stripping.

Bruce stared at her pale, reptilian skin and sighed. "It's so sexy when you refine gold and strip for me at the same time," he said, helping her out of her leather armor and clothing.

She kissed him and then jumped into the acid. Not knowing how long she would be gone, he took her gear and stepped back behind a column of crystal and rock not visible from the entry. He began looking around, noting the many pools throughout the cavern floor. "Not a good place for a human to explore. Bad place to get trapped." He took his bow and began shooting arrows at the ground to activate them. He pointed each of them at the entryway.

About ten minutes later, Syliri pulled herself up from the pool. "It's deep but generally, it grows hotter and seems to bend towards the hot springs area deeper into the mountains. The acid isn't as bad deeper. It floats here at the top."

She shook the acid off her body. "Hold onto my clothes for a bit." She smiled and blew him a kiss. "I'm sure you won't mind, right?"

Far outside, they heard a growl. In answer, the sounds of mining activity increased in volume. Bruce smiled at her nudity. "It's a good thing I'm not a jealous man. I'd guess that's Bull Stomper. Let's ambush him." He pointed to the many arrows and stepped back into the shadows. He pulled his cowl over his head and activated its magic that would help him blend into the darkness, even from enhanced or magical vision.

* * *

Bomoki looked up annoyed and said, "What now?" The soldier held a parchment bearing the annoyingly perfect seal and handwriting of Commander Sean, or the Commander as most of the people here called him now. The soldier held it forward but did not say anything. "Let me guess, another summons to some urgent matter no one knew about last time we met?"

Bomoki broke the seal and then looked up, somewhat angry when the soldier did not leave. "After you read it, I'm taking you to the god emperor," the soldier said. The soldier's tone of voice had a razor edge to it that suggested Bomoki had better get on with it.

Instantly, the mage's mind skipped through all the possible reasons he might be summoned to the god emperor... by Sean's seal. He snapped his fingers, "This is about the rain at Home," he speculated aloud. Looking at the letter, written in flowing cursive, Bomoki confirmed it. It ended with instructions to accompany the soldier to the throne by sunset. Glancing outside his small cottage at the base of Dragon Mountain, Bomoki saw that they'd have to run to make it.

Bomoki stood up and began gathering a few things together. "You ran here from there?" he asked the soldier, who nodded. "And you're good to run all the way back?" Again, an enigmatic nod. Strapping his large belt holding many different sizes and types of pouches to his waist, Bomoki reached at last for his shoulder bag that contained his spell book. "You know, with magic, we could get there a lot faster, and with a lot less effort. You game?"

The soldier's eyes immediately darkened with suspicion. Even though the god emperor practiced mortal magic at a level Bomoki coveted, as did the other dragon patriarchs, it always struck him with ironic humor that the actual people of Morbatten still distrusted it so much. Bomoki mimicked jogging in place. "I'm a mage. You really think I can run all the way up Dragon Mountain without a break? Come on. Let me buy you some food and drink, and then we'll magically go. We'll be there in time for sunset. I promise." Bomoki was already walking past the soldier. "What's your name?"

"Mahtran," the fighter said. "Horse Tribe."

"Well, while you might run there with no problem, I doubt you can carry me up there and I need to eat." Bomoki pointed to his desk covered with papers and rune inscriptions. "I've been at this all morning and barely slept last night. I've also walked that mountain more times than I care to remember. For me, it's an entire day. The god emperor knew I'd use magic. That's why it says by sunset. They expect me to use magic for us both. You see that, right? Hey, Mahtran right? - you know the tavern by the Temple steps, the one called 'Temple View?' I heard they got fresh fish from the ocean. I've heard it's delicious. Let's go there and eat." Mahtran followed, and Bomoki knew he had him.

Temple View, this early in the day, sat nearly empty but delicious smells already wafted throughout it and onto the muddy streets. With mud on the hem of his robe, Bomoki swore and wondered, again, why the god emperor still refused to pave the streets here in what Dar Tania described as the pre-eminent capitol city of the Isles. "Pre-eminent mud capitol," he said sarcastically while stepping over a puddle onto the front porch.

Bomoki walked in and sat down, telekinetically pulling a chair out for Mahtran. One of the children working to clean up from the night before blinked at the magic, mouth agape, and then ran over. "We want two large helpings of that white fish, the one with the large bone spike on its nose. Very large serving for my friend here."

The child paused, but Bomoki caught his hand and said, "You know, you really should hop to and get us food. We're starving. Plus, I'm your friend."

The boy's eyes dilated momentarily and then he smiled. "Bomoki! Of course! I forgot it was you. I'll be right back with your food!"

Bomoki looked up and grinned. Mahtran scowled and asked, "Did you use magic on the boy right there? I think you did."

Waving his fingers as if to conjure a coin trick, Bomoki laughed. "A little magic never hurt anyone. His father will be glad to take our money." Watching Bomoki's fingers, Mahtran failed to notice how suddenly Bomoki became his best friend. "Oh dear, I left my coin purse on my desk. Would you mind paying? I'll pay next time."

Hypnotically, Mahtran nodded and placed his purse on the table. "No problem at all. I really can't thank you enough, Bomoki. It's exhausting, all this running back and forth. This smells so good." He inhaled the scent of the cooking fish.

Bomoki continued to wave his fingers and at last stopped, replying, "It's not like you're a dragon able to fly to and fro. I bet they barely told you what this whole Home thing is about anyway."

The soldier's gaze remained locked on Bomoki's fingers. Even after the tavern owner came over and took drink and food orders, Mahtran continued to watch Bomoki's finger tapping back and forth on the table's surface. Mahtran looked offended at Bomoki's suggestion that he did not know. "Actually, I was there, Bomoki! Brook reported that, because they did not have time to study drainage from the rain, the earth elementals made roads right through some of the best agriculture fields. She also said that, in your haste, you did not end the weather spell correctly and the rain patterns are completely wrong now and won't become natural for several years at least."

"I bet Sean had a field day with this," Bomoki muttered.

"No, the Commander just listened and asked if Home could be assigned a different mage going forward." Mahtran took a long drink, his eyes still on Bomoki's hand.

This is bad, Bomoki thought. *Almost all of my pay is from Halfling projects.* "What did Alerius say?" he asked, signaling for more drinks. "Wow, you're really thirsty. Must be all that running plus how late in fall it is. Please, drink up!"

Mahtran mechanically reached for another tankard. "The great god emperor said he would like to speak to his impatient apprentice. And, that Sean needed to reset his Taysoran thinking about the role mages play in empires."

Bomoki smiled at that last comment. Bomoki had come to Morbatten from Taysor as part of the Queen's Way brokered through the war by Queen Alaura and her kingdom. *Roland's kingdom really*, Bomoki corrected his thinking. With several of the other kingdoms still raising and sending armies to the Winter War around them, Alaura had masterfully – *I bet the dragons helped her; she's smart but not Taysoran politics smart* – navigated the politics to keep Rowland's kingdom open for trading relations. Leaving Taysor was both the best and worst decision Bomoki had ever made.

Best because it freed him from his master in Taysor while giving him access to spells he would have had to research a lifetime to learn. Worst because every single day he cast spells for Morbatten's benefit that left him so exhausted he could barely study the ones granted him by Alerius. In Taysoran terms, Alerius' spell ability was above and beyond anything their greatest archmage could dream of. Possessed of a patience for magic research belied by his dragon nature, Alerius doubled Bomoki's casting ability in that first week of training. Alerius, unlike Taysor, felt and treated mages as a key part of the empire, rather than an eccentric cog tucked away for emergency use only. "It's a double-edged sword though," Bomoki said, clinking his mug against Mahtran's. The soldier, confused but enchanted, toasted back. "In Taysor, no one knew who I was or what I was doing. Here, everyone knows and if anything goes wrong, like this, I suppose I get taken to task for it. Oh well. Sean will have to deal with it until they get more mages." Bomoki guessed Mahtran had enough coin for their meals and then some.

By the time their food arrived, Mahtran lay unconscious in a drunken stupor. Bomoki tipped the tavern owner generously from Mahtran's purse. Bomoki ate quickly and then patted the soldier on the arm. He whispered to him, "You're going to remember finding me and sending me on my way, but you wanted to grab some food. You don't remember when, but before you got too drunk, you told me I needed to head on without you. You're also going to remember the god emperor told Sean I did everything correctly because the Halflings were taking too long."

Incoherently, Mahtran mumbled something that sounded like agreement. *Drunkards are always so much more susceptible to magic. I'm surprised Taysor never figured out the exact moment where drunkenness interacts with magic like the dragons here did. Taysor must look so narrow-minded to them.* Thinking this, Bomoki vanished from the tavern.

He reappeared on the open plateau in front of the large entry tunnel to the throne chamber. Bomoki thought of this as 'the gate' and resolved to start calling it that. This was where Alerius spent time with new mages, priestesses, and paladins. Up this high on the mountain, winter snow and ice dominated. Proximity to Alerius, though, kept the entire area around the entry free of snow and ice. A new class of paladins stood at attention, either the sixth or seventh; Bomoki did not care, while the humanshifted Alerius walked their line. Sean walked several paces behind. To their side, a group of priestesses sat on flat stone tables watching and ready to help. Bomoki smirked. Even a group of fighters working to become rangers like Bruce practiced up here. He looked around, scanning, and smiled. *No mages, just how I like it. Of course, less competent mages would make me look even better.* Thinking that, Bomoki resolved to send word to some of his friends with sloppy study habits.

Drawing near to the paladins, Bomoki noted Alerius stop in front of one. The knight, easily six feet tall, looked miniscule compared to the dark armored form of the god emperor. "Why do you want to be a paladin?" Alerius asked.

Standing tall and straight, the young man immediately answered, "Because my faith in Tiamat compels me to serve, god emperor!"

Alerius hulked over the man, "So, it's not the glory, the combat lust, the beautiful priestess Dar Tania, hmmm? Maybe Tiamat wishes you to be a farmer?"

"My purpose says otherwise, but I would gladly work the dirt if Tiamat requires it. Does She?" the paladin asked.

"Before Dar Tania, perhaps, yes. I know you. I know you all," Alerius said now scanning the paladins. "You were all born to be fighters but the tribes need food too. You grow. You have already grown. Look!"

Bomoki grew envious the instant an illusion of the paladin appeared before them. The eldar so easily, thoughtlessly, pulled magic into existence. Bomoki thought through what he would have to do, at least three spells over ten minutes to enchant the same illusion. The illusion showed the paladin. "Your name is Otor Ven," Alerius said. This omniscience also filled Bomoki with covetous desire. Alerius knew, could know, the entire sum of anything he focused on. By the god emperor's stance, he was doing it now. "You cannot hide anything from me, Otor. When you were ten years old, you had an accident that killed half of your family's chickens. Tell us, tell the class, what happened. Loudly, so all can hear."

Otor went pale and swallowed, feeling his entire past laid open and bare to the god emperor. Knowing he could not lie, but desperately wanting to, he answered. "It was cold. I did not want to close the chickens up safely. I told myself I would do it later. I forgot. They were killed by a fox. I blamed my sister. We ran out of food that winter, because of me. We barely survived. They beat my sister. I let her get beat. I helped beat her even though I knew I was at fault. I'm sorry for it. I have apologized to them all and tried to make amends."

"But, how can you make amends, Otor?" Alerius challenged him. "The potential light and sheen of your sister's love for you, the lost nutrition and suffering inflicted on your family, how do you make amends for lost time and growth?" The illusion of Otor wilted to show him and now his family as they slowly starved. Flesh sank from their faces and their ribs began to stand out. The family became lethargic. The illusion of the sister being beaten appeared. Her bruises and welts healed slowly, made worse by malnutrition. "How old were you?" Alerius asked.

"As you say, I was ten years old."

Alerius watched the sister's beating and then dismissed the illusion. "As paladins, you will have far greater power than a ten-year-old could ever dream of. The power Otor had, in this case, was to secure a routine and tedious chore for the family. You may find it strange that I, a dragon, would care about such things. Yet, I do. You see, for missing that responsibility, the entire family suffered. Now, multiply that responsibility to you as a servant of the empire, as a divine warrior. It's not safeguarding chickens, but the lives of those consecrated to Tiamat. The power to lie, to blame, to avoid the responsibility that Otor had as a ten-year-old is also magnified! If you conduct yourselves as boy-Otor did, if you selfishly or stupidly use this power, you will cause immeasurable harm to my precious and treasured children. I do not care about chickens except as food for Morbatten." So saying, the illusion of the family reappeared.

"I care about you, my children!" Their images went from gaunt to well-fed, to showing Otor entering the paladin ranks while his sister studied magic from a spell book. "For the want of chickens, Otor may not have been here today. There is a reason I separate the law into two: the law for the mighty and the Law of the Innocents. Otor is not alone here. Each of you have moments of shame in your past. See that you figure out and learn from it. In the law of innocents, Otor is a ten year old boy, lacking in wisdom and maturity to either secure the chickens, or stand up and own the beatings he directed at his sister. As an innocent, this is harmless. As paladins, though, pray you do not cross the innocents and children of my empire!"

The illusion showed the sister, studying from the book, wither and fade as starvation took her life. The mother, pregnant and large with child, suffered a miscarriage because of malnutrition. Otor, instead of as a paladin, toiled in the dirt with his countenance haunted by having lost his family. "Faith can exist amid suffering, but free will? You cannot make a choice to hear, to serve Tiamat when all your energy is directed at survival. Otor!"

The young knight snapped forward, full attention. "Slay these foul images and recommit in your very soul that you will never deviate from your purpose; that if Tiamat requires it you will die for Her Cause!"

At his words, and with a strangled yell, Otor drew his sword and attacked the illusions. They reacted as if real and though tears streamed down Otor's face, his steeled resolve cut his illusionary family to bloody ribbons. As his sister fell grasping at bloodied parchment, illusions sprang up all around the paladins. Without command, they drew blade and attacked their own private demons of past regret.

Sean did not look pleased by any of this. Bomoki walked up and waited for Sean to finish saying to Alerius, "Being a paladin is a bright cause, my lord. Revisiting the past, besides painful, it marks this moment for them in a dark way. Is this truly what you want for your knights?"

Alerius' face remained impassive and unreadable. "I want my paladins free of regret and past chains. The tribes are swept away. So too must they let go of things so petty that it might chain their progress. Tiamat wants divine warriors, not fighters hindered by the past."

Sean watched with Alerius while Otor continued fighting not just his family but other things in his life he regretted. A young girl, beautiful and yet awkward enough to show her age, rose up before him. He attacked the illusion as the story unfolded that they had been in love, but after making love, he had bragged about it and demeaned her to his friends. She did not know what had changed in him. The illusions showed it clearly; he considered her a conquest. "As a dragon, I see that regrets linger with my mortal children. By bringing this into the open, the paladins start anew. And the priestesses, you probably see this as humiliating to the knights, Sean?"

Bomoki pointed to another paladin battling a similar situation but this one involved a male friend, who had feelings towards him. The knight had completely cut the friend away and severed all contacts and then spent the rest of their time in the tribe belittling him. The illusion showed they were like brothers. Bomoki pointed to the image of the village boys nearly beating the young man to death. The now-paladin kicked his teeth in, apologized, and then ran off with the others. Bomoki spat at the paladin. "I was bullied like this in Taysor. I still hate them."

Alerius looked at Bomoki and said, "I'm sure you made them pay."

Bomoki laughed cruelly. "You have no idea, god emperor. No idea at all. Though, this was worse for the love they shared. I never had that type of a lover or friend." Alerius' evil smile told Bomoki that Alerius knew, in that moment, exactly what had happened to the bullies in Bomoki's past. Feeling his cheeks burn bright red, Bomoki looked at Sean and said, "You know what? Curse you. This is why I hate paladins and all religious functions. I hunted them down and destroyed their lives with magic. One committed suicide. The other two lost their careers, their reputations, their livelihoods. One is a beggar now and the other is in jail for a murder he did not commit. I regret nothing. My revenge against them is a dear and cherished memory to me." Bomoki hit his chest. "I'd do it again."

Sean looked away from Bomoki. "Mages like you are why Taysor has so few mages in positions of trust." The commander turned to Alerius and bowed. "My liege, I will go and tend to the rangers. How long do you see this exercise going?"

"Three hours at least. The magic will compel them to face their demons until all aspects of shame, regret, and deception are visibly slain. Or, they could remember what you taught them, Sean, and call on Tiamat to dispel the illusions. So far, only Shak and a few others have figured that out. It's disappointing. I do not wish to spoon feed them their progression." Alerius made a very human shrug to show he doubted the knights would, either because they had forgotten or because they would take the god emperor literally when he said 'slay.'

"Very good. Have you considered the report brought by Shak and Otor Ven regarding the snake creature and the hill giant? That something new would arise on the borders of Home after four years of quiet makes me think we should alert and arm the Halflings." With Alerius' agreement to do so, Sean rose from his bow and left.

Pointing at Sean's back, Bomoki said, "How did you get such a high-ranking Pragmatist to serve you, God Emperor Alerius?"

"I did not. It was all Dar's doing. It's her own particular magic – building trust and shared purpose. You would do well to learn this from her." Alerius stepped away from the battle field of paladins chasing illusions. "After all the delays with Summer's people, you rushed them. You disobeyed my instructions that both Summer and Brook convey their readiness. Summer's trust in Morbatten is not absolute. These, your actions, shake his tenuous hold on Morbatten, on myself, as being capable of honest dealing. Morbatten needs the crops they will produce. If this affects yields, I will hold you responsible. You and your power, not mine, will reshape their lands should it affect their crop yields at all. You will explain why you did this."

Bomoki felt ready for the confrontation but, whether by some magic that compelled truth or because he just did not care anymore, he found himself saying the real truth. "The entire project, as you have noted many times, is far behind schedule. The Halflings, they don't complain to you here – but there? It's never-ending with their sideways conversations and eye-rolling. They want their homes done. Their fields. Their crops. Their livestock. Their children. Too much or not enough sun. It's constant for years. I am not immortal like you, master. They weary me with their polite requests to hasten everything." Usually, this tack worked with Alerius. Bomoki changed topic a bit and said, "You just barely taught me weather magic and, while waiting and waiting there, it clicked." Alerius enjoyed seeing him, all of them, progress. *This might work,* Bomoki thought. "I was ready, Alerius! I wanted to flex this new magic, and impress them, impress you. For three hours, I called forth torrential rain! Remember how I could barely make it mist, while it was already raining a few months ago? And, now that it's done, they can politely complain about the things that any people living in any settlement complain about. Using weather magic, I hastened their transition from nomads to settlers to normal citizens."

Alerius growled and Bomoki felt his knees weaken. "This desire to impress me, insults me. I have lived since the beginning. Impress yourself. You would have to do something I had never before seen under the sun to impress me. I taught myself long ago to judge mortals by their own progress. In this case, you overstepped your bounds and while, yes – your magic has improved – you introduced more delay and risk into their settlement of Home and their trust in Morbatten. Instead of remembering it as the homeland granted them by Dar Tania, they will remember an impetuous and prideful mage who right-angled their roadways."

Alerius summoned a scroll case, which appeared in his hand. "Do you know what this is, Bomoki?" He opened it and pulled out the scroll. "It's a list of complaints and things broken or wrong since you hastened Home's completion. There are 100 items in this list. Somehow, you have managed to offend a race that defies being offended."

Bomoki groaned, "No, please. Don't…"

"Therefore, you will bind 100 earth elementals to the roads within Home before I instruct you again." Alerius had already turned his back on Bomoki and strode back to Sean. "Think of this as your atonement." A wave of envy shot through Bomoki as, without a word, a powerful *geas* spell forced his desire to learn into a compulsion to bind exactly one hundred earth elements to Home's roads.

Mentally, Bomoki screamed. He had readied several spells to help him escape, or to compromise. Sean was supposed to be in the discussion. Alerius hated Sean's self-righteous attitude, for which Bomoki knew the triggers, as much as he hated delays. Bomoki whispered furiously to Alerius' back, "You sided with Sean and the dim-witted midgets in this?" He added, "I know you can hear me. I don't care."

"If you want to learn conjuration magic and gate magics," Alerius voice came back to him, "you will learn to care. You are not, never were an innocent. I expect you to hold yourself to the higher law. If you cannot, you will leave. This is your last mistake in judgement. You are reminding me of something I observed ages ago: you can't teach caring or good judgement. Maybe you are simply unable to comprehend why you need to care."

Chapter 4 – Mysterious Parchment

For what, would you know?

Alaura could not get the question out of her head while she picked apart and copied the Merakoran book. "This part says the blind dragon became so powerful the sun king cursed his eyes with sunlight. I don't see a paladin king using curse magic. Sunlight, sure." Van grunted and continued about the large study, making note of various books he wanted to read, and writing them down.

The bookish priest seemed an endless pit of questions. Unlike the others sent by the King to her, Van's constant questioning reassured her that he had little pretense to act like he knew everything already. In the days since his arrival, he had yet to ask her on a date, flatter her, or bring up the topic of marriage again. By now, LeRoy had gone. Edwards was gone. Once asked to leave, they could not have left Morbatten faster. Day by day, Van though, he seemed to enjoy it. *Well, he enjoys my book collection at least.*

"For what, would you know?" Alaura said out, interrupting his long-winded question about whether Dar's dragons were present during Merakor's fall. "If you call them 'Dar's dragons' in either their or Dar's presence, you can expect something they call *multifixion*."

"You're still thinking about that? It's obviously a cursed page! Look at my hand! It's still not healed and has resisted Pha Rann's divine healing as well. I think it's best if you put it out of your mind and we destroy the page." Van rubbed his hand, wincing as blood soaked through the linen bandage. "It's been eight days. Even without healing, a paper cut would not bleed like this. It's cursed. What's multifixion? It sounds like many crucifixions."

Alaura tapped the blood writing and her eyes darted to the summit of Dragon Mount, where Ynt'taris laired. They had not been able to find time with her mentor. "If you hadn't upset Ynt'taris, this would be behind us already. Maybe it's not cursed at all," she guessed. "It could be vampiric, or necromantic. I wish we could discuss this with Ynt'taris." She picked up a book from behind her chair by the fire. Flipping a few pages, she pointed to a diagram. "This is multifixion. When you've mastered draconian, you can read this yourself. Essentially, the dragons figured out that a human soul and body can only be healed or revived from death so many times. It's different for each person. When they reach, whatever that limit is, they will reject divine healing. The god emperor calls this 'healing fatigue.' If you keep them there though, on the edge of death while attempting healing, their soul and body will literally rip to pieces. Even without necromancy, what's left of the body rises as an undead shadow. The soul is obliterated."

Van made a dismissive sound. "That sounds exactly like the stories being told in Taysor these days about a devil-worshipping society of mind-controlled humans. That's about the darkest, most evil thing I've heard in a while. You know that, right?" Alaura's flat smile bade him continue. "This is why there are a number of paladin orders marshalling forces to come and liberate Morbatten by killing the dragons."

"They can try," Alaura said confidently. "They'll fail. They won't be the first. I'm sure they won't be the last."

Van flipped through the book. "I need to learn draconian, that's for sure. And, my queen, you do have a kingdom back home in Taysor. Are you sure you want to be so casually tossing these atrocious ideas about like this?"

Alaura pinned the albino page within a much larger book, hoping to preserve the question showing red and wet in Van's blood. "The question, 'for what' - it suggests we offer something. Is that how you still read it, Van? It could also mean, at a higher level, some sacrifice paid for knowledge. For example, what if I were willing to study with Ynt'taris for the rest of my life to attain sage-level knowledge about the ice dragons? That type of condition satisfies the question though I don't see how the page would guarantee Ynt'taris' cooperation. It's just a page." She looked along the long side. "The ridges here suggest book binding thread and glue. Can you imagine if there's an entire book like this?"

Van pulled out a book, transcribed from Alerius' library. "So, the god emperor has a library that would dwarf the Great Library back home? Why don't you conduct your studies there?"

"It's truly huge. Dar showed it to me. She studies there all the time. While she has no problems, there are certain protections in place that, unless you're part of Tiamat's religion, make it very hard to be there." Holding a metal razor with tongs, Alaura cut the cursed paper. Nothing happened except a faint crease that smoothed flat before her eyes.

"I'd like to see it," Van said. "The protections push you out, I take it."

"No, they make it hard to focus. Eventually, I fall into a stupor and Syliri or another guardian escorts me out. It happens to Sean as well. We tested it with Bruce. He was less affected, but he also did not care that he was in a library. Rangers."

Van continued to make note of various books occasionally remarking about differences from the same book he had studied in the Great Library. "To think that, all these years, Dar's dragons -"

"Don't call them that," Alaura interrupted him. "They're very particular about hierarchy. Bomoki referred to them that way once and, besides embarrassing Dar, it created a lengthy 'discussion' about how Alerius does not want to be considered a part of Morbatten. To quote him, "Morbatten must stand on its own and be special because of its people, not because of my brothers and I." They're very sensitive about the topic. I say it was a discussion but, when you meet Bomoki, he'll tell you he thought they were going to eat him." Alaura laughed at the memory. "You had to be there, I guess."

"Well, still. They have these books without missing pages, damage from time, and the circumstances of how they were brought here when the Kinslayer War ended three thousand years ago. So much philosophy and debate could have been ended. If only we knew. The thing that I don't get is that Taysor considered this a haunted, cursed land full of these ignorant barbarians, but look! This book, even as a copy, it's perfect and I doubt an appraiser could tell it apart from the original. By the way, there's only one in the library and it's mostly water-stained, maybe blood stained. You can barely read half of it." Alaura looked up curiously. Van pointed to it, "It's the diary of Terest Nostram, first paladin king of Merakor. The debate rages around whether this person even existed."

Alaura eyed the cursed page, now pinned, and ignored Van. She said, "It seems harmless enough. What if we write that question with an implied offer of more blood." She let a drop of ink fall on the paper, the hundredth time she had done this. It splattered and then within seconds absorbed into the page as if it had never been there. "I've tried burning it with fire, ink; razors, magic blades. Whatever this is, it would be the lightest, most powerful armor you could imagine. I wonder if it survives dragon breath?"

Van shrugged. "Look, I'm game if you are, I have a condition. I want to put blood into a container. No open wounds. I don't want it to suck me dry again."

"We could ask it about that strange snake parasite the paladins found in the east," Alaura suggested.

Van disagreed. "We don't know what is so how would we verify this magic as being truthful. Let's stick with Terest."

Alaura pointed to her empty ink bottle and sent word for Lilli. Several hours later, with preparations made, Van sat down in front of the book and stared at the question elegantly scripted in his own blood. Taking the quill and dipping it in a bottle of his own blood, Van wrote:

For payment in gold, I would know if the first paladin king
of Merakor, Terest Nostam, was real.

The blood swirled onto the page and then vanished. A moment later, the question changed to a spiked and slash-cut rune. Another moment passed and the rune resolved into Taysoran Common.

I can show you. Gold matters not at all to me.

Alaura and Van both looked at each other. "Does it only want blood? Ask it," Alaura suggested. Van redipped his quill and wrote:

For the answer of Terest Nostram, what payment matters?

The ink absorbed more quickly this time and, with the quill running dry, Van had to re-dip several times to write this question out. Again, the swirl of the strange thorn-like rune that transformed into script they could read.

The only payment that matters is the soul experience of
those who bring me new information, new experiences, and
new powers under the many skies.

Van sat back and rubbed his head. He had begun to sweat and had a pale cast to his skin. Alaura signaled the priestess, who pulled Van's eyes open and looked at them. They sluggishly looked up at her and Van tried to smile. His skin felt clammy. "There's nothing wrong with him, but he is reacting to this as if being fed on by one of the undead called a Shadow. It's sucking his vitality even though it's not taking blood."

"Can you restore me?" Van asked. Lilli shook her head no. He stood and waved his arm around and after a second said, "Yeah, I feel dizzy."

Lilli touched his forehead and said, "You feel cold." Turning to Alaura, she added, "I am going to go and get Dar Tania. She is the only one that would be able to restore lost vitality, like this. Perhaps Commander Sean could as well, but he is training on the mountain with the next class of paladins. I don't know how long it will take to find Dar and bring her here. Please, do not do anything more with this cursed paper. Tiamat compels me to not touch it and I sense that Van's life is endangered should you continue."

Alaura built up the fire and helped Van walk over to a plush chair near its warmth. After Alaura got him settled in and brought him some food, Van noted, "I could restore myself but I can tell that Pha Rann would not approve of it given we willingly engaged after we knew the price."

Outside, the day spun overhead as Van faded in and out of sleep. Sometime past midnight, Dar arrived with Bomoki via his new favorite spell: *teleport*. Dar found Van still fitfully asleep in the chair, while Alaura read a book across from him by the fire. "Your fascination with Merakor never ends does it, Alaura?" Dar asked.

Alaura looked up and smiled though her expression darkened a bit when she saw Bomoki. "It was a fascinating time. Ynt'taris continues to teach me about what he calls 'nexal inversions.'" Bomoki muttered something and Alaura explained, "Tehra is supposed to be in the center of Creation, Chaos, and Warp. An inversion is when the gates move or Tehra shifts towards one. You should consider reading something besides spell books." Looking back at Dar, Alaura put her book down, "Merakor, as he said and I am learning, was the only time a civilization in Tehra actually caused one. Of course, you can hardly call it an obsession when you spend an equal amount of time in cleric training. Is it just me or do you grow fiercer every time you sequester yourself away with the dragons?"

Dar brushed a glowing red strand of hair back from her face. "If it keeps up at this pace, I'll be ten feet tall and able to stop an army with a wink and a blown kiss within a few years. Alerius tells me that Tiamat desires all the priestesses to act as Her Avatars here. I'm learning that the dragons have a rather strong streak of vanity when it comes to things like mortal beauty. Sometimes, I remember my life before. By now, I'd be married to the fourth or fifth son of some tribal chief's advisor."

Bomoki snorted and then laughed, trying hide it. "I see the same thing with magic between the three. They constantly debate whose magic is stronger. They're each so different in their specializations, but it does not stop them from arguing about it. Hello, Alaura. I see King Nathaniel is still trying to marry you off."

Van stirred a bit from his sleep and muttered something about black whirlwinds and screaming. Alaura pointed at him and said to Dar, "He's – his name is Van – he has been like for almost ten hours now. We want to continue our investigation, but these effects, they remind me of the lecture Alerius presented with Syliri about the various effects and powers undead have against us. Lilli speculated it's like a Shadow."

Dar walked over and touched Van's head. "Compared to the others, Van seems more of a bookworm, like you. I'm glad the others left," Dar said, referring to the other suitors. Dar focused on him and then smiled. "He is genuinely interested in you, Alaura. It seems his family did to him what you and Ynt'taris did to LeRoy. Show me this blood-draining paper."

Alaura uncovered it from her desk where they had it pinned. The blood-inked question gleamed as wetly as if freshly written. "Don't touch it," Alaura cautioned.

"The Queen does not want me to touch it," Dar answered.

Before either could do anything, Bomoki touched it with his finger. Nothing happened, "See? It's not touch that activates it. It's something else. Probably blood. Since you're experimenting, we should get a bunch of different people to write in it with different materials. Maybe it only responds to a cleric, or a mage, or someone magically inclined. I bet it would love the great hero Sean, just like everyone else here."

Dar had grown used to Bomoki's jealousy and ignored him. "Let me restore Van and then, if you want to, you can give it a try. Maybe you can learn something about it, like what it actually is?"

Bomoki sat down in front of the parchment and smelled it, studied it, while Dar began a prayer to Tiamat for Van's health. "Why would you ask about Terest Nostram? The dragons already know he was real."

"It's a test," Alaura said. "No point experimenting if it cannot tell us the truth or is only able to reveal things we already know."

Bomoki nodded and then sat back to flip open and study his spellbook. "I'm going to get some spells ready that might help."

* * *

Hrax Terrej noted an odd smell in the mine. It reminded him of humans, but another smell bothered him. This second scent had a cloying quality to it of serpents. *A human and a serpent or both?* he wondered. The idiot goblins reported nothing at all. When he reached the end of the mine shaft, he noted that all appeared as it should. Even the guard stood stiff and at attention. That was a welcome sight as he had grown tired of the constant groveling and information about the mine that just did not matter. Hrax growled sarcastically at the guard, "What? No report that the miners continue to mine?"

When no answer came, Hrax laughed but the unresponsiveness also bothered him. He growled at the goblin and then smacked him. The force of the blow pulverized the petrified guard and Hrax blinked in surprise and shock as stone fragments fell away from his punch. He whirled around looking for an enemy. The urgency and fear he felt, all at once, it was a new feeling he had not experienced as a Fecundus.

An arrow smashed into his forehead just barely missing his eye. With a sweep, he brought his wings over his face as two more arrows flew in and stuck in the wing. Both would have hit his other eye. Hrax looked around for the ambusher and realized the rock and stone throughout the cavern would be perfect. With a near-thoughtless gesture of his hand, Hrax cast a spell that covered the cavern with stone needles. This new power, something he could understand but not do before, happened naturally, easily. *This power, it will make them bleed and I'll know them by their pain. They're as good as dead*, Hrax thought gleefully. Thoughts of eating his first human made his stomach growl. Ylgolth had made it seem divine. *I'm still hungry.* Usually, a goblin or two would satiate him. This time, the fat hobgoblin and the ten females had left him wishing for more hobgoblins. Another difference, Hrax noted, was that the hobgoblin remained more strongly in his mind. The names of the goblins, which Hrax had never cared to know, came to him now. He could sift the overseer's memories and, when he found the parts where Hrax terrified him, those memories were most delectable.

Outside the acid cave, the goblin miners began to shriek as the rocks all around them became needles and razors. Hrax realized, *I need to be more careful with this new power! Very well, let them die and I will feed on their lifeforce.* Too scared to stop digging, they either dug until they died, or tried to escape and bled to death as the magical spikes lacerated and then pulverized their feet and legs to bloody mash. Hrax heard movement but, whoever or whatever had attacked him, wisely remained hidden behind the stone columns. His other power came to bear now and Hrax inhaled the pain, misery, and deaths of the goblins outside. It filled him with a level of power delicious to him. He wondered if humans would be even more delicious.

From behind the column, Bruce swore under his breath as the first pain lanced through his knee where he stood. Bull Stomper, clearly, was not a giant or a goblin. Syliri whispered to him a word that looked like a question, "Devil?" But the sound of shattering stone masked her words.

Bruce racked his brain but could not place the creature. It resembled a demon but with some frog-like attributes, especially its eyes and hands. Syliri not recognizing it, that meant it was not already in the god emperor's garden. The stone needles, he knew as a clerical power. They cut up into his feet. He had studied this in some seminar put on by Sean's Order. Bruce knew that if he moved at all, it would worsen. Already, his boots filled with and leaked blood. If he moved or made any noise, this demon would find him. The dying sounds of the goblins outside gave him little relief. *At least I won't have to kill them. Is a medusa affected by this magic?* he wondered. Bull Stomper inhaled deeply and strengthened. Bruce felt the vampiric pull of Stomper's magic consume the goblins' deaths outside. Against the dim lighting, Bull Stomper's muscles tightened and a feral grin creased his mouth.

"I smell you, human," Bull Stomper growled. "You and your pet snake. You can't hide forever." Hrax scanned the cavern. From the faint light of the acid pool, and further back from it, natural columns provided ample hiding places. The arrows had come from a cluster of just three though. He smiled. "I know where you are, approximately. Enjoy my gift."

From Hrax's outstretched hand, a fireball shot to the closest column by the acid pool. The detonation and heat blast filled that section of the cave with flames. When the magic energy ended, Hrax could only smell fire. "I can do this all day." He sent another fireball, this one at the acid pool. The detonation splashed and converted the acid to steam. It gave Hrax an idea and he sent another, deeper into the pool so that the explosion blew a large volume of the acid into the air and all around. Seven more and the pool began to boil. Hrax taunted them, "Unless you can breathe acid?" Another fireball struck the pool.

Bruce swore again, this time out loud, as the acid steam tickled his eyes and throat. "Syl? How do we win?" he whispered during an explosion. The lack of effective hand communication really made him angry. To send fireballs so lazily meant the monster either had a magic item or was just that powerful. As if to emphasize the point, three fireballs shot to the pool. Its surface now boiled.

Syliri remained in her humanoid form, and like Bruce, did not move. She mouthed to him, "Hold your breath. Don't breathe the acid. I'll distract it. You shoot it. And get farther back. The cavern drops down. The acid steam will be less, lower down." She did her best to use hand gestures to convey that Bruce needed to get further back and lower.

Bruce signaled 'okay.' He focused his will, and at the next explosion, he leapt back and down. It hurt, but by the third leap, he landed on normal stone. Bull Stomper remained within range of Bruce's arrows. With the next explosion, Bruce coughed and gulped clean air before going quiet and still again. This creature was smart enough to tell from where the arrows had been launched. Bruce retrieved and placed the first of what would be many more magic arrows, aiming them all around the cavern entrance. He then moved to set another volley from a different direction. He thanked Krentismar for the magic quiver that gave him limitless copies of his one real arrow.

When the next fireball arced out to the pool, Syliri caught it. She did not catch it in her hands, but stepped into the fireball's light and Hrax's vision. For just a moment, Hrax saw yellow eyes ringed by smaller snake eyes and his magic went gray. Though it still gleamed brightly, it looked dim and stony. Instead of an explosion, the gray fireball rose up and began to spin around Syliri. She stood there naked as the light orbited her. Hrax leaned forward to see against the bright light and acid fog. He mistook her for a human.

"You dare enter my home?!" Hrax roared at her.

Syliri walked forward along the edge of the acid pool, letting her foot step in. She could see that Hrax expected her to scream in pain. When nothing happened, she saw his battle rage and bloodlust calm a bit. "Who are you? What are you?" he asked. The tone of his voice became suddenly suave and masculine.

He must have noticed I'm nude, she thought. *I wonder if he has seen my hair yet.* She spoke to Hrax in her native tongue, a soft language full reptilian sibilant sounds and soft consonants. Hrax cocked his head at her and said in goblinoid, "I do not understand what you are saying, lovely one. Are you a sylph? A naiad perhaps? Another helper from Master Ylgolth?" Hrax pointed at her and wondered out loud, "Are you Bet Mirgul's sister?"

The fireball had been spinning so tightly over her head that it appeared to have stopped moving. Its light showed her snake hair clearly and Hrax pointed to it and grinned. "Medusae?" he asked. The sharp fangs of his wide mouth completed the frog-devil look.

Syliri nodded her head and stroked one of the snakes, which coiled around her arm. No doubt this was killing Bruce. Hrax stepped forward and she could plainly tell that she had aroused more than just his interest. She made a sign she hoped Bruce would see while he prepared an ambush, *Be ready*.

She pointed to him and asked, "Demon?" Splashing the water with her foot, she added to her question, "Acid demon?"

Hrax opened his arms allowing her to see him clearly. Syliri noted the same spiral markings on right shoulder they had seen with the hill giants. She pointed to those and tried the language of Hell.. "What are those?"

Hrax looked confused before answering her in goblinoid, "I do not understand these languages." He switched to Slaadi and asked her, "You are a medusa, correct? Do you serve Set?"

Syliri felt she had heard this language before but could not place it. The spiral markings and the language, they reminded her of something in her past. If Alerius were here, she knew he would say, "We have this in the garden. The creatures are called…"

Hrax took a step towards her, his arms open and carefully not doing anything threatening. He reached his hand out to her and said in goblinoid, "I'm not a demon. I won't hurt you. Take my hand and we can understand each other better."

Knowing it would kill Bruce, Syliri took comfort at least that he understood the language. *The more I learn about this, the better it will be when we return whatever it is to Alerius.* She put her hand in Hrax's.

Instantly, the cavern became one of gold. Radiant light reflected off golden floors. The stone columns broken by Hrax, and the intact stalagmites became chandeliers and furniture fixtures. In his hand, Syliri's own hand became smooth and alabaster, the perfect complexion to match Bruce's. She felt her snakes become brunette locks draping her shoulders. Everything she hated about herself became everything she ever dreamed it would be.

A dream, she realized. *This is my dream of the world after the maedar fell, before Time drove my sisters insane.* The beauty of the dream, the aching desire she felt for Bruce to see her this way… it all came together in her thoughts at once and she realized she held her breath. "What are you?" she whispered to the demon.

Hrax kissed her hand and wrapped his fingers through hers. "Your hand is perfect," he said. "I wish to hold it forever. I am Slaadi."

Syliri struggled to remember the levels. "Fecundus?" she asked. Green, or what they called Fecundus, was the only level she remembered. It was the weakest. Even with a green, Alerius had been careful in capturing it. His words ran through her memory; *With a slaad, you can never be too careful. They are master manipulators. The best way to interact with them is to attack suddenly with everything you've got. That's where I saw these spiral scars. From the green slaad we captured.*

Hrax thumped his chest and flexed. "Azuros."

Ah, Syliri remembered. *Azuros, a blue slaad. His touch is what pulled me into this dream,* Syliri mused. *Alerius would want a blue one.* He preferred these collector creatures as undamaged as possible, though maybe Dar could heal them now. As much as Syliri enjoyed being with Bruce, she really needed one of the dragons for an otherworldly creature like this. But, even her thoughts felt sluggish and alien, even to herself, here. She should be screaming in terror knowing she held hands with an Azuros. "It's too bad I can't petrify you," she lied. "You must have encountered one of my sisters as a Fecundus? I'm Syliri."

Hrax eyed her suspiciously but was distracted by her beauty. "The gorgon I met, she tried to stone me, but I killed her. She could not speak. How is it that you speak?" He ripped the arrows out of his wing and tossed them at her feet. "You can have these back. We won't need them. Your pet human, will he watch us make love?"

"I am a created being. The human mage who made me, he now decorates my garden. He did not want a mindless beast. He wanted beauty and power. It was his doom. The human serves me now and does what I want. What do you want, Azuros?"

"I am Hrax Terrej. I want all that is mine and more. Right now, I want to know this female divinity naming itself Syliri. If your creator were still alive, he would know my fury and the power of my dream. Stupid mage! Cursed creatures always meddling, always prying."

"But they have their uses," Syliri interrupted him. Hopefully, Bruce would be ready soon. "A family of birds now nest on the mage's statue, for example. The look of surprise on his face when I petrified him, it makes me happy in all my lonely days and nights. Tell me, Hrax, are there other slaads here – perhaps an Embros or Anthracos?" Hearing the word 'Azuros' had prompted her to recall the other levels. As a Blue, Hrax would have a mentor, or a guide. "My late mage taught me about the Slaadi. Is what they say true?"

Hrax flexed his arms and stepped into her arms. The dream touch masked her awareness that he was truly so close to her. "You know the colors. That alone is impressive. There are no others though I commune with my teacher through the pools like the one you bathe in." He pointed to the acid pool. "If I were to mate a gorgon, our offspring might send me to my next state." He licked his lips but clearly had no interest in murder. "What do they say about the Slaadi?"

Syliri sent a mental thank-you to Bruce for retrieving her clothing. She should not be glad to be nude with an aroused Slaadi, but it felt right. "If you ate me, you would never know the worlds of pleasure…" She stepped back, only now aware he held her, and turned to the side and put her hand on her hip. "Besides, they say that Slaadi accumulate lifetimes of experience as they grow. If you ate me, you'd learn only what other statues adorn my garden. How many lifetimes do you know, Azuros?"

Hrax looked around. "You have a beautiful dream full of gold." She understood him perfectly. "Am I the object of your desire, Syliri?"

When the word "desire" sounded in her ears, she became aware of his powerful masculinity. It made her swoon and he caught her by reaching around and clasping her upper thigh with his claws. A tiny part of her brain wondered why Bruce was not in this dream. As she thought it, Hrax's form began to change mimicking Bruce's. Hrax watched it. "With a modicum of control, you are turning me into your desire. I see. Very well. If this is required to mate with you, I accept your dream, Syliri. You have powerful will to even talk with me this long."

"What is this power?" Syliri asked. In the time it took to ask, Hrax became Bruce and she ached to be with him, to feel him. A flood of images of herself surrounded by children, human-haired children with human skin, filled her brain and her desire flared to the point that the ring gifted her by Alerius activated.

Hrax frowned at the ring and, still holding her hand, said, "We should remove this." His lips on her neck distracted her from his other hand pulling the ring off. She missed his hand along her thigh and bit playfully at him while he tossed the ring to the floor.

Bruce watched Syliri take Bull Stomper's hand. He expected something, like another signal to attack or for her to spin them around so his body would take all the arrows. Instead, she froze as if paralyzed. He would have been alarmed except for the unconcerned and increasingly happy look on her face. *No, it's even more alarming that she looks this happy*, he thought. He watched her look around slowly, and then with increasing movement. He could not launch his arrow volleys because she entwined her arms and legs around the demon's. *Is she trying to position him for a better attack?*

Syliri put her head back and the demon opened his mouth of fangs to her throat while the other pulled at the emerald rings on her hand. Bruce knew something bad had happened. Ignoring the needle rocks, Bruce called on his god, Krentismar, for aid and charged. Gravity worked to his advantage as he moved across and along the sides of the columns, silently. He saw the ring's emeralds flare brightly as the magic in them activated to strengthen Syliri's self-control, but she remained enraptured. He noted her heavy breathing and sexual arousal. He knew her well enough to recognize that. Grimly, he ran around the cavern by the entrance and then leapt at Bull Stomper.

Drawing his sword mid-air, the blue runes went red at the same time that Hrax's wing slammed Bruce back. The blow redirected his leap and sent him spinning right back into the needle stones. Grunting in pain, Bruce whirled and leapt out of that area. Hrax pulled the ring off Syliri's hand and

Bruce saw her lift her leg up and around the demon's waist. "Syliri! Snap out of it!" he screamed.

Back in the dream, Syliri found Hrax's mouth and they kissed, exactly the sensual snake-like dancing of tongues she most enjoyed. She felt her pulse racing and registered that Hrax had just removed her ring, but she did not care. It felt so warm, safe, and seductive. She felt him responding to her and lifted her other leg around him. She smiled into his kiss as he reached around and lifted her up so she could wrap both legs around him.

Somewhere behind her, a male voice called her name. It had an edge of panic and pain to it. It echoed in the cavern. Her mind noted that the golden room should not echo like a cavern. She noted that the Bruce in her arms, about to impregnate her, was not possessed of the voice she heard yelling her name. *Alerius' ring will reinforce my will if something bad were to happen. Only the maedar could drown me in Set's Dream like this*, she thought. Her mind wandered back to the waves of pleasure coruscating across her human skin and hair – *I have hair on my body!* – and she ground herself against Bruce. *Did Hrax take my ring off?*

"Syliri!" Bruce screamed. "What has happened to you? Come on!"

Bruce activated the *copy* magic that stored momentum in his sword and threw it at Hrax. Just as the sword was about to get smacked away, Bruce summoned it back and threw it again, from a different direction as he charged. Maneuvering himself to avoid the path of his arrows, Bruce kept throwing his sword trying to find a pattern.

The wings deflected and guarded Bull Stomper as if they had a mind of their own. It was maddening as Bruce darted to and fro. He knew Syliri would hate everything about this when she came to. Bull Stomper's facial expression changed in that moment. The calculating and dispassionate creature that Syliri touched became truly demonic as it pulled its head back and leered down at her. With her eyes closed and gasping in denied pleasure, Syliri reached up for him and begged for him. Bull Stomper seemed to feed on, even revel in her desire. The look in the creature's eyes, though, told Bruce that time had run out.

He threw his sword, trusting it would be swatted away and drew bow and fired his real arrow. The sword, activated with the prior throws' energy, shot towards the demon. As expected, the wings smashed it aside. The wing's deflection was the only pattern and Bruce's only real arrow shot with brilliant silver light trailing its path. Bruce held his breath, praying for it to strike true, but could not wait to see. He tumbled and landed by Syliri. Kelly, the cobra snake, found his hand and gently bit him and Bruce pulled, equally gentle but with enough force to pull Syliri off balance. "Thank you, Kelly," he called out.

Syliri fell back. Bull Stomper, not expecting lancing agony in his side, fell out of the dream back into the cavern where a gleaming arrow covered in runes had pierced his wing and buried itself in the side of his ribs. From all around the back part of the cavern, points of light erupted as Bruce caught Syliri and activated the arrow volleys.

Syliri clawed to return to Bull Stomper, but the sudden pull from the ranger and her snakes cooperating with Bruce, dropped her to the ground and she broke contact with Hrax. Instantly, the golden dream vanished. With the dream gone, her actions, all of them remembered, hit her. Still shaking from the passionate coupling in the dream, Syliri screamed in anguish, pain, and humiliation. Then, Bruce's arrows began striking all around them. Bruce pinned her to the ground and fumbled for the emerald ring. "It's too much, Syl. Help me, please!" Bruce begged her.

Syliri saw how close she had come to mating with a slaad. *From anyone's*, she realized Bruce had seen it all...*From my love's perspective*, she thought in despair, *I must have looked like a whore throwing myself at a demon.*

"It's too much." She heard Bruce yelling in her ear as arrows drove Hrax back from her.

"Yes," she said. "I cannot." She threw Bruce off of her, not caring that her toss sent him a hundred feet back into the cavern. Her gaze went yellow and she saw images of Hrax from her own and the snakes' eyes. "You toy with Set's Dream. Let me show you the peril of Set!"

Yellow energy blasted out from her eyes. Arrows still in flight petrified, only to shatter against Hrax where his body turned to stone. Hrax tried to fight the power of her gaze. She felt his will, strong even against her, try to resist and ultimately fail. Flickering torch light behind them petrified. Drops of water turned to stone. The horrible look of dread on Hrax's face froze forever and Syliri rose up before it, blasting it with the cursed power of Set's gift to the medusae. The gray stone crackled and began to opalize and still she lashed it with wave after wave of her power.

Bruce felt multiple ribs crack and only his armor saved him as he tumbled down to the cavern floor. The illumination of Syliri's attack was like nothing he seen from her before. Alerius' gift, the emerald ring, gleamed on the floor by her feet. Bruce tried to catch his breath and inhaled stone dust as the very air itself began to petrify and empty the room of breathable air. Bruce ran, trusting that if he could just get to the ring, it would help.

Krentismar, or maybe Tiamat, answered his prayers and he found the ring. Unable to reach Syliri's hands though, Bruce found Kelly in his face, eyes aglow with yellow light. Bruce felt his face clench and go tight. Kelly took the ring and coiled around Syliri's arm to put it back on.

The ground under him began to change and Bruce saw the acid pool begin to petrify. That was when Kelly and several other snakes lifted him off the floor. Broken arrows on the ground and spilled Slaadi blood became smooth rock. And then, the power stopped its fell intent. Bruce felt Syliri heaving for air too.

Kelly put him down and went to cover Syliri's eyes. "Oh, Bruce. What have I done? I'm so sorry. You must hate me."

"No, Syl. No, not at all. I will never hate you. You are my love. We'll talk and this will sort itself out."

"Bruce, I won't forgive myself. I do not deserve you."

"Syliri, you deserve every good thing this world can offer. I don't understand what just happened."

"It was so much worse than the maedar, Bruce. And I wanted to just keep going. Who cares about consequences, I want to destroy this so bad. All of it. Everything. Everyone." She dropped to her knees, her back turned to Bruce. "Please, don't touch me. I am barely in control of things right now. The god emperor will be so disappointed."

"Shhh, no. He won't. How could he? Syl, what is this thing?"

"It's a Slaad. A weaker one too. A weak one..., I'm pathetic!" She buried her face in her hands and dropped to the floor. Kelly dared Bruce to come near her.

"Shhhhh," Bruce said. "One thing at a time."

Chapter 5 – Brook Summerstone

Colored leaves crunched under Brook's bare feet. She loved it and kicked a pile into the air. The cool air, the mountain ring all around the east and north horizons, and earlier, she had seen one of the dragons flying high over what they now called Dragon Mountain. She traveled light. Summer had taught her how to find food from nature. Once she understood, once she connected to the land, it provided everything she needed even at the end of the fall season. "I love being a druid!" she sang out loud while she kicked another clump of leaves.

Heading north on the new elemental road, she made excellent time. All her life, she heard stories about dragons and how they destroyed the land. "It's hard to believe," she marveled, looking around. Morbatten looked clean, pristine, and ready for the great empire Dar Tania talked about in her sermons. "Dragons did this. I wonder what else I'll learn," she shouted out to the road ahead.

At night, she continued on her way by moonlight and with a softly-enchanted spell that gave her vision similar to an owl. One of her favorite things was walking at night like this; she could see everything in the sharpest detail. When she grew weary, another spell brought her the strength and endurance of a wolf. The spell combination made her feel like a perfect predator and she reveled in the feelings that came with it.

After continuing like this for almost six hours, she at last stopped by a clear stream of flowing water. Though the night fell chilly, she felt warm as if wrapped in wolf fur. Snacking on dried fruit, she leaned back and began braiding her long brunette hair into a tight ponytail. With her enhanced vision, she had no trouble seeing a humanoid form making its way towards her. With curiosity, she watched and noted that it must be another Halfling.

A faint voice came out of the darkness, "Hello? I'm traveling to Home and got a bit lost. I thought I heard someone by the river."

Brook almost laughed and called back, "You're on the right road. It's a little late to be travelling and lost. Did you lose your common sense too?" She sniffed the air with her wolf senses and did not detect anything amiss. Sun would rise in another four hours. "I'm Brook. What's your name?"

"Kaia," the answer came back. Brook saw that Kaia had reached the other side of the stream to where a rough stone bridge arced up over the water. This would be The Bridge marking the formal boundary between Morbatten and Home.

Dar Tania had insisted on a bridge. Summer wanted to build one where one side represented Morbatten and the other the Halflings. Summer already called it Friendship Bridge, a better name than Rescue Bridge. Brook imagined it would be covered with the journey her people had taken only to fall to ogres in the area Dar now called the Western Provinces. Though barely flowing now, in spring, this small trickle would become a rushing rapids.

With some guidance, Kaia found his way to where Brook lay back against a boulder looking up at the stars. Kaia seemed nearly blind in the darkness and with a hint of regret because she would lose her owl vision, Brook said, "We can make a fire. Are you cold? Hungry? What do you need?"

"Some food and warmth would be nice," Kaia said. Together, they gathered sticks and soon a fire pushed the darkness back.

Brook immediately noticed Kaia's black as the night sky skin. "I've never met or heard of a black-skinned Halfling," Brook said. "Is this another surprise by the dragons? Halflings of some tribal group?"

Kaia held his arms out and then smiled. "No, I have a taste of otherworld in my heritage." Brook noted the brilliantly white fangs, but still failed to detect any sense of danger about this strange Halfling. "The god emperor lets me live among the tribes, has for some time actually. Alerius suggested that I come down and meet Summer's people. You must be the druid everyone is talking about. Brook, right?"

She nodded. "I'm not trying to be difficult, but I feel like we'd have heard about you in the five years we've been here."

Kaia poked at the fire and watched an ember rise up into the air. "I mostly keep to myself. Trust me though. Those who know me know me very well. It's taken this long for someone from Home to become worth my knowing very well." He grinned at her. "Summer was close, but then he became complacent and stopped to focus his efforts on building up Home. You saw that. He's a natural leader, but lacks ambition to take Home to where it should be."

His words should have offended her. Instead, a vision opened in her mind of Home as a center of agricultural commerce. The giant roads that looked so bizarrely out of place now barely held wagon and rider traffic. Tens of thousands of Halflings filled her mind's eye and she saw what a Halfling city, aligned with nature, might look like. In that instant, all of her senses came alive and she felt an explosive mix of danger, safety, desire, and terror all at once. "What are you?" she whispered.

Kaia sat down being careful to avoid anything that might look aggressive. "Like I said, the god emperor lets me live amongst the tribes. Now that you're part of the tribes, it's time for us to know each other. More importantly, I want to know about you. Tell me, Brook Summerstone, if you could have anything in this world – like a wish – what would the druid hero of Home want?"

Brook forced herself to calm. "Sorry to disappoint you but I'm hardly a hero. On the other question, it's easy. I'd wish for the power to protect my people."

Kaia shook his head in disagreement. "That's too vague. Everyone wishes for generalities. Health, safety, power. No wish can protect your people from time, old age, or death. Protect them from What might be a better avenue of thinking. At least that would tell me what you're most worried about as a leader, a hero of Home. What are you so scared of that you feel it is your job to wish protection for all Halflings?"

Brook remembered a conversation between Bomoki and Captain Sean about this very topic. Steeling her resolve, she finished her ponytail and said, "It's not that. First," she held up a finger. "There are not that many of us. I love your vision but tens of thousands? I don't think there are that many in all the world." Kaia began laughing but signaled her to continue. "Though Bruce and others have brought us more than the original handful Dar rescued, we are a tiny number compared to humans. Second, we've been given a paradise... but what if it's actually a cage? And lastly, you assume I want to protect Halflings only as my people. The truth is that I want to protect Morbatten, if this is actually freedom and not a cage."

"I like your wisdom, Brook. You see, this is where Summer failed. He still doesn't see Home as part of Morbatten. Not seeing that, he puts the Halflings in a beautiful cage. It's not apparent now, but Morbatten will grow in leaps and strides. If Home does not similarly grow, you will become a tiny insignificant little corner of Morbatten's future. Cages come in many different shapes, sizes, and styles. Did you know that I'm in a cage? I'm essentially cut off from where I want to be. If I leave Morbatten, I'll be sought out and killed. If I go to where I wish to go before I am ready to kill the killers, I'll be killed. The god emperor has been very good to me in this cage that is Morbatten. How would you know for sure that Morbatten is or is not a cage to your liking? After all, if I remember this correctly, you were second in line to be eaten by the ogres after Summer. Now that was a proper cage full of suffering and torment. I bet it still haunts you."

Brook eyed the demon-Halfling more closely. "I've never told anyone about being next. How do you know this? If Morbatten is a cage, I like it just fine for now but something seems off. I can't quite put my finger on what it is. It just feels wrong, to me, in my gut."

Kaia smiled at her. In the moonlight, his fanged eye-teeth sparkled at her. "I can give you the truth but there would be two prices for it. The first price is that, knowing the truth about Morbatten, you would most certainly have to consecrate yourself to Tiamat. The second is that you'll owe me a favor, to be repaid later. Is that what you really want? Think carefully. My gifts come with a price. In this case, the knowledge you want would also come with a surety of your conversion to Tiamat."

"You can do this? How?" Brook asked. Kaia said nothing and returned to poking at the fire. She felt a growing sense of time urgency as if this strange encounter had a time limit. Her interactions with Dar and Sean had shown her that very different gods could exist in harmony but Sean's principled execution of doctrine with an eye to real people and situations always appealed to her. On the other hand, Sean's love – almost worship – of Dar Tania and her unflinching and uncompromising approach to Tiamat's edicts seemed so confident. *I'm not really like either of them*, Brook mused to herself. *But, I'd know and could tell Summer if Morbatten is a trap.*

"This deal you offer me, what if I don't like it?" she asked across the fire. "I don't know you or what this entails. It seems kind of silly."

Kaia continued to stare into and stir the fire. "But, I know you, Brook. I know everything." From the sparks and embers of the fire, an image of her as a small child appeared, swirling in the flames. Suddenly, a butterfly appeared and she chased it.

"No, I don't want to see this," Brook said. "I believe you."

"No, but watch. This is the part where you run right past the troll." The image showed her chase the butterfly past a cluster of rocks and earth. Even in the fire, it looked dug up and fake.

Brook waved her hand and the fire went out. "I don't want to see it. That troll killed my family. I relive that moment all my life."

Kaia's eyes gleamed a faint purple in the sudden night's dark. "When you were in the caves and knew your adopted father and leader would be eaten, I bet it really hit home in that moment: are you doomed to be next in a long line of doom? You know, not all memories have to haunt you. Dar, for example, she has really figured out how to leave her tribal girl self behind. Even I would bow knee to her these days. You could be like that. You could know – truly know – those things that bother you about this place."

Feeling her time was almost out, Brook blurted out, "Okay, I'll do it. Teach me about this cage."

Kaia stood up and she saw his hand swipe out at her. Instead of a Halfling hand though, a hand of ebony black, polished and gleaming in starlight, raced towards her. Just as it hit, she saw clawed talons speckled with red fire. The claws hit and passed through her leaving a faint sulphur smell in her nose.

Brook found herself standing high in the air and looked down at two enormous dragons. One she saw clearly as Alerius, the god emperor and fire-breather patriarch. The other she did not notice at first. Its form became apparent only when it moved. Trees had rooted into or around its body. Plants and other aspects of nature seemed to have bonded to it. Only when the giant tree near its body shifted did she realize something was there. Tracing that movement, that form, she uncovered the dragon. As if standing between the two, she heard them speak.

Alerius said, "Mallaforax, the time draws nigh that Merakor falls. I foresee the world trees burning."

The nature dragon - *is it a green dragon?* Brook wondered – replied, "The very River of Time burns. With it, yes, the world trees fall. I am surprised you care. What would you have me do?"

"We must find and preserve the seeds of the world trees in Merakor. I see eons will pass before we return. The Temple of Glass shall fall." The fire dragon's voice sounded sorrowful and Brook felt a stirring of emotion deep in her heart.

Mallaforax looked up at Alerius and said with shocked strain in his voice, "You want to preserve the world trees rather than the Temple of Glass? Really? I would know why. I will have the druids know to preserve the seeds. Westward, past Kinpeace, we will hide them for you."

"It is not enough, my brother. My consort tells me that, against what is to come, nothing of Merakor will survive unless we save it ourselves. I must ask you to leave Morilon and retrieve the seeds yourself. Ynt'taris, Spark, and I are too well known. We will draw attention. You, on the other hand," but the green interrupted him.

"I will go through the roots of the world and protect these doorways. Yes, I will do it when the portals are next open to me." Mallaforax seemed to lose focus as a swarm of butterflies darted through the space where Brook listened.

Alerius humanshifted and touched Mallaforax's snout. "The world trees are how we shall reclaim the Temple of Glass. I think of it as already lost to us."

"Truly, brother?" The sorrowful sound of their commiseration haunted Brook with its sense of loss.

Brook startled, back into the darkness of night by the fire ring. Kaia let her regain her awareness and then said, "The truth of Morbatten is this: Taysor and the elves, the other nations here: they are refugees. Morbatten is different because the god emperor carved it away from the Merakoran survivors so that, untainted, the Isles could have their own destiny. Part of that destiny is the truth that the pantheon of heaven is not responsible for nature; the dragons are. Mallaforax is the patriarch of the green dragons – the vapor breathers. As a druid, I expect that you'll ponder on this and know what to do." Kaia stood and brushed dirt and scraps of leaves off his pants and heavy cloak.

"It's a lot to take in," Brook said. "The Morbatten dragons, they know so much."

"Yes, they do. It's a shame there are so few who listen to them or study what they would teach." Kaia inclined his head to Brook and walked into the darkness.

* * *

Shak D'Rath sat in the cold sunshine. His full plate armor felt strange and restrictive to him but as Captain Sean hit him with a heavy club, he realized it had advantages. Sean had ordered him to wear a heavier set, closer to what the Taysoran knights wore. The Commander said, "All your life, your tribe favored fast movement and agility over armor except for shields and a few pieces you captured now and then from Taysor and Morilon. Now, with your goddess helping you, you must wear real armor. Make it part of you. Learn to trust it."

Sean struck at Shak, aiming straight into the helmet visor. Shak tried not to flinch but knew the Commander saw him pull back in anticipation. Sean dropped the strike to his gorget. It nearly knocked Shak over but he felt nothing except momentum from the strike. "You must trust it," Sean said. "If you're worried about your armor, you're not praying to Tiamat. If you're not praying to Tiamat, you're not operating as an inspired paladin. The armor is here because you will be able to face foes many times mightier than ever before. Tiamat must see that you do what you can, and have faith that She will handle the rest."

They continued like this for some time. The new class watched. This would be the Sixth Class as Sean accelerated the classes from one a year to three a year. Some snickered at Shak and Sean whirled on them. "You'll go through this too, except it'll be Shak leading you. Watch and learn but keep these things to yourselves. You're not barbarians anymore! You're holy knights. Act like it!" Sean spun about and the club he held erupted in bright yellow fire. Pha Rann's blessing turned the club into a holy avenger sword. Identical to the sword sheathed at Sean's hip.

Shak ducked at the last instant even though he had no way of knowing or seeing that Sean had transformed the brute stick into a holy avenger. "Well done!" Sean exclaimed. "Your battle instincts remain top notch. Now if we can just get you to trust your faith."

Sean tossed the club to Shak and the fire immediately went out. It left behind a boring, but heavy, club. Shak said, "How do I make this into an avenging blade? I did this against the giant. Here, I feel disconnected."

"You must gather your faith until you see only a blade. Your faith must be sure. You will not feel the splintered wood, or the cracks in the grain. You will not feel the weight. You will feel your sword. When you have it, call to your goddess and strike."

Turning back to the new class, Sean picked up a twig and twirled it through his fingers. "Tell me, could such a thing become a sword?"

Silence answered him while Sean pretended to use the twig like a sword. Finally, one of the initiates said, "For you, it could be."

Sean threw the twig at the speaker and mid-air it transformed into a burning long sword which stuck, quivering, in the ground just beside the knight's foot. "For you, it can too," Sean said. "For you, it has to if you're going to serve your goddess the way Dar Tania requires. Fighters fight with swords. You're paladins. You fight with faith."

The day passed in a blur with object lessons like this. When Sean indicated that Shak could at last dismiss them, he laid down in the grass and breathed deeply. Clouds drifting overhead in the golden sun coupled to exhaustion pulled at him. In moments like this, he found his thoughts often moved between Dar and this strange mission and role he played here in Morbatten.

Shak laid down next to him. "There has to be a way to go faster," Shak said. "I've been studying with you for five years now, Commander. I still cannot summon the blade. I feel stuck and don't understand why. My purpose tells me the Queen is frustrated with my being stuck."

Sean held his hand up to the sun and then closed his fist on it. "From a certain point of view, it's like you can hold the sun in your hand. But," he opened his hand again. "It's never really there. Dar wants to speed everything up too. I've been thinking on it. I have an idea. It's dangerous, for you and the clerics we'd need to support it."

"Have you shared it with anyone?" Shak asked, mimicking Sean grabbing the sun.

"No, where I come from, this idea is heresy. It's taken this long to get enough priestesses that it might work. The dragons would have to agree to participate too." Sean noted a cloud formation that looked like Dar. "I sense you have other thoughts on your mind. Tell me." Sean knew, already, about Alerius' order that Dar begin having children with the paladins. "It's okay. I know about Dar. And you. The god emperor told me." Sean sighed deeply. "Do you love her?"

Shak paused for a moment and then said, "Yes. No. It's different. We grew up in neighboring tribes. I knew of her, before Tiamat. I was at her Coming of Age, to watch as I would go the next year. There was a chance that she and I could have been betrothed. You've heard this too. She wasn't high enough in the tribal rankings to be betrothed to anyone, but still, there was a chance. I remember my tribe discussing how strange that the dragon god would test someone like her, alone. Usually, it was done as a group with great honor going to the one evading capture the longest. You can only imagine how surprising it was, to everyone, when we found the dragon god with Dar Tania. Then, Tiamat and everything else happened. I did not love her back then. As the high priestess, when she is near me now, I cannot help but love her. My purpose compels loving her. Yet, it is not the same love I have known for other girls."

Sean said, "I wish I could pretend to understand these things. I was pledged to my order when I was young enough to have had brief infatuations, but had never been with someone I truly cared for. My life, my work, it has distracted me, but still – I've had feelings like what you describe. I hear the chieftains are already fighting about the god emperor having chosen you as the first, Shak. What do you think?"

Without hesitating, Shak answered and said, "The chiefs are too narrow-minded and set in their ways. They keep trying to put this new empire into the traditions of the tribes. It won't work. Just like Dar, I was not high enough to be slotted for marriage. But, here I am – first of Tiamat's paladins. Religion is an odd thing."

Sean laughed, softly. Then, he burst into laughter. Confused, Shak chuckled a bit and waited for Sean to explain what was so funny. At last, Sean said, "In all my studies, I cannot think of a single time when a paladin said 'Religion is an odd thing.' Truly Shak, you have a way with words."

"Commander, the god emperor has asked me to do this. I do not want there to be bad blood between us."

Again, Sean breathed a deep sigh and stretched. "Shak, I've made no hiding that I love her. I've also not hid that I'm bound by numerous personal oaths that prevent my love from ever being more than distant admiration. I've also made it clear that I do not follow Tiamat's ways. There will not be bad blood between you and me. However, if you beat a fellow paladin to death like you almost did the other day, there will be." Sean smacked Shak's arm. "Will it be a marriage?"

Shak speculated, "No. They already told me that I will father, but not be a father, to the child. The child will be raised by the Warg Tribe, north of here in the flat valley Alerius calls 'The Ancients.' If I were not a paladin, this would be easier. After all, Dar is beautiful."

"You can say that again," Sean answered. "Hardship and challenge are part of what drives a paladin to be different. If you are commanded, you must do this. We do not need to speak of it again. So, Dar will be a mother. I suppose this should not be a surprise to any of us. I'll tell you what, Shak. Obey the god emperor and let's see if we cannot speed up your progress. I'll talk to Dar tonight."

"About the avenging blade, or me?"

"Both. It'll work out. Nothing will change with you and I." Sean leaned up on his arm and faced Shak. "You have my word as a holy paladin of Pha Rann. My sacred vow to you, as a brother in arms, is that your fathering a child with Dar will change nothing between you and I." *But, it might change everything between me and this new empire*, Sean felt a pang of concern.

"Thank you, Commander! I will redouble my efforts to do you proud."

"Meet me in the ethereal," Sean said.

It took Shak a moment to translate the strange Taysoran term for the flowing River of Time Dar described in her sermons. Shak took in a deep breath and focused on the rushing wind in the trees and dead leaves around the training field. The transition felt smoother. *I'm getting better at this*, Shak noticed. *Not as good as Dar and the Commander.*

Shak found Sean standing in the swirling energy. The flow seemed calm, almost glass smooth around Sean. By comparison, Shak's aura seethed shifting from color to color. Sean pointed to the shifting colors. "It's hard to be a paladin and sense your god's purpose when you're this troubled. This is one of the reasons why my group follows a vow of chastity, others forsake even more: wealth, material possession, and so on." Sean looked at his reflection in the flow of time. "Shak, calm yourself and see if you can calm your aura. There are things that matter to your goddess, to you, to the empire, to so many other things. But, only Tiamat matters for you, because you are her paladin. Unless you can focus solely on Tiamat, you're going to continue struggling with the avenging blade, with summoning a holy steed, with being able to heal and be healed. Let it all go because nothing matters except your service to Tiamat."

Focusing on Tiamat and guiding Shak to a different god, Sean's own aura blurred. Shak smiled and said, "I see what you mean. I did not realize that it was this hard for you to be with us."

"It's not hard. I want Morbatten to become the spear prophesied. I want to see what happens with all of you. Some knights go on epic quests. I am called bring forth an empire to defeat Set. I am content with this calling."

* * *

Van sat to the side of the parchment. Bomoki took up position right in front of it. A vial of blood, this time drawn from a fighter Dar asked to volunteer, waited for the quill. At a nod from Dar, Bomoki cast a simple spell that animated the quill. The pen floated into the blood and then moved over to the page. Bomoki, waving his hand as if to music, directed the quill to ask the Terest Nostram question.

Even with blood, nothing happened. The ink and words pooled on the page and then faded leaving the surface clean, same as with ink. Bomoki tried again going so far as to even recreate the strange runes and words. After three more tries, he looked up and said what they were all thinking. "Someone has to actually write the question." Bomoki grabbed the quill, dipped it in the fighter's blood and rewrote the question. Again, nothing happened. Bomoki sighed with exasperation. "Okay, with one's own blood."

"No -" Dar cried out but Bomoki stabbed his arm with the quill.

Bomoki repeated the Terest Nostram question while asking Dar for help. "Dar Tania, please be ready to heal me. I believe I am much weaker than Warner."

As Bomoki's blood dissolved into the page, new words began to form in the strange thorn-like rune. Too faint to really make out, Alaura cast a *scribe* spell to copy the rune. With each new dip and blood, the rune clarified until at last, it gleamed red. Like before, the rune swirled and reformed into Tanian Common language.

Terest Nostram was real. The first paladin king of Merakor, many considered him the exemplar against which all subsequent paladin kings should be judged. However, Terest lost his paladin blessings within two years of ascending the throne.

I know you now, Bomoki. For what, would you know?

Bomoki's hands shook with fatigue. Pale and sweating, he sat back as Dar tended to his left forearm. Where Van had been drained, Bomoki's experience showed the Darkhold stopped when the question was answered. When Van was tended to, Dar looked around to find them all shocked.

Dar, who only knew about Merakor incidentally, looked at their reactions and said, "I take it that this is a surprise?"

Bomoki began to laugh but his laughter sounded cruel and mocking. "Oh, yes indeed! Terest is revered amongst the paladins of Taysor. Your dear Captain Sean could wax poetic about his many good deeds. Makes you wonder how he fell, and why he failed atonement."

Van said, "It has to be a lie. Terest... there's no record of him ever losing his paladin powers."

Alaura, who looked lost in thought now, observed, "However, at some point in his story, the Mage Court became a thing. All the histories suggest Terest despised mages. There was even a song, a nursery rhyme about the king besting the mages. It made the mages look foolish and laugh-worthy." Alaura began to hum and then tentatively sang it:

> With flighty hands and easy words,
> The mages come, the mages came,
> The magic grows, the magic goes,
> But not so, the old king spanked their nose.
>
> With piggy snorts and piggy tails,

The mages come, the mages came,
The magic rose, the magic rises,
But not so, the old king poked their eyes.

"I don't remember the rest of it," Alaura said blushing.

Van interjected, "But, the Mage Court was to govern disputes amongst mages. A paladin could not-"

Bomoki had already leaned forward and wrote:

For more of my blood, for what did Terest fall?

After the blood and runes swirled, the answer appeared as a single glyph and then resolved:

Rape. For what, would you know?

Bomoki began laughing again. "The greatest paladin king of all time – rape!"

Alaura and Van looked at Bomoki darkly. Alaura said, "We are talking about a hero, one of the greatest heroes. Mind your tone, Bomoki."

Dar pulled Bomoki back and took the quill from his hand. "I think you've had enough of this. I can feel your life ebbing. It is time to stop." Bomoki nodded, too weak to resist and barely able to laugh though his body shook with his silent chuckling sneer.

But, Van pushed forward. "No, we must know for sure. This claim is an outrageous blasphemy. We need to know more so that the dragons can confirm the truth of it." He grabbed the quill.

Dar looked askance at Alaura but she seemed conflicted. "Just another question," the sage replied.

Van stabbed the quill into his wrist and wrote:

For more of my blood, prove that Terest Nostram committed rape.

The rune took a longer time than normal to swirl and resolve as it took more and more of the already-weak Van's blood. The room became light and airy as if a grand joke had been shared. The rune, looking at it, it made them feel happy.

In the Merakoran calendar, year 11 of the 3rd

full moon, Terest met an ambassador of
the elves named Sheress Un'kameh. He fell
in love with her and they consummated that
love in Year 12 of the 3rd half moon waning.
Sheress conceived Terest's child. Though
Terest sought atonement for breaking his
vow of chastity, the revelation of a half-elven
child in a time of new and fragile alliances,
was seen as a threat. Though Terest did not
order it, the mother and unborn child were
assassinated. Sheress, before she died, cursed
Terest with insatiable lust thinking he had ordered
her death. Subsequent children were killed.

You have visited me before, Warner van Struzer.
I sense your ill comfort with this tale of
Terest Nostram. Behold, the rest of his woe!

Cruel and mocking laughter erupted from Bomoki again. "Unbelievable! Dar, can the god emperor confirm the truth of any of this?"

On the page in the center of their group, new runes appeared transforming into both words and images. Before their eyes, and as if watching a moving illusion, the blood vanished and then reappeared to form a perfect likeness of Terest Nostram. The figure thrashed about, in spiked chains set into his bleeding skin. Banshees wailed and assaulted him from all directions. As if seeing beyond them, Terest's eyes met Alaura's and she knew. Terest's face grew in the page until they saw fine golden chains, barbed and hooked holding his eyes and mouth open. "He can see us!" Alaura whispered in disbelief. "He is alive!"

A banshee kissed Terest and he fell back against the chains in the banshee's embrace. Around the moving illusion, the names and ages of mostly elven women began to appear along with dates. For some, a child conception was noted. Such notations became crossed out and with a new date; *Assassinated by Terest Nostram.* Hundreds of names filled the page while Terest writhed in pain and pleasure under the banshee's attack. At last, one last name appeared.

Year 22, 4th quarter moon. Lolth visited
Terest and conceived a child named
Graz'zt. Graz'zt orchestrated the destruction
of Merakor after ascending to Lolth's
paradise. Merakor fell in Year 4,444 because
of Terest. He was consumed by
Mali Lynthraceae Vede Mecum.

From the portrait of Terest, a bloodied hand reached out to Alaura and then vanished in a swirl of blood. The room, except for the popping of steam from burning firewood, sat heavy and quiet in contrast to the amused sensation filling it earlier. Eventually, the original question appeared addressed to Alaura.

For what, would you know?
A universe of knowledge awaits, Sage.

Bomoki snorted. "I remember being taught about Terest. He was an exemplar of righteousness. So much evil. If true, this will turn history on its head!" On a whim, Bomoki wrote:

Is Mali Lyntraceae Vede Mecum your name?

Yes. In the languages I sense, my
name is Manual of Evil Fruit in
Taysoran, or Darkhold in Draconian.

Bomoki fainted. While Alaura checked on him, Van rubbed his head and noted, "Terest did die of unknown causes in Year 22 of the 4th Quarter Moon. If this Darkhold is lying, it's a very detailed and convincing one."

Alaura rifled through her bookshelves and pulled a scroll. Rolling it open, she scanned it and said, "There was also a lady elven ambassador sent in that year to the Mage Court. Sheress Unkameh, a princess of the Sylvan Nation."

* * *

All the goblins lay dead in pools of blood, soul-sucked when Hrax had inhaled their lifeforce. Not knowing what else might be lurking, Syliri and Bruce ran out of the mines. Hrax, magically shrunken and placed in Syliri's backpack, bounced easily. They encountered no resistance. When they reached the mine entrance, Bruce paused and asked, "I feel like we should search out Hrax's actual lair. Something like that might have powerful magic and other things we wouldn't want lying around."

Syliri shook her head, no. "A blue slaad could have a red or grey master. We might be able to face a red. A grey though? Alerius once told me that he did not know if he could defeat a grey. The Slaadi serve Set directly. The same way we use the River, the Slaadi live within Set's Dream. They channel it as their form of magic. The greys would be like how Alerius is to Tiamat. Alerius said that the greys seek a higher order Slaadi, one they call the Dark Slaad, powerful enough to awaken Set. I do not want to face a grey, not with you, Bruce. Not by myself. Not ever. Alerius was very clear to me on this. Alerius said that, should I ever find one, to not engage without him *and* his brothers."

Bruce almost argued with her but she took his hand and began running north. "I see, you want to cut straight to Morbatten? Okay, let's go." Bruce focused his will and suddenly, the steep and crumbly mountainside became firm under their feet. They ran at full sprint and left no tracks. Hill giants patrolling the mountain slopes did not see them. They ran all day and night, never stopping. If Bruce felt the strain, he did not show it. By comparison, Syliri's snakes fell limp and unresponsive as the night wore on, and still they ran.

* * *

Ylgolth relaxed in the acid pool. Since Hrax had opened the gate, he enjoyed the taste and scent of this world. The gate sat open in the center of the pool, masked by the vapors and a gentle caress from Set's Dream. In this world, everything seemed to be dying, in each and every moment. He relished in the quickly browning colors of the bright red and orange leaves. Hrax had called this slow moment-by-moment decay, 'time'. The hill giants, of course, wanted to worship Ylgolth, as they should, but after Ylgolth ate them, the survivors ran away. He did not care. The energies in this world bent and twisted around him in strange ways. Even here, in this toxic acid, small lifeforms held to the edges of the pools. "They try to live," Ylgolth observed.

Reaching out a finger, he scraped the strange orange slime off a rock. To his view, it writhed and twisted, too stupid to know Set's glory. "But, they hunger. It's enough."

Ylgolth spread wide his arms and screeched. All around, the orange slime mold began pulling together. When clumps the size of a goblin's head had formed, Ylgolth screeched and pulled them together and again until a small hill of orange-brown slime pulsated before him. "Child of Set, Ylgolth commands you. Find the hill giants and eat them. As you eat, you will grow stronger. That which you consume but cannot eat, bring back to me. When you are bigger than this, you shall divide as my children." Ylgolth's spread arms indicated a size about three times larger than its current size.

Psuedopods stretched out and the mold oozed away from the pool, towards the hill giant enclave. Pleased with the results of his magic, Ylgolth laid back into the acid and floated to watch the moons rise. It had taken hours to infuse Set's Dream into the mold, to shape it into a monstrous form capable of consuming all manner of life. Moonlight edged the clouds and Ylgolth marveled at the chaotic variation of this world. Under his gaze, one of the clouds began to change from harmless water vapor into a poison gas. He chuckled and whispered, "Let death fall where it falls. Set comes for you all."

* * *

The hill giants lounged around their bonfire. The cold night of clear stars and drifting clouds overhead barely caught their attention. The chieftain lay surrounded by his concubines. The witch across the way stank and he threw a glob of mud at her. She did not notice. All around, the other giants twitched and moved restlessly. Though asleep, the perpetual threat of attack and molestation made it hard to sleep except when they fell unconscious by exhaustion. The chief noted the sentinels around the camp and smirked. One leaned against a tree, probably asleep. "We'll eat you next..." the chief growled as he shoved the women off him and stood. Seeing his carved club buried beneath the witch, he stomped over and kicked her off.

The kick rolled her off the club. Awake at last, the witch cursed him. "Let it be. Let it be. The omens of ill-fortune are strong tonight but we are safe. The tribe must rest. Please, Oahg. Let it be."

"You call me Chief. Big boss. Call me Oagh again and I eat you next." He smacked her with the club. It felt good, so he hit the witch again. "Your bones break one day. You'll see." A final hit and he tromped off to the sentinel.

Disappointed to find the guard awake, Oagh said, "You lucky, Fist of Graves. If you sleeping be, we eat you next."

"I, Power of Bone! No sleep. Watching. Something wrong tonight." The sentinel pointed to the south, towards the goblin mines.

"Power of Bone? You keep renaming yourself. I like first name. You keep that one. Fist of Graves." Oahg squeezed his fist and hit the tree, shaking it. "Strong name. Bone not strong. Witchwoman bone's break soon."

"Chief, you not feel it?"

Oahg stilled his mind. Stomper had taught him that not everything seen could actually hurt him, like this tree. He patted the tree pleased that its bark felt like bark. He could see the tiny mouths in the tree trying to eat him. He did not feel what Fist of Graves felt.

"Bull Stomper once told me: You see the dream, pretty dreams of blood. Trick is to let dream stay in sleepy time. Be smarter than the dream. You smart Fist of Graves?"

The young giant shrugged. "Not smart like you, Chief. Smart like wolf, yes. I feel it, smell it too. Not a dream. I want fire. You okay with me getting fire?"

Oahg nodded. A fire seemed like a good idea. While Fist of Graves walked back to grab some of the large smoldering logs, Oahg called to him loudly. "Stomper says great god Set dreams terrible dream and we see it, but not real."

Fist of Graves replied, "Real sometime, like witch. Sometimes she make dream real and strange fire burns us, or enemies. Remember goblin feast?"

Oagh began laughing. The tribe still talked about it. The witch had promised a feast. The goblins had not wanted to jump in the pot of boiling stew. The witch called to her magic. It lit the goblins in purple fire and one by one, they self-butchered and fell backwards, dead, into the stew. They all saw the dream, and did not believe it until they began to eat. "Sometimes, real," Oahg called back.

Fist of Graves dragged three smoldering logs back and began smashing them to build a fire in front of his position. Feeling unusually chatty, Oahg said. "Stomper say that dreaming god shows us lies to make us fight. But we learned right? Now, no fight. We strong. Stronger than all clans. Someday, we eat them all."

Fist of Graves laughed and smacked his lips. "I taste their fat blood, Chief." With the fire burning, Fist sniffed the air. "I see flashing light. Look!"

In the crackling firelight, Oahg looked. He saw lights moving too. They looked different from the burning pain and fire of Set's Dream. He scooped up a small rock and threw it into the darkness. He expected to hear it smash a tree or another rock and then bounce, maybe roll. Instead, he heard a wet squishy sound. It surprised both of them. They each grabbed a nearby rock, placed by the guards for throwing. They threw the rocks as hard as they could. Again, a wet squelching noise. To the side of where they aimed their throws, a tree shuddered and then began to lean. Watching it in the firelight, the tree should have fallen with increasing speed. The giants did this often: how many stones would it take to fell a tree? It was a favorite game with them. This tree though, it leaned slowly and then began to shrink.

Fist of Graves sniffed the air, "Smells like hot water area stink." Oahg agreed and together they grabbed a large flaming log. Heaving it at the wet darkness, they both recoiled when they saw a slow wave of puke orange moving towards them. The front surface seemed infused with thousands of mushrooms that exhaled clouds of vapor. The falling tree vanished into the mass and then the ooze rolled over the burning log. It paused for a moment before the fire extinguished.

"It slow," Oahg said. "Wake tribe." He grabbed his witch-blessed club and walked up to the wave. Fist of Graves cried out for the tribe to awaken.

Oahg smashed the wall with his club. The ooze parted as easily as if he had smashed a mushroom. Small mushrooms immediately began to sprout all along his club. Disgusted, he threw it at the ooze and backed away to grab another log. On a whim, he ripped several trees into the fire. The wind was right, blowing towards the orange mushroom wall. He called out, "Make trees burn! Burn all!"

Behind him, the tribe began ripping trees down and passing them to Oahg's fire. Though the wall did not move fast, it moved forward inch by inch. While the fire grew, it seemed to back away and began flowing around the hot fire. "More fire there! And over there!" Oahg ordered.

With growing bonfires ringing them, the orange muck seemed to stop moving towards them. Instead, it slid sideways seeking the edge of the fire. The witch's voice grated, "Full of evil power, Chief."

Oahg looked at her and knew, in that instant, that she had to die and he would not eat her flesh. Smiling evilly so she could not see, he nodded and agreed with her. When his huge hands grabbed and threw the old giant into the wall, she shrieked but did not seem upset. The wet sound of her muffled cries made him laugh. The rest of the tribe joined in. Fist of Graves offered a bet on how long she might last, or even escape. The area consuming the witch thrashed about for a bit, becoming quite intense before going still.

No one took Fist's bet but all came to watch while younger giants absentmindedly tended the bonfires. Long past when the witch might have fought her way out, Oahg laughed and threw a flaming log at it. "Stupid witch, stupid mushrooms."

Fist and the others chuckled. They all felt disappointed that something had not happened. With the orange wall seeming to slide east, and the immediate threat of danger gone, Oahg began yelling orders to break camp. "We can't stay here anymore. We will move past this, whatever thing, and set up by the river!"

Oahg had made it halfway back to the camp when Fist called out, "Look! The hag lives!"

"No," the chief spun about to see.

From the orange wall, the witch's hand clawed its way out. Her veins, normally purple like a streaking bruises, bled orange-red along their course. When her face pulled out, her eyes met Oagh's with an evil and dim glare. "Kill it!" Oahg ordered. "It's not her."

He threw a boulder at her. It smashed into her arm and drove her back into the orange muck. The witch began to pull out of a different spot, her deformed and broken arm recognizable but functioning as if unhurt. The other giants now threw boulders in hopes of smashing her head. Fist hefted a rock and aimed, but at the last moment, he stopped. He had liked the witch lady. She had given him extra food when he was young.

While Oahg goaded the tribe into attacking, Fist carefully retreated. It felt dangerous and wrong. A good chief would have taken them away from this unknown monster. Bull Stomper would have. Fist shook his head. Thinking like this, it hurt. Fist saw the strange substance open and the witch hurled two boulders back at the tribe. Both hit. One fragmented and rained stone chips down around the group attacking the witch. Fist noticed the faintly illuminated spores as they drifted down around his clan. He had seen what happened to the tree and Chief's club. "I never liked any of you," he muttered. With nowhere to really go, Fist turned north and began to run. Behind him, blood-curdling screams and wet coughing noises began.

Chapter 6 – Sean versus Bomoki

Dar Tania found Sean sitting on the Temple Mount above the amphitheater. It commanded a clear view of the valley of Morbatten without putting Sean into the consecrated superstructure of the Temple itself. He seemed lost in thought, yet he smiled when she sat down by him. His armor sat on the grass to his side. The sweat of training had dried on his blue and gold silk clothing, leaving white salt rings in patches. But still, unlike the rest of Morbatten, he had no discernible body odor.

"You fight all day, and yet you never smell. I've noticed that Shak and a few of the others in the first class are starting to become like this. Why? How?" Dar did not actually care. She just felt awkward in this moment.

"They're becoming cleansed from this world. Their holiness to Tiamat will increasingly remove them from what you call the River. With Shak, I'm surprised it has taken this long. The tribal roots, they hold you all back." He ran his hand through his hair and lifted his face into an onrush of wind. It bore a hint of snow. Looking at Dar, he added, "It holds you back too, Dar. There are clerics in Taysor who, in these five years, would be able to recover the dead with ease."

"You're wrong," Dar said, taking his hand. "If I tell you, promise me you'll keep this a secret?"

"As always, you have my word." Sean withdrew his fingers from her hand.

Pouting when she felt him pull away, Dar said, "I train with the dragons out of the River's flow. Alerius tells me I have far surpassed the Taysoran clerics you mention. He has commanded me to not show my full strength amongst the tribes for fear that they would worship me."

Sean began to chuckle. "It seems the dragons have finally learned then. This totem worship of the dragons weakens faith for Tiamat. I'm glad you see this, that they see this. It has really hurt Shak and the other paladin classes. I predict it will be at least two generations before this cultural worship fades enough to be replaced by correct faith. You can accelerate it, but it comes at a cost. Speaking of which," he paused, seeing that Dar had been about to say something.

She smiled and took his hand again. "I like these talks, Sean. I miss having you around as often as you were in that first year. I, well, never mind. What were you about to say?"

He shrugged. "It's about Shak and the paladins. It can wait. All our talk these days is about them." Dar saw him look at her hand. Fire played along her fingertips.

Struggling to respect Sean's paladin boundaries, Dar lifted their hands and spread his fingers so they lay flat against her own. Her small hand barely reached past his knuckles. "You're like a giant compared to me." She let the fire entwine their hands and arms. Taking a deep breath, she rushed out her words. "The god emperor, he had commanded me to bear children with Shak D'Rath. He wants to mingle the first priestess with the first paladin of Tiamat. I can feel that the Queen wants this too. But…"

Sean interrupted her, "I don't know why you're telling me this. Your Goddess wants-"

"I want you," Dar said and leaned forward to kiss him. "I love you," she said through her kissing his lips.

She felt Sean freeze and a moment later, try to regain his composure. He did not kiss her back. The divine resistance to magic all paladins carry extinguished Dar's flames and heralded that she had become an enemy. He pulled his head back and cautioned her, "I've already explained this to everyone here: unless I relinquish my vows, I cannot do this. Please, Dar. You know how I feel about you."

"Then say it. Let me hear you say it, Sean. Tell me to not have a child with Shak."

"Dar, I… Tiamat is your goddess. I cannot be true to my divine nature and encourage you to abandon your own. Paladins, clerics – we make sacrifices. Sometimes, they seem more than we can endure, but at least this thing you're being asked to do has a clear purpose. Pha Rann rarely gives us such clarity." Sean gently caught Dar's shoulders and pushed her back to arms' length. "Until I can be truly with you, I cannot be with you."

Dar's eyes flashed an angry red. The whites of her eyes vanished and filled with a glossy crimson and then her own inner fire raged over Sean's paladin suppression of magic. "Even the messenger told you that you could!" Dar leapt on top of Sean and pinned him to the ground. "Your god said so! Be with me! Shak, the others, they would not dare! I am commanded to do this and must obey, but all I want is you. I am the high priestess of Tiamat; I get what I want!"

Careful to let his hands remain above his head in the grass, Sean mused on how much Dar had changed in the years since he met her. She radiated a divine power that far surpassed the most powerful clerics he knew in

Taysor. In his interactions with Dar, occasionally, the red dragon in her heart would raise its head, like now. He did not feel dragonterror, but he saw her frustration. "You're frustrated. I know that. I understand. It's going to be all right, Dar."

She poked him in the chest as her body ignited in flames, "Your god himself said you could!"

"I don't want to argue this. You know my position. Even loving you this much, I cannot." When she became this fiery, it filled him with a passionate racing thrill of excitement. He almost said, *I've never wanted anyone more than you. I love you.* But, he knew it would be a mistake. He had vowed, after the angel's visit, that he would stay and serve as a paladin of Pha Rann; he would keep all of his vows even if he served an unorthodox purpose in building Tiamat's own knighthood.

Unbidden, a female voice spoke to him. It said, "Sean, even your own god sent an angel to tell you this was okay. My dearest Dar Tania, she is fragile in this moment. She will obey but worries about you, a paladin of a foreign god. You might find that for which you have sought your entire life in her ember flames."

Dar remained crouched above, glaring at him. Her eyes off to the side as her fist slowly descended towards his breastplate. When it landed, it would dent his armor. Like a red dragon, her power increased with strong emotions. "Who is speaking to me?" Sean asked softly.

"Takhissis. Dar has given me her life, but she has given you her heart. You struggle with why my soldiers falter in their progress but Dar too falters, torn between her faith and her love. You love her. Love between Pha Rann's servants and others is not unprecedented." Sean looked around but could not **see** the Dragon Queen. "I mask myself from Dar so you too will not see me, Sean. Your heart wishes for this too. I intervene for Dar, for your love of Dar, and so that Dar might have this one wish fulfilled. Let her believe you do this because of you, not because of my speaking to you."

Sean noticed motes of dust slowly drifting in the air. *Takhissis must actually be here*, he realized. *This is not the River.* "Sacrifice is power." His words that he recited as a mantra felt hollow.

Takhissis' response did not surprise him. She continued. "Sacrifice can be power, yes. But, when it is love unrequited because of prideful obedience to a vow you are free from five years from now, it is only sorrow. The River will wash that sorrow into bitterness. You know I speak only truth in this moment, for Dar's sake. Sacrifice makes you less than you could be. Soon, you and my Dar, and my other children will be tried. My spear must be sharp. The sharpening stone is not sacrifice – it is desire. Sacrifice is your god's dominion, not mine. Dar is strongest in her desire. Look at how beautiful it is that endless love and desire dance in Dar Tania's heart for you. For you!" Sean felt a hand move off to his side and suddenly, he knew. He felt and saw Dar atop him, the regret she had not come to him sooner poisoned her soul. Her thoughts, her mantra, he heard it and felt it. "If this thing with Shak happens, Sean will be lost to me forever. Why didn't I tell him, show him how I felt sooner?"

"Without charm, compulsion, or guile, I come to you Paladin of Pha Rann for her and her love. It burns like the eldar stars did at the dawn of Time. Remember what the messenger said." The golden angel and its wings appeared in his mind's eye and he heard again, the words but this time he heard them the way Dar did. Even then, she was falling in love with Sean. He felt her love the way red dragons feel not just emotion, but the strong emotions suffuse through every cell until it seems they might die. "This is the fire of the gold and red dragons."

From behind Takhissis, a separate voice, that of Pha Rann's angelic servant, spoke. "You were freed of your vows and Pha Rann honors your stalwart heart. Part of Creation's goal is that you find and be with someone like this. Though a servant of Tiamat, her heart truly loves you and there is no evil in this, paladin. Takhissis, trouble my servant no more."

Sean felt movement and then She left. Sean marveled at the intervention of both gods and then felt the angel also depart. "Your commitment to your vows, Sean, is honorable and good. But, Creation is not absolute in its requriements. All were created to create, and Pha Rann gave you the gifts of emotion and love to better serve the worlds." The angel's words faded.

Sean became aware that he remained with Dar still frozen, Sean stopped his mantra and reached up for Dar. Her fist smashed into his armor, denting and heating it at the same time. Her words quieted at his kiss, she choked and tackled him back to the ground. Dar's frustration changed to shock as she realized he returned her kiss. Through their lips' embracing, she demanded, "Why?"

Sean rolled her to the grass and looked down into her eyes. Their frustrated and burning auras smoldered now, tentatively. He pulled her out of the River's flow and whispered into her ear. "Because I have always loved you. I will never regret you."

"Bright paladin, I have regretted every day we did not have this!" Dar leaned forward and met his gaze, full of passion and promise. Flowing back and forth in Time's flow, they at last collapsed to see day had wheeled to night.

Silent and holding each other as if they might never have such a moment again, Dar noticed Sean's armor scattered around them. She pointed to it and whispered, "I don't remember throwing armor all around like this."

Sean smiled and kissed her face, just to the side of her eyes. "Being with you, I cannot imagine ever being with anyone else." The tone of his voice rose in to that of the dutiful knight.

But, Dar kissed him back and put her fingers on his lips. She murmured, "No no, let this moment not be stained by duty. All our lives are obedience and sacrifice. Let this be the moment of Dar and her Sean."

"Okay, Dar. For us. Duty compels me to not belong to a Tiamat priestess." He hugged her and began tracing circles along the small of her back. It brought out goosebumps.

"No one has touched me since my calling, not like this." Dar went limp and leaned forward, resting her arms against his chest. She said nothing for a long time. The flames haloing her form danced until at last, she jumped up to gather Sean's armor plates. Some ten steps away, she turned and whispered back to him, "One day, you'll be mine forever." Seeing that he watched her, she blushed and then said again, "Forever."

The fire dragon still raged in her soul and Sean had to dismiss the possessive connotation of her tone. "When that day comes, I'll still be at your side, great Dar."

Dar had a sudden flash of Sean; he lay dying in sunlight while fires burned all around. Like a cold spear through her heart, she choked and dropped to her knees. Not wanting to concern Sean, she tried to make it look like she merely picked up another armor piece. *Tiamat*, she prayed in her heart. *What is this vision?*

A voice, not Tiamat's, answered. The voice fell along her skin like warm rain. Ashen smoke scent filled her nose and she prayed, "Takhissis, you do me honor in Tehra. Have you come to tell me what this vision means?" Dar noticed Sean, frozen and unmoving as he leaned forward to sit up. The tattoo of a golden sun in the center of spinning planets covered his back and Dar marveled she never before had seen it.

The Goddess replied, "You are gifted with the love of a paladin from a foreign god. Perhaps, this beginning becomes as you see, dearest one. I am come to caution you though. My path is one of fire and war. Though not certain, and I cannot know in this world for sure, you will be tested by our enemies in ways I cannot know. For behold, though I once had a Temple of Glass, it was broken and no priestess ever graced it chambers. You are my first priestess, treasured Dar Tania. Our enemies will seek to bend and break you in ways even I cannot foresee. Sean's death is not certain." The surreal woman of olive-hued skin and red flowing hair pointed to Dar's stomach. "What is certain is that you shall now conceive a daughter. You are to guard and train her as a high priestess. You are to continue guiding Morbatten in building my Temple, but, your daughter shall be your life's temple. While you may only ever truly love this foreigner, you are commanded to bear children with the heroes of Morbatten. You must accept this." Takhissis pressed her hand to Dar's heart. "And, you will be blessed with the powers of the dragons themselves."

Dar, her eyes switching between Takhissis and Sean, bowed her head and reverently whispered, "As you command, Goddess."

Takhissis kissed her lips and pressed her forehead to Dar's. The goddess said, "Dark moments gather in your future. You must steel yourself for the threats that may come from both enemy and the loss of love. Tiamat had hoped to protect you from this, but I see it must be. The red dragon is strong in you. See that you do not spend all of your love on this one knight." Takhissis blessed her and vanished.

Sean began moving again and looked quizzically at Dar. Feeling concerned, though he could not say why, he stood self-consciously and reached out for his breeches in Dar's hands. "Did I miss something, Dar?"

Dar almost shook her head and then passion overcame her for Sean. She dropped it all and ran to him. He caught her and they kissed again as Dar's fire rose up and over them both. So dark at night, with her fire reaching into the sky, Dar knew the others would see. The dragons of course already knew. "Sean, my love. Takhissis whispers to me that we shall have a daughter! You ask about duty; it is delayed. We can be together!" She pulled back as Sean went still. "I hope this makes you as happy as I am?"

Sean squeezed her and said, "I joined the Order so young. I had rather put the thought of children out of my head. You know this so soon? Already? I'm not doubting you, it's just so sudden. In Taysor, it takes weeks to really know for sure."

Dar began to laugh. Her bright and joyous laughter caught Sean up from the initial shock. "You're going to be a father, Sean! What will you name your daughter, something boring like a Taysoran name? What stories will you tell – hero stories of good gods or dragon stories of Morbatten?" She bit into his neck and then burst into laughter again. "Oh, she will be so conflicted!"

Sean began to laugh with her. "Give me some time to think on it. What name could be more lovely than yours?"

Dar raced back to his clothes and armor. "As long as you need, my love. As long as you need. Tell me, for being with me, must you now seek out the atonement that rightfully belonged to the brute prince Rowland?"

Sean closed his eyes and prayed. From his hands, an arc of sunlight in the shape of a sword appeared. "Apparently not, thanks be to Pha Rann." The look of contentment on his face made Dar fall in love with him all over again. Dropping the armor, they embraced again and loved until the sun rose over them.

* * *

Bomoki waited for Sean at Temple View. The only Taysoran tavern in Morbatten, it did a small but brisk business with those like Bomoki, who grew tired of the staple Morbatten diet of fire-grilled meats and sautéed vegetables. Though spices and sweet desserts were quickly catching on, actual chefs from Taysor remained rare in the valley. Bomoki pulled out a folded paper and wrote on it: *Discuss need for chefs and spices with Dar and/or Alerius.* Temple View liked Bomoki and turned a blind eye to how the mage always seemed to have a drunken best friend who paid for everything.

When the Commander entered, everyone turned and smiled, some even toasted him. Bomoki rolled his eyes. Sean, though a hero in Taysor, lacked the popularity there as one of many heroes. His Order lacked the flashiness of the Creationists and Spiritualist Sects too. In Morbatten, and largely because families saw him as the gatekeeper on their children becoming knights and priestesses, Sean had a practical popularity. Dar's obvious adoration of him bumped that popularity to unreal levels.

Sean sat down across from Bomoki. "I got your note. I'm glad you wanted to talk. I've some things too."

Bomoki waved his hands and an ale keg bearing Taysoran markings appeared, floating next to him from the shelves of the tavern. Pewter mugs bounced over next and Bomoki filled these, sending one to Sean. "I've never had any success with women. It's odd for me to watch these gorgeous women literally throw themselves at you – dour and aloof as you are – and it just makes them want you more when you do not notice them. I rather thought Dar might forcibly take you, Captain!" Bomoki raised his mug and took a drink. "I suppose there is no chance of the god emperor ordering any priestesses to be with a certain mage?"

Sean did not return the laugh or gesture but took a sip of the ale. Bomoki noted the immediate guarded demeanor. Sean said, "This is good stuff. If I knew you wanted to talk about women, I would not have come. What is on your mind?"

"The Halflings. We were there for far too long, Sean. They kept changing their minds. You're a paladin. You're supposed to be questing into hell to topple dukes and devil lords, not helping farmers decide where to best plant fruit trees. I'm a mage! I should be learning new things and strengthening the dim magical talent here. They now hate me even more and love you the same. So, you win. Not that I care but I felt it needed to be said." Bomoki took a long drink and then conjured cheese and dried meat. He sent some of these whirling over to Sean.

"Bomoki, you fail to understand. I don't track the world this way. Your actions with the Halflings, sure it frustrated them after years of preparations. But, it did not increase or even change the good or evil in the world though your attitude borders on what I might consider evil. The Cuthberics would certainly consider it so."

"And the Pragmatists?"

Sean assessed Bomoki to see if the mage just wanted to verbally spar. At last, he said, "Attitudes, in and of themselves, are not evil. You hurt the Halflings' feelings and diminished your own stature in their eyes. I see only equivalence. You finished your work early at the price of decreased respect. If there is evil there, it is not evil I need actively resist." Sean took the offered food and added, "With the dragon's punishment, I'd say Morbatten won."

Bomoki chuckled. "The dragons always win. They have the only thing that matters – power. But still, I saw the dark glance you gave me there in Home. My pride must be assuaged. I challenge you to a duel." Bomoki stood up and slapped the table with exaggerated bravado.

Sean raised an eyebrow and finished the food and ale. Rising, he said, "You want to challenge me?"

"Yes. I know I'll lose, but I'm curious to see how I fare against the legendary Sean." Bomoki stretched. "I don't suppose you'd be open to a non-fatal duel?"

Sean laughed, "If I killed you, the dragons would punish me far worse than you and the earth elementals. Terms?"

"I've thought about this all day. I get one spell, my choice. You get to be surprised by it. It affects me, makes me more warrior-like. I get one more spell, my choice. I want to see if I'm powerful enough to overcome your magic resistance. You get whatever you want except no sword. I'm not trying to kill you, though magic is flashy and it might look that way, and I'd appreciate it if you would refrain from killing me. Plus, I'm a bit dicey from the Darkhold," he said, pointing to his lacerated arm.

The lacerations there looked gruesome. "I'll explain it later," Bomoki said.

Sean nodded. "Very well, I accept your strange challenge."

Bomoki completed a spell that transformed his frail body. Before Sean's eyes, the wiry mage inflated with muscle. Not seeing anything requiring more armor, Sean stood his ground and waited, relaxed and casually ready for Bomoki to attack. Bomoki then began an incantation. It went fast, much faster than Sean had heard Bomoki spellcast before. Sean commented, "You've gotten faster. I pray to the great Pha Rann to bless me in my coming battle, to prepare my foe for Heaven, to let mercy shine upon the named challenger, Bomoki."

Bomoki finished the spell and blue ray of light shot from his finger to where it pointed at Sean's heart. The ray vanished as if it had never existed inches from Sean's chest. "May the warmth of thy light chase back the dark," Sean continued to pray as he moved forward to Bomoki, fists raised. Bomoki's morale deflated when the spell failed, but he quickly recovered to dodge a punch Sean aimed at his face. Sean began to pray. "Let light lift my heart so that I sing with battle!" Bomoki failed to dodge a kick.

Expecting the kick to hurt more than it did, Bomoki looked down and then caught Sean's leg. Twisting and throwing, Sean spun through the air but landed on his feet. Bomoki flexed his muscles and gloated, "So this is what a fighter-fight feels like!" He charged forward and tried to tackle the paladin.

Sean side-stepped and twisted Bomoki just enough that the mage landed on his back. By now, Bomoki would have normally been out of the fight. Strengthened by magic though, Bomoki rolled and recovered his footing. "You're not trying, Captain."

Sean shrugged, "Okay, but are you sure?"

Bomoki nodded and moved forward cautiously, trying to grapple but on guard against another kick or punch. "There's something I want to discuss regarding the paladins, all of them. It'll require your help," Sean said while moving forward to punch-kick Bomoki. Bomoki dodged and almost landed a counter blow.

Sean caught the counter-attack and his fist smashed squarely against Bomoki's left ear. Bomoki howled in pain and finally tackled Sean to the ground. Sean kicked the mage up and over his head, but continued to hold one of Bomoki's arms. Using Bomoki's momentum, Sean recovered his footing for just a moment before he spun around Bomoki's shoulder and locked it. "Tell me you'll help?"

Bomoki punched at Sean's leg with his other hand, but Sean tightened his knees around Bomoki's throat while hyper-extending the mage's elbow. "Ouch! Yes, yes, I'll help!" Bomoki signaled his surrender.

"You did really well. I noticed how much faster and fluidly you're casting spells. That's different. I've never seen that in Taysor before."

Bomoki returned to his normal size. The ale keg and food returned along with warm towels. "Yes, the god emperor calls it 'the difference between casting spells and being a battle mage.' He's trying to teach me something my master never did; you don't need to cast the entire spell. Alerius said to me, all the stuff you know is to help your human mind hold the magic until you're ready to release it. It's like this: you're thirsty and someone says, 'Fill the bucket with water. That way you'll have enough to drink.' But all you really need is a cup's worth of water. Spell-casting is like this. You can take the bucket approach, or the cup approach. Alerius told me I needed to start training with the paladins too. What do you need?"

Sean laughed, genuinely this time. "I need that. I need you to fight the paladins, with magic. Until they're dead, or they kill you. They won't kill you as you'll have guards. The priestesses will heal you as you fight. It's an idea I have to speed things up."

Bomoki raised an eyebrow and said, "I'll get to kill paladins and have it be okay?" He raised his mug and smashed it against Sean's. "I'm in!"

* * *

Ynt'taris landed by Alerius' mountain. "Brother, Syliri and the ranger, they run to us. Something is wrong."

From within the mountain, Alerius' voice came. "I shall see." Several moments passed and then Alerius appeared in the opening that looked out over Morbatten's valley. His human form looked south and said, "You are correct. They race and behind them, I scry only death. Since magic will not work, I ask that you watch. I will retrieve the two."

Ynt'taris bowed, "As you command."

Alerius watched the white patriarch rise up in the high clouds. For a moment, Ynt'taris noticed Sean and Bomoki locked in wrestling match. *He tests the warrior spells Alerius taught him, good.* The white patriarch noted Dar looking up at him. Her aura burned brightly with emotion as she walked up the path to the Temple.

Behind him, Alerius dragonshifted and sped to the Temple. Dar turned and waited while Alerius banked and then caught her into his claw, "Come daughter, danger threatens."

Dar nodded. In a moment, she borrowed Alerius' sight and saw. Syliri and Bruce ran as if being chased by demons. Though nothing chased them, the valley between the mountains far south, Dar guessed a four week ride by horse, longer if running, seethed with monstrous evil. *No, not evil; malice*, she realized. Syliri looked exhausted and she could tell that Bruce moved only by ranger skill and endurance.

Alerius explained, "You see Set's Dream. Something has stirred in the south. My dear Syliri will tell us what."

Morbatten blurred beneath them, and Dar exulted in the rushing of the wind. Somehow, it did not blind her. Somehow, she felt Alerius' movements as if her own. She saw the shocked faces of the people as they looked up, only too slowly to see anything other than their passing. Dar remembered and said, "They were to explore the southwards area, where you had noted gold and goblins. Your map named it Quattrain."

Alerius nodded. "Never before have we seen any sign of Set here. In Merakor, yes, but not here. A simple scouting mission, what the ranger told Syliri would be a 'hot date,' has become something deadly. Note, my priestess, how the land ripples in waves. If this continues, the mountains, the trees, the animals – they will begin to change. For thinking creatures like you, you will feel it as growing paranoia. But, it will grow until you cannot resist it. Your pregnancy will help though we have never seen how Set's Dream affects the unborn. You must use caution and stay back from it. Also, dearest rider, I am glad for you, to have this with the Commander. I had a dream that it pleased Takhissis and Pha Rann too. Perhaps, heaven is not so far away as the Dragon Wars suggested for our kind."

Dar remembered the glimpse Syliri had given her and Alaura of Set's Dream. That had been confined within Alerius' mountain, where it was always safe. To see it radiating this way, she could not understand it. Looking for a focus point, she saw that the center shifted randomly to eventually dance away from whatever she looked at. Alerius explained, "You won't find a center. Set is a primordial eldar of malign chaos. His dream shifts, desiring to stay in the center of your mind. This is how it begins, like a gnat stuck in the sweat of your eye lid."

As they got closer to Syliri and Bruce, animals and other creatures fled north and west. "It's like a forest fire," Dar said pointing to the mass exodus. A hill giant far to Syliri's south ran northwards. Dar felt a glimmer of curiosity in the dragon and then Alerius dived. In a heartbeat, he scooped up Syliri and her companion. The weightiness of their ascent from under the trees to the skies always made her stomach turn a bit.

Used to it, Syliri watched the forest recede and held tight to Bruce. It took him a moment to realize Alerius had picked them up and they were safe. Sweat drenched his clothing and his hair dangled as if drenched. When he finally realized he was safe, he took a deep breath and said, "Thank the gods." He immediately collapsed.

With a question in her eyes, Dar pointed him to Syliri. "We've been running for eight days," Syl explained. Referring to how exhausted he looked, she added, "I don't know how he does it. The mortal world has changed a bit since I last saw it this close." Her eyes crossed and she swooned. "Apparently, Bruce supported me more than I thought. I'm going to sit down."

Dar moved to the other hand which held Bruce. There, she pulled him into a divine sanctuary, a spell-like effect that allowed for peaceful rest and recovery. Two hours later, when they landed at the Temple, night had fallen. In spite of the darkness, Bruce woke feeling better than he had since the encounter with Hrax.

Alerius sat, humanshifted and waiting impatiently for their report. Syliri began, "Bruce, the god emperor picked us up. You've been asleep for two hours. I resisted his encouragement to tell him everything on the way here."

Bruce rubbed his eyes and stood on wobbly legs. "Woah, running for that long that fast. Okay, Lord Alerius, we found a group of hill giants and goblins in the valley you named Quattrain. As you guessed, there is gold there. The goblins were mining it. However," he said pulling the shrunken statue of Hrax Terrej out of Syliri's backpack. "This was leading them."

He put it on the ground and Syliri shaped the stone back to full size. Alerius circled it and they waited in silence. After a moment, he said, "I would name this is a devil except for Set's Dream chasing you from the south. This must be an avatar." His fingers tapped on the circular markings just visible on the stone. "These look like a Slaadi markings."

Bruce looked at Syl and then blurted out, "Syliri said you have a slaad in your collection. Is it the same?"

At the word 'slaad,' Alerius stepped back and blinked looking at it again. After a moment, he shrugged. "They all look so different. They don't really have a set form, ranger. As their power increases, they feed off intimidation and fear. Their form morphs to better suit their feeding." Alerius pointed to the statue, "Behold, what would most physically terrify goblins." He laughed. "In Merakor, they took the form of elderly humans until after they murdered their actual target. They then took that form. Insidious creatures, they are much worse than dopplegangers."

Continuing to circle it, Syliri almost said it was an Azuros, but Alerius waved her to be quiet. "The other one in the zoo looks like a muscular troll. This one, more elegant and devilish. Is this a red? No."

Dar asked, "Do red slaads breathe fire?"

Chuckling, Alerius shook his head. "No, they are colored as a sign of their control over Set's Dream. A red slaad can shape it like clay. Syliri," he said turning to her. "You and Bruce captured this mostly unharmed. This must be a green or blue."

"Blue, my lord," she replied. "We," she elbowed Bruce, "figured it must be recently transformed from green as well."

"Well done. I can see you shredded its wings nicely. Some torso wounds. You've gotten better at capturing them undamaged, Syliri." The one in the zoo, if they ever restored it, would immediately die from its wounds.

She blushed at the god emperor's praise. "Thank you, Alerius. Bruce did most of the work. His distractions allowed me to not damage this one as much as the other. Plus, it seemed to fascinate him – he named himself Hrax Terrej – that I knew about the Slaadi. Your teachings, my lord."

"Unpetrify him." Alerius' command did not surprise Syliri. She had been waiting for it. In an instant, she stepped into Hrax's face and touched his forehead. Undoing petrification went much more slowly. Having Alerius with them made it seem safe, even normal to revive a blue slaad. Alerius explained to Dar, "Fecundus, or green, is the newborn state of a slaad.

They progress in power, transforming as they do so, to Azuros and then to Embros/red. As an Embros, if they feed enough and acquire enough magical wealth to bribe their Anthracos master, they can be promoted to Anthracos. No one know how many Anthracos there are but I'd guess no more than ten if that. They don't really work together or trust each other."

The change back to flesh, once it started, went faster and faster. Syliri stepped back. "My lord Alerius, I told Hrax that a human mage had created me."

"This will be fun," Alerius noted while moving to stand before Hrax. The group felt a tremor of dragonterror leak through Alerius' calm disposition.

When the stony façade encasing Hrax crumbled away, a moment passed before he breathed. "Gorgona!" Hrax growled. "I'm going to rip out your spine." Twin fireballs formed beneath Hrax's hands. Maybe Hrax felt the wind, or sensed the dragonterror. He blinked to clear his eyes and looked around with increasing confusion. They focused on Alerius and then Syliri. "You said the mage was petrified!"

"Hello, Hrax Terrej," Alerius said.

The slaad sent both fireballs spinning to Alerius. They faded from existence almost the instant they left Hrax's hands. The slaad spun around and sent another fireball at Alerius. When it 'poof'ed out, Hrax whirled on Alerius with webbed fingers open, ready to fight.

"You will know your place or be forced to submit," Alerius stated.

Hrax sent another spell, this one manifesting as lightning, towards Alerius. Like the fireballs, it sputtered and vanished almost the instant it left Hrax's hand. "What sorcery is this?" Hrax growled. His eyes finally adjusted from being petrified. Before Hrax, a very tall human in full plate armor stood. A cloak of blood red cast with golden symbols billowed in the wind behind him. Syliri stood just behind his left shoulder. The armored mage had dark olive skin set against black hair framed the mage's brilliant red eyes, which glittered like rubies. The feeling of might and confidence exuded by this human made no sense. It carried an undercurrent of terror that should be delicious to him. From this intimidating human though, Hrax felt fear knot his stomach. A priestess whose hair and eyes burned with flames similar to the red eyes of the armored mage stood near Syliri. A human man, stinking of sweat, with a familiar scent stood nearby with a bow, arrow nocked and casually at the ready. As Hrax took it all in, the three obelisk stones on the hill behind became apparent.

"I've heard of this place. The goblins call it 'three spikes.' Why have you brought me here?" Hrax sniffed and confirmed what he heard. A group of humans ran up the hill. They carried all manner of weapons. Something about the armored mage bothered him though. He held up his hand in a placating gesture. "Tell me. I have done nothing to you." He glared at Syliri. "To any of you. Though, I thought you long turned into a statue with birds nesting on your head."

Alerius said, "I am the lord of these lands. You have attacked me twice now when all I did was have the gorgona restore you to life. Now you demand answers? Let's try this. What is the name of the *Anthracos* you serve? Polqeryx is known to me. Do you serve Polqeryx?"

Hrax listened and countered, "Polqeryx is dead. I did not know Polqeryx. I serve Ylgolth. Maybe you know that name?"

"I know Ylgolth as an *embros*," Alerius offered. "How did Polqeryx fall?"

Hrax chuckled, "You know almost too much of the Slaadi for my liking. Polqeryx was killed by Ylgolth, eaten to the bone. Ylgolth rules now."

Alerius pointed to the south, "Is that Ylgolth?" The southern sky came alive with Set's Dream as Alerius saw it.

"That is my beautiful master Ylgolth," Hrax said. Looking around, and then back to Syliri, Hrax continued, "If you would like, I could easily arrange a meeting with Ylgolth. You seem to know so much about us. Perhaps Ylgolth knows you, Master?" Hrax's eyes went wide and he dropped to the ground before Alerius, groveling. "You must be an *Anthracos* unknown to me. I am young in my learning." He looked up, waiting for a confirmation.

"I am Alerius. I do not expect the Slaadi to know my name. I am not of the Slaadi."

As Hrax came free of the stone, Dar stepped out from the River to see the exchange. A small glimmer of aura light spun in her womb. She patted it and turned her attention to the god emperor. Unlike the seemingly harmless conversation in the real world, the ethereal showed a different meeting. Though Alerius veiled his power and true nature, Hrax attempted to intimidate and probe for weaknesses at every chance. Letting Hrax think that he could not sense the ethereal realm, Alerius masterfully blocked such probes making them seem to accidentally fail. Dar saw Hrax's frustration mounting. Dar also noted how Hrax let his power slowly build as he interjected a spell's casting into the answers provided.

Just before Hrax could cast his spell, Alerius held up a hand and said, "You will fail."

Hrax blasted Alerius with a spell calling for him, for them all, to transform into rabbits. Alerius' slight grin preceded a giant fist that smashed into Hrax's face. Hrax felt the inhuman strength break his jaw, nose, and nearly kill him. Even as regenerative healing triggered, he felt that same fist close around his throat and lift him from the ground. "No one will remember Hrax Terrej. You're still a worm who accidentally dreamed of being an Azuros."

Hrax held himself against Alerius' fist, struggling to breathe. He tried to talk, but only gagging sounds came out. Alerius touched Hrax's forehead and suddenly, Alerius stood in Hrax's mind. Hrax tried to block him, but relegated to the side, he raged as Alerius sorted and filtered through the encounters Hrax had with Ylgolth. Then, same as the entry, Alerius withdrew from Hrax's mind.

He dropped Hrax to the ground and turned his back to address the others. "Ylgolth is real, and an Anthracos Slaadi. Hopefully, when this one is dead, Ylgolth will leave. It is unlikely, we must prepare to face this Ylgolth, and kill it."

Syliri's eyes opened wide and she leaned forward. "You have suggested but I never imagined."

Behind Alerius, Hrax jumped and attacked, trying to bite his neck. Fanged teeth shattered against Alerius' armor. "Syliri, please add this one to our zoo."

* * *

Ynt'taris landed outside Alaura's cottage. It had become so easy to land, humanshift, and pick up life in the small girl's form that Ynt'taris did not even register the time or energy spent polymorphing. The cottage inside was as always but the smell of blood alarmed the white patriarch. Inside, a crackling fire roared. Alaura sat across from the rude Taysoran who hated children. Ynt'taris corrected himself, *Seems to not like children. I will give you this benefit of doubt because my rider lets you stay where she cast the others out long before now.*

Both slept. The desks and tables littered with books and parchment remained as always. Ynt'taris' eyes immediately noted the small pot of blood and a blood-tipped quill resting to the side of a blank piece of parchment. The little girl walked over and found a pile of blood-soaked bandages on the floor. He noted Van and Bomoki's scent in the blood. *Bomoki*, Ynt'taris growled. *Leave it to that one to endanger my rider.*

Something about the mage bothered Ynt'taris and it was not the continual reports of impatient aggression and cheating.

Taking hold of Alaura's arm, Ynt'taris undid enough of the bandages to see deep lacerations along her left arm. The right arm was fine. "You must be Warner van Struzer?" Ynt'taris said to the sleeping man. He had many deep lacerations all over his arm. Because of the man's general health, the patriarch could tell Dar had healed him, but strangely, the arm lacerations had not healed. Dreamily, Van muttered something about Terest Nostram and then twisted his head to the other side.

Ynt'taris sat back and tapped Alaura. She mumbled sleepily and blinked her eyes. "Master Ynt'taris. I was hoping you'd come back days ago. We found something. I think the Court of Dragons will like it."

"Alerius often expresses concern with all the many ways humans kill themselves. Did you find a new way to die, by cutting your arm until you are dead?" Ynt'taris had never mastered human sarcasm or humor. But, Alaura understood.

She smiled faintly. "Always. So many ways to die. But no, look on the desk at the blank parchment."

Ynt'taris went back to the desk. Copies of Darkhold pages and runes, made in Alaura's own hand, littered the desk around a blank piece of old and weathered parchment. Ynt'taris scanned Alaura's copies and was alarmed to see the questions and answers about Terest Nostram. "Interesting," Ynt'taris said as he read aloud the names of the elven women and their children taken forcibly or otherwise by Terest. "These stories were all suppressed by Terest's successor and purged by the Mage Court."

"So, it's all true?" Alaura struggled to ask. "I didn't touch it, but tending to Van and Bomoki, it has been exhausting."

Ynt'taris picked up the parchment. It felt... alive. He sniffed it, licked it, and finally put it back down. The blood tasted like Bomoki's. "A writing material made up of eldar skin fragments, from those that died when time did not exist. I don't remember anything like this. Is it a new thing?" Asking the question, a symbol appeared in Bomoki's blood. Ynt'taris recognized it as an ancient form of cryptographic writing that became a way for the eldar to mark their creations. He read it even as the rune clarified into draconian:

For what, would you know?

Seeing the ill effects of Van's interaction with the parchment, Ynt'taris rolled and placed it into a tube. He nudged Alaura again. "I'm giving this to my brothers. Come, my sage. Alerius asks us to investigate the south." The commanding tone prompted to her to stand, barely awake. Poking Van, Ynt'taris said, "He shall stay here asleep."

Behind him, Alaura walked out, rubbing her eyes. Ynt'taris dragonshifted, picked her up, and flew south. "Alaura, you must awaken. There is something few sages have ever seen let alone studied. Though Syliri showed you a fragment of Set's Dream, our southern borders are threatened with a growing nightmare. We must investigate. Only an avatar of Set could do such a thing. There are no Merakoran books about Set's Dream, only poetry and campfire tales intended to scare children."

Ynt'taris moved up into the clouds so high in the sky they hazed the blue color. In their trail, actual clouds formed from the chill passage of the ice dragon. Soon, they crossed the Cordabad South River. A small gathering of the Fish Tribe appeared on the southern edge. They must have felt the dragon because they all looked up and waved. Masked by the clouds and borrowing Ynt'taris' eye sight, Alaura noted tribespeople but did not recognize any except for a paladin from Sean's first class. A minute later, Ynt'taris caught movement, spotting a solitary hill giant running towards the Fish Tribe's gathering.

Growling low in concern, Ynt'taris dipped down. The giant carried a large net and two clubs. One of the clubs draped over his shoulder by animal hides bounced. The other, which contained nails and spikes, showed recent action. Knowing the giant would pay no attention to a small white cloud high above, Ynt'taris looked along the giant's path and spotted a lone human male, unconscious, and entangled in a net upside down high off the ground.

"The giant is taking prisoners," Ynt'taris grumbled. "I do not know the paladins like Alerius does. The one down there, that you recognized, is he sufficient to handle a hill giant?"

Alaura thought back through the rosters and conversations with Dar and Sean about the relative strength and ranking of the paladins, and priestesses too. "Master, I remember those Sean considered strong. That one was not in the lists."

Ynt'taris dived, falling at the giant from behind. The dragon's strike eviscerated the giant along its backside. Not knowing what happened because of the numbing cold, the giant blinked and opened its eyes to see a giant claw positioned between his eyes. A human female leaned around the claw and in goblinoid asked, "Why are you hunting humans?"

Twinges of pain began to register through shock as blood began to color the ground around the beast. "Stomper, he want humans. Hungry." The giant's eyes traced the claw and saw the hand and arm fade back and away into the forest. Terror that would have curled the giant into a fetal ball knotted his body. Paralyzed by cold and already dying, the giant whimpered.

Alaura looked back at the white dragon and shrugged. "I can attempt to read his mind but I really don't want to if it's this stupid and simple."

Without another word, Ynt'taris pressed his talon through the giant's head. The effortless motion burst its skull apart. The dragon wiped his nail on earth nearby. Grabbing Alaura, and in less than a breath, they arrived at the entangled boy. Alaura had a healing potion and restored the young man to health. "We've killed the giant that attacked you, but there could be others. We cannot stay. Go tell the Fish Tribe to move farther north. This entire side of the river is dangerous." Alaura's words to the boy failed to register until the boy recognized her and then the white dragon. He dropped into a formal bow and then ran back to the river camp. He yelled a 'thank you' back over his shoulder.

Resuming their flight south, Alaura fell asleep. High above the world, the white patriarch craned his head to look down at her. She seemed so fragile. "You'd already be dead if not for my magic keeping you warm and alive," he whispered to her. "Alerius once told me about having a rider. I will never tell you, but I like this. Too long have I been away by my brothers to keep my own counsel and thoughts. You shall be a sage whose words reverberate downstream in Time's flow."

Cradling her more carefully against the wind, Ynt'taris turned his attention to Alerius and thought, "We are almost to Quattrain. Set's Dream is strongest in the mountains east, where you speculated Screem might take up residence should he wish to join us."

A second later, Alerius' voice sounded in Ynt'taris' mind. "Slaadi. Syliri captured and preserved a blue slaad. Its master goes by the name Ylgolth. May be Anthracos. Stay high and hidden. Confirm. We will attack together from a position of strength."

With Alaura safely asleep in the cradle of his hand, Ynt'taris climbed even higher, so high he could see the curvature of the world and the sky became black. From this cold height, the truth of the world became clear and Ynt'taris loved it. "So many blue waters, but so many cold places too." The white-capped mountains of the isles reached up just a fraction of their required height to try and touch him. The dragon's vision then focused down, past the drifting clouds, and along the mountain valleys to the hot springs.

"I see you," Ynt'taris whispered when he found Ylgolth at last. The hot springs and colored rocks around the grey slaad seemed to move and crawl even to this far-seeing vision.

Ylgolth looked up and said, "Yes, and I see you. Welcome to my nightmare."

Ynt'taris hit a small amulet on Alaura's necklace. The gemstone activated and she vanished. A heartbeat later, Ynt'taris, the white dragon patriarch of ice, felt the world move around him. So high above the world that nothing existed except his own body, Ynt'taris felt and sensed his legs and tail turn against him. He shunted the slaad's attack out of his mind as Ylgolth battled for control of Ynt'taris' reality. With nothing except thin air to work with that could threaten Ynt'taris, Ynt'taris laughed at Ylgolth's Dream. "Brother," he thought, noting how his own thoughts came back as roaring and charging sounds of attack. "It is an Anthracos. I am rather tempted to engage and destroy him now. He threatened Alaura."

Several moments passed into minutes, but Ynt'taris counted his heartbeats and knew the Dream's desperation to influence and control him. Alerius responded in three heartbeats. "Alaura has arrived and is safe. She sleeps and shows healing fatigue. I found the scroll tube you tucked into her robes. My brother, the only grey we have ever met was Polgeryx in the death throes of Merakor. Though we are stronger now, they are no doubt stronger too. At that time, I wondered if I could take an Anthracos. Tiamat whispered to me to learn instead. All I have learned is this: you might win. The surety of winning is by drawing them into our own battlefield, not theirs. Please, come home."

* * *

Brook stood on a tall hill and watched the white dragon rise up from the valley floor. Just a few hours before, she had seen Alerius speed south and then cross back north again. "That's a sight I'll never tire of," she said. She remembered how it terrified her after Dar Tania led them to Home. Now, knowing those titanic dragons were on their side, it comforted her and brought peace. "I never realized how peaceful it is to be strong." Looking around in all directions, she felt a change in the weather. The first snow would soon arrive. "I like snow." Most Halflings did not. In the long and desperate trip from their original home to this new Morbattanian Home, they had each experienced enough outdoor weather to last a lifetime. The snow here fell more deeply and with more chill than it had in their homeland.

Turning her gaze to the south, she saw the horizon blur against the mountains. It hurt her eyes to look at but she could not figure out what exactly about it hurt. A headache took root, but it immediately faded when she looked away. "That's weird," she muttered. Even in her peripheral vision, the headache grew again. Careful to face and only look north now, she guessed she had four more days of walking. "That's too slow. Damn you, Bomoki. I used to be okay with a four day trip. Now, all I can think about is teleporting everywhere." She shook her fist in the direction she imagined he might be. Probably that Taysoran tavern he always talked about, Temple View.

She calmed her breathing and began to cast a nature spell. It would call a familiar to her; a creature of the woods that would be her friend. She had found the spell in her notebook after the strange encounter with Kaia. It looked correct, though written in draconian, the strange language used by the dragons and now Dar Tania. The spell stretched her skills and she did not even know if it would work. "It'll work," she said cheerfully. Facing north, she began following the instructions. Casting this way, from a scroll, required a lot more concentration than the way nature magic usually flowed for her. When done, she looked around and wiped sweat from her face. Tucking her hair behind her ears, she wondered what kind of familiar would appear. "Something faster than walking, I hope. I could ride a bear. A wild horse, like those the Horse Tribe tended to wouldn't be so bad."

Several minutes passed and nothing happened though she got a bit nervous trying to imagine how Dar's people would react if she rode into the valley on a bear. Figuring must have made a mistake, she hefted her backpack and resumed her trek. Making good time, she recovered her stride only to become aware of a loud crashing sound behind her. With the forest all around bereft of leaves, she clearly saw a small tree shudder and then another away to her south. Whatever it was, it was coming straight at her on the narrow animal trail. She stepped to the side and calmed her breathing. She quickly enacted a *camouflage* spell and hid. Halflings excelled at hiding and this spell ensured success.

More crashing and tree-breaking sounds grew louder and louder until a hill giant stumbled into the general area where Brook had been when she went into hiding. The giant blinked, looking confused, and shook its head. It did not radiate any kind of evil but looked fearsome. He whirled, sniffing the air, and then shook his head again, batting at his ears with giant hands. Brook noted the spiral scars that started along a bare shoulder and rose up around his hairless scalp.

The giant did not stink as much as she thought they would. He carried a large club, a tree trunk really, onto which crude carvings had been made and then carefully healed and cured by fire. The giant snorted and shook his head again. Seeming confused and realizing it, the giant walked up to a tree, the tree Brook hid behind in the roots, and headbutted it. "Go away, voices!" the giant muttered in the goblin language.

He stumbled backwards and then smashed his head into another, larger tree. He did this several times before saying, "You say to find brook. What is brook?"

My spell summoned a hill giant? She almost laughed except fear for her life gripped her stomach. Tentatively, she called out in her best goblin. "Are you looking for me, for Brook?"

"The voices! Your voice! Where you at?" The giant whirled around, his face relaxing a bit. He almost looked friendly.

Brook stepped up from the roots of the tree. "I'm Brook. What's your name?"

"Fist of Graves. You Brook? You smash small. I hear your voice. I come. But, why? Why you call me?" He leaned back against a tree and then slumped down to the ground pounding his head.

"I'm going north," Brook explained. "Do you speak other languages?" She used Taysoran Common speech. "Do you understand this?"

Fist of Graves grunted. "Witch Lady, she teached me that talk. I go north too. Escape murder." He pointed at her and asked, "Friend?"

Brook laughed nervously, hoping her shrill laugh would not upset the giant. "I'm too small to hurt you, Fist of Graves. Yes, friends."

The giant held up his fist and squeezed it hard. "Friends call me Fist." He pointed to his fist. "Strong."

"Fist, would you like to go north with me?" Brook asked. In response, he opened his giant hand and held it out for Brook to step onto. "You're not going to hurt me, right?" she asked.

"No, not hungry." He lifted her up to his shoulder. Sniffing the air, Fist somehow determined north and began running. He went slowly at first so Brook could get a feeling for it. "This how kids ride. You small like baby." He increased his speed. When they came to a small river, Fist jumped it. Brook screamed and held onto his ear for dear life. When they landed, she slipped and bounced free.

Fist rocked back on his heels and pointed at her, laughing. "You cry like baby!" He tried to mimic her but when he saw her struggling to get up, concern crossed his face and he stepped over to her. "You hurt?"

Brook pulled some enchanted berries from a small pouch and ate them. With each berry, her wounds healed. Thankfully, no bones broke when she went flying and landed. The northern side of the river was covered in stones, which grated her skin and face badly though. Watching the wounds heal, Fist poked at the small pouch. "You stop bleeding. Magic food?"

She nodded. "There's a spell I know. It makes berries like this heal wounds. Do you need any?"

Fist shook his head, "No. No hurts. Sorry, I hurt you." He paused and then with a hopeful tone in his voice asked, "Heal sad?"

Brook looked up at him. At the word 'sad,' Fist's entire face changed. "No, these won't help sadness, Fist. But, maybe a friend to talk to will help. What are you sad about?"

Fist shook his head, a common behavior she recognized from the summoning spell for when he felt confused. "My family, witch lady, all dead. Orange wall killed them." He shook his head more violently this time and Brook noted a large tear fling sideways. He looked south and sighed. "All gone."

Brook realized she too was looking south, but with the forest blocking her view of the mountains, she felt fine. She ate all her healing berries and stood. She put her tiny hand on Fist's forearm. "I'm sorry you lost your family. Ogres killed and ate my parents just a few years ago. It still makes me sad."

Fist shuddered. "Hate ogres." The matter-of-fact tone almost made Brook smile. "They tasty." He sniffed her. "They stink worse than you, Brook."

"You're not going to eat me, are you?" Brook smiled hoping her charismatic smile and empathetic tone would help Fist decide to not eat her.

"Smell help Fist remember no eat you." He waved his hand at the height of Brook. "Bet you tasty." His stomach growled and he sniffed the air.

"We've been running for hours. Let me see." Brook looked around. The river had fish. "Do you eat fish?" Fist nodded and licked his lips. Brook walked up to the river's edge and showed Fist how to make a shallow stone circle in the water. She then cast a spell that would call fish to the circle. Immediately, a series of tiny fish leapt from the river to the water hole. Fist began to laugh, slowly at first, but it built as larger and larger fish appeared. Drook continued her spell until the hole seemed more full of fish than water.

At her gesture, Fist cupped his hands and swallowed water and fish. Scooping them in, he said things like, "So good," and "Mmmm, fishy." When done and without asking, he picked Brook up and began running again, being careful to not jump.

Looking back over her shoulder, Brook had a sudden vision of the river burning with war. Like Fist, she shook her head and blinked her eyes.

Around midnight, they blew past the Morbatten guards along the southern road. The guards gave chase but could not keep up with the giant. Brook had Fist stabilize her and she summoned birds to whom she gave a message to fly in front and behind, to let the giant pass. After that, the guards watched but did not stop them.

* * *

Alerius sat, meditating, in front of the petrified Hrax. Dar stood by his side. Dar looked content. Alerius could not recall a time when she felt this way. Her aura wavered gently between red and orange fire. *She will never know the cost paid to have Pha Rann remind the Commander personally of his vow's release.* It galled the dragon but at the same time, he drew comfort that this rock-solid paladin trained his own paladins. From beyond the River, Alerius saw time flow downstream into the future and imagined an army of Seans, serving him in Tiamat's name. That Sean knew this and proved such a stickler for his own personal vows amused the Court of Patriarchs. For years now, Alerius realized he coveted the Commander. *I'm beginning to fall like the other dragons*, Alerius thought wistfully. *When did I last covet like a fallen dragon?*

Alerius concentrated and listened until he could hear Syliri and Bruce as they lay together in a tavern at the bottom of the Temple Mount. Something had happened to her. Bad. He could sense it. Alerius felt Syliri's pain. His eyes never left the south though. The twisting haze along the horizon line of the mountains distorted the stars rising as night fell. In bits and pieces, he figured out that the slaad had touched her and pulled her into a mating dream. *I pried, but Polgeryx never described how Slaadi reproduce.* Listening to Syliri, it sounded manipulative, dominating, and would probably been lethal since there were no stories, anywhere, about Slaadi parents. Knowing that some humans struggled with mis-couplings, Alerius gained new appreciation for the ranger when all he heard was sympathy, support, and love undimmed by what happened.

He remembered saving Syliri before the Dragon Wars. He still held his theory that medusa stemmed from a dragon experimenting with a petrification breath weapon. *Syliri will recover from this*, Alerius thought. *It could have been much worse.*

The *maedar* though, the males of the medusa race, they enslaved all the females before Alerius could establish contact. *What if the maedar, as they told Syliri, really did create the medusae?* He eyed Syliri with his magic and wondered. *After all this time, she has found someone to love her.* Maedar experiments on the females created titanic beasts, terrible in their design. The Maedar pitted them against each other when not using them for harem pleasures. The most ferocious, they sent into the Abyss on quests to awaken Set. Syliri was one of those being prepared for the Abyss when Alerius met her. She had been drawn to his flame and he taught her. He conceded, *I studied her for a dragon connection. I suppose, after all this time, whether they are or are not connected to the dragons, it does not matter. Syliri will bring a new racial dominion to Tiamat.* Alerius withdrew from watching her with Bruce.

Syliri's rebellion against the maedar, when she called for it, overthrew and wiped them out to the last one. Alerius and the fire-breathers helped, but by the time the uprising's outcome solidified, Set's Dream took root in the gorgonas' hearts. The already-broken spirits of Syliri's sisters made them susceptible to falling into Set's Dream. Then, Time caught them gladly in its poisonous flow. *Not you Syliri. Not you. I pulled you from the Dream.* He could still feel the snakes biting at his fingers while he pushed her gaze away from him. Her power impressed him, even then. Hearing her, seeing her in the ranger's embrace, Alerius pushed it out of his mind. Her free will and emotions, especially loyalty and kinship with him, made her the crowning jewel of his early experiments to uplift Tiamat's dominion through worship. *The Slaadi must pose a special threat to her. Knowing this, other worshippers of Set would be equally terrible to her.*

The ranger posed no threat to her, except for emotional heartache. Alerius knew about that. For mortals, that pain lingered across generations, sometimes as many as four sets of parent-child relationships. It also could shape or break heroes. Like Syliri and Bruce, Dar now stood at his side with another Taysoran ever-present in her thoughts. Sean would never serve Tiamat, but he might serve Dar. Alerius stepped out of the River and from its side, he watched the spinning ball of lights that would become Dar and Sean's daughter. Dar's happiness and the newly-formed life in her womb washed over Alerius. He let it and felt the radiance of mortal love, hope, and longing. He savored it the way he had never savored any other birth amongst the people.

On a whim, he sent command to bring Sean and Shak to him. Shak arrived first at a brisk run, in full armor and gear. Alerius smiled to see it. "It pleases me to see that you do not rely on Tiamat to ease your daily life. That is the path of magic-users like Bomoki and the Taysoran priests. I do not wish to see my Temple become slothful. It reduces the quality of your lives and establishes a generational dependency for more of the same, but always worse."

Shak bowed his head and smiled at the god emperor's praise. He noted Dar standing to the side in a pose of reverent silence. Seeing just the two of them, Shak wondered if his summons would be to discuss the matter of bearing a child with Dar. The god emperor seemed conversational tonight. "My lord, you sent for me?"

"Yes. Weeks ago, I commanded Dar to bear a child with you, Shak D'Rath, my first paladin. You and she both spent weeks avoiding this command, and I let it be, for a time. However, I am now releasing you of this command until after Dar's daughter is born and weaned."

Shak struggled to mask the many feelings he felt at knowing Dar would have a child when he had been building himself up to it. He also felt the chastising tone of the god emperor's voice and found himself grow defensive. "I felt no imperative from the Queen." Shak said this, not meaning it to sound the way it came out. He paused. "I'm sorry, god emperor Alerius." He dropped hands and knees to the ground and bowed his head. "What I mean is that most of your commands are also co-prompted by Tiamat. In this case, I felt no such guidance. So, it has been easy to delay against other tasks you have asked me to tend. She loves Commander Sean and I, I need Sean to help progress my training." Shak's eyes darted to Dar who did nothing. Shak wondered, *Maybe she already spoke with the god emperor?*

Alerius kept his eyes on the southern horizon and nodded his head. "Ah, the good paladin and the evil priestess. At least, that is how his peers see it. For humans, the expression of love often breaks or kindles more love. It does not please me well to have my only capable paladin questioning my command because of the Mother's lack of a prompting. If I ordered you to slay the Commander, would you delay for fear of it hindering your training or Dar Tania's love? Explain yourself."

Shak wished for an easier topic. That Dar remained in reverent pose frustrated him. "I tried to talk to Sean about it. I tried to talk to her about, but she outranks me."

"Wrong. Dar outranks you in command of Temple matters. However, I commanded you both. Dar does not outrank me, and for this command, you are both equal, are you not? You are my paladin, or you are not. Which are you?"

Shak slammed his breastplate loudly and declared, "Your paladin, god emperor!" Dar opened her eyes, a look of serene peace filled them and it encouraged Shak.

Alerius stepped onto the ground. "I want our paladins resolute in their will, unbreakable in their vows, and devoted to the Queen. When I give an order," Alerius sensed Dar had joined the conversation and turned to her. He finished, "Obedience. Not questions, not delays, from either of you."

The tone of Alerius' voice almost made Dar laugh. She thought, *Very well my lord, let me take Shak right here so you can see it yourself!* Instead, she took a deep breath and prayed to Tiamat. An image came to her of walking into the Valley of Ancients and being greeted by many children, almost too many to count. In her mind's eye, she saw Sean's daughter. It made her sad that she did not see Sean. The other children were not Sean's; they lacked his blue eyes and fairer complexion. She had seen this image before. She prayed to Tiamat for strength and felt better. "Yes, my lord. It shall be as you say."

Shak also nodded in agreement. He caught Dar's eye and said, "I'm glad things worked out between you and the Commander." Dar closed her eyes and resumed her pose.

Alerius remained staring south. "The Commander will arrive soon. There are many things we must discuss."

"A different topic, my lord." Dar's rising voice tone suggested a dark topic. Alerius turned his head and looked at her. She continued, "Have you ever heard of the *Mali Lynthraceae Vede Mecum*, or Darkhold?" She struggled with the strange words.

"Yes. There are references to it scattered throughout my library. History suggests it as some kind of cursed source of knowledge."

"Alaura, she – that is, we found a parchment naming itself that. You write on it with blood and it tells you things. My lord, the Darkhold knows things that appear to be true."

Alerius stepped down from the air and walked towards her. "Alaura has this Darkhold?" he asked, his hand stretched out. When Dar said she did, Alerius' face went still as all around Dar a blaze of multi-colored lights erupted. "You remain untainted by curse magic. Good. Shall I presume the sage wrote in this?"

Dar shook her head. "The Taysoran priest Van, her new suitor, and Bomoki." Alerius nodded and indicated she should continue. "They asked about Terest Nostram, great emperor, hoping to test the truthfulness of its magic."

Alerius' eyes flashed red and then darkened. "From what you have said and your body posture, I can tell the Darkhold revealed new things?" Dar nodded. He checked on the Hrax statue again and then asked, "And what of Terest?"

"It said that Terest lost his divine blessings and compensated with magic to emulate paladin powers. He raped many elven women and had the children killed." Dar stated this but also asked it as a question. "His child, Grazz'zt, started the Kinslayer Wars, is what it said. Terest appears alive and trapped in the book." Dar shuddered as she remembered the moving image of Terest besought by banshees in hell.

Alerius nodded. "Very few knew this and fewer still know the heritage of Grazz'zt. Merakor did not occur all at once. Like most empires, it began with bloodshed and vile acts that history chose to forget. I'm glad to preserve the genesis of Morbatten free of this bloodshed. By our standards, Terest would be a monster. Let him remain trapped. Ynt'taris has already delivered the Darkhold page to me and I have it in safe-keeping. Anything else?"

Dar went back to her quiet pose. Alerius turned to Shak. "Sean is at least four hours away still. Come, join us, Shak D'Rath of the Warg Tribe. We meditate on the disturbance to the south."

* * *

Sean arrived at the Temple site just a few minutes after Bomoki arrived with Syliri and Bruce. Alerius did not wish to talk about the monster statue, so Sean asked for an audience. He began explaining his idea to accelerate training. As he spoke, the others crowded around to hear his words while Alerius remained, eyes closed, but listening. Sean said, "In my Order's early days, we practiced a form of training called 'Take It All Away.' We named it this because the premise, at least, is to fight until the only thing remaining is the fighter. Armor breaks. The weapon dulls or breaks. The clerics healing the fighter exhaust their faith. The fighter's ability to recover, even with magical aid, is spent. These happen one at a time. The assumptions of safety, that it's not real, that someone or something will intervene, these all get stripped away by the brutal and exhausting nature of the training."

Bomoki noted, "Makes sense to me. Mages train like this all the time, with the risk of backlash or mistakes ending our lives."

Alerius replied, "Commander, I have studied all sources of information throughout the world. There is nothing to suggest that this is real enough that it would even be in Pha Rann's doctrine, let alone enough to be labelled heretical."

Sean grinned, "I have sent a request to Lord Marshall Tomeist for a certain book to be sent here from the Great Library. You will see. Meanwhile, I propose we do this. You are already familiar with the problem of halted progress. The records also tell that the clerics supporting advanced faster than their peers."

Alerius opened an eye and smirked. "If this is true and it works, I will have to reassess my feelings about the Pragmatist Order, Commander. How does 'Take It All Away' work, besides the obvious? What do you need?"

Sean pointed to Shak and Dar. "I need the most powerful paladins. I need the most powerful priestesses. All of them must be present. Lastly, we need an element of surprise; we need you or one of your brothers to join. Sorcerers, like Bomoki, will help add to it as it forces the paladin to leverage more and more of his abilities to survive. To work, they must believe they are going to die. Some might. Our records show it became a blasphemous practice with the first casualty, what you call multifixion here. Because it was accidental, that's why the practice was forbidden as there is no real way to know exactly when, in this type of training, a paladin might fall. At that time, the entire Order had to undergo atonement for the unwittingly throwing one of Pha Rann's paladins into oblivion. However, with your limit testing, we know that Shak can endure twelve. Knowing this, we know where to stop. My Order's progenitors did not think to test limits before this training was tested. Of note, the paladins who survived, after atonement, and the clerics, all showed marked progression in their skills, training, and combat."

"Impressive," Alerius said. "Let's make it happen then, Commander. Please draw up the details. When this Slaadi issue is put to rest, we shall begin." Alerius snorted. "Take It All Away... in Merakoran, at least the original dialect of humans, that is the term we adapted here for 'multifixion.'"

Chapter 7 – Fist of Graves

Fist ran up the Temple Mount. Brook could not decide if she should go there or to Dragon Mountain. Sean had told her though that if she wanted to find Dar Tania, then the Temple site would always be her best bet. As Fist loped up the road and took advantage of the stone stairs already set in sections, Brook noticed a cluster of activity near the amphitheater. She pointed it out to Fist who veered towards it.

They entered a gathering led by the god emperor Alerius. Brook recognized his human form. As her gaze swept them all in, she was happy to recognize all but a tall and slender woman who looked different from the others. She wore a veil covering very long hair and stood behind the ranger. They all stood in relaxed but ready poses as Fist skidded to a stop, heavy with his breathing. He helped Brook down from his shoulder. Feeling everyone's eyes on her, Brook felt both self-conscious and overly aware of the hill giant. "I don't quite know where to begin. I'm sorry to interrupt." Remembering, she dropped into the formal bow.

Fist looked at her, but then sat back on the ground. "Drink?" he asked.

"No, Fist. Bow, like this," Brook whispered. Fist looked at her and seemed amused.

Dar walked forward with a large bowl. She prayed and it filled with water that she offered to Fist. As he drank and the bowl continued to remain full, Fist grunted and began to drink faster. The noise of his slurping made Brook wish she had not come here, to this group, like this. Sean eyed the giant and said, pointing, "Brook, you've made a new friend. The kerchki here do not kneel or bow either. The concept does not exist in their way of thinking. Why don't you introduce us while he's drinking?"

She smiled gratitude at Sean for helping her feel better. "Sure. I'm Brook Summerstone. What I mean is that this is Fist of Graves, a hill giant from the southern mountains. I met him on the road here. I'd still be on the road for days and days if he hadn't helped me. His friends, I, call him Fist."

The strange woman moved forward with a side-to-side swaying of her hips and shoulders that reminded Brook of a snake. "This is the same kind of giant Bruce and I saw in Quattrain. In fact, we saw this one. The chief and this one have these markings as did an old female giant." Syliri drew closer to Fist and said, "Bull Stomper."

Fist immediately dropped the bowl, splashing water down his front, and leapt to his feet. So abruptly did he tense that the others readied weapons.

Syliri pointed to the Hrax statue. "Bull Stomper won't hurt you," she said in perfect goblin.

Fist's eyes found the statue and he warily approached it. His straight line approach brushed up against Alerius. With fascination, Brook and the others wondered what would happen. Fist's contact with Alerius did not move the god emperor at all but bounced Fist to the side. Ignoring the god emperor and unaware of his actions, Fist approached Hrax. Finally, he tapped it. "Haha, Bull Stomper hard like rock. Nice carving."

Alerius said, "Not a carving. That's Bull Stomper, trapped in stone. He's still alive. Do you want us to release him?"

Fist's eyes grew wide and he looked back at Syliri and Alerius and then frantically began searching for Brook. Because of the group, he could not see her. Sweat broke out on his face and he fumbled at his waist for a heavy chain. "It's okay, Fist. I'm right here." Brook came running up to him. "You're safe. No one here is going to hurt you. I promise." Feeling bolder than she had before, she turned to the group. "Fist is my friend. None of you are to hurt him." Brook noticed the god emperor's flat expression and added, "Please, your majesty. I'll take Fist back to the wilderness on your command."

Alerius smiled and everyone else relaxed. "So long as you vouch for Fist of Graves, he is welcome here." A medallion appeared in Alerius' hand. "Here, Brook. This token around his neck will ensure he is welcomed here in Morbatten."

Brook took a golden chain with a symbol of Tiamat on it. Her fingers brushed accidentally against Alerius' hand and it burned her with heat. She jerked her hand back, smiling sheepishly. Being so close to the famous god emperor made her feel clumsy and self-conscious. Yet the symbol felt normal. "God emperor, we have not met but Summer sent me here to study and learn. I also bring a report of Home's progress." She started walking over to Fist to give him the medallion when she remembered, "Oh, here is the letter of recommendation Summer gave for me. I haven't opened it."

Alerius watched her with a slowly growing smile. "Brook, please. Give the medallion to Fist of Graves. Summer has already told Dar Tania about you. Since you are interrupting our council, tell me, are you going to be the first Halfling to consecrate to the Mother?"

She gave the medallion to Fist, who seemed deeply touched by the gift of wrought gold. Brook said, "You're putting me on the spot. I don't know. Well, it's not that but," she looked at Dar Tania. The fiery priestess smiled and shrugged as if to say, *It's okay to say yes or no.* Brook felt anxiety build in her and Kaia's words sounded as if he whispered them in her ear. Swallowing deeply, she said, "God emperor, is it true that Mallaforax used to head a druid order?"

Alerius' faint smile became a large grin. "I see you've heard some of our ancient history. Yes. This is true. We've been waiting for a druid to arise in the elven nation of Morilon to rekindle it. The royal family there though is actively suppressing those who might qualify as druids." Alerius walked up to Brook and circled her. Though it looked like he was taking in her appearance and stature, he actually viewed her from outside Time's flow.

Brook felt her entire life unravel under the god emperor's inspection. She felt herself judged and did not understand the criteria for judgement. After just a few moments, that felt like minutes, Alerius said, "I will not send a druid to my brother unless you worship the Mother. This is not a threat or ultimatum; it's a simple matter of fact."

Ynt'taris arrived, landing to the side of the hill and walking forward in his human guise. He heard Alerius address the group.

Alerius explained, "Druid magic is natural, of the land and creatures that dwell in it. It allows a druid to use that energy the way a mage uses magic. Because so much of what you see as Nature was shaped by the eldar dragons, there is a druidic sphere unique to Tiamat. Our Warg and Dire Animal Tribes are a testament to this truth. If Shak here ever reaches his next level, we'll see his destiny play out in this sphere as well." Shak bowed but curiosity burned in his eyes.

Alerius walked over to Fist, now wearing his Tiamat medallion. "Consider this hill giant. A normal druid would never summon or befriend such a creature. Preconceived notions of good and evil get in the way. For example, even though many animals eat their own young and kind, when hill giants do it, it must be because they are evil, right Taysorans? This is simply not true. The truth is this: they are so deep in Set's Dream that they cannot see good or evil. All they know is pain, terror, and the instinctive cry to battle or escape that terror brings." Pointing to the south, "That is Set's Dream. Fist was in Set's Dream. He did not see us the way we see ourselves. Now though, look at him."

An awareness gleamed in Fist's eyes and he nodded his head listening to Alerius. "I always different from tribe. Only witch, she named Bet, love me. Chief Oagh always send me on jobs to Bull Stomper. Always say Bull Stomper kill me. This," he opened his hands around the Tiamat medallion to the group in an expansive gesture, "it feels warm. Sleepy."

Alerius pointed to Fist, who fell over asleep with a touch of eldar magic. "Brook's summoning of an animal brought her a hill giant. This is Tiamat's druidic order. It works because it removes the caster from Set's Dream entrapping the monster. Instead of a demonic creature of terrible power, Fist saw Brook, as a Halfling, the way we see her. Though not harmless, you are probably the first curiously safe thing Fist has ever encountered in his life. This is why Fist has become more intelligent as you kept him fed on fish, and is so tired. Imagine living your entire life the way he has."

Alerius whirled on the Taysorans. "Taysor's never-ending quests to vanquish evil are doomed to fail because of Set's Dream. You think of yourselves as these holy warriors ridding the world of evil. In truth, you are removing scared, frightened, and tortured beasts from Set's Dream. The absence of the more powerful creatures your knights slay creates a void for the Dream to fill with some other monstrosity. This is why even your god named your empire as Morbatten's Shield. Did you really think these monsters see Pha Rann's holy light as their last living thing? Fools! They see you all as monsters and you let yourselves be part of Set's Dream."

The passion and anger Alerius radiated with his words began to tremble the bodies of those present with dragonterror. Brook had never felt it before and collapsed to the ground. All the most horrible things haunting her nightmares seemed about to rain down on her all at once. Dar ran to Brook and restored her. The fright passed as if a dark memory. Still, she held tight to Dar.

Alerius walked behind Hrax. "The next evolution of slaads, the red phase, allows them to throw creatures into Set's Dream just by looking at them. This one, Hrax, he is just barely at the level of beginning to understand Set. He must touch a target to trap them in the Dream and can only exert small degrees of influence, similar to a mage's *charm spell*. The greys though, this Ylgolth. They thrive on cataclysm. The more lives lost, and I'm talking all life not just human or Halfling, the more influence they can claim into Set's Dream. Set becomes aware of them. Where the Mother requires your faith and obedience, Set requires cataclysm and death. The flashier, the more terrible the disaster or war, the greater the Slaadi are rewarded. For Ylgolth to be here is troubling. We are not ready to be a spear any more than Taysor a shield."

Bomoki asked, "Will you destroy Ylgolth then?"

Alerius looked at Bomoki but before he could answer, Dar interjected, "No, we will. This will be a test, perhaps the first real test of the paladins, the priestesses, and the warriors. The people of Morbatten will fight this battle."

Bomoki shrugged. "You could ask the Darkhold. I bet it says you all die. From what the god emperor is describing, your people will march into Set's Dream and then turn on each other."

Alerius seemed both annoyed and pleased with Bomoki. When he looked at Dar, he beamed. "Yes, Dar! Armed with faith and consecration, you will anoint generals. Mortals, not the dragons, will teach the Anthracos to ware Tehra! You will serve this Ylgolth a banquet of pain. The Court will deal with Ylgolth should he put in a personal appearance."

* * *

Alerius dismissed everyone except Ynt'taris. Hrax, petrified and silent, stood with them. To the left, the sun rose on a misty day full of fog. Ynt'taris broke the silence at last. "Its master, this Ylgolth, he was able to cast me into Set's Dream from the edge of the world. He is Anthracos. What will you do?"

"Truly?" Alerius asked. Alerius reached out and Ynt'taris caught his hand. In a moment, images from Ynt'taris' mind filled his. Along the world's edge, there are few threats and Ynt'taris let the Dream take him for several moments before reasserting control of reality. Alerius continued, "My children cannot stand against a grey. My heart tells me this. You remember the Tower of Sorcery in the Arati Grasslands of Merakor? I knew an Anthracos there. When the dark elves came, Polgeryx conspired – successfully – to not only destroy the Tower, but the inhabitants and the attacking armies around it. The drow named it 'Circle of Desolation' because the devastation stripped the soil for miles in all directions. When I heard, I went to see and met Polgeryx. The grey was drunk on the lifeforces taken and mistook me for a fallen dragon. So, we talked. A grey, at its peak, would be a match for all of us combined. A normal grey or a new one, one of us might take." Alerius closed his eyes and whispered. "I am unsure. If the Dream turned us against one another, a grey could destroy us." The softly spoken words burned Alerius' mouth with shame and he clenched his fists.

Ynt'taris laughed. "You are unsure? We are doomed then. It must cut to your center to say this." Alerius said nothing and after his laughter faded, Ynt'taris added, "The Mother chastises me to be more like you: aware, not humble. The human word 'humility', this is not for dragons."

Alerius whispered, "Your qualities are no less important than the other dragons'. Your irony often underscores truth. In this case, yes, it cuts. I have not thought of Polgeryx in millennia. That a grey arises just upon our doorstep, now at this time, makes me wonder if the Pha Rannic messenger meant our confrontation to be this soon. A grey, Polgeryx said, can intrude upon Set enough to become an avatar of that one in this world. He said it happens rarely and pointed to the destruction around us. 'Even this was not enough to grant me the Dark Gift,' he said. I remember being deeply impressed. He did not say what the Dark Gift was. I had a sense it would be the difference between Dar Tania as a priestess and you or I as Tiamat's avatars. The way he said it, led to more discussion and Polgeryx clarified it was not vampiric, but rather some ability granted by Set. I guess it is a higher state for them, whatever comes after Anthracos."

Ynt'taris let the fire patriarch finish. "In that same time, my brother, I visited the ice giants. The drow were making overtures to them. I advised against their involvement. The promise of plunder was simply too great. Alerius, I begged them. I offered them power akin to your offer to the fire giants. If only Wenst Venqrst had the wisdom of Sar Jorek! Their alliance with the dark elves equaled a cataclysm for them from which they never recovered. The Merakoran ice giants, all of them, died. Yet, no slaad came to take credit. Set did not awaken and trammel the land with beasts. I say this because it cannot be known what appeals to Set, or the Slaadi. Maybe this Ylgolth will leave."

Alerius turned his head to the small girl standing next to him. "It is not our nature to let a beast like this linger near or know of our children. If we must, we shall gird for battle and end it. After so many generations, I am loath to risk my precious Dar Tania. Five winters now and we have just a handful of paladins and priestesses. Their progress and power have stalled. I cannot risk them in this state."

Ynt'taris nodded. "We could ask Hrax. We could ask the Darkhold."

Alerius whispered, "The Darkhold is known to Takhissis. Before Time, She wrote Her Name in it. Brother, this is just a page. There is an entire book awaiting. When assembled, the entire book is many times more powerful, knowledgeable, and less hungry. Each page hungers for more and more in its loneliness, to be whole and complete."

Chuckling this time, Ynt'taris noted, "And I thought I knew when you obscured the truth. All this time and you let it not slip at all that you knew!"

"Yes, watch." Alerius cast a spell and whispered, "Syliri, you are required." He then cast a second spell and a black doorway opened in the air before him. Through it, Syliri stepped. Bruce tried to come through as well but Alerius caught his shoulder and pushed him back through. "This does not concern you, Ranger."

Syliri looked at the two dread lords and then at petrified Hrax. She bowed and asked, "How may I serve?"

"I will undo Hrax's petrification. I wanted to offer you the chance, should you wish."

Syliri walked up to Hrax and touched the stone. It made her wince as she recalled the moment Set's Dream took hold and she did this to him. "I do not regret this," she ran the back of her finger along Hrax's cheek. "But, the undoing process, it hurts just as much. In some ways, it is worse because I have to enter the Dream first and then back this one out of it. It is a mercy the Azuros does not deserve. You might recall that more than a few of these broke to pieces in returning them to flesh. I could try."

Alerius nodded. "I wanted to give you the option to practice this. But, I need Hrax alive. Unless you are sure of the undoing, I cannot risk it."

Syliri bowed her head, not in shame but in contemplation. "It is all too raw for me, Alerius. To go into the Dream so often in such a short time, I do not trust myself."

"Very well," Alerius agreed as he summoned a stone table and opened the Darkhold parchment on it. "Please stay with me in case this should fail. Should Hrax break free, or should this," he tapped the parchment, "become untenable, you will petrify them." Syliri nodded and smoothed the snakes back from her face. Alerius pressed, "You are sure that his name is Hrax Terrej?"

Taking position behind the statue, Alerius put his hand on the back of the head. As the slaad turned back to flesh, Alerius took possession of it. When Hrax at last blinked his eyes and smiled at them, Alerius said through Hrax's mouth, "Syliri, please note that the powers and strengths of a blue are at least ten times that of a green. This blue is just a month old. You encountered him scant days after his transformation." Alerius closed his eyes. "He marked Fist and two other giants for the spawning of greens. He also marked many more goblins. It was all recent enough that it does not matter. There was never a spawning. The scars on Fist are from Hrax."

Hrax-Alerius walked up to the table and removed the single Darkhold page from the ledger holding it flat. Taking the razor quill, Alerius stabbed it through the faintly blue scales along Hrax's wrist. The scales sparkled iridescent in the morning light. Ichor-like blood oozed from the cuts and Alerius wrote:

I am Hrax Terrej and I summon all Darkholds to me!

The blood runes swirled slowly not quite forming runes before they finally resolved.

You are now known, Hrax Terrej. To summon
all Darkholds, you must voluntarily surrender
your soul to me. Do you consent?

Alerius said, "Takhissis told me about this." He laughed, "Within, Hrax is screaming in fear. He threatens me with Ylgolth's wrath." Hrax-Alerius wrote:

What more consent is required?
I offer my soul for endless knowledge
and power. Taste and know the vast
wastes of the in-between realms. I
write my name again, Hrax Terrej.

Alerius tore the flesh of Hrax's left arm so that blood began to drench the page. It was absorbed almost as quickly as it sprayed out.

With each blood spurt, the page replicated. On each new page, Alerius wrote: *Hrax Terrej.* Soon, his hand trembled and shook with fatigue and blood loss. When at last the pages stopped being added, Alerius wrote:

For pure and endless knowledge, Hrax
Terrej is the Darkhold.

Three hundred and thirty-two pages replicated in to the original. Dancing black and grey shadows encircled the book and where they touched Hrax, his skin peeled free to wetly slap onto and bind to the edges and outside of the book. Alerius grunted in pain as more shadows reached out. When all flesh had been flayed from his left arm, connective tissue and bone began to rend away and Alerius cried out in agony. The scream quickly turned from Hrax-Alerius to just Hrax. Behind, Alerius animated and grabbed hold of Hrax.

"Ynt'taris, help me hold him in place." Both dragonshifted and speared their talons through Hrax's shoulders. Where Alerius pressed Hrax's face down into the book, terrible crunching and chewing filled the clearing. The Darkhold peeled Hrax's body into itself one biological layer at a time. At last, only the hand and quill remained, which disintegrated into the book.

Ynt'taris looked down at Syliri and noted, "Your ranger would not appreciate knowing this happened. To spare you, I will tell him that I executed Hrax, which is very much the truth."

Syliri looked confused at this comment and asked, "Is Hrax still alive in the Darkhold? Bruce understands the danger of this creature. While he might not approve of your feeding it to an abyssal power, I doubt he would have issues with ending the Slaadi. I will tell him myself. Alerius, I find myself not wishing to keep secrets from Bruce. It is a new feeling for me, and uncomfortable."

"Very well, Syliri. It gladdens my heart to see you finding this connection amongst the fallen. Too long, too long you shied away from contact with the mortals. I'm happy for you. I ask that you embrace this discomfort. It can be quite thrilling to see the world the way mortals do."

"Yes, I understand," she replied.

Alerius continued, "As for The Darkhold, it is the center of the Abyss. When Demos-Gorgos pushed Set away, it layered the Gate of Chaos. Takhissis theorized that if a powerful being were sacrificed to the book, the actual book would come. The Darkhold consumes life to know about the many worlds and creatures of creation. But, it only knows what is consumed. It is not omnipotent, but its knowledge is powerful, and it always hungers for more." Alerius picked up the Darkhold and snapped it shut. Shadows cut out like razors from the book, too small to hurt Alerius, who cast a *sleep* spell on it. The book fell quiet.

* * *

Brook rode Fist's shoulders while Sean walked alongside them. Bruce followed with Syliri. Looking back, Brook wanted to ask the medusa so many questions but just could not. Seeing her interest, Syliri cocked her head and asked, "Yes?"

Brook tried to speak but stammered. Syliri walked forward and touched her face. "It's okay. I've always been part of Morbatten. We both serve the god emperor."

Bruce poked Syliri and said, "God emperor this, and dread lord that. Let it alone. He's a dragon."

Brook saw Syliri roll her eyes and all the scared parts of Brook vanished. "You're a medusa. How, I mean, what do you eat?"

Syliri began laughing. "I eat the same food you do, Halfling Brook. Though, before Time, we had cattle – gorgon bulls and cows, and chickens – what you call cockatrices. Like my sisters, they've all fallen to Set." She sighed. "I'm sure you might struggle to think a cockatrice tastes really good."

Bruce interrupted, "You've never told me about this. In all our travels, it seems like it would have come up. So, compared to chicken, how does a cockatrice taste?"

Syliri deadpanned, "Like chicken." Their conversation continued and when they reached the road leading up Dragon Mount, Dar Tania sat waiting for them with Shak. Dar melted into Sean's embrace as they greeted each other. Holding hands, they began to the five hour climb to Alerius' throne.

At some point in the long walk, Brook meant to ask Dar a question but instead blurted out, "Dar, I've decided to join Tiamat!" Immediately, she covered her mouth as if she had said a bad thing. She looked for a reaction from Sean, but the paladin kept his face carefully neutral.

Dar smiled at her. "You will not regret this decision, Brook. You do us all service with your faith. Mallaforax is altogether different from the god emperor and Ynt'taris."

"Really, how? Tell me everything, please!"

"Alerius and his brothers are fascinated with the mortal magic infusing this world. They see us the way other dragons see piles of treasure. That's not to say that Alerius does not love us or his treasure, he does. Don't ever take anything from him!" Dar laughed. When no one joined her except Brook, she smoothed her dress and continued. "Mallaforax, the Dread Lord of Vapors, feels the same about exotic nature. That is to say, there are creatures in the wild and unspoiled places of the world, such as unicorns, that Mallaforax studies. Alerius told me that Mallaforax converted a number of these and other fey creatures to Tiamat. The fey, in general, consider Mallaforax a type of sage and come from all over the world to consult with him. When you learn of these creatures, you'll come to know how miraculous this feat is. Also, where the patriarchs are aligned strongly to Tiamat, Mallaforax is actually aligned to both Tiamat and the god of these isles and world, Krentismar. While the elves think Mallaforax watches over them, the green patriarch actually watches over an indigenous race here called the Thri Keen. Imagine giant praying mantises capable of speech, magic, and civilization. That's what Thri Keen are. We don't see them. They're on different islands and underground but they once covered these islands."

With gentle prodding, Dar talked all the way to Alerius' throne chamber. When they arrived at the top, they turned to look out over the valley of Morbatten below. The southern distortion along the horizon was more clearly visible and they winced before turning in to the mountain. The large tunnel leading in along with the shorter sister peak to this one made them feel small. A dragon like Alerius could easily fly through this tunnel. Talon marks in the stone showed the truth of it. Brook expected it to smell like a dragon, or at least like a snake. Instead, it smelled like rock. The snow and ice on the slopes above never melted. Ice and hoarfrost clung to the upper sections of the mouth entrance. Just a few steps in however, the tunnel warmed.

"Where does the heat come from?" Brook asked.

Shak answered. "The god emperor is a fire breather. You're feeling the heat of his lifeforce."

"Wow," she whispered as they entered further. The tunnel inside was carved, smooth, and polished. It gave the cavern a glossy ambience of light that, when Dar summoned magical lights, brightened everything all the way to a massive double door set in heavy metal hinges and wooden planks hundreds of steps ahead of them. Like the tunnel, the doors would allow dragon flight. Miniscule human doors within these doors waited for them. Syliri stood by the opening with two fire giants. The kerchki always stood guard at this door. They ignored Fist. Fist marveled at them but, after flexing his arms and back, walked past the fire giants with his head held high.

When they entered, Brook craned her head in all directions. She expected a treasure trove of gold and gems. Instead, the polished floor changed from the mountain rock to gold ore. The chamber reached up hundreds of feet and she could not see the sides. Entering thirty paces, they came to a still pool of clear water. To the side of it, a throne emblazoned with golden statues of dragons sat empty.

Syliri pointed at a space to the side of the reflecting pool. "Alerius and Ynt'taris are waiting for Spark to arrive. We've set out some provisions. Make yourselves comfortable," Syliri gestured and a banquet set with all manner of food appeared. She and Bruce stepped away from the group and began a quiet conversation of their own.

Fist looked around and sniffed. "Smell nothing. Except that," he pointed to the food. "It smell good!"

The group made their way over to the food and though hungry, they soon enjoyed teaching Fist what he was eating. The giant had never eaten cooked food like this. Boar, fruit, vegetables, beef, lamb, cheese... while Fist had eaten these raw, or boiled with other things, he had never had it prepared to look and taste good. His enthusiasm occasionally overcame his ability to talk, and yet the giant did surprisingly well to follow Brook's example. At one point, Fist groaned and said, "Cheese!" with such enthusiasm that all present burst into laughter.

Sean joined Dar at the table and asked, "Have you had time to consider military preparations for Ylgolth?"

She smiled and took his hand. "I thought we might talk about names. You've had a day or two. What are you thinking?" Dar poured him wine from a crystal decanter.

Sean bowed his head for a moment. "Dar, I've been thinking on this. I never thought, ever, that I – we would share such a thing. I hope this does not surprise you though. My heart tells me that I must resume my vows." Dar's face fell with disappointment. Sean squeezed her hand. "If I'm not true to myself, how can I be true to you, our daughter, this empire? Think about your vision, Dar. You would do anything to realize the empire of dragons, right? It's the same for me. This is who I am." He kissed her hand. "I'll always be here for you, for the little one, for your dream. I would not ask you to leave Tiamat's faith or change..."

Dar twisted his hand with unreal strength. "Be careful, Sean. I am not asking you to change either. Love is not something you have to step down to from your lofty ideals." She struggled for a moment and then brightened her smile again. "The name?"

"There is a story in Taysor of a lady knight named Seline. She found herself in a strange land, a strange circumstance, and she found grace in Pha Rann's eyes. Where most of my class draws inspiration from Cuthbert and other heroes of that type, I always related more with Seline. Also, my mother's name was Seline. I think she would be pleased to know her name graced what I know will be a perfect baby girl." Sean looked down at Dar's hand while he said this. When he finished, he looked up and said, "If you hate it, I understand this child will be Morbatten's."

Dar pulled his face to her own for a chaste kiss. "I love the name. She shall be named Seline. The daughter of a high priestess and the dashing Commander Sean, boys will swoon in her wake and the dragons themselves will tremble at her grace."

The kiss left Sean wanting more and he silently prayed for strength to renew his vows. "Dar, I would see the new training implemented and tested. Then, I must go for a time to the Great Library to consult with my Order. I promise I will be back by summer harvest. Earlier if you send word. I would be here to greet Seline into the Valley of Dragons." He kissed her hand while she rose to check on the Court of Patriarchs.

Fist looked around and tore a shank of lamb off the table and offered it to Sean. "Here, eat. Make all better." He shoved it into Sean's breastplate.

"Food," he said. The force of the offering slammed Sean back into the heavy chair. He almost lost his balance except that Shak caught the chair before it toppled over.

Moving back to the table, Shak commented to Sean, "I overheard. You cannot know the relief I feel knowing that I am no longer required to stand between you and her. Many congratulations, Commander Sean. Your child, I cannot imagine it!" Shak raised his own goblet and tapped it against Sean's.

Sean smiled. "My friend, you do my child honor. You know, your god emperor will not let it rest until you too have fathered children. That is a huge difference in our cultures. It is one I have often discussed with the dragon Alerius. Someday, it shall be I clinking your cup." Sean raised his cup.

"Someday," Shak replied.

Conversation gradually returned to normal until the giant doors opened, moving on hidden levers and gears. A lithe dragon bearing large whiskers and narrow spines landed just across from them. Blue within blue eyes looked down at them and crackled with lightning before the dragon's form melted and collapsed into a human skein. Like Alerius, the human form remained too large to be a human. Instead of armor, Spark wore mage robes. He looked around at the group and walked forward to the scrying pool near the table.

From the immense darkness and shadows opposite the heavy doors, Alerius and the white dragon patriarch walked out in their human forms. Dar followed and closed the doors behind. Alerius walked over to the scrying pool and beckoned them to join him. Addressing the group, Alerius said, "Each of you have come to me with many things in your mind, and requests. It affects more than just you. Let's begin with the first. Brook?"

Brook timidly stepped forward. In the scrying pool before her, an image of Mallaforax appeared though it took a while to see him. An amphitheatre of carved stone rose up about halfway around a titanic tree with wide-arcing branches. The roots spread out almost as large as the canopy of leaves. Alerius waited for Brook and the others to take it all in. Long silent moments drew out before Fist pointed and said, "Not roots. Dragon."

Brook looked at where he pointed. A tangled clump of roots slowly resolved as a dragon's hand, knurled and twisted into the ground. Following that, Brook quickly made out the rest of the dragon. Alerius congratulated Fist, "We will talk about Fist in a moment but very good noticing the green patriarch. Mallaforax does not move about much and the world tree tends to grow around him. The elves of Morilon built the amphitheatre in an age where they thought Mallaforax would share more knowledge with them. Such a relationship never began because their king, Vel Pajor, thought this would be Mallaforax sharing with them, not the other way."

Brook pointed to where Mallaforax's head would be. "Am I to visit the Lord of Vapors?"

"Yes, but on the condition I named." Behind Brook, Dar Tania stepped up closer and put her hands on Brook's shoulders.

"I am ready for Consecration," Brook said. She looked nervous.

Dar began to hum a song and occasionally she spoke. "The tribes were all born into Consecration. You join Tiamat of your own free will?"

Brook nodded her head but it felt wrong. Feeling stronger than she had, she declared, "Yes!"

Dar then asked, "Your entire life, the experiences and knowledges you have had, those you will yet have, the quiet moments of your heart, do you consecrate the entirety of your being to Tiamat?"

Brook felt a pinch in her shoulder and realized Dar gave her a signal. Brook almost said yes, but paused. A name came to her and she struggled to form the words. Slowly, with Dar's humming, Brook said, "I do not pledge myself to Tiamat." Her eyes darted to the patriarchs with great concern but the dragons remained unreadable. "I consecrate myself to Tiamat-Zenrifia, the sacred name of the winds."

At the speaking of Zenrifia's name, Mallaforax's eyes shot open and looked at Brook through the scrying pool. The single giant iris of one eye then filled the pool until the pool itself went dark. In the darkness, and seen as through the magic, Brook saw her own reflection against the mirror of Mallforax's pupil. A slow rumble, as if trees grinding in wind, sounded through the chamber. "Brook, I will take you as my disciple. Come to Morilon. Brother Alerius, do not trouble me again."

The chamber went silent. The scrying pool cleared. Dar's humming continued, the only thing filling the emptiness of sound and sight. "Do you feel it, Brook?" Dar asked.

Brook answered, "I feel like if I don't head to Morilon, my soul will burst free of my skin."

"Then go, Brook. Leave behind the troubles of Morbatten and go to your new life as a Druid of Tiamat." Dar pulled her back from the scrying pool and turned her to Fist of Graves. "Fist will have problems with the elves."

"He is my friend. He is coming with me." Brook's factual tone drew a smile from Fist.

"Brook, friend. We go." He held out his hands to her and she ran to him. Bowing from his shoulder to the dragons, Brook waved good-bye. Fist ran out of the chamber.

Dar continued to hum while Alerius noted the circular scars on Fist and explained, "The circle cuts on Fist - he was marked by the Slaadi to bear a parasite. The marks enhance their intelligence and prepare them to become a slaad themselves. Hrax never completed the ritual though. There are two other giants and many goblins marked this way."

Alerius looked at Syliri and Bruce. "It is unlikely Ylgolth will attack us directly. Slaadi, by their nature, are most concerned with their own power and self-preservation. If Hrax had more time following his transformation, he would have prepared contingencies against his capture. It is nothing short of a miracle that you captured him when you did." Alerius looked at Bruce and added, "We had to execute Hrax. Even petrified, there are some creatures too dangerous to keep here. Azuros Slaadi are in that category. You did very well to bring us this one."

Bruce bowed and said, "High praise from you, Alerius. How may we continue to serve?"

"We need to know where the goblins you saw in the mine came from. That is where more slaads will birth from. Finding and killing them before they actually become Fecundus is much easier. The hill giants marked like Fist, they too must be slain. Ylgolth, if he finds them, can continue their consumption and transformation. Those marked, this way, they become more intelligent. Fist is not a typical hill giant. He knows it. The witch he spoke of, she most likely selected and marked him for Hrax. Either Fist is uncommonly intelligent, or the markings helped him become so."

Dar let her song fade and it drew them all into a silent reflective moment. Bruce took Syliri's hand. "We will seek out the goblins. It should be easy to follow their trail from the mines. Your maps show several excellent locations for a goblin warren, past the area you marked for hot springs. When we find them, we kill them?"

Alerius nodded. "If they've been infected or even marked for infection, the host will be far more powerful than you would otherwise expect. The green slaads that birth from these, you should be able to end them as well. If there are more than you feel safe handling, try to draw them into pursuit so that they meet our army here." Alerius pointed to a map that appeared in the scrying pool. The map showed a dragon's eye view of Quattrain bordered on the west by the Cordabad South River. "Dar, you shall position the army here." He tapped the edge where a shallow area of the river entered Home just south of Morbatten. His talon landed on a section of the river the tribes called "Crossing." The Fish Tribe preferred that spot as, even during the drier seasons, deep pools on either side of the shallow area resulted in easy fishing.

Dar bowed. Behind her, Sean and Shak bowed as well. Syliri lingered after the others had left. At first, Bruce tried to take her with him but waited patiently alongside her. When only they remained with the dragons, Syliri spoke. "My friends, are you sure you want me to go and revisit the slaads? If all we know is that Hrax's master is more powerful than Hrax, then I must ask – what if we encounter an Embros, or worse, an Anthracos?"

"You are worried about Set's Dream," Alerius stated. "Should you be?"

Syliri took Bruce's hand and pulled him closer to her, as if a shield. "You know I am. Though we linger for thousands of years, the time of the maedar is fresh still in my memory. The way Set's Dream moved, the way the Slaadi wield it, I have never felt this type of power. Is it weak to say that it frightens me?"

Ynt'taris turned and walked away. "It's only weak if you believe the Slaadi stronger than you. As an Eldar, you are only limited by your will." He gestured with his hand and faded from sight into the darkness at the back of the throne chamber.

Spark eyed Ynt'taris and noted, "You know, Syliri, that we all treasure you, even that one. It is wise to beware something you fear. That you fear Set's Dream makes you perhaps wiser than the great Alerius."

Alerius stepped forward and embraced Syliri. "I remember finding you, just as time moved. You were a wild and feral thing then, on the verge of becoming fallen. Across these millennia, I remember it. It is not weak to fear that dark nightmare. Syliri, you are part of the Spear. I cannot see what role any of us might play in the prophecy, but if you cannot or chose to not face Ylgolth, there will always be – forever after – the time before Syliri was unconcerned with the Slaadi, and the time after when she was afraid. Who do you want to be? This is an Eldar question."

Syliri hugged him back. "I would be strong enough to save my fallen sisters still trapped in the dream."

"Then, Syliri, you must confront these beings who wield Set's Dream. Defeating the avatars of Set, this is your test. You have this ring," and Alerius pulled her three-knuckled ring of gold set with smooth emeralds up before her face. "It steels your will and self-control. The contingency spell we enacted so long ago is also intact. That is your lifeline. We will not let anything happen to you."

"What of Bruce?" Syliri asked.

Alerius looked sideways to the human and smirked. "The ranger of Krentismar makes his own choices. He is already wanting to destroy Ylgolth, just like a paladin of Pha Rann would."

Bruce looked about to reply but held his tongue. After a moment with Alerius daring Bruce to say anything, the ranger bowed and said, "I choose to be with Syliri, no matter what."

Alerius tapped the three emeralds on the knuckle rings, one at a time. "If this should fail, you have the love of your ranger. Between magic and love, you are well-prepared to face any nightmare be it Set's or some other aberration." Alerius turned sideways so that Syliri could see Spark. "My brothers and I, we have never viewed you as being weak. Of the gorgonas, you are the mightiest. Never forget that. Long before you took this form, as a dragon, you would have been majestic and terrible to behold."

Spark bowed, as did Alerius, as he kissed her hand and stepped back. Syliri took a deep breath and softly pledged, "We will not fail you, god emperor."

* * *

Bomoki teleported himself, Bruce, and Syliri to a tall hill along the southern edge of Home. Snow gently fell in the afternoon light. "This is a welcome sight after that combat," Bomoki said. He looked southwards. The distortion, this much closer, tangibly hurt his eyes. Syliri veiled her face against it. They had hoped to use line of sight teleportation to get even closer to the gold mines. The snow limited their view. Bomoki rubbed his hands together against the cold. "I could take you one step further. There's a spot by the river I've visited. I don't remember where it is in relation to where you're going though. Weather magic won't clear enough of the area to matter. Besides, I think the god emperor would do more than punish me with chores if I used weather magic near the Halflings again."

Bomoki fidgeted for a minute while Syliri and Bruce waited. When it became awkward, Syliri touched Bomoki's arm and said, "My snakes grow impatient. What is the problem?"

Bomoki took a wand from his belt. When he opened it, Syliri and Bruce both realized it was actually a spell scroll. The mage smiled apologetically at them. "This is from the god emperor. We're dealing with the Slaadi. He said it more gracefully, but my understanding was something like 'you can never be too careful.' This spell will alter your memories. That way, if the slaads were to interrogate you, they will only see things that benefit Morbatten. If you're not okay with this, I am to take you back to the mountain."

Syliri took Bruce's hand. "I've been through this before. I trust the god emperor. So does Bruce."

Bruce frowned and asked, "How will our memories be affected?"

Bomoki grinned. He had already begun casting the spell. "You'll forget that Alerius is a dragon. He'll be an armored mage in service to the Queen Alaura, a possible Anthracos. You won't be sure if she is or is not. Every feeling you have for Alerius will be switched to her. This spell will end when Alerius touches you."

When the spell ended, Bruce said, "I don't feel any different."

Bomoki chuckled and watched the scroll burn to ash. "All hail Queen Alaura," he said. When both Syliri and Bruce agreed, Bomoki readied another *teleportation* spell.

They stepped into a clearing alongside the main river through Quattrain. Bruce looked around pointed east. "Those are the mountains. This saved us a week of travel. Thank you." Squinting through the snowflakes just starting to fall here, he guessed that they would need to head south along the mountains to reach the mine. "I can't tell how far but still this is good."

Syliri sniffed the air. "Something is wrong. Look!" She pointed to the trees around them. Though autumn had progressed enough for the trees to look inert and bare of leaf, they had an orange cast to their bark. The ground was devoid of leaves where it should be thick and crackly. Bruce tossed a rock at one of the trees and an orange spore mist sprayed out.

Bomoki sent a magic missile flying at the same tree. The glowing dart blew the orange muck away in a small circle. For a few seconds, they could see the natural tree bark. Then, the orange color reclaimed the tree's bark.

"That's not good. I'm guessing leaves, fish, animals, they're all diseased," Bomoki guessed.

Bruce looked around, careful to stay away from the trees. When he reached the northern section of the clearing, he covered his eyes from the snow and pointed. "There's something moving towards Morbatten."

They all came forward to look, but through the dim light of snowfall and the trees themselves, they could not see. Bomoki conjured a floating eyeball and sent it forward. "The spores, whatever triggers it, don't react to the wizard eye. I'm not seeing any animals, not even skeletons. Oh, wow." The mage took a deep breath. "I'm not even sure how to describe this. I'll try. There is a tall wall, maybe ten paces high, of orange slime moving north at a slow but steady walking pace, I would guess. Behind it, also walking north are hundreds of hill giants and several thousand goblins. They aren't reacting to the wizard eye either. I'm moving in front of the wall. Yeah, it's tall and maybe two paces wide. The forest within a stone's throw in front of it is being infected by spores." Bomoki suddenly screamed and dropped to the ground holding his head. Bruce barely caught him from smashing on the rocks.

"What happened?" Bruce asked. Bruce sniffed, "Do you smell that? Sulphur and earth. Strange scent for a river and forest."

Still clenching his head, Bomoki gritted his teeth and said, "The wall opened and a female giant covered in small mushrooms walked out. She shattered my wizard eye."

Syliri tugged Bruce's sleeve. "Bruce, they're coming for us."

From their north, a tree smashed down. Bruce helped Bomoki stand and said, "Can you teleport us over there?" He pointed to a foothill just barely visible on the other side of the river.

"Yes, but I'll need some time and focus."

A mold-infected log came hurtling over the trees towards them. The stomping tread of running giants came at them. Bruce picked Bomoki up over his shoulders when he saw the mage struggled for balance. "We don't have time. We're going to run and hide."

"I'll buy you time," Syliri called back. In front of her, the forest petrified. The weight of the trees caused them to fall, torque, and shatter. A venomous bow appeared in her hands and she shot an arrow into the chest of the first hill giant she saw. It should have petrified. Instead, the arrow went straight through its body and hit a tree, which turned to stone. "They're not affected by bladed weapons!"

Syliri twisted a ring on her finger and rose up into the sky. Using magical flight, she dodged thrown rocks. The wall continued advancing northwards along with the horde not attacking them. The hill giants, she counted fifty, raced towards Bruce. Within a minute, the fifty giants milled about beneath her, occasionally tossing stones at her. They moved when she moved. Her petrification had no effect. From her neck, she pulled a small ruby pendant off a necklace containing nine small and three large rubies. She dropped a ruby.

When the ruby hit the ground, it detonated as a magical fireball. At least the giants ignited. If they felt pain, they did not show it. Even as their bodies burned, they continued to throw rocks at her. She reached for a larger ruby but motion to her north caught her eye. From the wall, the birds consumed by the orange slime vomited into the sky. "I hope Bomoki has had enough time," she muttered. She flew south with a flock of diseased birds chasing her.

Syliri caught up to Bruce quickly. He stood in a clearing, bow drawn and ready to defend the mage. Bomoki cast in the middle of his spell. Seeing Syliri flying to him and the dark cloud of birds chasing her, Bomoki nearly lost his focus. He beckoned her to come to him. Holding Bruce's arm, Bruce caught Syliri, and they teleported.

The three of them immediately slipped, and began to fall down the side of the mountain. "I'm sorry," Bomoki yelled. "I lost sight of the hill you pointed to so I focused on these mountains."

Her magical ring of flying still in effect, Syliri caught and stabilized them. They floated against a steep vertical drop that turned into a chasm over a raging river. Far to the west, they could just barely see the birds as the flock dispersed and returned to the wall. "We need you to warn Alerius and Dar," Bruce said to Bomoki. "Dar, the fighters, they won't last an instant against that. A single dragon's breath by Alerius though and it'll be over."

Bomoki pointed to a flat ledge to their side. "It's not just that. The forest and all the animals, it's been wiped out. It'd be convenient if the orange slime keeps all the infected within it. What if it doesn't? It was smart enough to recognize my wizard eye. Clearly, it has consumed things with some strategic thinking."

Syliri put them down on a projecting boulder hanging off the steep side. Regardless of terrain, it moved forward. It only paused when it had to twist, like a worm, to cross gaps it could not fill with its volume. "Alerius and I studied molds, slimes, and the like for a time but because they did not exist in Morbatten, and because you can't really petrify them, we left them alone. Also, while the wall looks big, the actual creature is so tiny you cannot even see it. Alerius speculated that what we call disease is actually attacks by these too-small-to-see creatures of Set." Syliri asked Bruce, "Do you know where we are?"

He nodded, "We're close to the mine but farther east. I'd guess we're just north of the hot springs."

Bomoki had more questions though. "So, when I get sick, I'm actually being attacked by these invisible things?"

"Not invisible. Just very tiny. Smaller than dust. Right now, they've all come together, probably because of the Slaadi, and we can see them. But, yes. That is what Alerius guessed. He, we, never get sick so it wasn't something he could really study."

"So, a bug bites me. Would it be more accurate to say it attacked me?" Bomoki asked with some sarcasm.

Bruce caught his robe's sleeve and said, "You have a warning to take back to the god emperor. Get going."

Bomoki began casting another teleportation spell and said, "I'm going to summon a nose sniffle monster and send it after you, ranger." He winked and vanished.

Bruce held onto Syliri and she flew them up the mountain. Snow began to fall harder and harder until they conceded. "There!" Bruce pointed. "There's a cave we can take shelter in. We're not going to succeed at anything blind."

* * *

Ylgolth stepped into the goblin warrens. He morphed his form to look like Hrax. He found the goblins properly subjugated. They bowed and worshipped Ylgolth-as-Hrax, as they should. "Where are my favorites?" he asked a goblin groveling under his feet. A gentle push with the Dream and the goblin paralyzed in a rictus of fear.

Ylgolth continued towards the king's cave. The goblin tasted quite good and Ylgolth hungered for more. He helped himself to more snacks as he went. The king's area held the goblins marked for Hrax's worm. One was the goblin king. The others sat against a far wall. At Hrax's orders, these seven had food, drink, women, everything they would ever want. In anticipation of their transformation, they sat fat and charmed so that they ate, studied, exercised, and reproduced. They were beyond perfect for Ylgolth's needs.

All goblins in the cave fell to their faces before Ylgolth. "The time has come!" he declared. Ylgolth remembered how, before his ascendance to grey, he needed and even lived with these vile lower creatures. A small gate opened by his left arm and he reached into the square's blackness. He pulled out a handful of writhing, twisting tadpoles. The size of small snake, each held a tiny spark of Ylgolth, enough to capture the host's lifeforce and feed the birthing of a new slaad. "Fecundus," Ylgolth whispered. "This is your new world and home."

He threw the worms across the cavern. The seven marked goblins embraced the worms into their bodies. Hrax had done an excellent job conditioning these hosts. The other goblins present tried to escape. Their screams, and the pain they felt as the worms burrowed into whatever part they latched onto, made Ylgolth smile. On a whim, he turned the gate and sent it spinning back through the main warrens. The spin scattered worms across the caverns. "I wish I had prepared more," Ylgolth said wistfully. He caught up two of the worms and said, "Just in case."

Behind him, the king's cavern went quiet except for the chewing sounds of the worms as they consumed and transformed their hosts. Ahead of him, as Ylgolth walked out of the warrens, the sounds of agony gave him goosebumps. He looked at his arm. "I have never felt this pleasure before." He pinched his arm and laughed.

Outside, Ylgolth looked up at the sun. It wavered in his view where solar flares and eruptions from the star's surface pockmarked the glowing white circle. He required a different sun. It needed to be less bright, less golden. "The gods of this world, this place, they are stronger than I am used to," he growled. He should be able to baptize this world in his dream. "It doesn't matter. Within all I see, my dream is absolute."

Ylgolth looked to the north again. The slime moved, but slower than it should. Though sunny, a snowflake blew into his face off the mountain peaks. The sun felt warm, but the cold air, it slowed his creation. It had not affected the hill giants or goblins. Ylgolth flexed, paying attention to the white snowflakes drifting in the wind. A few landed but skipped off his reptilian arm. The heat of the hot springs had made it easy to not notice the ambient temperature differences in this world. He would need stronger life and warmer weather. He sniffed the air but smelled only goblin.

He looked north again. Something there shimmered to his view. Ylgolth squinted his eyes and focused his magic on magnifying what he could see.

Where Set's power paced the orange slime wall, a disturbance wavered the air. Ylgolth pierced it and saw, with great difficulty, roads and then settlements. A tall mountain set in the midst of two shorter mountains crowned a gently sloping valley cut in half by a river.

Ylgolth focused his power to see more. He saw a brief glimpse of dragon wings. *So, this world has dragons*, he mused. He tried to look again, but his attention was violently torn to the image of an armored fighter. Magical emblems and insignia scripted in gold on dark grey plate armor gleamed in the sunlight. The man, his face unhidden, looked at Ylgolth. He had dark eyes. Ylgolth almost took them to be completely black when he noticed they were actually red. Pale skin with jet black hair framed those eyes. A sense of confidence and power radiated from the warrior. Ylgolth whispered, "I'm going to consume you, foolish mortal." The whisper, sent with malice and cruelty, usually inspired terror.

The fighter kept his gaze locked with Ylgolth and replied, "You think Polgeryx dead." He shaped his hands into a symbol. Just before Ylgolth could comprehend the symbol, their gaze broke.

Ylgolth tried to refocus his eyes. The magical amplification made him see the ground, his own hands, anything he looked at in too much detail. It hurt. Against the confusing pain, Ylgolth closed his eyes and traced his own blood moving through his eye membranes. While waiting for normal vision to return, he pondered the brief encounter.

To have met my gaze, that must be a powerful mage. Ylgolth corrected his thinking, *He must be a very powerful mage. Perhaps the most powerful mage in this world. To have been in the correct time and place to do this*, Ylgolth exulted. *Fate intends us to meet! He's a human. So, I must be in the human realms. Hrax had not reported humans.* Again, Ylgolth corrected himself. *Hrax reported humans barely able to understand magic. Comparable to goblins, Hrax had said.* Ylgolth rubbed his face. *Had Hrax allied with this mage as an early gambit to overthrow me, his master? No, Hrax lacked that level of cunning. And, Hrax did not know about Polgeryx.* Ylgolth sat back against the rocks marking the goblin caves. *I ate Polgeryx. That cannot be Polgeryx, could it?* A knot of dread entered his stomach. It sat poorly with the goblin feast just an hour before.

The grey Polgeryx, his master, had excelled at disguise and polymorph magic. "Did I eat you but not really eat you?" Ylgolth asked while looking at the sun. Soon, the clouds would block it from the land and more of this snow would fall. His slime would move even more slowly. "I ate you! I'm certain! Hrax, you worm! You allied too early. Now, you're dead and soon your allies – and what they know – will feed me and mine." A whisper in the back of his head rose up, taunting him with revenge. "No, Polygeryx. You are dead. Shut up!" The voice in his mind went silent, but also sullen, impatient with waiting for a chance to rise up and take control of Ylgolth's mind.

Ylgolth rubbed his hands together to shake snow from them. Reaching up to the daystar, he imagined pulling it to the world. His dream flexed and it felt warmer but, unlike home, this sun remained fixed in its spinning path through space.

Such an interesting world, Ylgolth thought as he turned and walked back into the caves. The darkness there felt welcoming, like home. He walked into the first room and noted that two worm hosts fed on one that almost escaped. Both lay face-first in the midsection of a goblin, chewing loudly. A hand reached up to Ylgolth. It already showed webbing between the fingers. Ylgolth crouched down and looked more closely at the webbing. Sometimes, mutations occurred. This one looked normal, so did the one munching on the other side.

Ten goblins cowered in the shadows, trying to hide from the transformants. The stench of urine rose up when Ylgolth walked towards them. He reached out and grabbed two by their heads. "Weak creatures. Good news though! I'm going to make you all much stronger than you are now. Follow me." Ylgolth pointed to the two eating their way through the corpses. "Or, stay here and become their next meal. I'm going to the cavern where your king was. I want you to run through the caves. You should see more of these. Count them. Tell me if any of them look different than those two."

The eight goblins stumbled over each other in their haste to obey. Their terror, it inundated Ylgolth. "I haven't even shown them Set's Dream yet." Ylgolth moved further back into the cavern.

Twenty-seven Fecundus transformations proceeded. A goblin groveled in front of Ylgolth telling of one that looked red, that bled through its skin. "Take me," Ylgolth ordered.

Several caverns deeper in, a transformant seeping blood from its skin had killed five other goblins in the cavern. One had the markings of a chosen host by Hrax. Ylgolth watched it eating. Where the others chewed, this one sucked blood through the skin of the hosts. Its webbed and clawed hands broke and snapped bones while it ate. As quickly as it drained the blood though its own skin leaked it back out. Ylgolth pointed it out to the goblin. "It eats, but never fills. This endless hunger will never be sated. Do you know what this means?"

The goblin fell to the ground again and trembling said, "It means you will kill, oh powerful lord?"

Ylgolth smiled and reached down to the pat the goblin on its head. Just as the creature relaxed, Ylgolth slid it across the bloody floor at the transformant. "It means that Set blesses us with nightmares."

The goblin howled and screamed, scrabbling at the blood slick floor to stop its slide. When it hit the transformant, the goblin felt pain latch onto its leg. Its momentum spun it around into grasping hands. Ylgolth remained crouching and prayed to the dark god Set against the long screaming of the not-yet-dead goblin. He held his hands out towards the nightmare. "Great Set, bless this child that it shall fall into my dream that I may compel it towards thy enemies."

Heat waves of magic pulsed outwards from Ylgolth's hands. Under that energy, the nightmare twitched. A bleeding eye opened in the back of its shoulders. The eyes regarded Ylgolth. The spine crunched and a mouth opened in the middle of the back. Razored in a circle, the mouth moaned, "Daddy…"

The arms snapped becoming more like tentacles than bone. The goblin thrashing against the nightmare's left hand reached out for mercy to Ylgolth. "A fast death to feed my son," he said. The new mouth bit half the golbin's neck and face off. Ylgolth saw fang curves against bone into brain for a moment. "Yes, my son. Eat. Grow. Whatever you want. There is a mage I want you to meet."

While the nightmare ate, Ylgolth pondered his encounter with the strange armored mage. "How do you know Polgeryx? Did Polgeryx come to this realm?" Ylgolth could not shake it. "I ate Polgeryx's brain. I ate it!" He smashed the stone wall to his side, and then dug his claws into it. The sharp rock felt good. "Polgeryx would know. Dare I consult him?" All Slaadi consumed, their lives, their powers, existed within the greys. Tens of thousands of greens, hundreds of blues, and a score of reds could provide answers. "But, there is only one grey. I cannot risk losing myself to a ghost."

Ylgolth rocked back and forth for a while. Within his mind, the essence of those he had consumed lay locked and bound. It was the Slaadi way. His own master, Polgeryx, had told him, "Never access these. Like you, they want dominion. They can live again by possessing you. You've made it this far. Do not give any of them an easy path to your elevated status. It's a mistake equal to death."

Polgeryx had said this to him. The deal was they were going to destroy and consume another Anthracos, together. That one had lived in a world of plentiful magic. Feasting on magi, Polgeryx coveted that one's magical prowess. It was on the brink of ascending to the ebony stage, closest to Set. Ylgolth had instead betrayed Polgeryx and consumed him. "It's the Slaadi way." His words did not reassure in this dark place with a Son of Set taking form in front of him.

He had never seen or met an ebony transformant – not that he knew of at least, what the Slaadi called the *Atramenti*. "Could you be an Atramenti?" Ylgolth asked the darkness, thinking of the armored mage. The Atramenti could be anyone. They, he, it would know of Polgeryx and Ylgolth's consumption of that one. No one knew how many there were. Ylgolth preferred his natural form but the Atramenti could assume any form and hide it from all but the most powerful. Polgeryx, when consumed, had been living as a female elf amongst elves for centuries.

"Who are you? What are you, armored mage?"

Chapter 8 – King Reset

Alaura looked much better. Ynt'taris made her sit still while he retrieved a book she wanted to discuss. It alarmed the dragon to see his favorite human and rider so weak. "You look much better. Do I need to forbid you from using the Darkhold? I delivered it to my brother to save you from temptation. You, above all others of your kind, should know the path to knowledge is study and experience, not having the answers given to you all at once."

Alaura sipped at her hot drink full of healing herbs. She shook her head. "Master, I knew. But, the things it said!"

"Were all things you did not care about. In all our time, you ask about dragons, Tiamat, the eldar. Never have you expressed interest in Terest Nostram. Never have you asked me about Merakor except where it crossed the other topics." Ynt'taris sat down across from Alaura. His human legs barely reached the floor. "You must choose and focus, Alaura. You cannot be a sage divided in your knowledge. The thing that makes a sage great is their specialized focus. You may not see it now, but there is power in knowing much about a single topic than snippets of many. Even if you study your whole life, you'll never know as much as the elven survivors of Merakor do. And, they're just a few hours' flight west of us. On the flip side, the elves will never know about the dragons the way you might. If you had asked the Darkhold about dragons, I could at least understand." Ynt'taris looked around. "You're looking much better at least. Tell me, why. You knew it consumed blood. You knew it was at least evil if not cursed."

From the far side of the room, Van watched. Too weak to contribute and wary of offending the white patriarch again, he watched the interaction in detail.

Alaura took another sip and put her cup down. "You know how we mortals are. Our attention moves moment by moment. When confronted with the truth of this page, we couldn't help ourselves. Only Dar was able to resist it. Van is the one fascinated with Merakor. You already know Bomoki is fascinated with any magic that might accelerate his sorcerous powers."

Ynt'taris eyed her and stated flatly, "I don't like Bomoki. Be careful around that one. Even the god emperor has concerns."

Alaura grinned. "See, Master? Curiosity pulls at me again. You've never spoken so bluntly about Bomoki. What has changed?"

"He grows more powerful each day. For most mortals, the acquisition of power eventually stops being a draw. For a rare few, it continues until their death. Bomoki is this second type. When they become aware that power is as endless as the River's flowing, they seek to hasten their acquisition of it. It makes them dangerous as they race against time to acquire power rather than the wisdom to use what power is already attained." Ynt'taris summoned a different book. Flipping through its pages, the dragon tossed it to Alaura. "Galthrest is a good example of an elven mage like that one."

Alaura scanned the page. "The archmage Galthrest of Kinpeace. From Merakor, of course. Why have there been no archmagi here on the Isles?"

"Orankstakar is an archmage. So is Alerius. So is Spark." When Alaura continued to stare at him, Ynt'taris finally conceded, "Some might consider me one as well, though I do not wish it known, Alaura."

"So, only dragon archmagi are allowed? That hardly seems fair or real. None of the refugees coming here were like Galthrest?" Alaura folded the book closed with her fingers marking the page.

"Most died fighting in the Kinslayer Wars. A few came here and founded Taysor. They were wounded, tired of fighting, and the effort of opening such a gate for so many, it broke them." Ynt'taris leaned forward and touched her knee. "The truth, though, is this: Taysor does not push its mages hard enough to become archmages. They get swept into your paladin orders and mustered out to die in combat. Adventuring is a good way to gain and grow in power, but a terrible way to become an archmage. At some point, they have to stop and turn their studies inward. The discipline of combat is also different. It's about shortcuts and sudden destructive power. Research is slow and grinding. There are no archmages of fireballs, or polymorph."

Alaura nodded. Behind her at the desk, a quill wrote down their conversation. "So, tell me about Galthrest and how, this book said he was one of the mightiest of all sorcerers ever, he relates to Bomoki being dangerous. Please."

Ynt'taris smiled. "Sure, but not here. Come."

Alaura stood and donned a magical cloak the two had made for when she flew with the white patriarch. It protected her from temperature extremes. She also grabbed goggles set with clear sapphire lenses. At the last moment, she smiled an apology to Van and left.

Outside the cottage, Ynt'taris dragonshifted and lifted Alaura to his back. For a moment, Ynt'taris felt a presence watching him but it passed on to Dragon Mountain. It resembled the slaad. Alaura felt it too. "Alerius will handle it, rider." Ynt'taris flew fast and high to the north.

They rocketed into the sky. Alaura threw her hands back and watched as the valley faded below. They crossed the summit of Dragon Mountain and continued north. The Valley of Ancients, north of Alerius' mountain, gave way to the Shield Mountains. The Valley of Ancients rested much higher than Morbatten. Criss-crossed by frozen streams, free-ranging horses galloped away from their passage. The best of the tribes retired to this valley. Alaura had yet to learn why but suspected it must relate the Alerius' imperative that certain families have children in each generation.

Ynt'taris shot into an endless cloud bank. At his command, Alaura cast a spell that would mask their presence and send an illusion of them bursting out of the cloud's top to lazily drift back to Morbatten. Within the cloud, Ynt'taris found a tall peak and landed. "Not the tallest," he had once told her. "That would be too obvious." They entered the peak into a cavern of blue and white ice similar to Alerius' throne chamber. Ynt'taris lair was full of winter creatures that roamed freely though none greeted them. Alaura noted, long ago, that the creatures of ice preferred isolation.

Tunnels arced out in odd directions and angles. From one of these, a remorhaz appeared. Its alien face chittered at them and then left. It looked like a white-blue centipede with an almost-dragonlike head. Ynt'taris began to discuss archmagi with her. These moments, far away from what Ynt'taris considered spying ears, she loved. Her quill began writing the white patriarch's words.

"To become an archmage, it isn't an advancement in power. The difference between Bomoki and any other mage is simply power. In Merakor, you became an archmage when others began referring to you that way. You might imagine there were many self-titled archmagi throughout Merakor. Yet, for a few, their power became unequal to the point you could look at them and just know. It's just like when you see Alerius and Bomoki together. Is there any doubt as to which is the more powerful? If even a thousand years pass, do you doubt which remains most powerful?"

"I'm expecting you to tell me that, like Bomoki, Galthrest wanted to accelerate his power?" Alaura sat down and pulled the magical cloak tightly around her.

"Go ahead, Alaura. Your need for heat energy continues to not offend me."

She bowed her head gratefully and cast a spell. A globe of golden light sprang into being around her and then became invisible. Within the globe, she felt warm enough to remove the cloak. Finishing her spell, she said, "Power gains. That's not really my question. As you describe it, if power is infinite, they'd want a way to shortcut the end state of being most powerful or even all-powerful. Did they seek godhood?"

Ynt'taris coiled around her and laid his titanic head on the ground in front of her. "Yes, shortcuts. The bane of all mortals. Bomoki will seek, has already sought shortcuts like he did with the Halflings. Even you, precious sage, you seek tempting but distracting shortcuts, like the Darkhold. Galthrest became an archmage when he did two things. The first was what Merakor called *kinetic magic*. I'll explain in a moment. The other was something he called *shift magic*. Shift magic never became known because of the Kinslayer Wars. So, his claim to archmagery was based solely on kinetic magic." While speaking, Ynt'taris withdrew a perfectly smooth glass sphere, as wide as her warming globe, from nothingness into the space to the side of his head.

Alaura reached out to touch it but Ynt'taris pulled the sphere back from her hand. "All of creation has heat. If it came from the Gate of Creation, there is heat. However, because of this magic, I have removed all heat to the point there is none. This is as close to Oblivion as this world can be," the dragon said. "Watch."

Ynt'taris rolled the sphere to the side and slowly breathed ice at it. A single talon touched the top of the sphere where a curious rune lay. Alaura had seen the white patriarch breathe out many different kinds of breath attacks. This one came out slowly, lazily, and touched the sphere in a single line of icy mist. Anywhere else, it would have crystallized all the water out of the air and frozen the ground beneath it too. The sphere absorbed it. When done, Ynt'taris looked sideways at Alaura and said, "Kinetic magic absorbs whatever type of energy is directed at it. When released, the cumulative effects are quite spectacular. Here." A small glass bead floated through the air towards her. "Warm this first, then take it. While touching the rune, tap it as hard or as soft as you want on your hand or the floor many times. Once you do this and let go of the rune, be careful to never drop it. Come."

Using telekinesis, Ynt'taris lifted the large sphere and Alaura. They floated along behind him as he went back outside. The Shield Mountains wore a thick blanket of snow. At this altitude, it never melted. Alaura had seen for herself that the snow pack sat hundreds of paces deep in parts. A completely different world of creatures lived in and under the snow. This was Ynt'taris' true domain. They moved to a ledge dropping down a sheer three hundred paces. Alaura had measured it once.

"Watch," Ynt'taris commanded. He flicked the large ice sphere out from the telekinesis and it began falling. "I've been breathing ice lances into this for several hundred years," he explained. A second later, Alaura saw, and then felt a brilliant flash of white light exploding from below. Leaning forward to see better, she saw a pulsing sphere of grey energy and then all went dark. A moment later, a tremor strong enough to trigger avalanches across the slopes around them hit, followed by the strangest noise Alaura had ever heard. The sound of snow and ice compacting, but overlapping to the degree it rose in volume and hurt her ears. Snow lances arcing out from the sphere's blast raced up the ravine as each spike crisscrossed another. Ynt'taris pulled her back from the ledge when the chasm below channeled the spikes straight up past them. The snow-wet air crystallized around each lance. The ice spikes reached a hundred paces past them into the sky, before the energy expired. Not supported by the chasm's edges, the lances began to break and fall.

Ynt'taris craned his head over Alaura as ice shards, some as long and hard as spears, began to rain down around them. "Hundreds of years, I've infused my breath weapon into that *kinetic ice sphere*. This is the power Galthrest discovered. It works similar to how we charge magic items. The genius of Galthrest was figuring out how to enable the capture of nearly any type of energy. He kept this very secret. My brother," Ynt'taris alluded to Alerius, "his genius is sensing and capturing these things for his, for our own mastery. Since Galthrest's time, we figured out what materials can hold how many breath weapons and what types of spells or physical attacks. Spark and Alerius have extended it to human magic and materials. This is where the rune magic comes from. Such a gentle expression of Galthrest's genius."

Grateful for her protective sphere of warmth, Alaura had been tapping the small marble back and forth between her hands. She carefully followed Ynt'taris' instruction regarding the rune's use. He pointed to it. "Throw it at my hand. Don't touch the rune now."

She did. Instead of the gentle throw, the marble shot out of her hand too fast for her eyes to even follow. It made a sound like a whip cracking and hurt her ears. The glass marble shattered into dust against Ynt'taris' hand. "Wow," she said. "So, if I kept doing that, it acquires more speed?"

"The gnomes said it's not speed. It's something else they call *momentum*. It's the force of movement, of each finger tap released all at once. You barely have any in a finger tap but it adds up just like '1+1=2.' If you keep tapping it, the marble will, at some point, shatter to dust. The Court, we have tested and seen this same marble ignite and burn before it strikes a target. Like I said, different materials hold different amounts of energy. The gnomes explain it in terms that I never cared to understand. The breath weapon is easier to see. Each time I breathed ice at the kinetic sphere, it captured and then later released all of them at once when it shattered down there. The at-once effect is quite spectacular. You have no idea how deadly even common objects become when kinetically enhanced like this."

A metal marble, the same size as the white glass one, appeared before Ynt'taris. With a talon, he touched the rune and then flicked it with his other giant claw. He did this only a few times. "This is a special metal the gnomes refine with the dwarves of Stone. It's very rare. In Taysor, you call it *adamantium*, but the gnomes call it *tungsten*."

"Cover your ears, dear sage." After a particularly hard flick, Ynt'taris lifted the metal sphere up and then threw it down into the chasm of ice lances. The whipcrack echoes and reverberated as the metal ball seemed to vanish. It left a line of radiant energy in the air from where it left Ynt'taris. A moment later, the ice lances fractured and then crumbled. The other side of the chasm shook and then avalanches of snow and rock poured down. "Just a couple of full strength hits and this small thing becomes an unimaginable weapon."

Alaura checked her book to ensure she recorded everything as Ynt'taris spoke. Satisfied, she looked back up and asked, "As an archmage, did Galthrest guess his magic could do these things? Also, I understand your critique of Taysor, but across all the races and your own mastery, there has never been another archmage?"

"No, this has limitations. Galthrest was content with the magic you see in the ranger's bow. You cannot stack it and there are limitations by material. The elves obsessed over mithril and yet mithril, while able to hold a single spell's worth of magic, it cannot hold it cumulatively. In fact, it's one of the worst materials for kinetic shift. Consider it, Alaura. There are other archmagi in the world, but they see the same things you see. Even Galthrest saw it in the last days of Merakor. There is a complacency in the mortal spirit that, when desire is satisfied or distracted – like you with the Darkhold – you lose focus on what you really want and chase phantoms of Terest Nostram, a historical figure that simply does not matter to us. The Isles, they are complacent. Maybe the gnomes are not; Spark remains fascinated with their magecraft. Morbatten, the tribal people here were too caught up in the natural to see or care about magic. They saw dragons and were satisfied. That is all changing now. Dar's vision includes archmages that would tremble Galthrest."

Ynt'taris moved to the side and took her back into the cavern. "My brother, he figured out how to use the runes to store the kinetic shift by type of energy. You see, in Galthrest's life, all he ever did was figure out how to copy it. The ranger, Bruce, his bow and arrows work this way. He can shoot them. He recalls them before they hit. Later, they can launch as if shot even from resting in his hand. Imagine if he could repeat a single arrow this way hundreds of times."

Alaura resumed her more relaxed position levitating in the globe of warmth. "I take it that no one else knows of *kinetic magic*?"

"Everyone knows. Taysor uses it in its weapons all the time. They just haven't taken it to the level my brother has. I have." Ynt'taris' eyes gleamed at her. "The sudden destructive release is my own special twist. We shall discuss *shift magic* at a later time. Shift enables you to take energy and alter its location. Teleportation and gates work similar to this but shift allows you do things with it energy of any kind that, I have found, bends the mortal mind."

The sage smiled and laughed. "That's wonderful, Ynt'taris! I've always expected you were actually the strongest of the three dragons."

"You flatter me, sage. Now, I shall teach you *kinetic magic*. Prepare yourself." The white patriarch humanshifted and began explaining the foundation to Alaura.

* * *

Back in Morbatten, Bomoki collapsed on the cot in his small cube of a stone room. Outside, he heard Alerius discussing the orange slime with Dar, Shak, and the chieftains. They were readying their armies even though Alerius had concerns. Exhaustion hit Bomoki and he stretched back while conjuring a cantrip that would clean his body and clothes. He missed nice taverns, fine beds, and the beautiful women that would join him in circumstances like this back in Taysor. *Still*, he mused, *Alerius knows things I must know.*

Bomoki awoke from napping to silence. He felt better. Teleporting taxed him. He had only learned the spell a year ago. "I've never cast it so quickly and under such pressure," he grumbled. "Food," he called out. Moments later, food appeared, carried by an invisible creature. The food helped him feel better and he walked out in the hallway just off the throne chamber. It tickled him that no one else saw these many tunnels branching off Alerius' throne. *Well, Dar Tania and the other dragons see them. Syliri, obviously. Those that the dragons want to know. I wonder if they see tunnels I can't?*, he wondered. A disturbing thought hit him, *What is here that I can't see at all?*

He turned deeper into the mountain and entered an alchemy lab that would make any of his Taysoran teachers envious. Stocked with everything, it also held those unseen servants that made it possible and easy for a single mage to work alone. So far, twenty-four of the required one hundred earth elementals were conjured and bound. Bomoki could tell Alerius grew impatient.

"Focus on *gate magic*," Bomoki grumbled. Pulling up his sleeves he began the conjuration of the next earth elemental. The first time had nearly broken his health. That was four years ago. Now, it bored him and he imagined what creature he might call when he first mastered gates. He went through the motions flawlessly while his mind pondered the orange slime wall, and gate magic. Gates were key. While the earth elemental rose up in the summoning circle before him, Bomoki thought about how gates allowed two-way travel and a level of negotiation not possible with summoning circles like this. His mouth moved mechanically through the contract by which the earth elemental would agree to be bound to two things: the roadways of Morbatten and a controlling artifact. Bomoki had never seen the artifact but its name, in draconian, growled from his mouth. The earth elementals always wanted the same thing: gemstone ore. Finished with number twenty-five, Bomoki sat down on a plush chair and spun about and said, "Somewhere in this mountain, Alerius has his own lab. It probably looks just like this one. I'm going to find it," Bomoki promised. "This is so boring."

He conjured the twenty-sixth while fantasizing about getting an apprentice to do this so he could focus on more important things. It was one of his tasks: find more mages. Yet, so far, no luck except for himself and Alaura. Thinking about the sage, Bomoki almost screamed at the unfairness. "I'm working through all these earth elementals, teleporting everyone everywhere, and she, whatever she does, is free of this menial labor!"

Dar Tania's people had tremendous aptitude for combat and faith; they made excellent paladin and priestess candidates. While most were gifted with intellectual acuity, they just did not care about magic. Complaining about it to Dar Tania once, she did not offer him any answers. "Some of the candidates you interview, Bomoki, they come to me later and say that you're asking them to become gods. We do not want to become gods. We want to serve the Mother." Her answer infuriated him. Even now, he blocked it from his recall.

Bomoki wandered through the mountain complex. Room after room presented itself to him, but he knew them all already. He looked for something else. Knowing Alerius, access would be by gates. He had seen the dragon use gates both in dragon and human form. He turned a corner and entered what he thought of as 'the dead end room.' Forming a large circular column wide and tall enough for Alerius to stand and flex his wings, it had to be this room. Alerius did not have the patience to walk this far in human form. *The throne room must connect to this one by a gate. There would be other gates, or maybe any gate could access many other similar locations*, Bomoki thought while looking around for the hundredth time. Taysoran magic could open magical doors but they lasted only briefly and were limited to line of sight. The size of the gate varied by the skill of the spellcaster. The size of the dragons' gates dwarfed the best of Taysor.

Bomoki sat down in the middle of the room and tried to calm his mind and open himself to seeing everything. From that state, though he had tried before and failed, he just might find the one thing he always missed finding so far. An unknown amount of time passed until the blue dragon patriarch, Spark, walked into the room. He usually ignored Bomoki. This time, however, Spark spoke to him. "Bomoki, the emperor wishes me to show you something new. Listen."

Always ready for sorcery, Bomoki withdrew his spellbook and prepared himself. Most of his spell training happened like this, when he did not expect it. Against the curved wall, Spark pressed his hand. Bomoki could not tell what made that part of the wall significant. Around Spark's hand, the wall faded back into an alcove. "Enter," the blue dragon said.

The alcove contained the beginning of a round disc made of carved stone. A stone bench and tools ran along two walls. The disc appeared made up of keystones. Rough cut stones lay in the general pattern of a diameter three times longer than Bomoki's height. A single stone sat in its place in the disc, finished. Compared to the rough stones around it, this stone gleamed brightly. Spark said, "Go ahead. This is a work in progress for many years now by the Court. It has gone faster of late with Dar assisting but Alerius wonders if you might have more aptitude for it. Dar completed that one a few days ago." Spark pointed to the finished keystone tile.

Bomoki tried to pick up the shield-sized rock and found it too heavy. He could barely tip it up on an edge. He summoned small blue circles of magic. The circles floated near the stone and Bomoki tipped it back onto them. They held its weight. Once there, the stone lifted up magically and floated. Bomoki's own reflection looked back at him from its polished surface. Flecks of gems peeked through the glossy surface. Everything about the stone suggested potential for power. "What is it?" he asked Spark as he ran his hand along the mirror smooth surface. The runes caught at his skin and he traced them, caressed them.

"It's going to be a gate. Not just any gate though. This one will actually shift people, gear, whatever through to a desired location. It will feel like teleportation, but be profoundly different... if it works. Did Taysor or Alerius instruct you about nexal travel?" Seeing Bomoki grow curious, Spark continued. "We live on Tehra and the Tehran universe. Merakor called this world and the space around it 'the prime material.' There are many planes and universes. Each is connected to those adjacent. However, a few of them serve as focal points, what Alerius named nexuses or *nexi*. When traveling the planes, you can move to adjacent ones, or you can move through a nexus and bypass many planes. Think of it as a shortcut. I'm disappointed you do not already know this."

Bomoki began asking questions, but Spark signaled for him to stop. "When you use a gate, you have to designate *which direction*. Unless you know where a gate opens to, you don't just go through it. Moreover, each gate has an aura that, when you know it, tells you which universe it opens to. You've seen other mages summon creatures through gates. Those creatures that come through such gates are either contracted to come through when called, or else are foolhardy. A gate that can go both ways is not a gate. It's a *shift*. This shift will be special when we're done with it. You see," Spark blinked and appeared in the center of the stones. He pointed his finger in a circle. "Each of these stones will be able to change, to flow, to attune to a nexal gate. It allows the user to treat this and the endpoint of their travel as if a nexal gate, rather than what it should actually be."

"I understand the short cut, but why does it matter to use the nexuses?" Bomoki asked. He had taken the quill and wrote his own notes now while another quill wrote Spark's words. It even noted where Spark was, the attitude of his human body, and sketched the layout of the gate. Bomoki wanted to capture every detail.

"Tehra is a nexus, you know. The Astral is adjacent to us. Have you travelled to the Astral?"

Bomoki said he had and added, "I did it in Taysor, but it was inelegant compared to when Alerius took me."

"Did you notice the difference in your magic?"

"Yes, I struggled to remember my daily spell studies. The spells Alerius had me cast, they felt novice level. I felt weak."

Spark nodded. "That's right. Had you gone from the Astral to another, that weakness would be magnified with each threshold crossed. Born of this world – this dominion, you grow weak when you leave it. The same happens when others come here. As powerful as they might seem to you, you are experiencing a fraction of how strong they would be in their own realm. Think about that for a moment."

Spark conjured an illusion of spheres. "This is a map we put together of the gates." Spark touched one. "This is us, the Tehran universe. This sphere is wrapped all about by the Astral, which is actually all the space between all the realms. This is the nexus of Creation, Chaos, and Warp. Taysor names these Good/Heaven, Chaos/Abyss, and Hell/Evil." He tapped the Hell sphere. "As you know, there are levels within hell. Your doctrine says there are nine, but there are actually more than that, enough that you cannot count them. Pha Rannic clerics did not want to actually find out so they called it nine levels. Only Asmodeus knows the exact number. Tell me, Bomoki, how would you visit Asmodeus?"

Bomoki pointed and wrapped the Tehran sphere in glowing faerie fire. "Starting here, I'd shift to the astral." Spark held up a finger. "Then, I'd go the Hell sphere, its nexus right?" Spark nodded and held up another finger. "I assume Asmodeus is not in the first level. So, I'd have to go through the nine, or however many levels to find him."

"Very good. So, let's say there are nine, plus the astral. By the time you got to Asmodeus, you'd be ten steps removed from Tehra."

"So, I'd be ten times weaker?" Bomoki asked.

"No, when you went to the Astral, you were ten times weaker. It's repeated each step. With each step, the weakness grows until you're so weak you can no longer move. You feel it as a massive weight pressing in on you from all directions. Asmodeus feels that too, when he comes here. The gods don't like that feeling. This is why they-"

"Use avatars! I get it now." Bomoki walked up to the illusion and said, "I'm going to guess that Asmodeus has a nexus of his own? So he can be far from the first level but closer to these other places?"

Spark beamed at the mage. "Yes! Asmodeus is a nexal god. So is Demos-Gorgos. So is Pha Rann. The gods controlling these particular universes, or throneplanes, are much stronger than the others. Unimaginably so."

Without pausing, Bomoki continued. "And you want to build a nexus." He pointed to the stone circle around them. "This will connect to the other nexuses directly. With this, from Tehra, you'd be able to move directly to Asmodeus, for example. Do I have this correct?" Bomoki blushed and began smiling when he saw Spark's wide smile of approval. "That's some shortcut."

"It still would count as a step, but it bypasses all the intermediary ones. This is called *shift magic*." Spark touched the rough stone. "I know you're still working on the earth elementals for my brother. If I help you, maybe you can skip that work and start your apprenticeship on this gate?" Spark's human form raised its eyebrow at Bomoki. They both knew Bomoki would jump at this. Spark was surprised to see Bomoki thinking it through. "Is there an issue?"

Bomoki shook his head, no. "I have been punished for skipping some of the assignments the god emperor gives to me. If I do this, he will know you, or at least know that someone helped me. And you haven't offered to help me before." Bomoki hoped he sounded more diplomatically curious than accusative.

Spark picked up a rough stone and carried it to the stone bench. "Alerius is fascinated by mortal magic. I have different interests."

Bomoki waited a few moments to see if Spark would say anything else. At last, he said, "Very well, Lord of Thunder, I accept. How do we get started?"

Spark smiled at him from over his shoulder. "It's already done. Come, you're my apprentice now. This work does require mortal magic." As the two bent over the first stone tile, Spark began to explain the basic principles of rune magic, but as it applied to gates.

Hours later, Alerius found them still deep in discussion. The god emperor smiled to see it. Spark had been waiting for a human mage to get to a point where such a discussion was even possible. Even with his mastery of human magic, Alerius could not – and doubted any eldar could – craft the gate to function as a bypass. Their transient nature in the River of Time's flow confounded fixed magic like this gate. The gate needed to be absolute, known, and unchanging. Alerius fixated on that word for a moment – *unchanging*. He interrupted them. "Brother, in our design, we must change it. Rather than something to last the ages, I wish to make it brittle and fragile. The gate shall serve our purposes, but we must guard our children. The gate must be destructible."

Spark's eyes flared a searing blue, something Bomoki noticed happened with the Lord of Thunder when he felt challenged in any way. The two patriarchs stood still and silent. This also happened a lot and Bomoki knew they conversed, but somewhere else. He had seen Dar and Sean do this as well. The inability of those not tied to Tiamat's religion or otherwise divinely blessed like Sean to access what Dar called The River, it drove Bomoki insane. Several times, he had almost approached Dar to convert. Each time, he had reminded himself that of several hundred paladins and priestesses, only ten had so far proven able to step out of the River's flow. Bomoki wondered what Spark and Alerius discussed and why destructibility mattered. Whenever the two patriarchs returned from their outside-of-Time discussion, Bomoki knew he would need to be ready. He put them out of his mind and studied the gate stones.

The finished stone tile and its draconian inscriptions had been laid out in a manner Bomoki had never seen before. In just this one tile, seven runes appeared to overlap. A large central rune dominated the tile. Bomoki read that one as being tied to a location. The locator rune then held six other runes. These much smaller ones stacked vertically with three on the left side and three on the right. The right side rune column sat lower than the left side. *It must be some kind of order*, he thought. The bottommost right side rune had a magic circle around it. Given the two dragons remained immobile, Bomoki enacted a spell cantrip to improve his vision. Magnified, he now saw the characteristic marks of a summoning circle recreated in microscopic detail around that final rune.

Lost in his study, the mage startled when Spark asked, "Bomoki, what do you see?"

"Masters, I see a locator rune. The six runes on either side are not known to me and unreadable, even with magic. The bottom right side is encircled by a summoning mark. I see an implication of order. Do the runes move from top to bottom or zig zag?" Bomoki touched and traced the runes across the locator. The central rune began to glow. It made Bomoki withdraw his hand quickly.

Alerius and Spark chuckled. The deep bass of it had a reptilian tremor and Bomoki felt just a tinge of dragonterror. "You have nothing to fear. Your guess about the locator is a good one. We name that the Tehran Nexus. Each of these," Alerius swept his hand around the circle of rough stone blanks, "needs a Tehran Nexus rune. The smaller runes will touch along the disc and thereby govern interaction with the actual nexal gates. In other words, we're going to trick the gate into thinking it's not here, but somewhere else. That's how the shift should work."

Bomoki's quill had resumed writing everything. "How will this connect to the actual nexuses?"

"Right now, it won't. We have not yet exactly figured that out yet but have a theory. That's part of the research and experiment you're in. Are you ready for this, Bomoki? This work will confine you to this lab for a very long time."

Bomoki grinned, "I'm sure it will be worth it, Masters." Bomoki bowed to each. "How do I begin?"

Spark gestured and the rough stone on the table began to glow with faerie fire. The purple light enwrapped the stone and then moved off. "First, we need to engrave the Locator rune in the center of each stone." The flames flickered to show the rune. "While doing this, there are spells that must be continually cast. The spells depend on the nature of the rune." Spark pointed to the finished one. "This is the nexus that is our world, Tehra. We need one for the prime nexi first: Creation, Chaos, and Warp. Here is what they each look like. Do you have a preference?"

Images of the nexi runes appeared in faerie fire. Bomoki thought that Warp looked easiest and so chose that one. Spark nodded. "To do this, you must continually cast spells related to evil as well as their opposites. The *detect evil* and *protection from evil* are easiest. Light and Dark are easy too but mess up the work area's lighting, and it's important you get these perfect. Unless you are casting these types of oppositional spells, you cannot work on the Warp nexxus rune. While continually keeping this opposition intact, the *stone shape* spell must be cast and you will hold this in your mind during the other castings. This will slow you down a lot. It took Alerius and I both twenty days to craft the Tehran stone with Dar's assistance."

Bomoki sighed. "Pace. You told me that time would always be the problem with creating magical devices."

Alerius smiled at Bomoki coldly. "I'm glad you remember, Bomoki. Though there are ways to go faster in this work, if you do not understand the foundation, you cannot use the faster methods. It will take you sixty days to do just Warp's locator symbol, the same amount of time it would have taken you to finish the earth elementals. Do this task well, and around your recovery of spells, we will begin discussing gates and summoned creatures." Alerius turned and walked out. The god emperor looked over his shoulder and was pleased to see Bomoki and Spark totally engrossed in the gate's work.

Spark pointed to the finished stone. "These smaller runes are important. They create a cascade of magic across the locator. This is how we are going to confuse and bypass the adjacent travel principle. You will be tempted to remove material from the stone. Do not. Craft and sink the Locator but do not touch any of the material around it."

The glowing light of the locator symbol for Warp moved and fell to the rough stone on the bench. "Also, Bomoki, some of these are quite powerful. For example, Asmodeus controls Warp. Images, voices, phantasms may come to while working on this. Ignore them. Remember, the goal is to allow us to bypass the steps required to travel from here to other realms. Any questions?"

Spark began rearranging the laboratory to provide everything Bomoki would need for sleep, food, bathing, and servants to attend to his needs. Bomoki ran his fingers through his hair and watched it all. "What did the voices say to you when you did the Tehran stone?"

Spark paused in his spellcraft for a moment and replied. "The Tehran god, Krentismar, wanted to know why we were doing this. He told me it was dangerous. He tried to see what we were doing. I blocked him out. I serve only Tiamat. Though, he must have gotten through to Alerius and that's why we will make this gate very fragile. It makes sense. Imagine if Asmodeus came through our shift to this world?"

Bomoki rolled up his sleeves and began to work.

* * *

Bruce and Syliri moved cautiously, but quickly, over the increasingly barren terrain. Acrid steam from the geysers and hot springs in the sunken ground ahead stung Bruce's eyes. More than a few times, he slipped on the glossy rock. The strange mold and slimes usually growing here were noticeably absent. "I wonder if it was like a wave or if all the slime just pulled together into a blob," Bruce muttered as he slipped for what felt like the hundredth time. ***

Syliri picked her way carefully along behind him, watching his steps, and avoiding the slippery spots. "I could just carry you. Heat, acid, it doesn't bother me."

Bruce stopped and grinned at her over his shoulder. "Where's the fun in that? Sure, we could also get Amulets or Potions of Flight and skip all this stuff, but I like the natural world. It's slippery." He splashed some water at her. "And wet. This is my realm."

They continued for another hour. Syliri detected nothing but remained vigilant with all of her senses. Bruce signaled for her to stop. Not just stop, but freeze. Slowly, he crouched down. This had happened so many times in their years together that Syliri no longer questioned it. Her body automatically obeyed. *What caught his attention?,* she wondered. It was always something, like the hill giants weeks ago. One time, it was a rocky slope about to give way to a rockslide. Bruce had used the rockslide later to crush a pack of fiends chasing them. He reached back and beckoned her forward, slowly.

Syliri came up to the stone's edge and, like Bruce, turned her head sideways to look over it. A series of ledges dropped here giving them a clear view of the large hole full of rainbow-hued stone and plumes of steam. Boiling water in the cold air filled the depression with mist, but a gentle wind cleared it every so often. "You see it?" Bruce whispered.

She strained her eyes and did. The mist cleared and she saw a demonic creature lounging in a pool of acid. Black and grey mottled skin, somewhat like a dragon's, covered a lanky and angular body. Behind its gaunt shoulders, wings edged with bone spikes lay folded and draped. The wings appeared like a cloak. The creature's face, skeletal and stretched, where not extruding fang-like spikes, had been pierced by gold rings draping golden chains across his torso and head. Syliri guessed the creature might stand three men tall. "So, that's Ylgolth."

"Seems like it," Bruce replied. "You see the other thing too, to his right side and along the shoreline?"

She tried to follow his directions and then, there it was. Colored like the rocks, she nearly missed it. *How did Bruce immediately see this? While walking?* He'd been teaching her for five years to be a ranger, improve her archery, and navigate terrain like he did. *He does it so easily.* She realized that focusing on the creature automatically distracted her vision to the side as some type of magical repulsion.

As if reading her mind, Bruce whispered. "Unnatural creatures, those that don't belong here, they confuse the senses. I didn't see it at first. Ylgolth is so obvious. If you focus on him though, he'll become confused in your thoughts too. I think that's a chaos fiend or something similar to it. Whatever it is, it's warping everything around it. The result is accidental camouflage."

Syliri slipped down by Bruce and laid back to look at the sky. "A chaos fiend," she questioned. Bruce eyed from just over the rocks. In Tehra, Chaos with a capital "C" was always bad. It allowed Abyssal energies to warp the created and well-organized matter of the Tehran universe. Before being bound, Set did this to all Eldar he encountered. Anything they created, Set twisted into gibbering masses of mouths, eyes, and bleeding tissue. The creatures could only survive by feeding, or by having support from a powerful source of magic. Even magic unraveled eventually in their presence. They ate the unravelling. Syliri shuddered feeling too close to something not just fatal, but that could decompose her into oblivion itself.

Something felt wrong though. It was not just the strange creature or the lanky and bone-spiked form of Ylgolth. A single white cloud slowly moved to intersect the sun. She looked at Bruce, wanting to touch him and see if he was real, but dreaded he would not be. "Bruce, this feels wrong. If we were this close to a chaos fiend, it'd already be attacking us…"

No sooner had she said this than a solid form obscured the sun shining down on her face. The form twisted and a chittering sound along with teeth biting filled the area around her. Syliri's skin, her mind, everything went cold and frozen in that instant. Under her hands, the wet rocks began to move as if she held a wet writhing snake, or a handful of large worms. The cloud, so idyllic a moment before, became monstrous as white wings unfolded and a dragon twisted to dive at something nearby. Dragonterror and anxiety pulled at her heart, which began to race until she could feel her pulse in her eye teeth.

She looked at Bruce. Ylgolth sat where Bruce had been. The grey slaad leered at her, "I've never been with a medusa before. Your spawn could begin at the Azuros level. Imagine the pleasure of your motherhood!"

Syliri shook her head and reached out her hand to Ylgolth. *Bruce will be here. It will be Bruce*, she said the mantra in her mind over and over. *Bruce has not left me. This is a nightmare.* She remembered the horror of the time she spent in Set's Dream. It had taken too much time to destroy the maedar. She knew if she went back into that dark place, it would ruin everything she had spent her life building. She remembered Hrax and the golden dream of being all the things she was not.

The stone under her body erupted in cockroaches, their spikey legs digging into her skin as they swarmed all over her. *My beautiful human skin*, she wailed. *If this is Ylgolth and I touch Ylgolth...* Not-Ylgolth caught her hand. "Syl?" Bruce whispered. "Syl? It's me. It's okay."

With a gasp, she fell into Bruce's arms. "Oh Bruce, I'm so sorry." Syliri wept and hugged him tightly enough that he had to push her back so he could breathe. "Such terrible things, we need to leave. Now!" She scooted along the ground, pulling him back towards Morbatten.

"Shhh. There, there," Bruce whispered. He pulled her close and kissed her head. The snakes struggled free of her hair ties and attacked, but he ignored them. He flicked one away. "Not now Kelly, I need to be here for Syl." His skin felt hot and he pulled her up onto him as his kissing grew more urgent and forceful.

Syliri tried to pull back. "Bruce, not now. It's too dangerous."

"We're fine," Bruce mumbled into her neck. It bothered Syliri that her snakes continued to attack him; they never had before. A tiny voice in the back of her mind suggested they would not attack Bruce. As if reading her concern, Bruce kissed up her neck lightly and said, "We're close enough that everything is affected by Set's Dream, even the snakes. It's not their fault. As a ranger, I'm not affected hardly at all. Besides, it's not like this is any different than Hrax. What happened with him anyways?"

Syliri pushed back from Bruce. "Do you really want to know?" she asked. When he nodded, she said, "He was executed."

"I thought that must be case," Bruce sighed. "Why not just leave him petrified, my dear? Unfreeze him when you needed him. I rather hoped he might still be alive. He knows things."

The words, spoken in Bruce's voice, sounded so normal, but his use of "my dear" – that term, it was not something she ever heard him say. He would never ask her to unfreeze anyone. He knew it was dangerous to her. Syliri struggled to hold her composure because, just like that, she felt unsure of Bruce again. "Why unfortunate? I mean, it's just a slaad right? Alive, petrified, you'd be okay with that?"

Expecting moralizing, Syliri flinched inside when Bruce said, "He has things in his brain that would be useful. Even if dead, maybe we could revive him. What do you think, Syl?"

Her nickname, only Bruce called her that, reassured her. At the same time, the focus on brains, also a new thing for Bruce, brought her even more discomfort. *I need to test this*, she thought. *Set's Dream could be messing with us both.* She leaned forward and, struggling to remain quiet, Syliri bit Bruce's ear and said, "Tell me, I want to hear it, why do you love a monster like me?"

"Okay okay, but shhhh. We don't want Ylgolth or his son to detect us." Bruce flipped her over. "I love you."

She did not like being underneath Bruce in this place; too many worries edged her thoughts. His words, they went backwards in time and suddenly, Syliri knew. Bruce always ignored her question and simply stated the truth of his feelings, that he loved her. The reference to "Ylgolth or his son" confirmed it.

This is not Bruce, she thought. Fear and concern for Bruce flooded her and she had to exert extreme care to keep her snakes calm. Their biting at Bruce made sense now. *It's not Bruce; it's Ylgolth probably.* Too scared to open her eyes, Syliri moved to get out from under Bruce. He wrapped his arms around her and tried to prevent her and they fell to the side. Trained by Hrax, Syliri noted how brightly the emerald ring flared on her hand. In some ways, the green light felt like the only real thing. Everything else, even Bruce's touch, had a delusional quality to it.

On her side, and with Bruce caressing her cheek, Syliri broke his embrace and pushed back. "How do you know that's Ylgolth's son?" She tried to sound curious and teachable, but all she wanted was to run away. In her mind, already, the eldar nightmare of the maedar and how her sisters fell into slavery flashed image after image. She wanted to run but could not move.

Bruce reached up to caress her and swatted the cobra aside. In that moment, Syliri prayed it would be okay, that her Bruce would touch her and end the nightmare. The moment passed as iron muscles slammed her down and back against the stone ground. "Because, he is my son. You've been in my dream this entire time." Bruce's voice growled at her and dared her to resist. Iron arms held her down. "Since Hrax is dead, I will have to know what you know. Don't worry," Ylgolth said from Bruce's mouth. "This is only going to hurt beyond any pain you've ever felt." All around them, the dream changed and enhanced Syliri's ability to sense pain. Ylgolth's hand around her throat became spiked with needles. Ylgolth's other hand sprouted a transformant worm. Like a snake, it lashed out towards Syliri. Her own hair snakes batted it aside.

Syliri called on Set and threw her private hell at Ylgolth. She wondered, for a moment, if her power in Set would be strong enough. The Dream worked like eldar will. Her own self-doubt could undo her. She felt Ylgolth match her will. The Dream around them quivered and began to petrify and then Ylgolth reasserted his control. All of it focused against Syliri as Ylgolth sacrificed wide area control to strengthen and protect himself. "You're not just another medusa," Ylgolth spat in her face.

"But you're just another dead slaad," Syliri intoned as her entire face began to pull Ylgolth into petrification. "Either now, or later when you face my mistress!"

Ylgolth's wings swept up to block her gaze. When the wings petrified, Ylgolth tore one free and draped it over her. His other hand grabbed his transformant and punched it into Syliri's bowels. "Petrification is so basic," Ylgolth said as her gaze power ended. Already nestling into her bleeding entrails, the worm sapped at her will. "I can see why Hrax liked you," Ylgolth said as the first touch of Syliri's memories became available to him via the worm.

Set's Dream made the pain exquisite, every bit as seductive as Bruce's seduction just moments before Syliri realized the truth. As Ylgolth moved forward to bite into her head, Syliri embraced the nightmare in her that is the medusa version of Set's Dream. Its power allowed her to meld her body backwards into the stone. Ylgolth-as-Bruce slammed his face against the rock and howled. The worm twisting in her would have to wait. Syliri knew she could stay and fight Ylgolth with a slim chance of winning, or save Bruce. The only good option was to return to the armored mage, her friend, as fast as possible. Maybe the Queen could undo this? Only she could save them both from this level of power. With regret, she remembered how mundane the Fecundus' capture had been. *I should have paid more attention*, she chastised herself. The stone's embrace all around her melded form felt safer and masked the pain in her mid-section.

Ylgolth leapt to his feet and spread his arms wide. Set's Dream came crashing down on Syliri for the second time in her eldar existence. The rock did not protect her from the Dream and she felt its power gnawing away at her body and will, augmented by the infection in her. From within, the transformant worm began chewing upwards, looking for her, calling to her, "Mother…" She only wanted to find out what had happened to Bruce, but horrid images assaulted her mind. Once Ylgolth figured out what happened, Syliri knew: *he'll take me, finish me, and my dying body will unleash a horde of Slaadi on Morbatten.*

Through the stone, Ylgolth's voice reached her by the power of the Dream. "I've already marked your Bruce. He's weak. He'll spawn transformants, if he's lucky. They'll be weak. Nothing like what you will bring forth." Ylgolth's lust breathed out at Syliri and the stone began to reject her. "Just a taste, Syliri! It can be so much more than this! You could be my queen, my endless queen. Our endless children would rule as kings of the world without end!"

Syliri knew her time was running out. *Bruce! I'm so sorry! I'll come back for you, I promise!* Within the stone, she morphed into her titanic gorgona form to speed her passage through the rock. Even merged with the stone, she felt hands trying to pull her back to Ylgolth. Without the ring to strengthen her will and remind her that the Dream was just a vivid hallucination, she would no doubt be groveling before Ylgolth, willing to do anything to save Bruce. *Thank you, my Queen. Thank you for saving me from this. I never thought anything could be worse than the maedar.* Following Queen Alaura's, really Alerius', guidance, Syliri bent the Dream and asserted enough control to make Ylgolth think she was coming to back to him. She escaped.

Sensing her escape, Ylgolth sent one last cruel image to her mind. A naked Bruce, his body laying one side, sat naked under the Chaos Fiend Ylgolth called his son. Cruel talon claws marred his torso with deep bleeding wounds. His jaw, broken, jerked side to side as he convulsed. Behind her, Ylgolth screamed into the sky, "Run Syliri! Run! Tell your masters that Ylgolth the Violator has filled you with Azuros!" Malicious laughter chorused the dream around her and continued long after she burst from the rock and raced north. She could not help herself. Her hands cradled the wound in her belly and wept. She could feel the worm in her. She could hear its busy teeth. Echoes of her desires to have a child with Bruce mocked her as the Dream shifted her despair to Slaadi eating her from the inside out.

For the second time in her long life, Syliri prayed to Tiamat for help and wondered if, this time, the Goddess would answer. Dar Tania came to mind and a glimmer of hope filled her heart. *Even if the Queen does not, Dar very well may.*

* * *

Ylgolth grinned wickedly at the medusa's flight. Buried so deeply in Set's Dream, she could run forever. Ylgolth screamed out after her, twisting his words to hiss at her the way a cat might at a mouse. "Show me your master. Tell him that I come to spoil all that is his!"

Next to him, the human's body jerked and thrashed as the chaos nightmare of drooling mouths and tentacle tongues chewed away at Bruce's body and soul. It took a considerable amount of focus to keep the fiend on task. "Ruin his mind, my pet," Ylgolth said reassuringly. "Just his mind." The human proved surprisingly resilient. The goblins immediately fell into Set's Dream; most creatures did. An echo in Ylgolth's mind, this human – naming himself Bruce – questioned everything: *This isn't real. That was a rock before. That's sunlight not fire. I've been captured and this is a spell. Stupid mages.* The glimmers of Bruce's real thoughts amused Ylgolth.

So long as the human held onto his fragile thread of continuity between what had been real and what his senses now screamed at him, he'd remain resilient. Ylgolth patted Bruce on the head. "It doesn't matter. You all fall. Even if you don't," Ylgolth let Bruce hear his real words. "Even if you resist this till the end, your flesh will give way to a swarm of transformants. Think of them as worms with teeth, eating into your muscles. They'll start with your feet and save your major blood routes, heart, lungs, and brain for last. Your agony, it will allow them to feed on your very soul. You'll arise scattered amongst hundreds of new consciousnesses, all linked to your brain as they feed – as you feed on yourself. Can you imagine the glory of this gift? Set must love you very much. Also, the woman you love, the medusa, she is infected too and will spawn many Azuros. You killed Hrax, my new Azuros. And so, I kill you in his name. I took your woman in his name. We'll talk again, soon. I'm going to offer you an end to this agony then. Start thinking about it. Until then, enjoy this gift..."

Bruce's mind had latched on to Ylgolth's voice. It reminded him of Hrax. The words, terrible as they were, reassured him that he still lived. Everything he saw, it could be dismissed. None of it was part of the natural world. Ylgolth's words about Syliri were almost too much. *When did I fall to this beast?*, he wondered.
It was when I slipped. That had to be it. I slipped on a stupid rock! I never slip. He remembered thinking that and instants later, he detected Ylgolth.

Page 184

Try as he might, he could not remember anything after that. *Why can't I move?*, he wondered.

Syliri had shown him Set's Dream, in Alerius' cave, with Dar Tania years ago. It helped. He knew this was not real. The blunt talon cuts that tore his skin, his broken jaw where Ylgolth had grabbed and then dragged him by his mouth, those hurt. Those were real. Bruce focused on Ylgolth's words, the only words that mattered – *And Syliri got away!*

The first image of Syliri's embracing Ylgolth filled his mind then, by Ylgolth's command. The duality of Ylgolth's cruel pleasure and Syliri's careful love began to shred his sanity. He knew Syliri would never betray him. *Even if*, she would not consummate a relationship with a slaad. He knew from Hrax that she would not. Sounds, touch sensations, and the things he loved best about Syliri began to assault him now, twisted by Ylgolth's dream.

Through Ylgolth's dream, Bruce felt something bite his right shoulder. A cold yet burning sensation spread from there. In the power of Set, Bruce saw himself out-of-body. He saw the chaos creature reach down with a mouthed tentacle and bite his shoulder. He noted the flesh around the bite pulse like candle wax melting. By the time the tentacle withdrew, the beginning of an eye slit appeared and then scales appeared, one by one around it. The Dream amplified the horror of his body's ruin. He begged for it to stop. "I'll do anything! Save her, please god!"

Ylgolth patted him on the head. "There is no god above Set." With each word, Ylgolth stabbed his fingers into Bruce's right shoulder. When he was done, bleeding holes made a spiral pattern. "Set is All. For Set, I take all that is mine – you are mine – and more."

The images in Syliri and Bruce's mind of a female power behind the armored mage bothered him though. "I've never heard of an Antramenti or any other Anthracos taking a female form. Still, her servant mage defied me. Is there an Antramenti here?" The thought bothered Ylgolth. His mission here had started so simply. Hrax had found gold. The Slaadi needed gold to hold enchantments as they moved between realms. "Confronting another Anthracos without my own children here... it's suicide." Still, Ylgolth felt that he must learn more. His own master required it.

* * *

Dar Tania stood at the head of Morbatten's army. Soon, the Battle of Crossing would commence. Her knights and priestesses stood in position around her. Sean, gleaming in his Pha Rannic armor, looked like a miniature sun moving about the lines. His radiance hurt her eyes and Dar wondered if Sean saw her the same way. Her halo of fire burned brightly all around. She felt regal and all-powerful in this moment. Their daughter's aura occasionally touched her own and streaks of silver and gold inflected throughout her own body's aura. She sensed the paladins around her notice but none mentioned it.

Shak stood behind her. Thinking about him, she felt immediately chastised by Alerius' words. She took little comfort from her time with Sean, knowing and dreading all the days it took before Alerius finally said the words she knew must be said. At face value, things worked out. For the future, she remembered the vision of herself in the Valley of Ancients. She would have just one child with Sean; his words of returning to his vows lingered in her mind. She shrugged the feeling aside while watching Sean speak to the fighters. *I will not regret being with the one I love,* she vowed in her heart. Again, she felt chastised. Unbidden, the image of Sean's death flashed into her mind.

She watched Shak berate the fighters. Their job was to rain arrows into battle, but they wanted to charge in with sword and shield. Though her people had armor now, and better weapons, the bulk of their army remained tribal. They did not like standing in units. The chieftains did not like their tribes being stacked into archery, sword, and cavalry units outside of the tribal boundaries of blood relationships. Shak looked so handsome.

Shak, the only paladin of the hundred to access the River and draw an avenging firesword, shifted back and forth on his feet. His armor, a contrast to Sean's polished set, showed dragons in bas-relief and framed each section etched in gold draconian script. Shak's candidate knight, Otor Ven, stood to his side. Craning her head back to look at them, Dar smiled. She did not understand why, but whenever she did this, the paladins cheered. This time, their cheering held an edge. Takhissis whispered to them of war.

"Paladin Shak D'Rath," she said, her voice loud and clear. "You are clear on your instructions?" She heard him slam into formal stance.

"Yes, Dar Tania! All is ready! We will not fail Tiamat or your trust in us!"

Her pregnancy chose that moment to make her queasy. She prayed and it alleviated enough, for now. "I do not require assurance of trust. Tiamat requires victory. A simple 'yes' will work in the future. Do you understand?" The older priestesses, who had been midwives before, had told her she might feel bouts of emotion early in the pregnancy.

Shak and Otor cried out, "Yes, Dar Tania!" At their response, all the others joined in, shouting 'Yes!' until even the soldiers to their sides joined.

To the paladins, Dar winked and said, "We haven't even started combat and here I am barking at you all like a pregnant dog."

It worked. They all held her in too close to the same regard they gave the god emperor. She unclasped the gold and steel emblem of Tiamat handing at her throat. She lifted it high so they all could see. "I pray to Tiamat for you, for us all. Let the burning fires of Her Might fill our hearts and lead us to glory!"

The rubies in the emblem sparkled in the sun. As one, the group took a deep breath and felt tension ease. The coming anticipation of battle filled them, not with dread, but with divine strength. Across the gentle valley, the trees shuddered as the orange muck approached the Cordabad River.

Barely visible at first, once it came into the open, the orange slime pulled itself towards the river so slowly but inevitably. At the water's edge, tendrils began to arc across the flowing water. Dar signaled. From behind them, forty catapults launched barrels of oil. The barrels smashed into the arms, along both sides of the river, and upstream. The ooze retreated and then, sensing nothing in the attack, it reached out to cross the river again. Reloaded, the catapults fired again.

"Shak, charge." Dar's words, spoken quietly enough that only Shak could hear, galvanized the young knight.

Shak, alone, charged forward to the ooze. When he was halfway between the army and the river, Dar called out more loudly. "The rest of you, forward!"

100 paladins and 400 priestesses advanced down the hill. Seeing their attack begin, Sean ordered the archers to fire. Hundreds of flaming arrows arced up and fell towards the ooze. Pools of oil ignited, and then the river ignited underneath the orange blob. With half its mass on either side, the ooze pulled itself towards them even while burning in half. The third rain of barrels began to fall, and then Shak's sword cut into a tendril anchoring the creature on Dar's side of the river.

Dar prayed and a tornado of fire exploded around Shak. The heat and shockwave of the flamestrike ignited unbroken barrels stuck in the ooze. Though the slime reached out to attack the burning paladin, its mass burned away within three steps of Shak.

Shak sprinted about, the flamestrike centered on him, as Dar exited the River. From the ethereal, she poured her prayers, faith, and – after a pause – hope for her child's future into the vortex of flames. Where Shak went, the ooze broke apart. Dar became aware that Shak regarded her from the River's banks. He mouthed to her, "I will always love and serve you, my Dar." He fell back into Time's flow.

The first wave of paladin initiates hit the orange wall. The priestesses behind them blessed the paladins with resistance to the oil fires raging all around. Some of the tribal witches were strong enough to call a flamestrike and blasted these at tendrils coming across the river. Compared to Dar's, the fires from this group looked dim, barely noticeable in the sunlight. Yet, it protected them from the slime creature and the burning oil, which turned the battlefield into hell. Dar blinked tears from her eyes; she had not been ready to hear Shak in a time like this.

Singing a hymn of flame, Dar's bright alto voice uplifted into a yell for Takhissis to drench the battle in fire. The vortex of fire dancing around Shak split apart to protect the paladins around him. Dar reached down in the flowing current of Time and cradled the moment of Shak's words. "I honor you too, brave knight."

Below Dar, the battle raged along the shores of the Cordabad River. The burning oil, the flamestrikes, the paladins, and the continual volley of catapulted oil and burning arrows seemed a level of carnage that, by itself, might win the day. Sean ordered another archer volley, "Target the tendrils on our side! Catapults, re-target: the trees on the other side of the river. Raze them all!"

The siege engineers, wearing only loincloths, heaved the wheels of twenty catapults forward. Stronger ropes to increase distance snaked up through the pulleys. Logistics teams, mostly made up of older men and women who wanted to help, passed burning pitch forward to the siege machines. Sean felt a surreal moment of paused time watching the quiet efficiency of the crews. Everyone wanted to help. Sure, those deemed by Dar Tania to be too old to fight had their feelings hurt. Unlike Taysor though, they choked it back and worked as one in the support units. Even the tribal chieftains and their fighters, whom Dar had ordered to stay as the third reinforcement wave, they ignited their next volley and took aim. Some of these, Sean knew, hated him. Most hated or at least felt lost in confusion that Dar had become their ruler overnight.

The moment passed when a flash of heat washed over them. Burning white hot, brighter than the sun, Shak's flamestrike arced up thousands of feet into the sky. The chieftains, about to let loose their volley, paused. As the column of fire rose up, dragon wings and an image of the god emperor seemed to rise up from the fire and then burst apart. A rain of fire fell all around the battlefield. Sean pointed to Dar and cried out to the fighters, "Behold! Your priestess!"

Dar knelt on a hilltop to their left. Her hands up towards the sky, she prayed. Sean could imagine the song she must giving voice to. "Men of Tania! Lend her faith. Join in her song! You know it!"

The younger fighters and the siege crews began first, their song becoming brighter and stronger as more and more voices joined in. Sean knew the song and even he wanted to join. From their position, they watched drops of fire fall and ignite the stones and boil the river.

"Fighters! Draw sword!" Sean ordered. Behind him, a thousand swords jumped from their sheaths. Sean waited for the fire to end, marveling at its magnitude. Taysor had stories of firestorm spells like this but not from a cleric as young as Dar. The instant the fire ended, Sean screamed, "Charge!"

Sean's white stallion whinnied and then raced down the hill. Pitch arced, over their heads to explode amidst the trees on the far side of the Cordabad. Amidst the fire and smoke, Sean noted the wall charred with gaping holes. It shuddered and began to break apart. From the fragments, hill giants and goblins with an unhealthy orange cast to them rose up and began to attack. In their center, a hill giant hag stood, untouched by the flames all around. She cackled and pointed to the shuddering forms rising up out of the ooze. *No*, Sean realized. *This must the witch lady Fist of Graves described, this is Evil.* Her aura seethed. *She's raising the dead that were entombed in the ooze.*

Sean aimed for the witch. He figured, given the Slaadi's backing of this attack, that she would prove herself an unusually gifted hill giant witch, a slaad, or a demon. A priestess healed caustic blisters covering the skin of a young paladin as he fought a small pack of goblins. Sean's holy steed jumped over their heads and kicked one of the goblins. It fell dead. "Protect the third wave!" Sean shouted at her. Without divine aid, the normal fighters would burn to death in this battlefield. She nodded and signaled to the priestesses around her. As one, they blessed the fighters with resistance to heat and fire.

By the time the giant witch noticed Sean, Morbatten's line of combat reformed before a line of sick-looking hill giants and goblins. As the third wave charged into and through this line, and to the hag's dismay, the Set-controlled mold zombies fell to pieces, cut and severed by blade and cauterized by fire. The third wave cut and pushed and then dropped to their knees with shields raised. The paladins and priestesses advanced at charge, leaping over the third wave amidst blast of fire and slashing metal. While the Set zombies did not retreat, they fell.

Dar continued her firestorm prayer focussing on Shak D'Rath. She noticed Lilli take the hand of a small priestess child, and together they walked forward across Morbatten's battle line. Both held medallions of Tiamat in their hands and, while singing to Tiamat, wherever they pointed, the zombies fell apart into mounds of inert slime.

Sean studied the witch, looking for how to best attack. She held a gnarled staff and pointed it to and fro. Reanimating magic lurched the fallen giants back to life. It pulled cut arms and amputated legs together into mounds of flesh that returned to combat. A small wall of ooze formed around her. Still a hundred paces away, Sean saw Shak drive forward with three other paladins. He almost cut his way through to the giantess, but her staff struck him square in the chest. The blow smashed him back into the three and they fell to the ground. A small but visible shockwave from the hit helped Sean bury his thoughts that it might be just a giant.

Sean recognized Otor through the haze of battle. The young knight threw his shield on the wet slime and used it as a step to jump at the witch. Sean imagined he could hear Otor's prayer to Tiamat. As Otor stabbed into the witch's face, his sword ignited in dragonfire. The smile of pride on Otor's face, the look of joyous surprise by the paladins all around, turned to horror as the giantess turned and caught the blade sideways in her teeth. Chomping down on the blade, Sean saw her face blister, but she shook her head side to side and threw Otor into the air just as her staff hit his body. The young paladin, the second to draw an avenging blade went flying askew to smash into the rocky ground and bounce into the burning river. Otor's sword's fire extinguished.

Sean called to Pha Rann as his charger jumped the wall. His sword, igniting in a halo of noonday light, sliced down at the staff. "Pha Rann, let thy truth be seen by all!"

Before him, the hill giantess' form melted to reveal a lanky and twisted form of too-long arms and legs. The creature had a sense of looking female but what might have been hair revealed itself as fleshy growths from its head and back. Rows of fanged teeth and wart-like protrusions of pink boils from which hair grew made Sean ill. A head-shaped mound, adjacent to her bent-forward neck, writhed as if something were trapped inside, trying to escape. "I've never fought a hag before," Sean yelled while slashing towards her head. Just as he anticipated a clean decapitation, the hag ducked and struck at his horse with her staff. Long claws full of decaying flesh and gore swiped at his horse but slammed instead into the horse's armor. Still, the blow threw them both aside. Sean dismounted mid-air and rolled to his feet. His steed, trained for this, landed and moved to flank the hag.

"You wish to see truth?" the hag cackled. "Behold Ylgolth's Dream!"

At her words, Sean and every fighter who heard her bellowing cry felt their weapons twist and writhe in their hands. Serpents of many fangs bit and spat poison at them. The ground upheaved and vertigo raged. Many of the newer fighters fell to the ground or tossed their weapons aside.

Sean closed his eyes and prayed to Pha Rann. "I reject you." His calm words belied the concentration in his face. He stepped forward and slashed side to side. The hag dodged back and, thinking he left his head undefended, she slammed her hand down to crush the tiny human. Sean's sword cut up and severed her forearm. Shrieking, she kicked out and slammed the heel of her foot into his breastplate. The kick knocked Sean back into the orange wall of slime protecting the hag.

The fell creature raised her other hand, black lightning crackling around it. The wound of her severed hand had already closed. The first talon of a fingernail regrew in its stump. Soon, she would be whole again. Sean blinked, trying to clear the mist of spores from his eyes. Though his divine halo kept him safe, charred dust rained down around him. He whistled and heard his charger attack the hag. The sound of evil magic rose up before him and he knew he had just a short time left.

From just outside the wall, Shak regained his feet. He saw the hag transform and smash the Commander. Shak focused and, calming his mind, stepped out of the River. In this altered place, the hag loomed large and disgusting over Sean, who glowed like an angel. Shak had never seen the Commander this way. A hint of wings around Sean in the ooze, which looked black and oily here, struggled to break free. The hag's amputated hand showed a phantasm as energy from the River rose up and regenerated it. Sean's horse reared up, steadied by wings. Here, it looked like a pegasus. Shak looked at himself and saw the darkly-shadowed fire of his own aura: no wings, no bright halo. He felt a moment of envy and then the hag raised her hand. Grey energy swirled up from the River into her palm. She would attack Sean at any moment. Sean's words echoed in the ethereal. "I reject you."

Without thinking, Shak charged at her against the River's current. Those fighting alongside Shak stumbled as Shak moved so quickly they lost their hold and balance on him. They knew he attacked the hag and turned their heads just in time to see the young Tanian jump onto the hag's spell fist. Shak cried out, "I reject you!"

The blast that should have struck Sean, struck Shak instead. It seemed he might retain his hold and then the vile spell detonated. Shak rose up and tumbled head over heels into the air. The hag's arm disintegrated to a brown bone spike bleeding marrow and maggots onto the stony ground. The explosion obliterated the ooze wall. All around, paladins took cover under their shields, and then charged forward.

Sean's steed steadied itself against the explosion and drove forward to pummel with its hooves. It rocked the hag, who turned and bit at the horse. Her jaws of cracked and stained teeth, elongated like a snake's, clamped down on the horse and swallowed its head. Blood fountained around its neck as the body collapsed in rigor mortis. The hag spit the decapitated head at Sean who had finally regained his footing.

Sean, like Shak, moved out of the River's flow and attacked the hag from outside of Time. A blinding streak of attacks and counter-attacks accelerated with the hag somehow keeping pace. Her other hand, regenerated now, used her staff to block and parry. With each blow, Sean recovered and charged at her.

A chieftain, just arriving at the scene, tried to watch and then waded into the combat with sword swinging. The hag blasted him backwards with a sweep of her arm. The chieftain's sword broke against her skin. With crunching bones, his chest collapsed and he fell dead. Other fighters attempting to enter the battle, retreated when they saw the chief fall. Priestesses advanced forward in a ring around the paladins' fight against the hag. A priestess prayed over the chief, but said, "Only Dar can save him. He is beyond my faith."

Advancing down the ridge and careful to keep her arms lifted to heaven, Dar healed a wounded paladin and said, "Help me walk. I'm exhausted." They stumbled towards the combat. "Hurry. We are running out of time." Her arms shook from fatigue and the paladin held her right arm as a priestess took the other. Her firestorm long since spent, smaller flamestrikes spiraled about Shak and Otor, but she had to keep them away from Sean. "I never thought holding my arms up would be so hard."

"The Commander has us do this early in our testing, for those of us who value strength over stamina. You're doing great, high priestess." The paladin's worshipful tone caught Dar's attention. She made a mental note to learn his name and remind his class later that glory goes to Tiamat.

Sean slashed and stabbed at the creature, amazed she countered him. His earlier assessment that the hill giant must be a hag quickly upgraded to what Taysor called a 'night hag'. These shape-altering creatures of the Abyss gravitated to conflict and strife. With a grey slaad present, it made sense. Possessing supernatural strength, resistant to elements and magic, their only hope would be in brutal combat. Sean dodged a staff attack and remembered that Alerius did not yet have a night hag in his collection.

Smiling grimly, Sean uplifted his heart in prayer and redoubled his efforts. No matter what he tried, he could not get a clean attack in unless the hag was distracted. Shak had saved his life. He knew it. Even if he survived the *disintegration* spell attack, Pha Rann whispered in his heart that he owed Shak D'Rath. His horse had saved him too. So close to ascending as a Pegasus, it hurt Sean and he blocked it from his mind. It had not been his intent to fight Tania's battles. Watching the hag block his own attacks while felling any paladins that got within range, Sean realized, *A night hag is a worthy foe, a mighty death.* He shook his head. *It is not your time to die, Sean. You have a daughter to look forward to.*

He unleashed a furious series of blows designed to open the hag's left flank. Just when Sean thought he had a clean stab, the hag's other arm regenerated and caught his sword blade. Ignoring the fire, the hag lunged forward and head-butted him. In that moment, he felt something pierce the armor over his heart.

Sean's soul sang out to Pha Rann and he drove his blade down into the hag's neck. Searing cold agony pierced his sternum. He felt himself tumbling backwards, and caught the hag's hand still at his chest plate. She had let him think his strategy worked. Her dirty finger nail punctured the plate armor over his heart. He wanted to say something glorious, epic, even bard-worthy. But he gagged on his own blood.

What felt like a wet snake wriggled into his breastplate and he blocked the nightmare from his mind. Blood froth spilled from his lips. "Worth it," he said. "For Dar and Seline!" he screamed through the blood froth of his lips.

Sean threw the hag back into Time's flow and locked her hand to his breastplate. Her body tumbled to the ground as she scrabbled at the rocks to recover her balance. A gaping slash across her neck left her head titled at an unnatural angle. She popped it back into place as regeneration began to recover her form. Sean dropped onto his back clutching at his heart. He never let go of the hag's hand over his armor though, and pulled the hag off balance.

Paladins coincidentally near their reappearance attacked as one. They cut and stabbed into the hag as others tackled her trying to pin her down. Unable to move with Sean desperately holding her to his body, the paladins pulled the hag back towards the burning river, which continued to burn as the catapults fired more barrels upstream. Sean blinked through the haze of smoke and pain as phantasmal beasts swirled through the air around him. He blinked and they vanished but everything looked brown and white. His body twitched and he wondered how he still lived. A tail slipped through his fingers into his chest where never-ending agony split his sternum and stilled his heart.

Dar stumbled to Sean. The Pha Rannic paladin's aura faded several of her steps ago. He had turned his face to her and mouthed, "I love you, Dar." His eyes took in the sight of Shak leading the paladins in a desperate charge to fell the hag. "Tell Seline, I lo..." His weakly golden aura ended and then exploded in purple and green tendrils of dark magic. Like an octopus, the energy burst from his heart and coiled around his body.

"No, no, no." Dar whispered a prayer to Tiamat as she took her last step and dropped to Sean's side. A hole in his breastplate the size of three fingers gaped open. Blood leaked weakly from Sean's unmoving heart. It just twitched. The hag's finger had left an orange slime around the hole. Sean's body convulsed. With that spasm came a malevolent pressure of evil. Dar looked around at the battlefield. The priestesses, those still standing, supported the paladins against the hag.

"Combine with me," she whispered to the paladin supporting her. Behind, the chiefs and the fighters rushed the hag and began piling on, hoping to restrain her so the paladins could finish the creature before it regenerated.

"I don't understand," the paladin replied. Like Otor, he showed the fatigue of being revived from death's doorstep.

Dar remembered this one. He had finally passed the test after three failed attempts. "Wess, you must combine your faith to mine. This will hurt." Dar forced him to combine with her. *So weak*, she thought. *I hope he survives this.*

Dar placed her hand on Sean's forehead and prayed for him. Within his chest, the transformant worm had already chewed through Sean's heart tissue. All it needed, Dar could tell, was a call from Set's Dream and it would awaken in Sean's corpse. "Wess, we will restore the Commander. However, we need to remove the parasite in his heart."

Dar ripped Sean's breastplate off. It took too long. To her side, the hag threw seven paladins off of her as her armless body heaved, still regenerating. The knights hacked and cut even as the rest of the army gathered around. No sooner would the hag almost break free than fighters threw themselves at her. Dar would get no help from the priestesses. The sun overhead dimmed and her heart sang. *Alerius?*, she prayed. It was just a cloud drifting across the sun. In a moment of silence, of crackling fires, and metal boots against stone, the hag's voice screeched out with amplified dread. "Arise!" the hag screamed. "Arise!"

Shak punched into the hag's mouth and then summoned his avenging blade to pull it out through her skull, and still, the hag fought on. Sean stopped convulsing and the dark aura pulled back into his body. He took a breath.

"No, no, no," Dar screamed. "I can still resurrect you, Sean!" Dar pressed her hand into the gaping chest wound and ripped Sean's heart out. The transformant immediately attacked her. Wess lost his composure to see the now arm-long worm thrashing at Dar. It broke the combination. Dar mashed the worm into the super-heated rocks below them. She imagined it screamed in pain as its wet body sizzled there. Wess drew his sword when he realized he had broken his connection to Dar. Shame draped his countenance and he turned and ran from her.

Though free of the transformant, something held Sean still in its sway and Dar prayed to Tiamat asking, "Is it your will that I restore Sean?"

The answer immediately came, "Your enemy has marked Sean as a vessel, sensing your love. Sean is lost to Set's Dream. To kill the hag, to save Sean, you must kill Sean." Dar felt a tremendous empathy but also a resolute and iron will in those words. She remembered Alerius requiring immediate obedience. The tone of this revelation suggested it as an immediate requirement.

She almost said, "But, I love him. Seline…" A wave of serene and divine love washed over as if to ask her what Sean would want in this scenario. Blanking her mind to her own feelings, Dar began to pray over Sean but reversed the words to the spell that would have revived him. Dissonant and painful to her throat, the words flowed with tears. At the last wincing syllable, the evil presence around Sean and the hag vanished with Sean's last breath. The fighters continued to hack and dismember the hag who fought on. Her evil power diminished greatly when Sean's body at last fell still in death's embrace.

A gentle whisper in her mind followed the silence of her spell. It said: *I know you love him, my daughter. He knows it too. Never before have a Pha Rannic paladin and a priestess of a Hell Lord loved. You shall write this into the Book of Genesis; you must begin my scriptures, Dar Tania.*

Dar fell across Sean, her last erg of faith spent, and wept for him. She wept for them both. Since becoming a priestess, she had learned pain of anatomy, of the physical, and spiritual. Sean had been her rock. His constant love and support had been her sanctuary. After years of yearning and his stupid vows, to finally be together… to see a future… she clenched her fist still dripping Sean's heart blood. "Not like this, Sean." She remembered the first time he had touched her, to wipe a tear from her face after her first confrontation with Prince Roland five years ago.

At last, the hag fell and stopped moving. With her collapse, the last of the slime and its creatures went inert. Heralds went up to cease the catapult bombardment. Bloodied and wounded, the fighters fell back to collapse in the arms of those ready to take their turn against the hag. Slowly, the realization of victory hit them. Cheering broke out followed by more and more. The swiftly moving river washed the filth of combat and oil downstream and the fighters jumped into the water to wash themselves clean.

Dar saw this through a lens of tears. It was unbearably beautiful and glorious. Unable to express her wellspring of emotional agony, Dar lifted her head to the sky and sang. She sang for Sean, for Otor, for the Heroic Dead fallen that day and those lost. The image of Wess running away in shame; *We have so far to go still*, she thought. *All paladins will participate in cleric training so that they know, from now on.*

Upon hearing her song, they joined her. The song had a triumphant edge to it. No one saw or heard Dar's private agony of loss. Their high priestess simply cradled the head of their valiant Commander. All across the battlefield, priestesses worked to stabilize and heal the wounded. That Dar Tania knelt by her beloved Commander Sean struck many with a poignancy etched into their memories of that day.

Shak D'Rath, bandaged and barely able to walk with a priestess' help, found Dar surrounded by a ring of paladins. She whispered the prayer song having fallen hoarse hours before. They parted for Shak. Someone called him, Shak, 'Commander.'

Shak looked down at the two and bowed his head. "Never before, never after, shall there be – will there be a love like this one. High Priestess, we remain here, yours to command. Commander Sean, may your soul rise into the glorious sunlight you taught us."

The soft humming of the paladins lent voice to her song.

Chapter 9 – Set's Dream

Alerius watched the battle from his throne room. When Shak spoke to Tania from outside the River, Alerius lost his composure and dragonshifted, grateful for his solitude. As his paladins, his priestesses, his fighters fell to the slime, he ached to blast them with his fiery breath. Leaning forward and chuffing, Alerius watched his precious Dar flamestrike Shak. The vortex of fire pleased him. It showed her progression from doing this in isolated safety to being able to do this in the midst of combat. Shak's improvisation of the flames to carve into the mold pleased him too.

Each unfolding of the battle inflamed his desire to rise up and burn his enemies. Each soldier, each of his children's deaths – it enraged him. "Ylgolth, thief!" Alerius spat into the darkness of his mountain. When Otor's sword ignited, Alerius nearly backflipped and the mountain trembled with his excitement. "A single pass and the slime burns!" he screamed. "Just a single pass of my fire!"

A female voice whispered to him for the darkness. "Alerius, my love. You must let them do this, alone, the mortal way."

"I know!" Alerius roared back. Echoes scattered from his roar, magnifying and reverberating until it sounded as just a dull roar.

A female human clad in armor with a red halo of flame for hair appeared from the scrying pool, which bubbled and hissed with the heat of her entry. With lips and eyes of fire, she touched Alerius' knurled claw and said, "My love, you must."

Alerius' eyes dilated and focused on the female. For a moment, rage battled against the desire to submit to her. Alerius, after a brief struggle, dropped his head. "My lovely Takhissis, I must be sorely tried, if you are truly come to me."

The goddess of fire incarnate, Takhissis, kissed his claw. "Yes, Tiamat fears for you, and your children. I am sent to be with you during this time. You have many strengths, but letting this happen when you might intervene, it is always your sorest trial."

At her words, Alerius' eyes refocused on the pool. The image showed the hill giant witch burst apart as a night hag. Sean's attack failed. Shak went flying. At the sight of Shak, Alerius voice trembled. "My only paladin…"

"Shhhh," Takhissis assured him. "The young knight still lives. Listen, you can hear his heartbeat. He loves our Dar."

Sean' renewed attack drew a quizzical sense from Alerius. "None of these things justify your coming here, beloved. There is something else?" His eyes saw the hag puncture Sean's breastplate and press a Slaadi worm against his gambeson. Alerius began to tremble as the implications fell into place, one, by, one. His eyes flickered to look for Dar. She stumbled forward with the aid of a novice paladin. Alerius saw that she knew, that she prayed for what she knew to be wrong. He saw her lips mouth out his name, "Alerius!" At that moment, Alerius felt his rider's blackness and despair.

Takhissis intruded into the mutual agony. "You are the incarnation of passion, rage, and lust tempered by a genius understanding of this new world awash in Time. But, in all your centuries of nesting here in Morbatten, with your *morbat*, you have yet to taste the depths of mortal emotion. It is beautiful, ephemeral, and not something Tiamat believes you can endure on your own, not without interfering. Yet, this is the Rider Dogma we explored together before Time."

Takhissis' hand languidly pointed to the pool where Dar destroyed the transformant. In the scrying pool, and all around them in the throne room, Dar's anguish rose up like a flamestrike of despair around her. "Mortal despair, my love. You must find the beauty in this too. Passion denied, like Dar and Sean's, can be just as powerful a crucible as your rage, my husband."

Alerius' pupils contracted to pinpricks. Alerius watched Dar collapse on Sean. He felt Dar's loss, poisonous moment to the next moment, excruciatingly slow in its murder of her love. "She can revive him," Alerius said these words with an undertone of hope, of asking Takhissis to make it so.

The human goddess shook her head. "The Slaadi infection is rising up in Sean's breast. If we intervene now, if we deny Dar this, she will remain your high priestess, but she will never become the goddess you and I both see she can be. This is her temper. This is her crucible. Tell me, my love, would you have a high priestess capable of obedience only when freed of all threats? Must the dreadnought of flame that is you, must you always save the day?"

Alerius rose out from the River of Time. There, his beloved Takhissis burned with the red passion of a thousand stars. But, Takhissis was not his focus. He cast his gaze down to the battle. From across the span of distance, Alerius heard Tiamat whisper to Dar of Set's evil. When Dar's first uttered word of the prayer that would revive Sean began, he held his breath. Then, Dar's voice twisted the prayer to slay what remained of Sean's lifeforce. He saw that Dar Tania remembered his words about obedience and she saw what he missed, that the hag had taken root in Sean's body. Alerius, god emperor of Morbatten, the patriarch of fire breathers and avatar of the kerchki, the first eldar to say to Tiamat to rebel... "I am all these and nothing. I am alone in my Dar's pain."

Alerius, mightiest of the mighty, collapsed to the surface of the River's flow and watched as Time pulled Dar's voice downstream and destroyed the love of her life. Takhissis let go her human form and laid her titanic head atop his. "It pains you to see this play out, again, but you are not alone this time. I still see you as I faded into Tiamat at the beginning of Time. Oh, how you raged, even in your submission to Tiamat! I love you for it. Tiamat honors you for it! Dear Alerius, it is not just you who find your treasured mortals so beautiful. Tiamat finds you and your pain, in these moments, precious. You remain mine for all the endless flows of Time, and I remain yours. Let Dar mourn. Guide her from despair back to health and strengthening her resolve. This is a fragile place, and she may blame you. You must be strong. The life of a heathen, like Sean, is a small price to pay for our own paladins and a high priestess freed of such entanglements. Reward her faith, beloved. Restore all of the Temple of Glass to her in the years to come. Tiamat removes this injunction against her love for a foreigner. We would see Seline walk in Dar's footsteps."

Takhissis ground her head against Alerius' so that their horns interlocked. Twisting her head so that her eyes rested atop Alerius' own, she gazed into his soul and felt him tremble. Every part of him struggled to refrain from throwing her off and racing to Dar's side. The nature of the fire breathers always called for immediate action. Takhissis held his gaze and matched his small movements as if to say, "I'm here. I'm not leaving. You must let this be."

The River froze around the two until Shak's voice added to Dar's croaked whisper of Sean's hymn. At last, Alerius moved to cast Takhissis off, but he found her gone. The River flowed. Time passed. The god emperor remained, as always when Takhissis left, alone.

* * *

Bruce found himself in a strange place. Nothing appeared solid. He remembered a mountain, hot springs, and stone formations familiar to him. He remembered a moment of pain. Like a nightmare, he recalled bits and flashes of Syliri's sexual ecstasy with him, no; that was the nightmare part. He saw Syliri meld into the rocks and run for help. The grey slaad, this Ylgolth, must have captured them both. *And she escaped?*

It felt hard to think straight. Overhead, the sun blazed in waves of pulsating heat. Bruce remembered a chill autumn day, but everywhere, the ground shimmered as if baking under a desert sun. Suddenly thirsty, Bruce dunked his head into a pool of water. It felt cool against his feverish skin. He drank. The geysers erupting around him triggered a memory that he should not be able to drink from this pool.

Feeling better, Bruce scanned the area. His equipment lay in a neat pile where he had left it. After their love-making, Syliri must have folded his things before escaping. *No wait, that's not right. We would not have been intimate here.* A small note protruded from his quiver. It was from Syl. It read: *Keep an eye on Ylgolth. I'll return to Alerius and bring help. I love you.*

He could see the faint signs of her departure to the north. Syliri could move fast when not trying to be quiet, even faster if she dropped her humanoid form and travelled as a giant serpent. That was when he noticed the landscape all around him. It seethed with dark intent, as if something terrible would ambush him at any moment. Though clearly he had been unconscious and fine, it made him worry for Syliri. She did not have his outdoor sense. He decided to track and join her. Nothing could hide from Alerius. Alerius would wipe out Ylgolth and they'd go back to their happy times wandering the natural places of Morbatten.

"Tell me about the armored mage," a voice said to his side.

Bruce whirled and looked but saw nothing. "Who are you?"

"I'm Ylgolth. I've hidden myself so as to not alarm you, Bruce. I'd rather you not run away like Syliri did. Tell me about the mage, or the Queen, and I may just let you go. After all, Syliri needs you. You have no idea how much."

The landscape twisted and Bruce saw a flash of Ylgolth and Syliri together. Bruce shook his head and felt his heart drop. "Did you and Syliri, no. I mean, you two?"

The acid pool where Bruce had just slaked his thirst moved as something titanic shifted invisibly. "She thought it was you, but she's smart. There are medusae in my own domain but they are nothing like her. She's special, but you know that. Like I said, she needs you. The question you should ask, before your insanity returns, is if you want to delay by fighting me and losing, or answer my questions about your masters and save time?"

Bruce found himself nodding and agreeing with Ylgolth. "That makes sense. She does need me. Part of me wants to kill you for hurting her, but other parts of me understand that she thought it was me. I guess that makes it okay." The hot springs stopped twisting, reacting to Bruce's calm logic. It helped him think clearly. "And, we did kill Hrax so, I guess it's only fair." The words rolled from Bruce's tongue feeling alien.

"Indeed," Ylgolth said. "You killed my son and so Syliri must provide me another son. In my home, we have a saying for this: *equivalent taking*. Now, about the Queen and the armored mage. Tell me about this one."

Bruce's mind quickly ran through all the things he might say. "There's a lot to tell you, but in this equivalent taking, tell me first, what happens to Syliri?"

Ylgolth made a chuckling noise. Bruce's heart fell as if the sound were terrible, but his mind heard it as joyous. "She will nurture and give birth to many of my kind. Of course, if you help her, you can remove them before they mature and eat her from the inside out. You know how it is. Removing them so that she survives, it makes her stronger as a mother. Other parts of her might suffer as Slaadi grow on both flesh and intelligence. But, the maedar already measured this for her kind. Bruce, this is important, if you leave even a single transformant, the cycle will start again. A medusa like Syliri could endlessly birth transformants."

Thinking of Syliri as a mother made Bruce feel happier. "Okay, thank you. I'll tell you everything I know about them." A wave of nausea struck Bruce from behind. When he recovered, he realized he could not. Realizing this, the landscape shifted like ocean waves and Bruce fell to his knees vomiting. Nothing was real or natural. He felt the smooth rocks under his hand. They did not move.

"Tell me," Ylgolth commanded.

Bruce looked up at where he imagined Ylgolth's eyes might be. "They're going to kill you. Don't worry. He's just a mage. Powerful though. Not as powerful as she is…"

Bruce swept up his gear and began to run. He ran for hours and then through the night. The wind against his face, the heaving of his lungs, it all felt deliciously good. Even though the land all around heaved unpredictably, he found that by concentrating on the task of tracking Syliri and catching up to her, he could push the anxiety of everything else aside.

It was almost sunrise when he caught sight of his first problem. The land rose up in this part before gradually dropping to the river. From the crest of the rise, he looked down and saw Syliri's trail. He could just barely make out home far to the north. With better light on a clear day, he knew it'd be right there to the north – the three mountains. Along Syliri's route, Bruce saw a flock of aerial creatures. They must be tracking her as well. No doubt, they would wait for her to rest and attack.

Feeling galvanized by the impending danger to Syliri, Bruce continued on at a sprint. By noon, he gained on the flying creatures enough to recognize them as wyverns, two-legged miniature dragons with poison barbs on their tails instead of breath weapons. Of more concern, a conspiracy seemed to have arisen with a land-based group of monsters moving to intercept Syliri just at Morbatten's southern border. Bruce could tell that Syliri would never make it. Worse, he caught a glimpse of the land pursuit and thought he saw the telltale sign of a land shark, a large one. Syliri would not be able to petrify a land shark. Another part of his mind wondered, *What is a land shark? Syliri should be able to petrify anything. Why do I keep questioning basic things?* Bruce paused his thinking for a moment in confusion and then remembered, *Ylgolth wants to be with Syliri too. We both love her. That's right. I'm confused because Syliri is running away from the only love that can give her children. She must be confused too.*

Bruce prayed to Krentismar. Immediately, his body filled with power from the wilderness twisting around him. The raging currents of flowing purple water, the whip and crack of the dusty wind, they gave him strength. Bruce gripped his sword and began to cross the land in leaps and bounds. *The green sky overhead must smile on me*, Bruce rejoiced as his first jump cleared nearly forty paces.

* * *

Syliri knew she ran through Set's Dream. The horrendous torture of every sense, she had left it behind when Alerius saved her. Recognizing it for what it was did not make it any less nerve-wracking. Every visual change in the landscape forced her to remember what it actually looked like. The lava ahead of her – just a small stream. The impossibly tall giants reaching down for her – trees. The burning smell of cooked flesh and tortured cries of murdered children – autumn wind and crackling leaves underfoot.

Syliri wished for a god to pray to; even her friend, the armored mage, had Tiamat. But, Tiamat always felt wrong for the medusae.

If she had her geography right, she would reach Home any mile now. She crested a hill and paused to catch her breath. No matter what she did, she could not quite recover from running. Looking back now, she saw the southern horizon shimmer and then the stars ran together into a phantom leering down at her. Before her wide-open eyes, the apparition twisted into a maedar. Seeing the long destroyed male race of her own kind, Syliri felt a moment of gratitude that they had all fallen to Time's poisonous tide.

Gratitude's moment became terrible as the phantom actualized and reached down to her from the skies.

Syliri screamed and fell backwards, clawing away from it. "You're all dead!" she screamed. In her terror, the snakes coiled up to strike at the phantom. All around, trees petrified as her gaze swept the area. A stone leaf fell on her head. Fearing it an attack, Syliri swept her gaze around her in all directions. The cloud petrified and fell as stone dust, creating a snow-like effect. Hapless birds caught in her gaze dropped and shattered on the stone trees surrounding her. Syliri saw the maedar begin to break apart and then winged bats dropped and fell. She breathed a sigh of relief knowing that the attacks would renew any second.

A sword bit into her side and she spun about, writhing back from the pain to gain distance. A dark assassin wielded a sword wet with her blood. She could feel the evil intent of Set's Dream twisting the creature's will. No doubt, it saw her as some kind of monster as well. Syliri's blood boiled and she hissed forward with the creature full under her gaze. He dodged behind a stone tree. Her gaze caught part of his boot and she saw him smash it to gravel to free his leg. It would not matter. A medusa in a stone forest at night; this was Syliri's perfect hunting ground.

Syliri activated the ring on her left hand. Enchanted by Alerius, the ring summoned her bow. It understood her true size and appeared in her hand as large as a ballista, arrow nocked. Her arrow smashed into the tree behind which the assassin hid. Using the fragmentation as cover, Syliri slid forward with her gaze at full power. Her assailant had already moved elsewhere. A quiet but frightening thought pierced her focus, *What if this is a maedar?*

From all around, the forest lit up as if with fireflies and then a hundred bright points raced towards her. Arrow after magical arrow slammed into her. Many missed their mark and she moved to let her body's terrible skin take the brunt. The few coming to her face, she petrified to stone and they smashed harmlessly against her upper body. The attack felt familiar though. *Bruce?*

Another sword attack ripped along the backside of her tail. It cut far more deeply than she had felt in thousands of years. Every instinct in her screamed out, *Maedar! Run!* The part of her mind still resisting the Dream begged to know if her attacker was Bruce. By force of will, Syliri retracted her petrification gaze and returned to her humanoid form just as a second volley of arrows lashed at where her head had been. A targeted shot like that, it was definitely Bruce.

"Bruce?" she called out into the darkness.

She dropped her bow and knelt on the ground. Though it still twisted and writhed against her knees, she knew she would rather die than harm Bruce. Her giant serpentine body faded to humanoid size and she fell to her knees.

"Your surrender is pointless, demonspawn!" Bruce called out. "I know your tricks! You dare attack the woman I love and you must die."

He's trapped in the Dream. I have just one chance. "I am wounded," she answered. "My death is certain. I would see the face of my slayer before I die and return to the Abyss."

She heard Bruce halt in his approach. "What is this? A spawn that recognizes its certain fate and accepts it? What manner of sorcery is this?"

Syliri let her sigh be heard. "I am tired of fighting. Ylgolth harries me to continue but I miss the vast plains of my homeland. May I see your face, Bruce? Then, you may end me as you see fit."

Bruce circled to her front. She saw him set arrow after arrow pointed to her torso. He called out, "I will grant you this request."

Syliri kept her head bowed, eyes on the ground as Bruce instructed her. He approached, keeping a buckler shield between his eyes and her own. Syliri whispered, "Ylgolth wished for you to feel slain by your love. I have no medusa-like attack. It's a spell, bound to this ring. Shall I remove it?"

Bruce said, "Remove and toss it to me."

Syliri did so. "I'm powerless now, and homesick. End me before Ylgolth finds out I have betrayed him."

Bruce drew his sword and stepped to the side. *He's going to send a volley to weaken me before he strikes*, Syliri realized. *Can I withstand this attack? I must.* "Tell me, Bruce – do you see only a monster here?" Syliri flinched as twenty arrows shot out and peppered her torso like porcupine quills. She groaned and leaned forward.

Bruce darted forward to strike the killing blow. Syliri left the flow of Time, and caught Bruce in the ethereal realm. Her gaze unleashed, Bruce petrified just as his sword tip touched her breast. His momentum carried him forward and, though Syliri caught him, his sword impaled into her heart. She screamed in agony. "I love you, Bruce!"

That was when a single unearthly voice boomed throughout the forest of stone plants. "Contingency." *That voice,* she thought. *It sounds like my friend...*

* * *

Spark and Bomoki were interrupted in their work when a loud noise blared throughout Alerius' mountain caves. "Syliri's Contingency," it said three times. It took Spark a moment to shift from working on the locator rune and teaching Bomoki to this alert. They had been working for days, without sleep, occasionally getting reports about the army's preparations and battle. Bloodshot and exhausted eyes looked to Spark for guidance. "What does this mean?" Bomoki asked.

"Aeons ago, the three of us crafted a spell that would preserve Syliri from death. That magic has at last been activated. Come."

Spark touched Bomoki and they vanished from the laboratory. Bomoki made a mental note to ask about the *contingency magic* later. Reappearing in the throne chamber, they found Syliri and Bruce embraced. Bruce stood petrified in the act of attacking while Syliri's gaze remained in full force. Speaking to Bomoki, Spark said, "The contingency will heal her, but only temporarily if she is cursed, poisoned, or diseased. She needs our help. Why would Bruce attack her?"

Spark sniffed the air. The cavern held the presence of Alerius, though the red patriarch was nowhere to be seen. A scent of burning flowers lingered too. It reminded Spark of the eldar times and he shrugged off the nostalgia. Telekinetically and with great care, Spark pushed Bruce back and away from Syliri. When distance showed the bloodied tip of Bruce's sword impaled in Syliri's heart, Spark seemed to deflate. "So, that's what happened," was all he said.

Spark let the Bruce statue fall to its side, cracking where it hit the polished tile floor. Walking around, they saw the many arrows quilling Syliri's body. "Syliri, it's Spark. You will release your gaze and we will aid you," Spark ordered.

One by one, Syliri tore the arrows from her chest. Her eyes never left Bruce's. Spark saw a shift in the focus of the snakes and, following it, he noted a portion of the ranger's arm where the stone struggled to take hold. From that area, an eye slowly opened in his flesh. Syliri groaned in agony and clasped her hands to her heart. "Set! I come for you!" she screamed. The reptile hiss in her voice reverberated around the cavern. She looked up at Spark, her eyes wide and terrible in their fear. She clearly did not know where she was or who was in the room with her.

Spark cursed and a globe of magic armor sprang into being around him and Bomoki just as Syliri's gaze activated. The yellow horror of her gaze hit the sphere protecting Spark, which saved them both. "Notice how her gaze manifests similar to a dragon's fire. Alerius was fascinated with her kind before Time. He wondered, and still does, if medusae are not some offshoot of a dragon type. The males, the maedera, were cruel slavers so enamored with Set that they fought over the best of the medusae, like Syliri, and experimented on them for pleasure. Syliri most likely sees us as maedera. She seems deep in Set's thrall. Bruce too, I'd guess." The magic shell encapsulating them began to turn to stone. "It's so rare that she unleashes her all that I forget how powerful her gaze really is."

Spark pointed at her and his other hand made a symbol in the air. "Sleep," he commanded her.

Syliri shuddered at his command, her eyes darting around for some unseen enemy. She continued to resist and so Spark sent the symbol traced in blue light towards her. When it hit her, she fell unconscious. Bomoki, exhausted though he was by working nonstop on the gate, managed to trace and copy the rune symbol and magic into his spellbook.

From their side, as Spark walked forward to check on Syliri, a floating ball covered in eyes around a giant circular mouth attacked them. Maybe because it was not attacking with magic, or because Syliri petrified some of it, the ball creature passed through Spark's protective sphere. Bomoki startled and fell backwards almost tripping and falling in his haste.

Spark sensed it just in time and counter-attacked with a staff he summoned into his left hand. The Son of Set went sailing into the upper reaches of Alerius' cavern. Spark watched it carefully as he enacted another spell. This one created giant floating hands that reached out and caught the beast as it recovered and spun back at the two sorcerers. "If you're not too busy taking notes," Spark said to Bomoki, "please begin animating physical objects to launch at this chaos spawn. Whatever touches it, is going to warp. Look at the force hands. They're already melting. My staff too."

Bomoki had indeed been taking notes about the force-hand spell. Spark slammed his foot down on the tile, which fractured and fragmented it. On the blue patriarch's command, Bomoki sent these hurtling towards the beast. It nimbly dodged the larger fragments, but when the smaller ones blinded the eyes they hit, Bomoki realized they needed sand. "Master, fragment more tiles to smaller pieces!" Some of the stones bounced off what remained of the hands, which looked like candle wax melted by a blast of flame. "What is that thing?"

Spark tossed his staff away as eyes began opening on the part that contacted the creature. The monster dove at Spark.

The Lord of Thunder summoned mage armor to appear and protect both him and Bomoki. Using the mage armor's gauntlet on his arm as a hammer, Spark slapped the beast away as far as he could. Bomoki readied the rock dust. Spark said, "It's a nightmare from Set, from Ylgolth I'd guess. They serve as anchors for Set's Dream. We didn't see it because it was feeding Syliri and Bruce's dream, which looks like it involved murdering each other." Spark's tone of voice held just a tint of sadness. "Now." Spark cast off the mage armor. Though it protected him, like the staff, eyes erupted all along the plates of conjured metal.

Bomoki continued to throw debris, but most missed. The fiend danced about in unnatural directions, seeming to defy normal movement. "Master, we need something else," Bomoki said, pointing to tentacles erupting from the staff and mage armor.

Spark nodded and suddenly hundreds of wands appeared like a wall before them. Spark snapped his fingers and they all discharged at the fiend. "Bomoki, magic will work, but which one?" Some of the energy filled the monster with power, healing wounds, and even spawning additional eye stalks. Spark pointed and faerie fire illuminated one wand. It had no apparent discharge but the magical flames flowed in a straight line and showed parts of the fiend vanishing into black dust. "Disintegration, of course," Spark said. A moment later, all but the one wand vanished and Spark summoned another.

Bomoki blasted the graveled tile at the nightmare. Spark added his own force of will and, together, they drove stone projectiles at the beast. As its eyes were torn to pulp, it rotated and came in for another attack. Spark enacted a spell familiar to Bomoki – telekinesis. Just as the mouth tilted to latch onto Spark, Spark pulled the Bruce statue in front of them. It effectively speared the nightmare on Bruce's stone sword. The beast made a gibbering sound that for a moment sounded like the word 'father.' Eye stalk by mutated bit of flesh, the Son of Set melted off Bruce's stone sword. Spark passed a wand to Bomoki. "Disintegration," he said. Together, they unleashed the wands on the gory bulk of its body. "Bomoki, when we're done, find anything touched or changing and disintegrate it. Quickly."

Spark broke Bruce's stone sword and disintegrated it. They found arrows near Syliri also mutating. Portions of stone tile touched by Bruce, Spark's staff, and so on, they all had to be destroyed. On several of the arrows and stone tiles, the eyes had grown large enough they looked like they might detach. Bomoki asked about it. "Master Spark, these grow and then drift free? Can Ylgolth see us?"

Spark shrugged. "I've not studied these. They're too dangerous. One mistake and you're lost forever." Spark walked back to Syliri and checked her skin. "She seems untouched. Maybe the *contingency* spell saved her. I bet it activated just before she mutated. Bruce is as good as dead."

Bomoki pointed to Bruce. "The ranger is not so lucky." He pointed to bulges visible in the stone where Bruce's armor and gear seemed ill-fitted. From the side of his bracer, an eye cast in stone stared at them. "Is there a cure?" He pointed the wand at the eye and almost triggered its dire magic.

Spark stayed Bomoki's hand. "No. Syliri must make this call. She is too close to my brother, to me, to take her only love away like this. Listen to me, Bomoki: This is why Set was bound. Set cares nothing for any of us whether we serve Creation, Chaos, or Warp. It's all mutation and death. Everything you need to know about Set can best be explained by the alliance of Pha Rann, Demos-Gorgos, and Asmodeus to bind Set into never-ending sleep. To bring them together, that was the only time it has ever happened. You see, Set does not create or destroy. He mutates it all into destructive forms."

Bomoki pointed to the cracks in Bruce's form. "The petrification can be undone though. In stone, the chaos is slower. I don't understand this."

Spark nodded and with sadness said, "Normal stone would not even slow the chaos infection. It unravels matter. Syliri thought, as an eldar, her gaze and will could hold Bruce like this forever. Maybe that is what she will do. Among her sisters, it is common that they petrify those they love most. Syliri says they consider it a gift of immortality. They think they are saving the creatures from death. As for undoing Bruce, to what end would we undo it? We would have to either kill him immediately, or watch him die and then fight more of these things. Look how far along these are."

The chaos lesions along Bruce's body showed at least seven eyes ready to open. Though Spark far overmatched the single chaos spawn, Bomoki realized they had been lucky. "If Bruce had come here, normally, would we have detected the spawn?" Bomoki asked.

"No. We would have been caught completely by surprise. As it was, I arrived ready for something powerful enough to trigger Syliri's contingency. I'm surprised my brother is not here. Syliri is a favorite of his."

"Why eyes, Master Spark?"

"They see Set's Dream. The more eyes, the more of the dream they see and the faster the host is pulled into chaos. Tentacles and other mutations of the senses or movement are the same. To pull into the Dream, to eat the Dream. It doesn't matter. It's all sick. If you imagine Alerius, but like this, and the size of a world, you'd have a good image of what Set looks like." Spark stood the Bruce statue upright. "Go back to the gate, Bomoki. I'll wait here for Alerius and ensure Syliri stays asleep."

* * *

Ylgolth watched with fascination as these strange humans tore his slime creation to bits. After encountering Alerius, he knew Bet Mirgul would fall but she should have managed to slay many. Sure, the one knight looked like the most powerful of the lot but the hag should have been able to destroy the entire army. The priestess, she had been unexpected. Nothing in Hrax's reports or his knowledge from the goblins had prepared him for divine opposition.

Ylgolth had to admire the hag's plan though. It almost worked. If the knight had recovered the hag's soul, the priestess would have died too. Frustrated that the strangely-armored mage did not appear in the battle at all, Ylgolth tried to figure out which god stood against him. The burning fire and haloed auras suggested something of fire, but none of Creation's gods manifested that way. The one paladin, that one was most certainly Pha Rann. The others baffled him. "Polgeryx probably knows," Ylgolth spat. "Maybe this whole thing is a ruse to allow Polgeryx to take control." He chuckled. "Good try, Polgeryx but you'll have to be craftier than this. As Bruce said, it's just a human mage."

Ylgolth sniffed the air. He imagined a faint tinge of smoke as the last hill giant animated by the slime fell to iron swords. *These creatures*, he thought, *they are very strong. With just a few of these, I could ascend to an Atramenti.* He cast his eyes around, suddenly wary. The Atramenti, whether just one or many, they had spies everywhere. Ylgolth found himself regretting that he used all his transformants on the goblins and, though enjoyable, had wasted himself with the gorgona. He consoled himself, *Well, one made it.* So weak from the gate's crossing, they had only yielded only one Son of Set. It would be some time and many souls more to consume before he could create more. He doubted that Syliri would birth any. It would take great luck and so far this world seemed intent on denying him.

Ylgolth thought back to the armored mage. The one who withstood him would make a powerful host for his ultimate Atramenti form. Self-preservation instincts kicked in and Ylgolth questioned the wisdom of setting his sights on such an unknown target. Envy for that one's power warred with caution and the entire confrontation played through his mind. Unable to see the battle by the river, Ylgolth focused on the ranger. Bruce had completely succumbed to Set's Dream – *to My Dream!* Ylgolth exulted in the moment and flexed his arms and wings to the sky.

The goblins arrayed behind Ylgolth swayed slowly side to side. They mimicked Ylgolth's movements but sloppily, as if drunk. The transformants controlled them and would soon grow strong enough to eat their way out as Fecundus Slaadi. When the goblins fed, either on each other or these humans, they would begin to take their true shapes. "I regret I did not interrogate Bruce about everything else he knows." The goblins all nodded their heads to each syllable, drooling. "You can't understand this now, but knowledge is everything. After your rebirths, you will crave it."

The goblins that survived Ylgolth's carnage had followed the Slaadi transformants and now stood with Ylgolth. To these, Ylgolth spread his arms and smiled. "I require your servitude." His words filled their minds with images of war and feasting on flesh. The visions showed them conquering and defeating the humans Ylgolth spied through his mold-infected hill giants. Human flesh would taste sweet. Human blood would scorch their throats with intoxicating power. Slowly, the seductive dream caught hold. It replaced terror and uncertainty with confidence and rage.

One by one, the goblins' countenances changed from anxious fear to aggressive obedience. When Ylgolth's Dream claimed the last one, Ylgolth sent an image of the priestess with burning hair to their minds. "This one. I want this one. I want to know this one. This one is key to the armored mage; I know it. You will go east and rally more goblins to our war. Your way will be smooth and fast. Those resisting, you will slay and eat. The rest will join you. When you have become a mighty flood, you will turn north and capture humans for me. Your bite will make them obey you." Ylgolth projected this last notion to the goblins. At his words, their teeth began to drip venom. Their muscles swelled. Spikey hair sprouted from their heads like porcupine quills. "I am Ylgolth. You are mine. Now, run; obey!"

The goblins turned and ran east. The transformants continued drooling, nodding their heads to their master's words. Ylgolth checked the eyes of one and then licked its salty and blood-caked face. "Not quite ready. You need to eat. Come, we will move north, but not too quickly. I wish to see where this battle happened at the river. Maybe the army will still be there. It is time my dream touched all the humans. Bruce was not enough."

* * *

Brook Summerstone and Fist of Graves stood at a fork in the Cordabad River. Ahead of them, to the west, a mountain peak, split in half, rose up from gentle but rolling hills. North of the mountain, large foothills continued as far as they could see. One fork of the river flowed along the edge of the northern half of the split mountain, creating a deep boundary with the foothills. The other fork flowed away to the south, but that flow looked small. Neither knew anything about this area. Fist lowered her to the ground.

"Hungry?" he asked. A gentle tone in his voice suggested concern for her. The farther they got from the Slaadi curse, the more observant and thoughtful Fist became.

Brook stepped off his hand onto the frozen ground. "Yes. My people are always hungry. Fish?" she asked. Fist could not eat enough fish to fill his appetite. Traveling on the river's banks had been a blessing. For one, stones and obstacles that would challenge Brook barely slowed Fist's pace. Also, her druid craft allowed her to spellsing the best fishing songs. Fist already sat back, watching with anticipation.

At her call, the fish practically jumped out of the river. They always got a few big ones but this time, they got so many, Brook had to stop the spell early. "There you go. Let's try cooking all of them this time, okay?" Fist shrugged, and dropped a handful about to go in his mouth. He cleared rocks as big as Brook with a sweep of his hand to make a clearing of level ground. Travelling for days now, Brook found that Fist carried her so gently, she was not tired at all. Horse riding made her body ache, but this was luxurious. Another spell and fire kindled in the sticks and branches Fist had already placed in a fire pit.

While she cleaned the fish, Fist found flat stones to act as a cooking surface and placed them over the fire. "I do good job," he said proudly. "Cook fish taste more yummy." He licked his lips and poked a larger fish. "Too small for me help."

Brook patted his hand. "You're doing great, Fist. It seems the farther we get, and the less hungry you are, the more you are learning. Do you remember this letter?" She drew an 'A' in the dirt by the fire. It took him a while, but he finally said it correctly. This time, he did not smash stones against his head. "I bet you'll be able to read and write in no time at all!"

Fist smiled at her. "Write name: Fist." He made unintelligible squiggles in the sand and they both laughed. "Not Fist, not yet. Someday. Bad nightmares fading. Sleep feels good."

Fist had really bad dreams. Their second day on the trail, Fist had suddenly stopped moving. Worried he had died, or something else bad, she had been relieved but annoyed to find him sleeping. He slept most of the day, warmed by the sunlight. *Sleep was another thing getting better*, Brook realized. Regular food, sleep, and distance from Hrax and this new threat, Ylgolth, seemed to allow Fist to become intelligent. "Take your time, Fist. You're important to me. Food, sleep, whatever you need. I want you strong, and I want to see you write your name!"

They ate, cracking jokes back and forth. If Fist had the intelligence of a toddler when they first met, he had grown to a small child now. Every so often, a glimmer of what he might actually be would come through in a flash. This time, in the midst of singing a children's song about chasing butterflies, Fist said, "No butterflies in dream. Flying creatures of teeth, attack eyes. I hate them." The word 'hate' had such murderous rage that it darkened the mood of their dinner. Fist shook his head and added, "Then, I see. I remember butterflies as child, before Bull Stomper. Before the dreams. Makes me angry. Never go back."

Fist responded best to hugs when his past haunted him. She hugged his forearm where it rested on the ground in front of him. Like an ape, hill giants had overly large forearms. He smiled and patted her hair. "Never go back, Brook. Never ever."

Night brought with it a suggestion of coming snow, but full and feeling safe, they laid back and Brook explained the stars and twin moons to Fist. He pointed and tried to say their names, but the draconian words faltered in his mouth.

A soft voice interrupted them but carried no sense of threat. The strangeness of it caused Fist to spring to his feet in a somersault to land between the voice and Brook. "I've never seen a Halfling with a hill giant before. What exactly are you two?" he asked in a language Brook thought she recognized but struggled to understand. The intent of the question was clear, at least.

Brook's spells with the plant life around them would have alerted her if anything with hostile intent approached. It took her mind a moment to register the language: *Elven*. Her parents had tried to teach her Elven.

She called out to Fist, "Shhh. It's okay. We're safe. No dreams here. I promise." Fist did not relax. When Brook walked around Fist, she found an elf in grey stone-colored leather armor. A cloak mimicking the autumn leaves draped his back and hooded his face. He held his hands in the open before him. A long sword lay sheathed at his waist and a metal bow draped his shoulders.

Trying to remember her Elven pronunciation and words, Brook answered. "Friends." In her own language, she said, "I think that's how you say 'friend' in Elven. Um. I hope that wasn't pretentious." She looked at the elf. Her five years with Dar Tania had them all speaking the tribal language of those humans. Dar called it Common, but the Halflings had their own language they called Common, which was a dialect of Taysoran Common.

The elf smiled and said slowly in Elven, "Friend. Yes. Your accent is fine." He switched to Taysoran Common and continued, "You seem to understand me better than you speak. Okay. I was told to come east and find two unlikely companions. When I saw you use druid craft to eat dinner with a hill giant, I figured you two were as unlikely as I would ever find in these wilds. I'm Trenlis Venfermis, or Tren. What are your names?"

Fist finally relaxed. When he unclenched his hands, two giant rocks fell to the ground. Tren smiled and pointed to them, "Glad you didn't have to use those."

Fist pointed his thumb to his chest. "I – Fist of Graves. That Brook Summerstone. Friends." He did his best to imitate the Elven word for 'friend' but like draconian, it came out sounding all wrong and grumbly.

Tren grinned at the attempt. "I never thought I'd see the day when a hill giant attempted *Elven*. Bravo, Fist."

Brook nodded. "That's right. We are friends. We were sent by the god emperor Alerius to find a land called Morilon. I am to meet the Lord of Vapors there, Mallaforax."

Tren's face became unreadable when she mentioned the god emperor and green dragon patriarch. "I'm sorry," she added. "Did I say something wrong?"

Tren pointed to their campfire. "Do you mind if I sit down? I've been scouting for you for days. I could do with some easy food. Running and hunting, at the same time, it's harder for us non-druids." Brook pointed to the fish keeping warm by the fire, and watched him eat. Fist wandered off to the river and dunked his head in to drink.

After a time, Tren looked up and said, "Your use of the term 'god emperor', it tells me that you respect for the dragon. Is this true?" Before Brook could really answer, Tren continued. "Morilon has very different feelings about the dragons. While I've never interacted with them, I've spent my whole life in the shadows of the one you're on your way to meet. I suppose I'm indifferent, but as we – well, you – meet more and more elves, you'll want to either temper your enthusiasm, or not talk about it at all. Most of my people and the royal family especially, feel the dragon is a jailer. We've had enough issues that could have been solved by the dragon, and well, the dragon did nothing. My kind will also have some issues with your giant friend. Speaking of, how did that happen?"

Brook sat across the fire from him and a minute later, Fist brought more wood. His strength allowed him to limb trees and then crush the logs into splintered kindling. They burned brightly and easily. It made the cold night and this new companion at their fire seem normal. "I want to hear more about Morilon, and why the elves do not like the dragons. But, for Fist, he's my friend. The god emperor," she put particular stress on it this time to see Tren's reaction, "said he would come with me. If the elves have a problem with that, they can take it up with the dragons."

Behind her, amidst the sound of more tree limbs snapping, Fist grunted. "Brook friend too. Dragons tasty."

Brook gestured to Fist and said to Tren, "That's his word these days for not-friends but not enemies either. 'Tasty,' it suits him, don't you think? I was travelling from Home – that's what my kind call our area in Morbatten – to visit the god emperor. Fist just sort of found me. That was just twenty days ago but I feel like he's a big brother I've known my entire life."

Tren took his boots off and stretched his toes to the fire's warmth. "I've never heard a single story of a good race befriending hill giants. Actually, Morbatten's revelation that fire giants have been here, and in the numbers seen by Taysor, were shocking to us all. Now, I meet you coming from Morbatten with a hill giant. Is this common in Morbatten?" Tren had a hard time saying 'Morbatten.' The consonants and inflections Brook had become used to sounded funny and she laughed.

"You have heard a lot but it seems you really don't know anything about Morbatten, do you? Let me tell you this. I was imprisoned, my friends and family being eaten by ogres and cannibal humans right in front of us, and Dar Tania rescued us. They gave us a safe homeland. Even by our standards, it's a paradise. My people are recovering and every day, more Halflings arrive to join us. We've never had this before. Morbatten and the dragons are for my people what Fist is for me - a big brother no one will mess with. You know, most newcomers arrive with the same concerns I hear you saying. After a few months, there are still concerns but it's about weather patterns and crop yields."

As if to punctuate her words, Fist punched a dead tree. It fell with a crash, creating a wind block for the night's cold. He smiled at Brook to see if he had done it correctly. She gave him a thumbs-up and Fist chuckled while mocking the tree's weakness. "If all hill giants are like Fist, I would befriend them all."

Tren looked at her sharply to see if she joked. "You're serious? We'll be traveling together for the next few weeks." He eyed her. "I'd guess that it takes us twenty days to reach Morilon."

"How fast could you do it by yourself?" Brook asked. When he said it would take 10 days, Brook stated, "I might be small, but Fist moves fast. We'll do it in 10 days. I don't' want Mallaforax waiting even a single day."

Just behind her, Fist laid down cradling a rock to his head for a pillow. His body warmth already warmed her. With the fire in front and Fist at her back, she felt great. Tren felt it too. The elf nodded. "Ten days then. I must reconsider my stance on giants. Along Morilon's borders, they prowl and raid. They consider us, like you, a delicacy."

Fist mumbled, "Elves, tasty. Yummy. Never had elf." His drowsy voice had already given way to sleep. His body remained tense though. Brook patted him on the head and instantly, Fist's body relaxed, appearing to deflate.

"He has bad dreams. Beyond nightmares. The farther we get from the southeast, the better, and smarter, he's becoming." Brook pointed to the marks on his shoulders that ran down his chest and back. "If the giants on your borders have any marked like this, I will tell you – they aren't in their right mind. They don't see you as elves. Food, yes. But more than that, they see as murderous enemies. They think they are defending themselves from you. At least, that's what happened with Fist and his clan. He's getting better though. The God Emperor Alerius and the dragons, they are fighting against it, helping Fist."

Tren listened to her with a curious expression. "So, you're saying that the monsters on our borders might all be like Fist?"

Brook smiled and patted Fist's arm. "I don't know. But, think about it. If you weren't sleeping, always under threat, and the world around always pushed you to paranoid overreaction, we'd all be monsters." A sad look crossed her face and she remembered the cannibal humans helping the ogres. "Then, there is true evil. The ones who see the world the way we do and choose to be monsters."

"Are all Tanians like you?" Tren asked.

It caught her by surprise. "Tanians? What do you mean?"

Tren laughed. "Your nation is called Morbatten. Your high priestess is Dar Tania. If you mix them up, you get Morbattania. In Morilon, we've shortened it to Tania. You're a Tanian, or didn't you know that? Taysor calls you that too." Tren grinned at her.

"Tanian," Brook said rolling the word around in her mouth. "I like it. I think Dar will like it too. What other nicknames do you have for things? Is Morilon called something?"

"Morilon is what the dragons called the forest we settled into. We call ourselves *Velese*. The kingdom to your north, we call them Sorans." Tren looked up at the stars dotting the sky overhead. "We had names for everything back in Merakor. Here, it all seems lost, forsaken somehow."

Brook whispered, "*Forsaken*. In draconian, the language Dar Tania speaks with the dragons and prays in, that word has another meaning. It's complex though. Dar told me it means, 'the place you wish you were not.' It has something to do with Time and how the world works."

Late into the night, Tren told her stories of Merakor and how the Velese, the elves, came to Morilon. Because Alaura and Dar were talking about it, Brook perked up when Tren mentioned that the king's daughter was killed by 'the blind dragon'. Brook asked, "I've heard that term before, but get the sense it's not actually blind."

Tren folded his arms and pulled his cloak more tightly around his body while he unpacked his bedroll. "That's right. Blind to mortal anguish. It's a long story for another time. You must rest if you are to beat me to Morilon."

Brook snuggled up against Fist's back with the moon high overhead. A feast of late season berries and roots sat ready on the cooking rocks with leftover fish for breakfast. Tren added more wood to the fire and laughed at himself. "We'll begin our run whenever you're both ready. I've never travelled with a hill giant before. This will be fun."

* * *

Alerius re-entered Time's flow with a sickening crunch in his gut. His treasured moments with Takhissis came hardly at all. The cost of her coming to even the ethereal realm of Time's flow made it so they never spoke in person. Over the aeons of time since he gave her up, he was forced to accept divine revelation, like Dar hearing Tiamat in her heart, as the closest he would ever get. Then, as Merakor rose and the trials and challenges of Alerius' dream increased, Takhissis came to him only for comfort and to steel his will against the challenges only she could see from out there, beyond Time's bitter flow. The painful knowledge that she came to prevent him from intervening in Dar Tania's despair highlighted the role he and Dar had yet to play in shaping the religion.

Direct intervention, he already knew this from repeated failures with the tribespeople, always – always – created dependency. How many times had he lectured Takhissis and Tiamat on this very principle? The irony of it being him, again, that must not intervene punched his heart. For a blinking moment, Alerius envied the metallic dragons their dispassion. Then, the moment passed. The jewels of a fully-matured society sparkled many times greater than any given individual in Morbatten, yet Alerius loved the sparkle. "My children, they will outshine Merakor!" he roared into the dark corners of his lair. "I shall see both!"

He knew. *How many experiments have I patiently conducted in each generation? Trust and hope are the basis of a mortal's ability to make decisions, I know this. If I intervene to shape these or force them to make the 'right choice,' it takes away from the power the mortal would otherwise have. I must watch and encourage, but only intervene when absolutely required.* His emotions, incensed by Takhissis and Dar's distant anguish, broke his ability to speak but he could hear his own words in memory. It stung that Takhissis had parroted his own words to him. Takhissis had kissed him and said, "Beloved, I see now what it cost you to let me go. I love you for your strong heart. You will endure this too. You must."

Feeling her, smelling her, seeing her had helped. Now, in the lonely absence of her departure and back in this dark world floundering in the poisonous flow of this moment falling to the next, Alerius put his head back and screamed. His roar of loss, frustration, and anger ripped out of his heart and became a blast of fire lancing up into the cavern overhead. The fire's intensity rose until globules of molten glass began to rain down around him and still he pushed his hurt and Dar's hurt into his breath weapon. The heat in the room increased until secondary and radiated heat boiled his scrying pool.

My scrying pool, he thought detachedly. *Something is wrong*. His body alight with living fire and eldritch heat, Alerius' eyes focused and saw it. Syliri lay unmoving. A blue sphere of light enwrapped her body. Green blood boiled and hissed in a circle where it had spilled out of the protective magical shield. *Spark's magic protects her, why? Why is she not moving?*

The pain, which already threatened Alerius with unquenchable fire, caused him to trace and see each of the arrow wounds. He followed them back, splitting his mind out of the river's current, to see Bruce's sword and the contingency Alerius gifted to Syliri so long ago. Time snapped back into focus and he noted her shallow breathing. Her love, like Dar and Sean, he saw Bruce. To his dragonsight, Bruce looked warped and ugly. He also saw the telltale stone fractures and chaos warp in his stone form that spelled his death. Either would slay him if he returned to flesh.

"Syliri." Her name spoken against the slow grinding of molten stone echoed in a moment of quiet. Syliri, and flashes of her from the Dragon Wars, as they toured Merakor, and their aeons together assaulted his mind and became mixed up in Dar's funeral song for Sean. Syliri was his friend. He had plans for the treasure that was Syliri's life – to be a goddess in Tiamat's dominion. Until Dar, and then Bruce, Syliri had remained in his mountain. Alerius counted time and saw it: five years of love between her and Bruce, against an endless circle of seasons. Like Alerius giving up Takhissis, Syliri too had lost her consort.

Alerius licked the Bruce statue and tasted the foul magic of Ylgolth and Set's Dream. "Syliri. No," he groaned. Worse than Alerius' own giving up of Takhissis, Syliri would have to decide what to do with Bruce. Unsure of himself, Alerius raised a talon to end Bruce.

From behind, Spark's voice came on the winds of magic against the raging thermals in the throne room. "Brother, I would help but cannot endure your fire."

"No need, Unzx'Cthczen. I hear your words and Takhissis prepared me for this." The word 'this' echoed and reverberated in the cavern. Spark's name, in draconian, rumbled from Alerius' mouth and fed into the echo like thunder. *No, she did not. She distracted me to save Dar from my help.* Realization fed the anger growing in the god emperor's heart every bit the equal to the last great battle in the Dragon Wars when he had realized Takhissis would be lost to him. "This… this…" it kept echoing until Alerius could not take it anymore.

With spread wings, Alerius shot out of his lair into the sky. The fireball of air in his wake transforming into plasma made him glow like the sun itself. Looking around for a target, Alerius saw the smaller peak east of his mountain. Dar planned to build a castle there, to house and train more Seans. *Takhissis, Dar, Syliri…*, he thought and held their names in his mind. His rage continued to rise, threatening to unravel his Tehran form. He realized, deep in shock, *I'm about to ascend. I can't do this now and leave Dar alone.*

With no outlet for the snarled emotions in his heart, Alerius turned to the small eastward peak. A few of his people lingered near the Temple side. They stood with their hands over their eyes against Alerius' ember radiance. The narrow beam of fire that shot from his mouth and eyes to the summit, connected Alerius to the mountain with a red and gold thread of energy.

From a distance, the thread seemed to move slowly until it touched the mountain. A shockwave of heat visibly moved the air around the beam and then plasma ignited around the line. The top of the summit vaporized and Alerius pushed his fury into the earth. Part of his mind connected the fact that his children at the Temple were running away. The rest of him glorified in his power and raged, "Die! Burn! All shall burn!" This eldar part of him, so destructive he rarely let it out, came bursting out of his skin. His grey scales outlined by liquid yellow of burning flames. He imagined Ylgolth and pushed his fury against the mountain peak. Biting out threads of fire, Alerius raged, "Ylgolth! You shall die! You shall all die! I will find you!"

Each word, punctuated with a blast of heat, echoed and resounded throughout the Valley of Morbatten. A feeling, indescribable and beyond the dragonterror the people of Morbatten only sometimes felt, permeated the empire. For those closest, the emotion of terror and fury proved too much and they collapsed in the act of running away. For the paladins and priestesses, they heard it as a battle cry to war and their hearts leapt as they swelled with pride and vigor. None knew the name 'Ylgolth' but they all knew, this Ylgolth would die. Animals, birds mid-flight, even those already asleep, fell to the ground. For those few remaining conscious, they thought they heard the sound of the god emperor calling to Dar Tania.

Ahead of him, the mountain shimmered under coruscating waves of energy. Where touched by Alerius fire, the rock vaporized and then burst into new arcs of fire. Around the destruction and below in the valley, everyone stopped and walked out to see the new sun burning just over their heads to the north. The ground trembled in small quakes and a bassy thunder echoed throughout the Valley of Morbatten.

Farther away, the Halflings cleaning their fields from autumn's harvest paused. They felt the power to the north and saw the blinding yellow light. "What's that?" a farmer asked his friend.

"Who knows? Probably more magic experiments." Everyone nodded. That must be it. In the last three years, since Bomoki's arrival, Morbatten had become accustomed to bright lights and strange noises near the Dragon Mountain.

North of Alerius, in the Shield Mountains, Ynt'taris halted in his lecture to Alaura about the Dragon Wars and doctrine of Consecration. He cocked his head as if listening and then trembled. "I'm sorry, Alaura. My brother needs me. We must go."

When Ynt'taris arrived with his rider an hour later, the eastward summit no longer existed. Rivulets of lava ran down the now flat side of Alerius' mountain. Nothing remained except blackened glass pools. Thermal drafts scorched up from the plateau. Alaura pointed to Alerius. He sat, now in human form, on the edge of the escarpment in front of his lair. He stared to the south.

Ynt'taris landed and found Spark leaning back to the side of the main tunnel. The lightning patriarch stood just outside of the rain now falling softly. Bomoki stood behind Spark in a protective sphere. Sensing it, Ynt'taris dodged behind Spark's conjured force wall. The heat from Alerius and the now-gone eastern peak hurt Ynt'taris. Snowflakes intermingled with ash. The heat from the shattered mountain and the pulsating thermals around Alerius made it dangerous to get very close. Ynt'taris thought about subtracting some of the heat, but Spark waved him off.

After pondering various actions, Ynt'taris humanshifted and sat down by Spark. "What happened?" he asked.

Spark pointed south. "Dar Tania's battle at Crossing. And, Syliri against Ylgolth. It all happened all at the same time. He rages now. You know what happens next, brother." Spark pushed images of Syliri and Bruce to the white patriarch, who shuddered.

"Syliri is our sister," Ynt'taris seethed. "Ylgolth will face the Court of Patriarchs." Ynt'taris words met Alerius' at the same time.

Alaura watched it all and wished she could see what the dragons shared. Bomoki though, looked exhausted and in a state of shock. "I understand how you feel," she said. Not knowing why, she embraced him. "It makes you realize how small humans really are."

Bomoki nodded and then hugged her back.

Chapter 10 – The Pragmatist Order

Alaura sat upon Ynt'taris' back in a regal gown befitting a queen of Taysor. Van held onto her for dear life. Underneath them, the land rolled under the spread of the white patriarch's wings. Van said, "His wings! They must be three hundred paces across!" Van pointed to the curvature of the horizon, at a lightning storm irradiating the tall clouds in pockets, and for the hundredth time said, "Words cannot describe this." It made Alaura remember her first time with Ynt'taris, when the patriarch had taken her away from the prince.

At the center point of the Shield Mountains between Taysor and Morbatten, Ynt'taris began to dive. Only after they pierced the clouds did Van see Taysor. The last northern mountain of the Shield seemed to glow golden and Alaura said, "That's where Oranstakar resides. He's the dragon that watches over Taysor."

"The Allegiance of Blood, you mean?" Van asked. "I thought that was a fable. Something we hear to distinguish us from Merakor."

Ynt'taris began laughing, his mirth audible through the roaring wind of their dive. Alaura patted Van's hand on her waist. "Your ignorance is cute. I was like you when I began studying with Master Ynt'taris. The Allegiance is real. The god of this world required it of our ancestors as assurance none would bring the Kinslayer War to the Isles."

Protected by the spines along the white's back, Van adjusted his goggles and yelled back. "So, there were spies in the refugee groups! I knew it."

Alaura nodded. "Same as how the Slaadi, rakshasa and others infiltrated the lower levels of Merakor, many of them retreated with the refugees away from the front lines. According to the dragons, almost a third of the refugees failed the Allegiance. Their blood stained the shores of the Isle of Mondsa. The stories in our histories about the oceans of blood, that was Krentismar's thri-keen slaughtering the infiltrators."

Ynt'taris pulled into a gradual bank circling the tall central tower of Taysor's king. Smaller towers and keeps stood in a ring around it all interconnected by broad highways atop intersecting walls. Palace guards gripped their weapons and fidgeted nervously while the white dragon circled around their keep. Ynt'taris did this a few times, letting them take in their own puniness compared to his majesty. At last, he dropped the herald banner of Queen Alaura. Making one final turn, he landed in a courtyard and humanshifted to his preferred form. A bright sun dress and ponytails amidst a flurry of falling snow helped his human form evade the guards. By the time the palace guards reached Alaura and Van, Ynt'taris was nowhere to be seen.

They came cautiously, holding long pole arms bearing anti-dragon enchantments. "Where is the Beast of Roland?" a captain demanded of Alaura.

"Master Ynt'taris wished to see Taysor while I attend to business with the Pragmatic Order. Please convey my warm regards and well wishes to High King Nathaniel. I would be on my way." Alaura turned to Van and winked at him. "Ynt'taris would love to know they called him the 'Beast of Roland.' He feels that Alerius gets all the best appellations." Van offered her his arm and they began to walk past the guards.

The captain and his guard searched the courtyard and sent out runners. "Queen Alaura, riding a dragon to court is hardly..."

"Appropriate. Yes, I hear all the queens are seeking out how to make a better first impression. Yet, I must tell you that should Ynt'taris or the others hear you describe them as modes of transport, you can rest assured that you'll be eaten." Alaura got her bearings and walked to the eastern towers. "Captain, we'll be with the Pragmatists. Surely, they can accommodate us. Should you find Master Ynt'taris, I suggest courtesy rather than pole arms." She looked closely at the dragon-slaying runes on the pole arms and sniffed. "I see you've been upgrading your weapons. They won't do you much good against a patriarch."

The Pragmatist Order resided in a short but broad keep. From the street, it appeared as a massive multi-storied building covered in statuary and landscaping that ran up its high walls. Ornate stained glass windows, showing the mythologies and heroes of the Order, adorned all open surfaces. Built for both military and official purposes, the part-palace and part-fortress appeared inviting and intimidating at the same time.

A contingent of knights bearing Alaura's banners rode up to the entrance just as they turned the street corner alongside the compound. All of the paladins present when Roland died had stayed on with Alaura, much to her delight. Their number grew slowly. Like her, they held a respect for Morbatten the other Taysorans did not care to possess.

Their captain, a middle-aged man named Harding, pulled up alongside and dismounted to walk with her. "My lady, we saw your approach by dragon and followed. You really should send word so we can give you a proper escort here in the city. Lord van Struzer," he nodded. "Good to see you again, sir."

Alaura put her arm through Captain Harding's and said, "I believe dragon escort sends the message I wish Nathaniel to understand." Alaura touched Van's shoulder. "Captain Harding, I'm glad you two already know each other. Should I presume your knowing each other was part of some royal vetting process?"

Harding chuckled. "You have no idea the frustration the King has with you, my Queen. Both LeRoy and Edwards came back like sulking dogs. Van was in the court when the King discussed your situation with both. And, it was not much of a discussion unless Nathaniel yelling at them counts? I'm rather surprised to see him returning with you. It will warm his majesty's heart."

Van tilted his head at Alaura and addressed Harding. "We've been rather busy. While the issue came up, we've been heavily engaged in dealing with a cursed piece of paper and a Slaadi army to the south of Morbatten. You should come visit, Captain. There's a lot more to do in Tania than house-sitting Roland's tiny shack."

"Speaking of," Alaura interrupted. "How is the embassy plan moving?"

"We have bids ready for you to review. I actually contracted fast riders to bring copies of the architectural plans to you, but securing the parchment against the trip to Morbatten has been difficult and not many riders want to go. I'm glad you're here. Will you have time to review?"

The rest of the knights bowed when they walked up to them. Harding gave orders to the three youngest to watch the horses while the rest accompanied Queen Alaura inside. Just before entering, Harding pointed to the goggles. "You may wish to remove those. While striking, they clash with your regal outfit. Van, I would have expected you to dress up."

Van stood the side with his arms folded, watching. "In my short time with the Queen, I've come to appreciate her view that some of this Taysoran culture is silly, if not unnecessary." He reached into his backpack and withdrew his official clerical mantle and vestments. "Whoever thought that white is an appropriate color for field work should be executed." Harding nodded. Alaura's first act as Queen had been to remove all ceremonial armor and weapons to either sell them or upgrade them to combat use.

Harding walked up to Van and adjusted his leather armor and handed him a polishing kit. "It's a better look, but to be sure, apply some polish. You can't pull off the battle cleric look if you can't take care of your armor." He pulled tightly on a shoulder strap and suddenly Van felt several places become more comfortable. He took a deep breath and laughed at how he could breathe more easily. "Seriously? Ask for some help. Our Queen knows how to adjust armor." Harding quickly helped Van pull his cleric garb over the armor.

The entry hall to the Order featured vaulted ceilings supported by flying buttresses. Outside light filtered through the windows casting different images on the floors and walls depending on time of day. Right now, the image of Cyril Nostram battling a chain-wielding demon chased the image of Queen Abigail bowing before an angel across the central area of the chamber. Both famous Pragmatists from Merakor's history, Cyril won the battle against the fiend and ultimately married Queen Abigail. They had many children after Cyril retired from being a paladin. Their son became the first Pragmatist King to sit on the One Throne of Merakor. Alaura had never visited before and found the stained glass and their images fascinating.

Captain Harding, a member of the Literalist Order, noted, "It's said that the images change with the weather as well. I've never been here either."

Squires sat along the wall before tall double doors carved throughout and set with gold filigree. Statuary and books lined the entry hall. By the squires' easy banter, Alaura could tell they were friends. They rose and bowed at her approach. "Queen Alaura, do you wish us to interrupt our masters? They consult with Lord Tomeist for well over an hour now."

Alaura noted a sitting area beneath the windows some ten paces away. "It has been a journey to arrive here. Thank you for the offer. My group will wait over there. When your masters are done, if you would convey my desire to speak with Lord Tomeist?"

The bowed and waited for her to sit before they resumed their casual banter. Van looked around and relaxed. "This is a lot more comfortable though far less fascinating than our trip here."

Harding remained standing, vigilant in this place though not required. The Orders each had their own palace, which sat on sanctified ground. No one could remember the last time anything bad had happened to Taysor and so, over time the palaces became more functional and less military. While waiting, Harding briefed Alaura on kingdom matters. "Demolition of the Roland palace is proving more expensive. I suspect you have enemies that are driving up cost and creating delay. We continue to investigate but only see a common thread: whenever we are close to a deal, something bad happens with the workers and they withdraw their bid or we never hear from then again. It may be easier to renovate rather than build from scratch."

"Dar Tania has a vision of what their temple will look like. It is magnificent. In keeping with the Queen's Way, I want my palace here to serve as an inspiring embassy for discourse between our peoples. Renovating it is what every queen does. We must sweep Roland and the Absolutist legacy of that place away." She folded her hands and took a deep breath. "If needed, Master Ynt'taris would only be too happy to help."

Harding's mouth creased into a wry smile. "I doubt the King would appreciate any more destruction by the dragons. But, yes. If we cannot do this correctly, we may need to hasten your plans."

Van made a shocked sound. "Captain Harding, it rather sounds like you've converted to the Pragmatist way of thinking! A miracle?"

Harding bowed and Alaura explained, "My late husband and the Literalist doctrine threw the good captain and his entire unit into atonement when Roland used one of their avengers to strike down Dar's chieftains. You've heard this story I'm sure. Commander Sean personally intervened with the Literalist Order on their behalf."

"While my heart wishes to recapture the literal meaning of the scriptures, it opened my eyes to realize that we all faced demotion to Squire for the act of a spoiled noble." Harding made a fist and struck his chest plate. "Until it happened to me, I did not realize how arbitrary that felt."

Van leaned forward, "You must have great respect for Commander Sean. He was well-regarded here and in Morbatten."

Harding frowned and Alaura caught his hand. "I have so much on my mind, dear Harding. I forgot to tell you in a more appropriate way. Commander Sean fell. It's one of the reasons we are here."

At her words, Harding's face became stone and darkened. After a moment, he released his clenched fists and said, "I would hear this story in detail. I idolized Sean and rather hoped he would have taken me as a disciple."

Alaura stood and gave the captain a hug. Around them, the other paladins who had all been saved from atonement by Sean's intervention, bowed their heads in silence. She promised them all, "You will hear this story with Lord Tomeist, in detail. If time does not allow, then tonight at the palace."

They returned to discussing the embassy plans until the grand doors opened. The two knights and their squires paused and bowed to Queen Alaura before continuing on their way. They found Lord Marshall Tomeist walking towards them. Heavy plate armor gilded along its edges in magical runes moved fluidly with him. He carried his sword at his belt. Though old, he moved with energy and purpose towards them. At his command, the grand hall closed. Drawing near, he said, "Pardon an old man his cramped legs but I rather feel like not returning to my office. I have asked that lunch be provided while we speak. I presume this is about Sean's request for our 'heretical books?'"

Alaura and her party stood and greeted the old paladin with great respect. "That is one of many things to discuss. We have a mix of matters, made complicated by sad news."

Tomeist gestured for them to return to their seats and began to pace. "You don't mind if I do this while we speak, I hope?"

Alaura began. "Lord Marshall Tomeist, before we go into detail I must share our news with you first. I'm afraid it may steal the very air out of this room." Tomeist turned to face her and she continued, "Commander Sean is dead, fallen in battle against a mighty foe – a night hag. He saved hundreds of Morbatten's fighters and who knows how many innocents by engaging the hag. His fight enabled the entire rest of the army to eventually defeat it. Though I will tell you, it took well over three hundred of their best fighters almost an hour to destroy it. A grey slaad is involved and we will discuss this more later on. I am happy to oblige any level of detail you wish." She produced a letter, pressed and sealed by Sean's signet ring. "This letter conveys his wish to be buried in Morbatten and that his armor and sword pass to his daughter Seline. The mother should not surprise you; it is Dar Tania."

Tomeist's eyes grew both wide and sad at the last part, but he nodded. Though rare, it was not unheard of for Pragmatists to father children. Alaura bowed and continued. "Like I said, we will go into detail later. On behalf of Commander Sean and my authority as the Queen of Halkenwood, I ask that the Pragmatists certify and join Morbatten's war against a grey slaad naming itself Ylgolth. To ensure that Morbatten is suitably ready and trained, I further ask that the Heresy Library be opened and shared with me that Morbatten may train their paladins. Lacking clerics, except for Dar Tania, I also ask that the Pragmatists lend clerical aid to Morbatten."

Tomeist resumed pacing as Alaura went into detail on each of the points. He asked questions a few times but mainly listened. When his squires brought in lunch, he signaled for a break and refused to discuss Alaura's matters at all. After lunch and when they were alone, he resumed pacing. "Alaura, you have done a good job summarizing Sean's requests over the years. So far, I have been content to refuse him in silence. The grey slaad though, this changes things. The thing lacking in all of Sean's requests was an evil of sufficient scale to overlook the indiscretions of supporting Tiamat, on our borders no less! I was there and saw things transpire with Roland, but unlike you with your wide-eyed curiosity and naive acceptance of their ways, I saw the undercurrents where they flowed to evil. Yes, Pha Rann wants us to support Morbatten against Set. Of that, there is no question. But, Pha Rann leaves us free to serve Good as we see fit. Tell me, do you have proof that this grey slaad then serves Set?"

Alaura withdrew a book containing sketches of the chaos spawn trapped in stone all over Bruce's body. Tomeist recognized the ranger and covered his mouth. "For two such heroes to fall, it breaks my heart." He sat down. "I have been ready for Sean to either bite off more than he could chew and be slain by the dragons outright for years now or to retire. More than a few of his letters to the Order discuss the young lady Dar Tania. But, Bruce too. It is too much. I accept this proof."

With a tone of grave solemnity, Alaura said, "The hero Bruce was caught this way as he slew the love of his life. If this is not Set, I do not know what to name it. It is said that when prophecy begins to stir so do the forces opposing its fulfillment. For my part, I have no doubt that Bruce had fallen into Set's Dream. In some ways, I see Taysor as being blessed, yet again, by the presence of a strong southern neighbor. Sean set the precedent with Pha Rann's blessing and intervention at their Temple site. I would invite the Pragmatist Order to step aside from the Winter War and ally with my house in helping continue Sean's vision." She looked at Captain Harding and added, "With the Pragmatists, the Literalists would no doubt join this alliance as well."

Harding slammed his breastplate and bowed to Tomeist and Alaura. "There is no doubt. The messenger, just five years ago, stated for all to hear at Tiamat's temple site that Taysor is to be the shield. But, we are a small Order, Lord Marshall. We would march under your banner."

"Typically, I would call a council. However, Pha Rann fires my old bones with fervor. I see the rising smoke of battle and can taste victory. No council is needed. The Pragmatists will fight with you, Queen Alaura. It will take two days to muster. How about your Order, Captain Harding?"

"With your endorsement and example, we too shall be ready in two days! My Queen, I would leave to make them ready." He bowed at her dismissal and ran. All but two of his unit went with him.

Servants appeared and Tomeist began dictating instructions. "Let the bells ring. Let them ring," Tomeist proclaimed. "I will go pay a courtesy visit to High King Nathaniel. Before I do this, tell me, Queen Alaura, are these dragons truly so wondrous? Will they welcome our aid?"

Alaura smiled. "They are practical and care only about outcome. They will see this two ways: your aid ensures victory, and that this represents a continuing fracturing of Taysoran politics. They will try to use this to their advantage. They will also see this as their being obligated to the Pragmatist Order, a debt they have felt since they began their association with Commander Sean. Who better to find a good purpose in that than you, Lord Marshall?" She took his arm. "Surely, you would not leave me alone in this magnificent building? It is high time I visited the king in person. My last visit was over the corpse of Prince Roland."

Tomeist caught her arm. "Since Sean is no longer with us, I must ask you: to what end did Sean ask for the heretical training books? This is what I expected you to discuss. In keeping with his wishes, I retrieved these and reviewed them. While our Order will not use them, I cannot help but think a different god, or Goddess in this case, might find use for them. I have conditions the dragons must agree to."

Alaura signaled her guard to wait outside. "Harding, please prepare the group to visit the High King. Maybe, have a messenger sent to let Nathaniel know I am coming?" She turned back to Tomeist. "I'm sure that if the Pragmatists would start referring to the dragons as something more noble, the god emperor would consider your terms." She patted his hand and asked, "What terms, Lord Marshall?"

"These are absolute terms and must be agreed to for all time. First, Tania's knights are enjoined from any action against a Pha Rannic paladin except unless they are provoked first. Second, upon provocation, the animal law of 'bite back' shall apply. Lastly, Commander Sean describes aspirations he has tried to instill in the paladin and clerical orders. These principles must be inscribed in the Temple of Tiamat for all to see, so that they forever remember that a paladin's divine purpose, even accounting for godly differences in theology, is to protect and advance the world and its peoples through Honor and Justice. Do you think the dragons, umm, the Emperor Alerius, could agree to such terms?"

Alaura wrote them each down and brushed her quill along her lips, lost in thought. "I believe so. It depends on presentation. The Court of Patriarchs reacts poorly to demands and conditions. If I present these as affirmations of Sean's life, then it won't even be a problem. Alerius held great respect for Commander Sean, even in disagreement. As to the paladins, there is a hatred for Roland's Order. The Absolutists and the dragon knights, I don't ever see them getting along. They will most likely insist that whatever happens in the Winter War is exempted from this agreement. My lord, I need this concession. Otherwise, this becomes less of a discussion and more a presentation of demands."

Tomeist walked her back into his office. A chest sat in it. A single book rested on velvet padding inside. Alaura read the runes for "Take It All Away" and kissed Tomeist on his cheek. "You have great faith in me, Tomeist. If I might suggest that you bring this? Dar Tania will host a funeral the likes of which you cannot imagine. Both she and Sean had hopes of an alliance, if not friendship between the Pragmatists and their country. Who else than the Pragmatists to hold Pha Rann's Shield when the time comes to strike at Set?"

* * *

Ylgolth looked through the eyes of his marked goblins. They did not disappoint. Cave and crag burst forth with goblins and orcs rallying to the banner of the one strong enough to take the northern valley. Oral tradition told of fierce but delicious humans there who could only be taken by war parties, and then only in small numbers. It told of a protector so fierce they named it 'fire demon.' Because of the fire demon, none dared cross the river. Instead, they waited for the foolhardy to wander south.

With word arriving by these stronger and enhanced goblins, news of battle spread and war hosts rallied to join Ylgolth. In their minds, Ylgolth appeared as a fearsome and titanic demon equal to the protector of the humans north. Rumors of gold and treasure flowing there made it extra enticing. Ylgolth fed his dream to these desires for novel food, power, women, slaves, and treasure. The goblins and orcs responded well. Then, stone giants and trolls rose up from the mountains around the hot springs and joined the hosts. Seeing the stone giants, Ylgolth deeply regretted wasting all of his transformants on the goblins. "At least I enjoyed my last tryst with the gorgona," he laughed cruelly.

Automatically, behind him, the goblins laughed as well. Even though the transformants grew in intelligence quickly, it began from the baseline of the host creature and the goblins were truly pathetic. It would take these nearly twice as long to evolve to the Fecundus state. Hrax, one of his best, had entered Fecundus almost ready to transform. Feeling particularly cruel, Ylgolth pressed the Dream and the ground turned into biting insects. The goblins broke from their fast march into running. Another easy push and the fear of their being hunted accelerated the goblin horde so that they could almost keep with Ylgolth's march.

Whenever any fell dead from exhaustion or other accidents, Ylgolth called them back into his service and used the Dream to suppress the daylight of this planet. The natural sunlight could not be completely expunged, but it did enough to keep the shoddy bodies together. Snapping at one that impaled itself on a tree branch, Ylgolth said, "After all, if this mage is an

Atramenti, I must arrive with a proper entourage. And, if not, I will need all of you as fodder and distraction."

Ylgolth thought back to his last transformant. Hidden in a clay pot after Syliri pre-emptively escaped, Ylgolth chose to impart a copy of himself to that one. "If I die, I still live. It won't be but will be me." It gave him a small measure of comfort. This world felt so unbalanced compared the ease of the Dream's movement back home. Should that happen, his clone would know to leave this place at once. "Only survival matters."

They crested a ridge and saw the sparkling river. The slime was gone, washed clean by the weather. Scavengers cleaned up what the weather missed. Before them, burned out stumps of trees lay smashed backwards by the siege catapults. Ylgolth squinted. Gleaming glass sand swirled and looped in cursive showed how the fire vortexes had moved against his hag. Ylgolth swept his hand and the charred and still smoldering forest burst apart and away from his army to give them a clear and easy path to the river.

To their east, a horde of orcs cheered. Led by the marked goblins, Ylgolth strode forward to meet the war host leader. The orc looked brown and strong compared to the grey-cast green goblins. Tall and strong... *Well, stronger,* he corrected himself. "Where I come from, orcs do not taste good. I am Ylgolth."

The orc leader smashed a flanged mace on the ground. It blasted a rock there to fragments. "I," he stated while flexing his arms and chest, "am War Host General Og Unfreti. I bring you 950 warriors all! We come to war with the humans and claim the bounty you send us as visions. I," he smashed his chest again, "also bring fifty stone giants and a hundred trolls, but they are slower." The orc dropped to his knees. "For this gift, mark me yours, I pray you."

Ylgolth regretted again that he had no transformants, but marked the orc nonetheless. His webbed claws spiral-scarred the orc who took the pain without even a slight look of discomfort. Ylgolth's eyes took in the host of orcs and he lifted his arms high. To the orcs he sent a different dream. All around them, the goblins jogged in place too scared by their dream of biting ground to let their feet linger. To the orcs, Ylgolth sent images of their teeth morphing into fangs, their size increasing, their muscles bulging with power. The visions relayed through the transformant goblins now became direct from Ylgolth's imagination.

The orc host began to cheer and shout as they smashed their weapons on shields. Some of the orcs began body-slamming each other. Their grunts of head smashing rang out and Ylgolth took this sound and energy and turned it into a glorious vision of might and power. The orcs became drunk with it. Over their din, Ylgolth screamed, "We march north!"

Before him, the river parted and the horde crossed the banks. Flowers left by Dar where Sean fell, and other tokens left for other fallen warriors were trampled to mush, unnoticed.

* * *

Dar Tania came to and found she lay on the stone table under the three obelisks of the Temple. Blankets and flowers lay all around her as if a pyre though she quickly remembered the Taysoran tradition of gifting flowers to those in ill health or mourning. She leaned forward and found her body ached. She tried to stretch, but sore and stiff muscles from the battle hurt too much. She blinked in the sunlight and looked around to find Syliri lay next to her, and Alerius. The god emperor drifted in currents of magic with his eyes closed but facing the valley of Morbatten and south.

"God emperor," she tried to say, but her throat had torn and bled in her hymn for Sean. Feeling panic, she touched her belly and felt the dancing aura of her daughter, alive and well.

"Don't talk. You pressed yourself so hard that, though not wounded, you are beyond divine healing at this time. It will be some days before you can speak naturally. This is similar to what Sean proposed with his 'Take It All Away' method. You'll find that, from out of the River, you may pray to the Mother and will be just fine."

Alerius stepped down from the air and turned to her. His face looked different and Dar realized she saw pain, compassion, and then she noticed the column of smoke that rose high into the sky adjacent his mountain. The smaller peak was gone and the whole valley smelled of smoke. Ice that normally clung to the mountain was gone. Molten rock, still glowing red, ran up the side of Dragon Mountain and several rivers of molten rock dripped down its slopes. "We'll talk about it. I cannot right now, your pain is still too raw for me. I created this nation because of the beauty of the mortal spirit." He swept his hand out across the valley. "All of it is beautiful, but when my beloved rider's spirit fell with her Sean, it was more than even I could bear." He took her hand and turned her face to Syliri.

Dar noticed, now, that Syliri was unwell. Even for a medusa with green scales, her complexion looked sallow and enervated. Multiple wounds across her torso and a closed but a slowly bleeding wound in her mid-section leaked droplets of blood with each pulse of her heartbeat.

"You want to ask what happened. Save your voice. There is so much pain that occurred during your battle and I must tell you, caution you, that another battle is even now running towards our valley."

Dar's eyes opened wide and she took Alerius' gauntleted hand. It was the first time she ever heard him describe this place as anything other than his own. She lifted his hand and kissed it. "Syliri and Bruce were captured into Set's Dream. Though not dead, Bruce may as well be. These wounds you see on Syliri are from Bruce. She tried to save him. This is what is wrong with her." Alerius pointed to the obvious wounds. "Your priestesses could not heal her entirely. She lingers near death. Do not heal her just yet. I have her asleep."

Alerius dropped to his knees before them both and Dar felt a wave of dragonterror rise up around them as Alerius struggled to contain his feelings and lock them back inside his inscrutable face and always-calm demeanor. "I have prayed for a priestess through the aeons to help with just this and now, here we are. The not-obvious problem is that Syliri has been infected by a Slaadi worm. It is growing in her and suggests that she was taken by Ylgolth." Dar, still holding Alerius' hand, felt the dragon wanting to burst forth. "Until the worm is removed, she will linger near death. If you are up to this task, this terrible thing I am asking of you, we can restore Syliri. But her heart – like your heart – is broken. You may hate me; I would not blame you."

Dar tried to open Alerius' closed hand but like lifting a mountain, she could not. All around them, a phantasm of Alerius' true dragon self blasted outwards in waves of terror. It did not affect Dar, but Syliri stirred. Dar put her hand on Syliri's forehead. Down in the valley, the people would no doubt feel this. Eyeing the smoldering remains of the eastern peak, Dar realized they had been feeling this for days now. For long moments, Alerius trembled until he felt Dar's lips of fire on his forehead. Takhissis voice came to him and said, "My consort, you have a priestess now. Help her find strength to overcome her own sorrow by serving you, Syliri, and the people. You have not much time before Ylgolth arrives."

Alerius looked up and found Dar's eyes right before his. She caught and held his head, resting her forehead against his. Just like Takhissis had. Without speaking, Alerius finally felt what his cherished mortals called 'faith' and 'hope.' Dar pulled the mighty patriarch out of the River and steadied him against the flowing energy that roiled about with both of their emotions. A dark stain of shadow streamed away from Syliri. The eldar medusa aged and died in the poison of Time's flow.

Dar looked upstream and summoned the vision of Sean's death and caught it into her heart. "So that I never forget my first love," she whispered. She pulled Alerius' rage and caught it into her soul. "So that I never forget the love of the fire patriarch." She found the image of Alerius reacting to Syliri's plight and fixed it in her mind. "So that I never forget the love of dragons." She caught the torrent of Syliri's battle and Bruce's torture. "So that we can make the Slaadi pay for what they have done." Her steel voice colored Time's flow around her and carried the last of her words downstream. "What dark vengeance shall be wrought, beloved Consort of Takhissis?"

Focusing now on Syliri, Dar pulled Syliri just out of Time's flow. The slaad transformant nestled in her womb painfully contrasted with Dar's own Seline. It made her weep to see such a horrible thing there and she shielded Seline from its dark purpose and energy. "This must die, suddenly so that it cannot fight back or use Syliri's soul to shield itself. It is already aware and hiding itself from Syliri. Alerius, Syliri must die. I've never resurrected an eldar, but Tiamat whispers to me that it is possible."

Alerius shed his human form and revealed his true self along the River's banks. Downstream, the River's flow ignited with fire. Standing in a current of flames, Dar cradled Syliri's head and began to pray to Tiamat for her restoration. With Sean's memory in her heart, the flames all around her praying erupted in the image of her holding Sean just like this, and the reversed echo of her anti-prayer tore the ethereal. Still, her voice rang out loud and clear. Just before finishing it, she nodded to Alerius.

His talon, like a spear, pierced Syliri's belly and skewered the Slaadi worm. Dar pushed her hand into the broken flesh and yelled, "I have it!" She ripped it out. The memory of doing this for Sean made her ache. She resolved that she would not lose Syliri, her friend. Syliri tried to take a breath, but died in that moment.

The snake-like creature was covered in gore-filled quills. Webbed and clawed hands scratched along Alerius' talon while the head twisted in agony trying to bite at its attacker. Holding it against Alerius' claw so it could not escape, Alerius breathed a slow line of ember fire. Dar felt is as warmth even as the transformant disintegrated to ash between the talon and her hand.

When it was all gone, Dar completed the last verse of her prayer. Health and vigor flooded into Syliri's body. She awoke to find both Dar and Alerius cradling her from opposite sides amidst a torrent of liquid fire. The cool human tears of Dar and pinpricks of flame from Alerius brought forth her own tears. Gently, Dar lowered them all back into Time's flow.

"Is Bruce?" Syliri asked.

"It's bad," Dar said. "Morbatten is being invaded by Ylgolth. The god emperor needs us. I know you are tired, but I would ask that you help us watch over Alaura and Sean's people. They are coming to help. My people must fight their own battles, but we are too small to risk everything and we barely won against the night hag. Watch, Syliri. Pray. Should we need the brave fire giants, I will send word. Until then, watch and pray. You shall command the kerchki and ensure that Ylgolth is ended."

Syliri reached out and touched Dar's face. "You were the first human to love me," she whispered. Syliri noticed the darkness in Dar's eyes, which usually gleamed as pure red fire. "This," she touched Dar's eyes. "What happened?"

Dar tried to say, but could not, and clenched Syliri's hands. Wrapping them in his hands, Alerius humanshifted to embrace them both. "For what has happened, please do not hate me." Back on the Temple beneath the obelisks, Alerius turned and almost collapsed against the stone marked for the fire-breathers. "Vengeance is all I can offer." He vanished.

Dar pulled Syliri to her and tried not to cry, her hoarse voice making it worse. "Sean too?" Syliri asked. Dar nodded.

Dar felt Syliri freeze and her skin grew cool in her arms. The green scales of her complexion went stone white as even her snakes went still and unmoving. Syliri was beginning to retreat into stone, away from the world. "Oh Syliri, no. Please stay with me, with us. Ylgolth…"

"Deserves worse than death." The reptilian hissing of her voice promised revenge, for them both.

"Yes," Dar agreed. "Dark vengeance. For this and other reasons, I would ask you to stay." She took Syliri's hand and moved it to her belly. "I'm pregnant, Syl. Sean is the father. I want Seline to know you as her aunt. Who will teach her archery and the ways of the wilderness if not Syliri?"

Syliri's complexion moved away from stone though she remained frozen. "It sounded like Alerius almost apologized. Does he blame himself?"

* * *

Ylgolth's flood encountered its first abandoned settlement. It lay amidst open farm fields and perfect roads though no houses anywhere. The roads at first welcomed them. The fighters were unaccustomed to traveling on roads, but then and in spite of Ylgolth's dream, the road began to oppose them. A trip here and there toppled entire columns. Holes opened up and then the road would split and divide the army. Without careful attention, one branch would end up hundreds of paces from the other. Though Ylgolth had filled their minds with images of livestock, plunder, and food, none manifested.

They pressed on until the roads crossed the same river. The land, rougher here, still had perfect roads but the settlements grew more numerous. Ylgolth ordered them to burn the homes and set the forest ablaze. The ill power of Set's Dream compelled the normal east to west winds to blow north as their rearguard.

Rising up a section of the cursed road, Ylgolth saw a column of smoke reaching up into the sky from the north. Unfreti pointed and said, "We saw this first ten days ago. Volcano?"

Ylgolth squinted but this area remained remarkably immune to his power. "I have seen volcanos. They have grey ash that rises like clouds. This is something else."

The horde pressed on for hours before a runner caught up to the forefront. "Masters," the orc heaved. He had stripped off his armor and weapons to run faster. "Our rear flank is being attacked by wargs, and horses," he struggled to catch his breath. "They bear human riders. They are striking at us with poison and letting the fire finish those who fall. The undead are consumed by fire before they can arise and rejoin the horde."

Unfreti beamed at the runner even as Ylgolth cursed. "You have done well to catch us and give us this bad news." The War Host General's mace, bearing razor sharp blades on its numerous flanges, decapitated the runner mid-sentence.

Ylgolth ended the forest fire realizing his enemies turned what he thought would be an advantage into a weapon against them. *Clever*, he mused. *Atramenti clever*. That small knot of fear increased.

They marched on, this time wary for being flanked. Unfreti pulled the war host together into a phalanx formation with heavy shield bearers on the other edges. This slowed them even more than the road already did. Unfreti cursed frequently as the road twisted. After two hours of marching, they returned to the scorched line marking where Ylgolth ended the fire. So focused on their deliberate march and wrapped in the deep forest, they lost focus on the sun and somehow, marched in a giant circle.

The war host began to murmur. Unfreti had been hearing it for some time but prayed Ylgolth did not. Now, the grey Slaadi trembled with mixed emotions. "They think these tricks will stop your great army, Unfreti!" he roared.

In response, the army screamed. Ylgolth realized the error he made in letting Unfreti lead his army. Though they acquired new orcs by the minute, and the long circle allowed for another thousand at least to join, Ylgolth pushed and the second strongest orc suddenly saw Unfreti as a weak and enfeebled leader. When the second attacked, Unfreti easily smashed him but Ylgolth's dream pressed others to rebel. In minutes, Unfreti's dead body twitched and reanimated in the dream. *Another transformant host wasted*, Ylgolth sighed.

Though the army seemed incensed and ready to fight, Ylgolth did not know how far they would need to go before they reached their foe. With the moon rising, he signaled for camp. Unlike the hot springs and mine area, this area teemed with life too stupid to flee the Dream. Within minutes, all manner of forest creatures and livestock stumbled drunkenly into the army. "A feast, for my great warriors!" Ylgolth declared.

* * *

Shak and Otor knelt on a hill top. Five priestesses behind them blessed and prayed over them while they pressed the strange Taysoran device to their eyes. Each held a conical tube that magnified the image pointed to many times over. "Telescope," Shak rolled the word over in his mouth several times. "I can see their leader."

Otor moved to point his own telescope in the same direction as Shak's. "I count at least a thousand orcs, maybe more. Yes, I see the leader now too."

Shak flexed his back, which popped loudly. A priestess moved forward with concern. "You need to be careful, my lord. After so much healing, not even Dar Tania would recommend you being out here."

Shak popped the tube down to its compact size, appreciating its clever design. "Dar Tania would no doubt be here with us, were she able. Besides, it's time we stepped up and showed the Court of Patriarchs and our high priestess that we can act on our own. Tiamat blesses our course of action."

Otor agreed and smiled over his shoulder at the priestesses. Though not as pretty as Dar Tania, each had a quality that made them beautiful to Otor. He hoped they saw him the same way. "It's a good plan. Were the Commander here, I can hear him still saying, 'I like the strategy. Paladins could, but should not lead. Caution and inspiration must rule all your actions. Still, I like it.'" Otor pushed his chest out as he said it imitating the Commander's Taysoran accent. Everyone smiled.

Bomoki snorted. "Sean would never say that. Were he here, I can assure you, he'd tell you this is an idiot's plan. Still, since Sean is not here, I fully endorse your breaking with the Commander's rules. Testing and exhausting your enemy works well when you know what you're up against." Bomoki pointed to the south. "You don't know what you're up against."

Shak's eyes narrowed and for a moment, Bomoki wondered if the young knight and new commander of Morbatten's armies would attack him. The mage made a mental note to back off Shak D'Rath until such time as the young knight could be understood in more depth.

Shak pointed to Bomoki. "You said this was a good idea. Were you lying to us?"

Bomoki held up both hands, "No, no. It's a good idea. I just disagree that Sean would approve. Even in Taysor, paladins do not lead strategy; they carry out tactical orders. You guys are too ready to charge off into battle. Your individual strength does not translate to larger army tactics. I myself have heard Sean lecture you and two other classes on this very topic."

Shak's annoyance reached a dangerous point and Bomoki took a step back, hands up. "Look, your idea will work. But I beseech you, run the plan and let's then move back to the main army. That is still your plan, right?"

Shak took a deep breath. "Yes, that is still the plan. Though, sitting here now and watching them feast, heading back to the army smacks of retreat. A paladin does not retreat. Dragons do not retreat."

Shak and Otor removed their armor and stretched as the priestesses blessed them with the speed and endurance of dragons. While they did this, Bomoki removed miniature catapults from his satchel. Each sat cocked and loaded with burning oil, ready to fire. Shak picked one up. It fit in his palm, weighing no more than what a grown chicken might weigh. A small red rune inscribed by Bomoki's hand glimmered along the neck of each. "These will explode as we requested?" Otor pointed to the rune. Bomoki nodded. At last, Shak and Otor bowed before the priestesses after loading the catapults into satchels.

Veroi, Dar Tania's chief acolyte and a daughter of the Fish Tribe, finished their blessings. "Last of all, Shak D'Rath and Otor Ven, we bless you in Tiamat's name. You shall move in silence until such time as you choose to break it. May the dragons watch over and bless your efforts."

"Thank you, Veroi," Shak said. Though her blessing lacked the sledgehammer effect of Dar Tania, Shak was glad to have another priestess backing them up.

Veroi cursed at him. "You just broke the silence." She cast it again. Shak opened his mouth to thank her once more but, at a warning look from the priestess, kept quiet and gave her a silent double thumbs-up of gratitude.

The two paladins took deep breaths and turned to run towards Ylgolth's army. At the extreme range of the catapults, they set up four and aimed them at the enemy horde. Another fifty paces, they set up another set of four. They did this three more times. The last was close enough to the horde they could hear the loud feast and brawling orcs through the trees. They touched a rune on each mini-catapult and marveled as they enlarged to full size. As per their plan, they aimed the outer two high and at the edges of the horde. The middle two they positioned to aim just a bit more towards a center. If all went as planned, the orcs would be funneled into a straight line, ideal for the other catapults to inflict maximum damage. The forest would also ignite and burn.

Shak and Otor grasped each other's wrists and they bowed their heads reverently, asking Tiamat to bless their purpose. At the same time, they fired the outer catapults. In the dark of night, the barrels full of oil would not be detectable until they burst apart. Moving to the center catapults, they fired these as well. With Tiamat's blessings and strength on them like a mantle, they worked quickly to reload the outer catapults, with fire this time. Halfway through cranking the first, fire ignited along the tree tops and burning oil rained down on the army's flanks. The feasting and carousing stopped and turned to loud yells of alert and painful cries of those burning. When the next two barrels ignited, the horde's sentries spotted the fire of their catapults. As one, the horde roared and charged towards the two paladins.

The whiplash and kick of both catapults firing felt good. The orcs saw the fire this time and moved into that straight line funnel. The paladins cut the rope just enough that it would snap and fire on a delay. They ran fifty paces back and fired the four ready catapults there.

The orcs ran fast, charging the catapults. After being harried all day through the burning forest, the orcs were ready for action. The front line reached the catapults moments after they fired. In dismay, they found the four catapults unmanned. "The cowards retreat!" The orcs sniffed, catching the odor of humans leading to the north and west. "Come!"

The stream of orcs racing by the machines could not resist cutting at them with ax and sword. The first detonation of Bomoki's explosive runes triggered the other three to detonate. The force of the explosion cut the advancing line of the army off from its main column. It also masked the second line of catapults and their barrels as they arced high up and fell into the midst of the orcs. The sight of a wagon-sized barrel landing and bursting apart made an orc laugh at the sight of a goblin being crushed to death. The liquid inside, though, ignited in a flash, sucking the air and concussing those on the outer edge of the circle of fiery death. Seeing the explosions in front and explosions all around, the head of the remaining column halted even as those further behind pressed forward. Stone giants bellowed and waded through the fire in hopes of joining a fight at last.

Ylgolth cursed the stupid creatures and took to the air. From his height, he saw the two paladins run to and fire the last four catapults. Perhaps sensing his scrutiny, the two paused and turned to look at him. Ylgolth recognized them both from the river battle. They had played key roles in defeating the hag. He grinned and sent his glorious dream at them. The eye along his shoulder dilated to focus on something appearing behind Ylgolth. Enraptured in the dream, Ylgolth saw it too late. A black doorway of magic opened behind him. Through it, a barrel came hurtling at Ylgolth along with a blast of lightning.

The sudden impact and burning oil sizzled with electricity. Ylgolth shook the crude elemental attack off though it stung. His regeneration would heal this by the time he feasted on the two humans. Their cleverness though, it confirmed that they must be enthralled to an Atramenti. If not, Ylgolth would cherish and save these two for when he next created transformants.

Still alight with fire, Ylgolth dove at the two paladins. Still too far away, he noticed doorways open next to the humans and they vanished. Ylgolth's roar echoed across the valley of burning forest. The scent of burning orc flesh made his stomach growl. Halting his dive, Ylgolth saw that almost a third of his army burned. *Without scoring even a single capture or kill, these humans eliminated a third of my host… and they interrupted the feast that would have solidified the loyalty of the host to me. No doubt, the orcs now see me as complacent.* A paranoid voice grew in his mind. *How did the armored mage know about Polgeryx?*

Chapter 11 – Humiliation

Shak and Otor reappeared next to Bomoki and the priestesses. Bomoki finished his *teleport* spell and they all vanished before the grey slaad might follow their dimensional travel back to this point. Otor opened his eyes and found he stood in a cleared space before a divan chair on which Dar Tania sat. She looked grim. Otor had joined the second class, a time of never-ending joy as everyone discovered new powers and capabilities daily. He remembered the joy in Dar's face whenever the Commander came by, or when any of the paladin initiates passed a test. Otor noted her focus southwards where the line of oil fires burned many miles away. Wess, the knight who had run away from Dar, stood at her side and would not meet Otor's or any other paladin's eyes. By flickering torchlight, Otor had a revelation. *It's not just that the high priestess loved the Commander. She loves even those who fail. She truly loves us.*

Strengthened by the thought that Dar knew how to redeem Wess, Otor bowed to the ground formally and waited as Shak delivered his report. Bomoki confirmed it. Dar smiled, though her eyes showed how much the smile cost her. "Well-executed. I'm impressed. For the cost of the catapults, we have demoralized the slaad's army. We will break the orcs and, as a bonus, clear the eastward mountains of all goblinoids. Ylgolth shall die." A feeling that Shak and the knights recognized as dragonterror trembled in the undercurrents of Dar's intent. He shook it off, but before he realized it came from Dar, he instinctively looked and expected to see the god emperor. The others felt it too and even Bomoki took a step back and eyed Dar with new eyes.

"This fight is personal to the god emperor. As per the plan, we will focus on the mortal armies with careful attention to any with the spiral markings. Our Taysoran allies with Queen Alaura will clean up their eastward command." Dar waved her hand to the side and the council dispersed.

Bomoki walked up to the divan and took a long drink from a wineskin. "You were right, Dar. This is fun." The realization that she possessed dragonterror still roiled his thoughts. He had long considered her just the pretty face of Alerius' recruitment of Taysoran skill to Morbatten. *What else was I wrong about?*, he wondered.

Ignoring him, Dar called to Tiamat to flamestrike the area some fifty paces in front of them. Alaura stood there on the hill, alone. She wore clothing like Dar's from the river battle. Floating in the air next to her, the Darkhold floated adrift in its own dreams. The flame column reached up into heaven. Ylgolth would see it. They awaited Set's Dream.

High above the hill, Ynt'taris growled at Alerius. The two dragon patriarchs hovered and watched from their impossible altitude. Spark ensured they remained obscured from detection. "I do not like leaving my Alaura unattended, contingency notwithstanding. Syliri's contingency was hardly protective."

Alerius growled back. "Careful, Ynt'taris. Tread carefully with me on this. Though I love you dearly, my flames hunger for any challenge. Pray it is not you my flames reach out to consume."

Ynt'taris nodded and moved back from a sudden burst of heat from the fire patriarch. Miles to the south and east, they noted Ylgolth view and then scry the flamestrike. Predictably, the orc armies changed their general northern march to charge the hill as well. Ylgolth went invisible. "Too easy," Ynt'taris said. He sent his own vision to Alaura so she could track the magical disturbance clearly visible to the dragons.

The Hrax statue, what was left, stood repaired in stone next to Alaura. The hag's staff in her hands, Alaura forced herself to look calm and relaxed. Three metal balls of strange workmanship revolved in the air around her head. Each bore the kinetic shift rune. Each metal ball had been charged by one of the three dragons with intent to Ylgolth. They crackled with the distinctive energies of fire, lightning, and ice. "I'll be saving the ice for last, Master Ynt'taris," Alaura whispered.

The Darkhold stirred in its sleep as Set's Dream washed over them. To ensure Alaura's safety, Alerius had cast a powerful illusion of the real world to help stabilize it. The sage shrugged the Dream off noting how the horizon and ground seemed to breathe as if alive. Willingly embracing Alerius' illusion, she wondered what it would all look like fully in the Dream. It would have to be worse than what Syliri showed her years ago.

The Darkhold, though, responded to the Dream and awoke. Shadows began spiraling out and clawing the air around the book as it fell open and its pages began to flip. Alaura's skin crawled whenever she heard the book whispering to her. "Alaura, for what would you know?" She could imagine that if she opened it, the red words would sparkle at her in fresh blood.

* * *

Bomoki appeared on the rough road between Morbatten and Taysor. They were right where Ynt'taris had said they would be. Lord Marshall Tomeist and fifty paladins of Pha Rann sat around campfires taking their rest from a day's hard ride. Their squires prepared meals and Bomoki wistfully remembered his days in Taysor where road travel meant well-cooked meals that tasted delicious. Morbatten focused on strong meals to fortify the body. It always left a dry taste in Bomoki's mouth.

Bomoki raised his hand to greet the guards. "Always on top of your game, my countrymen." Bomoki bowed. "I am Bomoki, apprentice to the god emperor Alerius. The white dragon patriarch, Ynt'taris, told me that you might be here. If you stay, you will miss the very battle you seek. I am ordered to take you to the end game."

The Lord Marshall walked forward. "Bomoki, the betrayer." His words, often whispered in Taysor, had never been said to Bomoki's face. However, Bomoki noted the words were curious, not hurtful.

"So I am told. The Queen's Way has not been invoked since the days of Merakor." Bomoki turned in a circle. "Do I look like a betrayer, of Taysor, of anything?"

The Lord Marshall stepped forward and offered Bomoki his hand. For a just a moment, he detected a flash of evil within the mage's heart. Tomeist saw the mage standing atop a hill looking out over the valley of Morbatten, a ram's head wand in his hand, laughing with malice. Tomeist blinked and the images were gone. The mage seemed torn on taking the knight's hand. When he finally did, all Tomeist felt this time was ambition. The mage coveted power. "No, but you seem overly-eager to chase the magical arts. I am Lord Marshall-"

"Tomeist, youngest brother of High King Nathaniel. Yes, I've seen you many times as a young boy. For a time, I thought I would be a paladin, but my overall ill health proved that an idle fantasy." Bomoki bowed. "My lord, even now, two hundred novice paladins and two thousand barbarian fighters go up against a grey slaad named Ylgolth and a horde of orcs, giants, and undead. Though the god emperor personally fights, he humbly," Bomoki bowed lower to hide his smile – as if Alerius would humbly anything, "asks that you and the brave Pragmatist Order travel with me to where the grey slaad may have a contingency. Though not guaranteed to see action, the god emperor will deal with Ylgolth and the armies with the orcs."

Tomeist listened in an attitude of prayer. "If we go with you, will we save the day or at least help? And to where are we going?" Tomeist signaled for his armor and weapons to be brought to him and for the camp to break.

"In the east and south mountains, that is where we first discovered the Slaadi. They seem to like having contingencies. God Emperor Alerius asks that you and your knights help ensure the slaad menace is eradicated." Bomoki met the lord's eyes and smiled. "Though not sure, I have found that my master, Alerius, is almost always correct. While it may be saving the day, it will ensure the day is saved and the future is freed of more Slaadi."

Tomeist nodded. "I remember meeting the dragon years ago with the prince's ill-fated embassy."

Two hours later, and just as Dar was flamestriking Alaura, Tomeist signaled their readiness and Bomoki opened a gate, far beyond the ability of any Taysoran mage. Bomoki knew that someday he would be able to do this without the god emperor's gifts enhancing his powers. He held the gate with his magic and then widened it again so that they paladins could pass through it four abreast.

"Bomoki, this is unheard of. I'm impressed." Tomeist's words gave Bomoki goosebumps.

The Pha Rannic Pragmatist and Literalist Orders passed through the gate and reappeared in the hot springs. The horses struggled to retain their footing on the suddenly wet and slippery rocks. Bomoki, with a flair to impress, ignited a pile of goblins in faerie fire. The pile of fifty-some bodies lay a hundred paces from them. "My lord, this is what we were asked to investigate. The Slaadi infect hosts with what Alerius calls a transformant. It turns the host into a slaad. However, in this case, it could be something more. Do you wish to bide your time or attack the sleeping goblins? I assure you, they are bound in slumber and are linked to Ylgolth's life. When that dark life ends, Alerius believes that whatever this is will begin."

Tomeist prayed. He saw a portal open and a creature moving within it. He turned to his men and explained his vision. By popular vote, a Pragmatist tradition when time allowed, they agreed to wait for what they all considered to be the larger prize. Part of the decision was not wanting to attack and kill sleeping goblins. The other part was their desire to face an epic foe. Quietly, with their clerics behind the main line of knights, the squires withdrew with the horses to safety through the gate and the knights took up a semi-circular position. When Bomoki noted the acid nature of the liquid pool, they shifted so that it might not be used as a weapon against them.

* * *

Ylgolth paused in his approach several hundred paces away and hovered in the air. Using Ynt'taris' dragonsight, Alaura thought the slaad looked disappointed when the Dream did not affect her. Alaura twirled the staff and looked right at Ylgolth. Pointing the staff to him, she beckoned him to come.

Ylgolth blinked and nearly rubbed his eyes. This new figure, she was not the medusa or the armored mage. Though she appeared like a mage, the hag's staff, the hint of her from his other visions, and the book of pure chaos seething next to her suggested an unknown factor Ylgolth was not ready for. There had been just a hint of this figure in the ranger and medusa's minds. They had referred to her as "Queen." He switched his vision to look at magical auras. While the female's aura barely registered anything except unusual intelligence, her overall aura so near the chaos book and the three bright points spinning about her head like a crown, created a titanic presence that loomed much taller and larger than it should. Ylgolth's mouth dropped open. The shape of her magical aura looked familiar. "It cannot be; Polgeryx?"

Ylgolth flew closer and in a sudden bout of fear, blasted a forked tongue of lightning at her. The lightning struck a protective sphere enclosing Alaura and failed to even touch the hilltop. In response, Alaura took the hag's staff and tapped the metal ball orbiting her head. Charged by Spark, the ball shot like lightning at Ylgolth. A loud sonic crack exploded like thunder all around.

Taking cover behind his wings, Ylgolth barely had time to protect himself. He rejoiced that his natural and magical armor protected him. But, when lancing pain erupted through his wing, shoulder, and out his back, he realized how mistaken he was. Golden chains wrapping his torso exploded and links rained down to the ground with his blood. In disbelief, he caught his fall and touched the pain. A hole through his wing, through his shoulder, bled. Though regeneration started his body's repair, the speed of the attack and its ability to pierce through his many protections struck fear into his heart. Two similar bright points of magic remained to circle the sorceress' head. Realizing he might not endure another attack, let alone two, Ylgolth landed thirty paces from Alaura and fortified the Dream to further protect him. He did not feel the Dream responding to the Queen's command though. *Maybe she is so powerful she does not need the Dream?* Ylgolth marveled.

Alaura struck the staff on the ground and said, "Welcome Ylgolth, betraying thief of Polgeryx. Like a carrion beast, you slink in the shadows and fail to know your place." Alaura remembered Ynt'taris advice to mimic Bomoki when saying these words. It helped.

Ylgolth's eyes narrowed and he looked at the spell globe of invulnerability around her. "When last we fought," Alaura continued, "you caught me by surprise. This time, I rather think it is you who will be surprised." She tapped the ground with the staff and the area all around the hill lit up with suppression runes. Ylgolth stood within the perimeter. "Unlike our many confrontations, you will not be able to leave this one."

Ylgolth tested this and felt its truth. "Your magic has increased, Polgeryx. Or imposter perhaps. But if I cannot leave, then neither can you!" Multiple images of Ylgolth appeared all around the hill and as one, they charged Alaura.

With Ynt'taris' enhanced sight, Alaura never lost track of the original as he blinked and went invisible again. Alerius' charged stone shot out and blasted the grey slaad. The stone pierced his abdomen and Ylgolth doubled over in pain. Unlike the first one, this metal sphere detonated within his body. In shock, Ylgolth watched his legs shred and char as his upper body spiraled away from the ground. The burning inferno of the explosion slowed his regeneration.

Alaura tapped the staff to the ground again and enacted a spell that amplified her voice. "Ylgolth, for the crimes you have committed against me, I condemn you to die. My Fecundus slaves will eat you, and increase my power! But, I alone will eat your brain and unify Polgeryx as your master."

Ylgolth screamed as his upper body twisted through to the air to fall on the ground. Alaura's words reached him as if spoken into his ears. To lose to Polgeryx after all these centuries of being the victor. It enraged him. With one wing broken and the other burning, Ylgolth screeched for magical aid. No aid came. He screamed again and opened a gate. It would summon his Embros to him. With great anticipation, Ylgolth pointed to Alaura. When the first stirrings of the gate showed a red scaled claw coming through, Ylgolth shouted, "Kill the imposter!"

But, the armored mage came through the gate. "What sorcery is this?!" Ylgolth shrieked. "You're supposed to be…"

The mage reached out and drew dark energy from the book and answered, "Your slaad, yes? I'm no slaad, but I serve the ones you only sense in your own nightmares." Alerius caught Ylgolth's regenerating wing and ripped it out of his shoulder.

From the other gate, Ylgolth sensed movement and desperately reached out to augment his Embros with Set's Dream. When a small girl with white eyes stepped through, instead of the hoped-for Embros, Ylgolth knew he had lost.

This is the power of the Atramenti. I was foolish to seek this out. Embros! My clone, live and continue all that is mine. In shock and pain, Ylgolth sent his command to his transformant clone by the acid springs to activate. Only an Atramenti could so overmatch him. Ylgolth looked to Alaura, but she was gone. Instead, he looked straight into the eyes of a very angry Syliri. Magical suppression blasted him from the armored mage and Ylgolth felt his mind paralyze. The last thing Ylgolth heard was the armored mage saying to Alaura, "Great Atramenti, did I prove my loyalty?" The armored mage seemed to draw power from that book.

The book, it caught Ylgolth's slowly petrifying heart. As a last act of despair, Ylgolth's mind seized on the abyssal book. It did not just seethe with fell power, it lit the night sky with it. *Every bit the equal of Set's Dream... If I can get that book's power,* Ylgolth thought. *I want it, all that is mine. This book...*

In an instant, the book appeared before Ylgolth's face. It opened to a page containing fresh blood and many words. Knowing time was limited, Ylgolth scanned the page. It read in the chaotic style of the Slaadi's infernal language, "For endless power, for the midnight skies of Set's Nightmare, what is the cost to awaken Set?"

Alerius grinned; it had been tricky to get the Darkhold to display the last part of their negotiation in the infernal language of the Slaadi.

The answer read:
Write your name and have all that you wish.

In haste, Ylgolth touched his bleeding finger to the page and tried to write his name. His intent was enough. The small girl's hand punched into his spine between his shoulder blades with cold and inhuman strength. Paralysis set in as Ynt'taris severed the slaad's spine. Regeneration barely held him alive but he touched the Darkhold's page. Syliri loomed in his face and the grim power of her petrifying gaze continued to slowly eat away at what remained of his body. While regeneration would repair the physical damage, Syliri's gaze nullified the power in his flesh. Worse, he felt his lifeforce being pulled from its connection with Set into Syliri's experience with Set, where the predators become prey and Set is everywhere watching. Ylgolth felt his mind wanting to freeze, to stop, to avoid any movement that would call Set's attention to him.

"Please," Ylgolth choked. "My name is Ylgolth." The two dragons watched with expressionless faces though grim satisfaction filled their hearts. Ylgolth felt the book's power charge every cell of his body. With that extra vigor, Ylgolth revoked the petrification and paralysis of his body. Invulnerability and omnipotence struck Ylgolth's mind with images of the titanic Mother of Nightmares bound deep in the Abyss' center. His body's regeneration accelerated. In a heartbeat, Ylgolth felt his entire body reform.

"It was worth it!" the grey slaad screamed, clawing at Alerius.

The mage caught Ylgolth's hand as if not even trying. "Know my name and know your doom, fool. I am Alerius. Take the certainty of your death to the Darkhold forevermore."

Alerius? Images of the fire patriarch of Tiamat, of countless battles before Time, of Polgeryx sitting in counsel with the armored mage flashed to his mind with that name. Deep within Ylgolth's consciousness, the consumed Polgeryx began to laugh. A single thought bubbled up from Polgeryx, "Alerius, my friend. Thank you for this revenge."

Ylgolth began to scream as, like Hrax, his body began to move into the Darkhold as if being pulled one thread of gore at a time. The Darkhold's feeding took many minutes given the slaad's regenerative powers, which Dar reinforced with divine healing. Syliri and her snakes bit into Ylgolth's neck and filled him with poison as her petrifying gaze unleashed all her wrath at him. Only by the power of the Darkhold, did the slaad resist her gaze's power. Kelly tore Ylgolth's eyes. No sooner would Ylgolth feel a renewed flash of invulnerability than some dire wound would wrack him with pain. The fire-haired priestess continued to heal him. She even blessed him with Tiamat's endurance and courage. It confused Ylgolth to feel a strange god healing him, the Abyss empowering him, and this Atramenti's servants murdering him all at the same time. It went on and on.

"I will be the last thing you see, Ylgolth," Syliri hissed into his face. Venom from her words blinded him and his face went numb as stone only to break apart as Syliri head-butted him. Just as his spine regenerated enough that he could feel his legs, Alerius grabbed and disintegrated his leg from the foot back up to his spine. Just as the book granted Ylgolth power to resist fire or petrification, the small girl would lance him through with ice. He died. He died so many times. Each time, the fiery priestess would revive him. Each time, he would fight to thinking he might escape only to die again. Even the slaads in his memory, possessed by consumption of their brains, expressed horror and delight at Ylgolth's pain. Polgeryx mocked him relentlessly.

At some point, Ylgolth felt a strange sensation. The rise and fall of blades, the lull of pain and healing, the agonized screams for aid to the Atramenti, stopped. Everything froze and Ylgolth felt another new feeling in this strange world – certainty of permanent death. The priestess called for his resurrection, with hate darkening her countenance. It failed and she smiled at him from death's dark gate. "It is time for you to die, Ylgolth the Failed."

Void opened like a flower in his soul and everything became despair and pain. Ylgolth saw it: the Gate of Oblivion. For him, it writhed with cruel and mocking faces of those he had slain. They spat at him. Ylgolth's soul and body shredded and then fell to dust. The shadow that arose from the gate seemed confused. Dar Tania caught it with Tiamat's power and, off-handedly, pushed it into the Darkhold, just shy of multifixion.

Alerius ripped a sheet out of the book and wrote in his own blood:

As promised, I deliver to you a single unique life that is many thousands from across all creation. Know that I am Alerius, fire patriarch of dragons and chosen consort of Takhissis-Tiamat.

Slaadi – Ylgolth, many.
Consumed by the Darkhold. I know your name now,
Alerius of Takhissis-Tiamat.

In the plains below the hills where the Darkhold ate Ylgolth, Shak led the armies and the fighters of Morbatten in a night of bloody slaughter. The screaming and yelling continued through the night until near dawn, when the survivors tried to escape. They found their escape cut off by the undead raised by Ylgolth through their long march.

* * *

Bomoki remained with Lord Marshall Tomeist. After another hour, Bomoki whispered. "Dar Tania tells me that Ylgolth is about to die." He chortled. "This was the first time I ever saw the god emperor worry about a challenger. A grey slaad. He has no idea what waits for him in Morbatten."

"That powerful, are they?" Tomeist questioned.

"You have no idea, my lord. None at all. Each of the dragons would rival the mightiest archmagi of Merakoran legend. And, on top of that, they are then also eldar dragons. I remind myself ,often, to think of them as unascended gods." Bomoki cocked his head as if focusing. "If you wish, I can create an illusion of what their priestess Dar Tania sees."

On Tomeist's head nod, Bomoki chanted softly and an image of the battle at the hill burst forth in soft blue light. "The Queen fights alone?" Tomeist asked with concern. She sent the first metal sphere shooting at Ylgolth and Tomeist whistled. "I have never seen anything like that before." The bullet's shockwave continued well past Ylgolth into the night sky.

"This is magic I have not yet been taught. Someday," Bomoki promised. "Someday it will all be mine."

Tomeist patted the mage on the shoulder. "Milk before wine, my friend." The Taysoran adage for patience fell on deaf ears.

"This attack, it obliterates magical protections because there is no magic in the actual projectile. You must imagine it moving as if thrown by a god. The Queen Alaura started to explain it to me once, but she was abjured by Ynt'taris to not discuss it with any. I have no doubt she understands the magic. While I toil in experiments and research, the 'great Queen' is tutored in far more interesting and powerful magics."

The Alerius bullet shredded Ylgolth's body in half. Bomoki added more detail into the illusion. Alerius' instructions were very clear. "When this is over, I want Taysor to understand the folly of ever challenging Morbatten in any way other than the Winter War. Do you understand?"

The illusion scaled to show the relative size of Ylgolth versus the Queen Alaura. Bomoki expanded the field of combat to show the area from where Dar Tania watched and then added Master Ynt'taris high over the battlefield. "The one they call 'Spark', the blue dragon patriarch, he watches from the dragon's mountain to ensure we are all able to know and communicate. Also, lightning apparently heals the Slaadi." The illusion expanded again to show Shak and Otor Ven leading the charge against the orcs. "That book," Bomoki lied. "It was brought as a weapon by the Slaadi. It contains much of their power." Already, the Darkhold consumed Ylgolth into its pages.

* * *

Across Morbatten to Quattrain, Set's Dream ended. The goblins immediately turned to run, scattering in all directions. The orcs, feeling the death of their leader as a weakening of their own strength and resolve, saw the oncoming Morbatten fighters and the wall of fire, and undead, in their path of retreat. As one, the host screamed and charged to attack the paladins.

Around the Pha Rannic knights, the atmosphere changed. The goblins, trapped in slumber by Ylgolth's dream, woke up. Something in their midst also stirred. That was when the screaming began. A goblin almost escaped but a bone-ridged tentacle pulled the hapless creature into the pile. "This is not yet it," Bomoki cautioned.

From the center of the acid pool, a furious roil and bubbling erupted. From it, the hand of a slaad rose up into the night air. "That's what we're here for." Tomeist nodded and quietly passed word down the line.

Bomoki watched and heard, for a moment, Bruce complaining about the need for effective hand signaling. It almost made him laugh. "My lord, I'm going to enchant this entire area to look as it is. I realize you may feel you do not need illusionary aid, but..." All around them, the area upheaved as another Ylgolth pressed his dream into the area. The fifty paladins, the ten clerics, and the fifty squires felt reality twist and writhe with angry hunger. A moment later, Bomoki's spell reasserted a modicum of control over the area.

Ylgolth rose up to stand on the surface of the acid. "I see you," he said.

Noting that this Ylgolth did not wear the gaudy golden jewels of the other, Bomoki clutched the rod he had used to control the earth elementals in Home. He stamped it on the ground with authoritative force. When the metal clad foot of the rod hit the ground, the far side of the hot spring split and began to drain the acid, slowly. The ground underneath the paladins shifted, becoming firm. Bomoki whispered, "The god emperor likes to control every variable of a combat."

Ylgolth swept his arm wide, dragging his wing like a wedge through the acid. It created a splashing wave towards the knights and the goblin pile. Bomoki imagined a wall of earth protecting the knights but not the goblins. With Ylgolth still in the acid, they could not effectively engage... yet. The acid obliterated the goblins and left a young and red-appearing slaad shoving goblin flesh into his mouth. Four tentacles ending in eyes wavered from his back like twisted wings. Blood and gore stuck in the bone ridges. Like Ylgolth, this one looked around and pressed Set's Dream at them.

This time, they felt the ground twist and nausea washed over the group. The two Slaadi locked gazes. The black one in the acid said, "Serve me, Embros Ylgolth. Together we can defeat these humans. Imagine the power of their feast!"

The red slaad, leaned forward to crouch on all fours, the way a cat would when pouncing. It hissed back, "Imposter! Ylgolth told me that I am the one true Ylgolth!"

The grey slaad exited the pool too quickly for them to see and the two Slaadi tumbled back to slam into a rock wall. Bomoki reinforced the rock as five paladins crouched behind and near the wall's top. "Good strategy recommends that we fight the victor," Bomoki said to no one at all. The paladins charged.

Lord Tomeist felt a vigor and spring in his step as he charged. Though not as glorious an enemy as an actual devil or demon, the Slaadi sat near the top of the hierarchy of evil and definitely at the top in the worship of Set.

Fire and protective magic glowed into being around the lord, as it did for each of the paladins. Their swords began to burn with sunlight fire. When they leapt into the battle, the area glowed as if noon arrived. The slaads remained focused on each other, inflicting wounds and seeming to draw health, vampire-like, from the wounded other. Back and forth they went. Deeming the grey slaad the greater foe, Tomeist prayed and leapt into the air. Divine wings sprang from his back. At that very instant, a spell from the mage hit him, accelerating his movements and enlarging his form by almost double. Tomeist rejoiced and thrust his sword into the grey's back.

At the last instant, eyes embedded on the grey's wings caught sight of the paladin and the grey rolled aside. Beneath the grey, the red slaad twisted just enough to avoid Tomeist's sword. The other knights fell onto the Slaadi. The more experienced veterans arrived, born on winged leaps that Bomoki accelerated. The eyes, still focused on Tomeist, blasted him with a burst of glowing white missiles of pure magic. They burst apart like silver fireworks against Tomeist's faith, with no effect. The red sent a fireball spitting at him and though it detonated, the flames did not harm the Lord Marshall. It did burn the grey slaad, and the two turned back on each other.

Bomoki slumped down on his belly to watch the fight. He had only a single teleport spell left and could barely contain his racing heart. *Alerius, as you guessed, another Ylgolth has appeared at the pool.*

The answer came back immediately. *Not Ylgolth. The Anthracos clone themselves and seed throughout the universe. They advance in power by consuming themselves. I'm sure the Atramenti are like this too. The grey you see, is a clone. The red is a clone. The real Ylgolth is watching through the grey's eyes on the other side of the gate. Do not doubt it. My apprentice, when the Taysoran fighters end them, you are to send the head back through the gate. Ensure the red sphere is inserted into the head's eye socket.*

Bomoki tapped the small box in his belt nervously. After seeing what Alaura did with these to her Ylgolth, he did not like holding one so casually. *Remember, you must retain skin contact with the rune at all times.*

The battle, due to the slaad's regenerative abilities, lasted far longer than Bomoki would have expected. When Lord Tomeist at last cut the grey's head from its shoulders, and the red fell under a tide of paladins, Bomoki stood and had the earth elementals assist him moving down. He took the head, hoping the knights would not notice. Tomeist did. "What are you doing?"

Bomoki looked up at the Lord Marshall while he finished cutting the eye out. "A message to the Slaadi, from the god emperor. It should ensure the Isles are never encroached on by their kind again."

Tomeist almost turned away but stopped himself. "May I?" He reached out with his hand, as if feeling, towards the ruby gemstone marble in Bomoki's hand. The air around it glimmered with fire and Bomoki recognized the paladin technique for detecting inherent good or evil. It responded with fire.

Bomoki held the marble towards Tomeist. "Since my first day, any attempts I have made to similarly identify good or evil, they fail. The god emperor is a creature of fire. Do you sense anything?"

Tomeist shook his head. "I sense only anger and flame. I apologize for the delay."

Bomoki inserted the marble into the skull. When the marble was seated securely in the brain matter, he removed his finger from the rune. He looked up to where he knew Spark watched and held the slaad's gate open. "Let me know if I should not proceed with this."

In response, a forcewall of magical light sprang into being, illuminated with gently flickering lightning that crackled along its length. It reached out from the shore to the gate. Spark's voice sounded in his mind, "Ynt'taris and Alerius both said to stress this: do not jostle the marble. Be very careful." Bomoki took a step towards the magical bridge, but found that his courage faltered when he looked at the gate and knew it opened to more Slaadi.

Though he had rehearsed this with the Court several times, and in his head since this night began, the prospect of taking the skull through the gate – now when confronted with it – made his limbs weak. He swallowed. *All I have to do is walk through the gate, boldly gift the skull to whatever is there, and teleport away. That's it. C'mon Bomoki, you can do this!*

He took a few more steps, when suddenly, the Lord Marshall took his arm. Holy radiance filled the area around him and uplifted his heart. "Pha Rann bless you, Bomoki. We will complete this errand together."

Bomoki gulped and followed the paladin across the forcewall. It flickered and Tomeist withdrew his divine suppression of other magics. "What will be on the other side of this gate? Do you know?"

Bomoki tried to swallow and wet his mouth, but nervousness made it dry. "The dragons, they say that it will be the slaad's word," Bomoki stammered. "I mean - world. Sorry. Ylgolth's planet if, if he is truly a grey." Feeling a firm resolve and calm from Tomeist, Bomoki's voice strengthened. "Alerius thinks their highest form – their god, if you will – the Atramenti create and send their clones as greys into the universe. We could come face to face with their god."

"Wouldn't that be Set?" Tomeist asked, genuinely curious. That same question from anyone else would come across as condescending.

"It could be. I don't know. The Atramenti, Set, no one has really been able to study them." They reached the gate. Bomoki wanted to keep talking as a delay, but Tomeist pulled him through. "The god emperor thinks the Slaadi do not actually want to awaken Set."

Bomoki expected a passage of some kind. Instead, they stepped through to stand on a brown field of blowing sand. It cut into their skin. The dry air carried crystal shards. Both of them felt the weight of gravity and weakness. It made them stumble. Tall brown and black crystals rose up to an alien grey sun. To their left and right a ringed moon rose as another, banded in brown and red, set. Footprints in the sand showed the path Ylgolth trod to reach the gate. The gate itself sat on a circular dais of stone, several steps above the drifting rivulets of blowing glass. Bomoki flexed his fingers and marveled at how greatly diminished he felt here, and remembered Spark's lecture about traveling. Compared to his experiments as a student, he felt the weight of the universe pressing in on him many times more ferociously than the Astral had. Bomoki realized how very far from Tehra they must be.

Curious, he turned to look at the gate and noticed a single glowing rune floating over it. It was the locator rune for Tehra. He pointed to the rune and said, "Tomeist, that is how the Slaadi came to our world. I have just one spell left to return us home. Please, I beg of you, destroy the rune."

Tomeist nodded. Divine wings burst from his shoulders. They seemed overcharged and larger here. Again, Bomoki thought to the lecture on planar travel. Tomeist might be weaker, but they were perhaps a step closer to Pha Rann. Hence, the wings had more power here than in Tehra. The contrast between his own and Tomeist's power caught Bomoki's attention. *Maybe it's a paladin thing*, Bomoki wondered.

Tomeist rose up and summoned his avenging sword. In this realm, the sword appeared as if a ten pace long lance of golden fire. Bomoki shielded his eyes and had an epiphany. "Paladins are even stronger when they take their fight to the home worlds of their enemies. It's not about nexal travel at all." Alerius' interest in paladins and the nexus gate project jumped into Bomoki's mind though he could not connect the pieces as to why Alerius would want more paladins and a gate like the one they worked to construct.

From behind, a bitter voice startled the mage. "Yes, curse them. Curse them all."

Bomoki whirled, holding the head and the Rod of Earth Elementals before him like a shield. Through the grit in his eyes, he saw Ylgolth but also not Ylgolth. Tall and lanky like Ylgolth in Tehra, this creature moved more like a spider on six arms and legs. Golden webs that Bomoki realized were thin gold chains draped its body. Behind the mage, a cracking sound and flash of light told Bomoki that Tomeist had successfully destroyed the Tehran locator rune.

"There are more, always more," Ylgolth said. "You have no idea how many of my children walk your world."

Bomoki remembered Alerius' admonition to boldly present the message. Enfolded by Tomeist's wings and seeing how the radiant sunlight of those spiritual wings blinded the slaad, Bomoki held up Ylgolth's head. "I have a message for the Anthracos and Atramenti, not just of Ylgolth." Bomoki held up the head and spun in all directions, assuming others watched. He then placed it on the edge of the platform. "We have killed three Ylgolths now. We are ready to kill all of you. An alliance of Pha Rann the Creator, and Tiamat the Glorious are pointed like a spear at your very heart. Trouble us no more. Our fight is with Set, not the Slaadi. We offer you Ylgolth's head as a warning, and also a promise of more death."

Bomoki bowed and enacted the teleport spell. He and Tomeist vanished. As Bomoki cast the spell, he heard Alerius' words casting with him, altering and changing the spell. The locator rune, which Bomoki had labored over for weeks, burst forth in Bomoki's memory. A key phrase of the spell altered and power beyond anything Bomoki had felt or known changed the spell to state recall to an alien place whose name Bomoki could not recognize. Bomoki made a note of the changes and swore to remember it exactly. Panic still struck him, though, and then he and Tomeist appeared on the hill beside Alaura. The mage fell to his hands and knees and began vomiting. The alien air and glass sands of that place began disintegrating out of his skin and lungs as a brown mist.

Unaffected, Tomeist smiled and bowed to Dar Tania and the Queen Alaura. "It is good to see you both again."

* * *

The Atrament'ylgolth watched curiously as the puny mage tried to teleport away. With the gate severed, such a spell would not work. That it did, when the mage and the paladin vanished, had been curious. It should not have been possible, not by any rule of magic or divine intervention. The slaad's body rotated through the sand to clear unstable areas and approached the gate platform. The decapitated head of Ylgolth sat there in a puddle of coagulating blood and gore. Twisting its vision, the Atramenti noted a tiny point of magic and withdrew fearing a trap. When nothing happened, it hissed. From the sand all around the platform, legions of Slaadi rose up, shaking free of the dirt. Four greys stood before countless hosts of Fecundi organized into thrashing masses. Azuros kicked and stabbed into the masses keeping them generally intact.

One of the greys, on a signal from the Atramenti, moved forward to the head and picked it up. "There is a gemmed ball in the brain." Several spells later, the grey said, "The magic is a lower level rune inscription. That's all there is. Perhaps it is a gift?"

The Atramenti slowly distanced itself from the platform. "Perhaps, but we have not survived this long by presuming our enemies give us warnings or gifts. That their teleport worked… this should be a trap. It is obviously a trap."

The grey Ylgolth nodded and summoned an Azuros. "This is a trap, but we must consume the brain that we might know where and who these creatures are in the Tehran realms. You are to consume the brain. If not a trap, or one you survive, you will have a grey's powers. Congratulations on your impending transformation."

The grey then retreated behind the sand dunes and crystal columns. On a whim, the Atramenti transferred its consciousness and soul to his favorite grey and ignited the Atramenti's host body alight with magical energy, to give the trap a target if it worked that way. Wishing for other decoys, the Atramenti suppressed his innate paranoia for a moment. Focusing hard on it, the ebony slaad suppressed his own magical power.

On command, and with a look of resignation, the Azuros picked up the head and bit into the brain. Its eyes gleamed as power and knowledge filled his mind. He wanted to eat more, to eat around the rune-inscribed marble. The Azuros called back, "Alerius is the correct name of our foe." He almost said more; Ylgolth's knowledge flooded his mind though and he hungered for more power. A hiss from behind by the grey compelled him to get on with the trap part. He reached in to grab the gem and touched it.

A whining screech filled the area around the platform. So loud the Fecundus nearest the head dropped to the ground and covered their ears, the Atramenti saw the Azuros drop dead. In a straight line that then curved towards the Atramenti's decoy body something moved impossibly fast. No magic, but as it moved, a single ribbon of Slaadi fell dead until it reached the Atramenti host.

With enhanced vision, the Atramenti saw a tiny hole appear in the navel of the host. Another hole burst out the other side and then it arced back. *Tehran magic should not work like this here,* the Atramenti thought. To see better, the Atramenti called on the Dream and slowed Time's flow. The object was conical, similar to an arrowhead, but made of the strange material, which apparently did not lose potency across the planes. It had almost no magical signature at all yet acted in a most magical way. The only magic seemed to be that guiding it to strike at the most magical creature there. Atrament'ylgolth thanked Set for the ever-present paranoia that, in this case, saved its life.

The second time it entered the decoy, the sound stopped. The host petrified. "What magic is this?" Atrament'ylgolth marveled. A second later, a detonation blew the host to pieces. In slowed time, the Atramenti saw the division of the realms waver and then fracture as the blast shredded reality. Somehow, the Tehrans had sent their magic, with barely discernible power, into the Slaadi worlds. That it contained enough power to destroy a grey slaad and shred the dimensional separation of the Abyssal realms was impressive. Watching the mayhem, the Atramenti pondered what it would take to do this while also shielding the destructive power and petrifying magic. *More power than I have alone. The Atramenti have this power here, but in Tehra? No, this is too much,* Atrament'ylgolth sent this thought and observations into space to the other Atramenti where they hid, lords of their domains.

Fire and flame pulsed throughout the targeted slaad. Shockwaves blasted out from it. Lesser Slaadi incinerated, leaving shadows in the sand as their bodies protected the dunes from melting to glass. Atrament'yloglth signaled and the greys abandoned this dominion for another, safer one. Behind their departure, the demonspawn that haunted the in-between spaces of the Abyss poured through the fire to attack the remaining Slaadi. A small voice in the Atramenti's mind whispered, "This is the fire of the one named aler Alerest. I'd recognize it anywhere." It was Polgeryx, an ancient Anthracos that almost ascended to Atramenti.

Atrament'ylgolth ordered, "Polgeryx, provide all memories of Aler Alerest." Images of Alerius sitting in human form, like an armored mage, with Polgeryx in the twilight of Merakor's destruction filled the Atramenti's mind. The roiling maelstrom of chaos blasted into their new dominion through their escape gate. The greys closed it off, before warily eyeing each other. Only one could be the Atramenti. "I am not dead," Atrament'ylgolth said. "You serve still. Go, find the greys of this place and identify them to me. This shall be our new world."

The Atramenti paused and then called out, "Let word be sent throughout. No slaad shall go up against Aler Alrest, for our collective safety. So order I, Atrament'ylgolth."

In the silence, the wind howled all about. The world lay unspoiled before them. Insect creatures scurried about in the ground, in the air. The Atramenti dug into the moist soil, reveling as it began to consume and gather intelligence. Soon, higher life forms would feed it everything it needed to know to dominate this place. He focused and called out, "Send word to our Tehran comrades. Let them be watchful and report all that they know about this Aler Alerest. The Atramenti would know where and how this magic is accomplished. We have infinite time to acquire this new power that should already be mine, be ours."

Around them, disembodied voices echoed in chorus as a handful of Atramenti concurred. Atrament'ylgolth wondered for a moment, as he always did in these moments, *Did the voices really sound their concurrence, or was that just a genetic memory from the countless Slaadi consumed across an endless lifetime?*

Chapter 12 – Court of Patriarchs

Alerius found himself joined by Ynt'taris and Spark on the Temple mound. Heavy winter snow fell and though the still smoldering remains of the eastern peak kept snow from sticking there, the valley of Morbatten sat quiet. Alerius allowed himself to humanshift and sat upon the top of the stone tower marked for the fire breathers. The other two followed his lead.

Hours passed until at last, Spark broke the silence. "Our apprentice, Bomoki, he works tirelessly on the gate. I would hazard that, between his keen observations and memory, and the hints we have given him, he may have already begun piecing together the magic of *phase shifting.*"

Only the blizzard force winds answered for a time until the young girl atop the ice breather column spoke. "My brothers, you laud greatly Bomoki's achievements. I fear you gloss over his true nature: a power-hungry miscreant drunk on eldar magic and the access you give him. If ever a corruptible human existed, it is this one. I see in him the same attributes that drove Ool to madness."

Alerius spoke immediately. "Ool is madness. Bomoki may succumb to the allure of undeath. All mortals, at a certain point, must come to terms with the poison that is Time in this realm. So long as he completes the gate's missing pieces, I care not which way Bomoki chooses to end or prolong himself. Dear brother, if I take your objection at full value, I would question Alaura. Either as our apprentice, or as a lich, Bomoki shall complete the shift gate."

Ynt'taris hissed and then inhaled deeply. "Alaura is," he conceded, "equally susceptible though her nature lends itself to not-necromancy. Bomoki, I can see that one rushing headlong into it without regret or second thought. It would be to our detriment."

"The teachings you so freely share with your rider, Ynt'taris, are also to our detriment. From the same point of voice," Spark countered. Alerius nodded in agreement while Spark continued. "We have cherished our secrets for so long, I find a certain pleasure in sharing them and watching it ignite the mortal mind with new possibilities. It reminds me of a lightning storm within their mind."

"Firestorm," Alerius stated.

"Ice. Yes, I see that. So, are we to continue on this course?" Ynt'taris asked the other two.

"Painful though it has proven – do you remember any other five year period of such turmoil within the tribes?" Alerius asked.

"No, it is unprecedented," Ynt'taris answered. "Syliri is dear to us all. She is recovering?"

Alerius looked up at the night sky and focused on the snow rushing towards his face. The thermals wrapping about his body pushed the snow away from him but he found it beautiful. "Add some lightning to this storm and it would represent our hearts," Alerius said quietly. "Syliri, like my precious Dar, she mourns for herself and Bruce. Though we have broken her from Set's Dream, her kind is especially susceptible to Set's power. It lingers with her. She has added Bruce to the Garden, against my request that she slay the ranger. She says that the people must see what chaos spawn do and how they take root. 'My heart is stone,' she says. 'You have none of my sisters in this place. Let me and my Bruce remain here forever.' For an eternal being, that five years means so much, this is the remarkable thing about this world, this single blue gem in the vast planes of space."

Spark added, "I have spoken with her. There is a chance to undo the chaos. It is a spell we have long researched, my brothers – the ability to unwind the fabric of this world and reshape it as we did before Time. I have shown her our research. Her despair makes her intelligent. Within minutes she pointed to the sacrificial clause. She forbade us doing this for her Bruce. As she put it, 'Even if this works, Bruce is mortal and he too shall die, again. As the god emperor says when consumed by mortal emotion: *I am alone.*' She thanked us and said she would consider it, but only if she could make the sacrifice herself or we found some other way. If she restores him, I estimate that Bruce would have just minutes of free thought. Perhaps, by keeping him in stone, Syliri would prolong his days with her. Medusa look at stone and life the same way. Maybe to her, he yet lives."

Ynt'taris leaned forward and asked, "The Darkhold Project may know how to undo chaos spawning."

"It may," Spark said. "For now, I have locked the Darkhold in my inner sanctum. Bomoki, Alaura, others – they have shown themselves corruptible by it. When we have mages loyal to Tiamat, I suggest we bring it forth then. It is dangerous. As we discussed, brothers, I copied the Ylgolth page many times. The Darkhold does not need the same page and has since spit them back out across the universe. Because Ylgolth believed he was destroyed by an Atramenti, the tale of Aler Alerest and the Atramenti of Tehra no doubt falls like this snow across the Abyss."

Alerius cautioned Spark. "See that you are, dear Lord of Thunder, not corrupted by it as well. I found it worked against my desires the same it did the Taysoran men. Let us also place a contingency upon Bruce, to disintegrate him should he birth a chaos spawn." When finished speaking, Alerius signaled a change in topic. He opened his hand and illusion ignited. Dar Tania appeared within the magic. She sat on a plush rocking chair by a crackling fire. Seven priestesses sat before her, listening. Her belly showed almost four months pregnant. "She is more beautiful in her motherhood than I dared dream possible. Each day, Seline dances and mimics our high priestess. Dar grieves still, though with each day, the excitement of sharing stories about the Commander with Seline gives her hope and focus for the future, not the past. Listen…"

Alerius' words faded and Dar Tania's voice synced with the illusionary image of her class. "There shall be multiple books in Tiamat's scripture. Each book will have a focus. We have already discussed the genesis story of how Tiamat came to be, and also a book dedicated to the five cardinal dragons, and the mortal emotions they encompass. A book of paladins, of course, must be there and for priestesses too."

A student interrupted and asked, "Only females, high priestess?" Ynt'taris recognized her as Lilli, the cleric attending Alaura since last winter.

"Please, call me Dar. High priestess is too much of a mouthful. Tiamat is female and so the priestesses serve. You ask about men. Tiamat commands them to serve as paladins. My heart whispers that a day will come when both male and female clerics serve but not now."

They all laughed and one, a small girl no more than eight years old, finally stood up to get their attention. "Ana," Alerius breathed at the illusions. "She has the weightiness of prophecy about her, my brothers. Tell me you do not feel it."

Ana bowed and said, "High priestess and priestess, too many words. If we must call you Dar, maybe we can have a rule that we are all Dar. Dar This and Dar That. Would I be Dar Ana, Dar Tania?"

Dar leaned forward and brushed the child's already intense red hair back from her face. "I like that, Dar Ana. Come," she patted her lap. "Sit with me and let me tell you a story from the Book of Genesis."

As Ana climbed up, the small girl giggled and said, "Of course, I'm not as beautiful or as powerful as you, Dar Tania. Maybe there needs to be something in-between for me to grow into, like R'Dar? Can I be R'Dar Ana?"

The priestesses chuckled at Ana's precocious questions, but agreed. "Of course, R'Dar Ana. I like that too. Now, let me tell you a story. The Mother whispers to me that, for one of you, this story has special meaning. Did you know that in the Dragon Wars, the wars that separated the colored dragons from the metallics, that only two dragons dared to rise up and attack the All Father? Anyone want to guess?"

With the innocence of a child, Ana said, "The god emperor, of course." The others nodded and after a pause they speculated it must be Spark or Ynt'taris. It turned into a debate and the two patriarchs swelled with pride to hear their merits and strengths lauded as reasons for their challenging the All Father.

Alerius interjected, "At some point, we will set the record straight as to your roles during this time. I would wager that Alaura figures it out, unprompted. Challenging the All Father makes the Dragon Wars sound trite. We all, the matriarchs included, played roles. Mayhap there shall be other books."

Ynt'taris bowed and thanked Alerius for his faith in his student. The illusion resumed and Dar Tania said, "His name is Bvocpharan Mae'yl, though the god emperor names him 'Crimson Burning' in draconian. Crimson was part of a hatching just as Time first stuttered. Born on the threshold of the world we know, he hatched at the same time two others did. Alerius names those other two Armageddon and Arminoth. These three each became leaders of fire breathers and were the first to pledge loyalty to Alerius and Takhissis. To hear the god emperor describe it, Crimson's breath channeled the Gate of Creation into a lance of fire so hot it could cut the planet in two. When the Dragon Wars erupted, Crimson attacked the All Father and was cursed to lose his eldar magic. Of all that remain of the eldar dragons, Crimson is the only one unable to wield magic, and to humanshift as does the Court of Patriarchs."

Ana tugged on Dar's sleeve. "Tell me, Dar. Tell me: if the All Father stole Crimson's voice and magic, what happened to him?"

Dar pulled her back against her shoulder, seeing the sleepy look on the child's face. "We don't know. It's a mystery that haunts the Court to this day. The All Father cast Crimson away, out of Heaven and where he fell and landed, we still do not know."

Back at the Temple, Alerius smiled at the illusion and it parted to give way to the gate. Bomoki worked on the second of five hundred rune tiles. "At the ninth tile, we shall hasten his work. Soon, my brothers, soon. The eldar dragons will come back to Morbatten. Crimson, my friend. The fires here are warm and await your stoic heart. Wherever you and your kin are, hear me. I am Alerius. You will be found. We shall bring you three home."

Spark and Ynt'taris bowed their heads and joined Alerius in stating this fact: *We will bring you home!*

After a moment, Spark and Ynt'taris both spoke at the same time. "Brother, with concern, in this sequence of events, you have aged more than we have ever seen except when Merakor fell. These mortal emotions, you must bear them with greater care."

Alerius held his right claw forward and noted the deepening of colors there. "Yes, I have aged. The eastern summit is no more. Syliri is wounded. Our Taysoran heroes are dead. Time flows and we remain as always, a bulwark against its murder. We must consider the long view of this: Sean the Hero, exemplar of Pha Rann chose Morbatten and Dar Tania over Taysor's ways. Though Seline is but one child, we shall tell the world of Sean's many children with Dar, of his love for the paladins, and of his bright heart's alliance with Tiamat. The story of Sean and Bruce will echo throughout future generations as a clarion call to heroic service in Tiamat's name. The aging is worth it. This sacrifice of my body ensures an increase in faith."

Spark nodded. "Have you considered why the paladins did not draw fireswords in the battle at the river? The heretical book Alaura brought us suggested that only dire peril would advance them."

Ynt'taris spoke. "The book said dire peril and heartfelt appreciation for the miracle of divine intervention. Leave it to Pha Rann to write such pithy things into a book his own worshippers deem heresy."

Alerius answered. "It is surprising that our children take for granted the divine power of the Mother. Perhaps we need to restrict it from them for a time. Shak D'Rath will execute the book's instructions bereft of divine love. Bomoki must focus on the gate."

Ynt'taris added, "Alaura promises to bring more mages. Bomoki, alone, is dangerous to us."

* * *

Tren watched as Fist carried Brook into the giant white marble stadium. Built in the early days of Morilon, when they anticipated great partnership with Mallaforax under the rule of Queen Raina Pajor, the stadium formed a half circle around the southern edge of the world tree. Mallaforax named the tree 'Earth and Sky,' and the stadium itself had come to bear that name. The trip from Merakor to Morilon, though, taxed Reina and old age and grief for the past claimed her life before the rest of the stadium was ever completed. Her eldest son, Vel Pajor, blamed many things for Reina's death and the elven exile to the Forsaken Isles. He blamed the weakness of the elves in not seeing the growing decay in Merakor's roots. He blamed the alliance and its heroes for not doing more. In Morilon, he blamed the god of the world, Krentismar, and the dragon Mallaforax for not saving his daughter's, and later his mother's, life.

Raina had devoted her life to nature magic. Though not a druid, the Queen's passion for living things had, at least, touched and helped shape Morilon. Many Merakoran plants and trees took to the soil and it brought a measure of peace to know the dark elves had not destroyed all of their fond memories the homes they forsook. The great stadium doors, shaped by living roots of the world tree itself, they only ever opened for the Queen or during times of great need. When Mallaforax summoned the elves since, they had to walk around the edges of the stadium, or more recently, a mage stood guard with the fighters and would fly over the walls to hear and consult with the dragon.

Tren should have been surprised when the doors opened, but his nine day journey with the two unlikely companions taught him how jaded he had become under Vel Pajor's rule. When the elves have lost their savor in life, all days blur together and the immortal press of time brings only ennui. If Tiamat could inspire a hill giant to laugh – to say nothing of befriending a Halfling – then perhaps Vel's narrow vision for their own race, the natural heirs of laughter, required re-examination.

The doors to the stadium opened. The mage and the fighters on patrol where the grand boulevard met the stadium stared in disbelief. Thick mist from the world tree's roots wafted out of the three story tall doors. A moment later, the acrid sting of chlorine gas reached their noses. One of the elves muttered about dragon stink, but Tren told him to be quiet.

The dragon's voice rumbled out of the stadium. Built for perfect acoustics and even though not finished, Mallaforax's voice sounded like a wet landslide. "Tren Venfermis, ranger of Krentismar, you may enter too. My druid and her giant shall require assistance, from a friend."

The mage looked at Tren and pointed to the doors. "You can't not go. You must. Our nation's charter requires absolute obedience to any non-evil commands by the dragon."

A warrior said, "It's not a command. Remember the last time there was a command. You can tell. This is an invitation."

The mage looked annoyed. "Command, request; it's a dragon talking. Tren, you must go."

Fist and Brook turned and were waiting for him. The Halfling, looking smaller than ever against the stadium door to the dragon, waved him forward and yelled, "Hurry! You've got to see this!"

Above the stadium, the world tree's branches reached up through the elven canopy. Golden veins throughout the trunk helically spiraled into great branches. Golden light raced up one of these veins and the canopy of leaves overhead pulsed. The green leaves, each the size of a shield, sparkled and then turned red, white, blue, black, and a jade color of green.

* * *

Dar wandered the darkness of Alerius' mountain chambers. The aftermath of Ylgolth had left the boisterous empire quiet. While she welcomed the quiet, and noted her priestesses did too, it concerned her. Morbatten had no stories about quiet times. She turned left and heard noise ahead. The Garden, a large complex of alcoves, each containing a single statue of a former-living creature, loomed ahead. The noise could only come from Syliri. "Syliri, I've been looking for you for hours."

Dar flinched when she heard a stone smash against stone. The crack boomed and echoed. "I'm worried about you."

Dar found Syliri kneeling in front of the Fecundus statue. Adjacent, Bruce rested in a new space. Syliri did not sweat, but broken stone fragments from shattered floor tiles and the heaving of her chest told Dar that Syliri had been here for some time. The Fecundus statue looked as it always had, though its base and walls around showed Syliri's wrath. Dar prayed silently, asking Tiamat for guidance. "How do I help Syliri?"

Dar reached down and put her arms around Syliri. "We've both lost so much. Please, let's not lose each other."

Syliri touched her hand. It trembled and with a voice twisted by her petrification gaze, Syliri hissed back, "You do not know how hard it is to resist Set's call. I hear him, everywhere. I never knew the slaads could do what they did to me, to Bruce. I can go back. I could be with Bruce. In the Dream, the few minutes we have could be eternal. The Dream is that powerful."

Dar pulled Syliri's head against her breast and stroked the snakes. A glint of green light drew her attention and she saw the emerald ring lying by Bruce. Half the gem surface had turned to stone. "He loved you, Syliri. He still does. The god emperor once told me that mortal love is a magic all its own. It's possible that there is magic at play here, because of his love, that we just haven't learned yet. After all, you and the Court, you've been isolated for so long."

Syliri choked, half laugh and half sob. "Mortal magic with an eldar? If I could, I would give up everything to be with Bruce, even for a lifetime." The cobra hissed at her and she flicked it aside. "Everything!" She shrieked and Dar felt Syliri slip back into Set's Dream when her arm began to petrify.

"Shhh, please. Don't. I know you wanted so many things, but do not threaten my Seline. I lost my love. Let this be our bond of sisterhood." Dar gave Syliri a half-second to stop and breathed deeply when Syliri regained control. "How are you this strong, to pull in and out of the Dream when your heart is clearly breaking?"

Syliri said, "I'm not really in control, Dar. I just don't want to hurt anyone else and I'm tired of feeling so much pain, all the time." She reached her hand out to Bruce and whispered, "The golden dream..." She began to weep. "I'm not strong. You have no idea. What you consider strong in me is merely Set dragging this out, hoping I come back to Him. There's the dream of power..."

Syliri's eyes flickered to Dar's, then the Fecundus, then Bruce. She wiped her eyes and stood up, brushing dirt from her knees. "Tell me, Dar. Is it weakness to wish for a final farewell?" Her voice grew confident too quickly. "Wouldn't you wish for a final good-bye with Sean?"

Dar hesitated and then said, "Syliri, I can't imagine what this is like for you. But, yes. If Sean were trapped this way, I'd want him to know I still loved him. I'd want to know what he wants. With Bruce though, don't you already know? He'd tell you he loves you. He'd apologize for not seeing you through Ylgolth's power. He'd try to end his..."

"His life?" Syliri's eyes gleamed, illuminating her face with yellow radiance. The snakes coiling about her went fully alert, seeking about for an enemy, before turning as one. They looked at Syliri and she closed her eyes.

"Syl, no!" Dar shouted, lunging forward. She caught Syliri's hand and felt the stone magic take hold in her fingers, but then nothing happened.

In the silence of the moment, Syliri's flat voice stated, "No matter how many times, I am unable to end myself. I may as well sacrifice myself on Set's altar, which is all I see when I try." A curl of anger rose in her voice and she lifted her head to the cavern and screamed out Set's eldar name.

Dar noted her left hand remained cold and unable to move, but cradled Syliri close to her, unwilling to let her go, to feel alone.

"Why?!" Syliri screamed out again. "Why me? Why did you make me the one to see my sisters fall? You left me alone!" Syliri walked over to the Fecundus and punched the wall to the side of the alcove. The force of the blow became visible and Dar braced herself as air and noise cracked over and past her. A jagged gash opened in the wall and Syliri healed the stone even as she punched it again. "You want me so bad, come and take me, you bastard!"

Dar walked over and picked up Syliri's ring. The god emperor's words came to her mind as fresh as if just spoken. She recalled the bright, sunny day. She stood in his claw as he showed her the world of Morbatten, the Shield Mountains, and Oranstakar's lair. She saw the world he saw and tasted prey in the wind. In this dark cavern, she imagined the warm sun on her face. In the calm of that moment, even with wind racing past them, Dar asked Alerius about Syliri. "She is an Eldar, but seems so much weaker than I understand Eldar to be. I do not mean this as disrespect, but aren't the Eldar essentially gods?"

Alerius lectured her for hours after her question. But, the part about Syliri stayed with her. "Syliri was the first of Set's creations to rise up against him. She is like me in that I was the first to rise up against the All Father's plan to leave this world for Pha Rann's heaven. I understand why the Eldar might seem gods to you, but in time, you will understand. To many in the tribes, you are now a god. You wield healing life and death. On your command, armies rise. Aren't you a goddess? You see, as a god, Set does not understand rebellion, or worship, or even life really. Set understands only the pleasure of destroying others' creations. Think of a child playing in dirt. The child makes a castle out of mud. Another child comes and steps on it. I have seen this happen millions of times. This is Set."

Alerius landed on a mountain summit. The high air and clear skies showed a commanding view all around. Alerius pointed his talon in an arc. "This is the castle built by the child Pha Rann through the dragons. In draconian, "dragon" means "shaper." Well, that was our intent when we constructed a mortal tongue for us to converse with you."

Dar had not wanted to interrupt Alerius. After some time, Alerius continued. "Syliri, as the first to rebel, taught Set that sometimes the maker of the castle fights back. Sure, we had been fighting back the entire time, but Set created the medusae. He made the maedar. That one of them would reject him, his own castle-maker, hurts him. That is Syliri. She knew. There are many Set wishes, but He craves Syliri. She might be able to wake Him from his bound slumber. The power she wields, she knows, but what you cannot see, Dar, is how easily it comes to her. Her use of Set's power brings her back to Set. Only when she is totally in control is she able to use it as she wishes. Other times, her use touches Set and bit by bit, He claws her back to Him. The emerald ring I gave her, it fortifies her will and self-control. This is true. It also masks her from Set by bending Set's Dream and masking it to look like one of her sisters. If Syliri were to ever unleash her full power, it would destroy her and she would no doubt rise up as a priestess of Set unlike anything the world of Tehra has ever before seen."

Dar thought about this and asked, "You keep her by you to prevent this from happening?"

"You mean, why not kill her and end the risk, Dar?" Dar nodded. "Because, like you, Syliri is one of those I consider my friend; I treasure my friends above all else. Syliri is my friend. I value this mortal feeling more than any treasure I have ever captured."

Dar remembered blushing, grateful for the sunburn along her cheeks. She re-opened her eyes to see Syliri leaning her head against the wall, heaving for air. "Syliri," Dar said. Not getting a response, Dar walked up to her. "Give me your hand."

Syliri did not give it, but did not resist when Dar took her hand. "Ages ago, during a time I can only fantasize about, your friend Alerius made and gave you this ring." Dar slipped it back on Syliri's hand. "I love Alerius and am bound to serve him. How I envy you! You get to be with him because you chose it. You choose it every time you come back from Set's Dream. I had no choice. My options were middling life in the Horse Tribe, no doubt birthing babies for the next generation of fighters, or to run away like so many have."

The green stones twinkled and Dar kissed the ring and Syliri's fingers. "I know you're hurting," Dar continued. "I'm hurting too. I need you, my friend. I need my sister back."

Dar took and pulled Syliri away from the Fecundus to Bruce. Dar pointed to Bruce's lips. "He once told me that, should you ever petrify him, he would not look terrified of you. You could look at him, his grim expression, as being trapped in the Dream and not seeing you. I see something else though. He looks resigned to me. He knows he is infected. He knows Set has messed up his mind. He knows that if you don't do this, he might kill you. This is Bruce's final act of free will where he says, "Syl, I love you." Look at his smirk and tell me I'm wrong."

Syliri looked up and studied Bruce. She ran her fingers along his lips. "It's true," she replied to Dar. "This is the first time I've seen one of my statues not trapped in horror. His lip here is curled up like he's trying to smile."

Syliri began hyperventilating. Resting her hand on Bruce's chest, she tried to calm herself. "He knew. He knew! Do you know what this means?"

Dar nodded. "It means we could revive him, for a while at least."

Syliri's eyes flickered back to the Fecundus. "A moment can become an eternity," she whispered. "Dar, I'm going to unpetrify the Fecundus. If something goes wrong, kill it. Kill me. Swear you'll do this!"

"I have no issue with the Fecundus dying. Go ahead, but what is your plan?"

"The slaad can touch both of us and stretch a single moment out into forever. It'll look like a moment to you, but for us, it will be an eternity. Then, I'll return them both to stone, or at least understand Bruce's wishes."

Dar prayed and felt no guidance from Tiamat. She agreed.

Syliri touched the Fecundus and began unmolding the rock of his form. She left his lower half petrified. The Fecundus groaned in agony and Syliri slapped him. They had moved Bruce near the slaad. Syliri unpetrified Bruce while Dar explained to the Fecundus what they wanted. "Basically, you can do this and we will consider increasing your liberty or ending you. Or you can refuse and we'll kill you slowly."

When Bruce unpetrified with the slaad's hand on his head, he awoke in Set's Dream, in Syliri's golden dream. Syliri stood before him arrayed in a shimmering gown of golden threads. Bruce looked at the eyes erupting along his arms and stomach. "Syl, what is... why haven't you ended me? I killed you."

"No, Bruce. I need to be with you."

Outside the dream, Dar watched the slaad carefully. Praying to Tiamat, she could sense the slaad's intentions. Whenever it shifted at all, Dar touched the slaad with Tiamat's power causing lacerations and blisters to erupt along its skin. Though they began healing quickly, the slaad cursed at her. "I see you're with child," the monster said. "I bet you'd be delicious for my master."

Dar shot back, "Which one? We've killed two Anthracos. Give me another name and we'll hunt that master too."

"I don't' believe you," the slaad said as it returned its focus to stabilizing Syliri's dream.

"Believe me. Don't believe me. I don't care. But, if you do well, I will bring you something to eat with knowledge of what has transpired in the world since your last awakening."

That caught the slaad's attention. "Truly?" it asked, licking his lips.

"You must consider that your life, the life of the Slaadi, may not be the best place for you in the world. I'm building an empire here. As I understand it, you've been in stone for at least 2,000 years." Dar glanced at its placard. "Yes, almost 2,100 years. You're nowhere near Azuros. Maybe you should consider allying with us. Give them the best dream ever. Impress me by serving Syliri now. Let me know before we return you to stone."

Just heartbeats later, Syliri opened her eyes and returned Bruce to stone. Syliri breathed deeply and thanked the slaad. Dar could tell she struggled with deep emotion. The raw edge of earlier had softened.

"What did Bruce say?" Dar asked.

Syliri smiled. "He said that he wants to be here when we figure out handsign language. He also answered my most important question."

"Which is?" Dar prompted.

Syliri touched Bruce's stone mouth, now set in his charismatic and full smile. "That he sees no monster."

The slaad snorted. "That one is touched by Set. You should end him now before he infects us all."

Without looking, without losing her serene smile, Syliri backhanded the slaad. The force of the blow decapitated the creature and bounced its head back against the wall. "Dar, we had a lifetime together. Come, sister. Let us make a statue of Commander Sean. We shall make it larger than life and set it upon the Monument of Heroes. You have yet to name the trail up to Alerius' lair. Let us name it the Monument of Heroes. I will place Bruce beside him."

"Yes, I can see it. The Monument of Heroes shall rise up to the Throne. I love it, Syliri. Someday, when I am gone, I want my statue to be placed facing Sean's."

"I promise, Dar. Enough of this. Bruce told me to tell you that Sean collected books and maps. The training book has a quest in it Sean meant to take the first paladin class on. Bruce said that you need to decipher the

map and ensure Shak, and I'm quoting Bruce here, "doesn't mess it up."
Apparently, it helps the knights summon a divine steed."